MW00484551

Dreamland Diaries

BRUCE BALLISTER

All rights reserved. No part of this book may be used or reproduced by any means, graphic, electronic, or mechanical, including photocopying, recording, taping or by any information storage retrieval system without the written permission of the publisher except in the case of brief quotations embodied in critical articles and reviews.

This is a work of fiction. All of the characters, names, incidents, organizations, and dialogue in this novel are either the products of the author's imagination or are used fictitiously.

Dreamland Diaries, Revised edition
Copyright © Ballister Books 2021
Direct inquiries to: ballisterbooks.com

Cover Photo by Kathryn Stivers Photography,
Author Photo: Katie Clark
Back cover starfield, NASA's Hubble deep space observatory
all rights reserved.

ISBN-13: 978-1733257152 Softcover Trade
ISBN-13: 978-1733257169 eBook
LCCN: 2021903585

Printed in the United States of America

Dedicated to my wife and best friend, Christine

This 2021 edition is a minor update, necessitated in part because the original was never anticipated to have a sequel. That sequel, *Orion's Light* was created by reader demand and does require a follow up novel to complete the story, a final chapter if you will. To bridge some of the minor discontinuities, between the original concept and the following storyline, minor tweaks have been made to this original.

I hope you will enjoy *Dreamland Diaries*, and that you will follow up with *Orion's Light*, and the final chapter, PASS-FAIL.

Other works by the author include a fresh look at Cli-Fi, or Climate Fiction with a Sci-Fi twist. *Room for Tomorrow* takes a hard look at where the climatological trend lines go. It's horrific to say the least. In *Room for Tomorrow*, Parker Parrish gets a look at that horror show in a small farmhouse bedroom in the hill country of Southern California. That room and its secrets may hold the key to our global salvation. The plot line progresses on two parallel timelines spaced one-hundred-ninety four years apart. Find your copy at Amazon books or ask for it at your local bookseller.

Ballister's foray into non-fiction includes *Welcome to the Zipper Club*, an account of his experience with heart disease, triple by-pass surgery, and the road to recovery. It is a short, fast, and personal account meant to inform and advise those who are anticipating a coronary artery bypass graft, or CABG, and the consequences of open chest surgery. The ebook is especially accessible, if you need this book in a hurry for yourself or a loved one.

Reader Reviews of Dreamland Diaries:

"As a library administrator living in North Florida, I was Immediately captivated by the lyrical descriptions of the "old Florida" coastal environs and towns I have loved for over forty years. Ballister has managed to create an engaging story of family, history, and intergalactic power struggles that takes you from battle scenes in space to a cracker house in Wakulla Beach, to Area 51, to government agents who will stop at nothing to get their hands on a mysterious artifact..."

"This book keeps you on the edge of your seat throughout. For me, having never actually set foot in the region of Florida where this book is set, the time taken by the author to describe the natural environment helped to paint a great picture of the area. These descriptive sequences flowed nicely with the overall narrative and, at times, forced you to keep reading to find out 'what happens next'! I found it to be a wonderfully organized piece with a great ending that sets up nicely for a sequel. I would highly recommend this book to anyone interested in sci-fi/fantasy literature."

"… the discovery set in motion a nine year-long adventure for Brad that included a rogue government agency, murder, flight, extended family relatives, interstellar combat, artificial intelligence, telepathic conversations, finding mom—twice, kidnapping, Area 51, Hurricane Kate, and finally Tom Brokaw.
Oh yeah, there is a love angle to sweeten the plot—between cousins, distant enough cousins so as to avoid an improper family relationship, but just barely. What began as teenage interest matured over time into a—, but wait, I can't say more lest I infringe upon the storyline. You are going to enjoy this one folks."

"It is a real page turner from the beginning."

Characters, from the ordinary folks of North Florida to the shrimpers and fishermen of Apalachicola, are so well drawn that readers may feel they could climb aboard and be ready to crew. The unpleasant and very scary government agents are totally believable. Soon, the suspense builds and doesn't let up until the mind-boggling conclusion, which left me salivating for the inevitable sequel. "Diaries" was one of my most satisfying reads of the year. It would make an awesome movie. Don't miss this one!"

Dreamland Diaries

Parts 1 and 2 of the Four-part Series

Part 1

Chapter 1

The unexpected always happens.
Proverb

May 25, 1976
Near Wakulla Beach, Florida, 7:15a.m.

The boy walked down the narrow game trail with an uneasy feeling that something was watching him. Sun-bleached blonde and already tanned a rosy auburn that would darken by full summer, he wore a white tee and cutoffs over high-top sneakers. Although he knew the familiar pine flatwoods landscape had been disturbed by the storm, something else— something not of these woods—unsettled his usual curiosity.

The night before, a tropical storm, not deemed worthy of a name by the National Hurricane Center in Miami, came ashore on the nearly uninhabited big bend of the Florida coastline near the St. Marks River estuary. Unlike almost every other part of the state's coastline, the big bend's resident population was composed mostly of alligators, deer, bear, wild hogs, myriads of insects, and other creatures, instead of humans—though there were a few. Just before sundown, a thin, dark funnel had descended through the sheets of rain. Spun up by the differing speeds of rain bands that fed the tropical storm, the small funnel cloud reached toward the water's surface, sucking up a tower of spray. The frothy white base seemed to move almost independently of the sinuous, writhing column of grayish-white spray.

Beautiful, awesome, lithe, and dangerous, these formations were understandably sometimes called "water sprites." The waterspout danced toward the shore, unnoticed by the few local humans who had taken shelter. Small-craft warnings had kept the Apalachee Bay free of watermen. The funnel lost its water source as it crossed over the grassy flats near the shore, and soon lost touch with the surface entirely as it crossed into the ragged tree line, dipping here and there to wreak havoc on the planted pines and cabbage palms of Wakulla County. On its last dip toward the surface, it snagged the craggy top of a bald cypress that stood forty feet above its neighbors. The tree was battered like never before in its five hundred years. The twister's suction pulled and twisted until finally, when too many of its roots lost their grip on the soaked, sandy soil, the forest giant had shuddered and tipped.

As the funnel lifted back into the cloud base, the ancient sentinel fell. Within the deafening roar of wind, the crash went unheard by all except the nearest creatures. The osprey family that had ruled the rook for the last three seasons took deep cover and weathered as best it could on the ground. Its aerie lay smashed and irretrievable across a swath of low scrub and palmetto.

Within hours, the unnamed tropical storm crossed the narrow neck of Florida's panhandle to soak southern Georgia in much-needed rain. The winds quickly died along the coast, and a waxing moon rose near midnight, blanking all but the brightest stars. Most of the forest's inhabitants would recover from this disturbance in the annual cycle of life. The new opening in the canopy above would afford opportunities for lesser species to seek the sun's energizing rays. Life would continue with little change except for ragged limbs strewn on the ground, the torn foliage, and the forest giant downed and dying. Nearby, a patch of titi scrub surrounding a small pool of groundwater spread its narrow branches to the newfound sunlight.

The uncommonly clear air following nature's ultimate rinsing machine had removed every impediment to vision save the humidity itself. Luminous, nearly horizontal shafts of morning light had turned the moist, blue haze a muddy yellow. The morning quiet was punctuated by the erratic dance of buzzing insects. The leaves that remained on their branches hung limp and still. Creatures—furry, feathered, and armored—stirred after a day and a half of hiding in cracks, and crannies. A gull crept out of a sheltered hollow and stretched, flaring its wings as it hopped into the clear. It fluttered and took off for breakfast on the beach.

The boy paused near a clearing, trying to sense what was different in his familiar woodland, besides the minor destruction dealt by the storm. Approaching fifteen, Brad Hitchens was tawny, strong, and above all in the woods, observant. His favorite trail had not been marked with paint blotches like the formal wildlife refuge trails—it was a combination of deer and small-game tracks connected by his own shortcuts, formalized almost a decade ago by his mother. The coastal flatwoods provided new smells and sights that morning after the storm. His trail, little more than a slight brown line drawn in a carpet of ferns, was obscured and crossed with broken-off branches and a few downed trees. One of his favorite haunts, called the Cathedral of the Palms by old-timers, was only a short distance into the woods past an old sawdust pile left over a hundred years ago by loggers who'd stripped the forest of its longleaf and southern yellow pines.

The area was unusual in its ground cover as it lacked the near-total brush cover of saw palmetto found in most of the planted pine stands surrounding the refuge. Approaching the grove of mature cabbage palms, he was relieved to find most of them intact. Their canopy had been thinned somewhat, though. He thought that for the first time in years, the moss on the south side of the trees might soon die from unaccustomed sun exposure. Loosened palm fronds littered the ground. Sensing someone—something— he quickly turned to look behind him for a glimpse of whomever, or whatever. Nothing!

Downed pine branches and palm fronds strewn in all directions obscured the deer trail leading out the other side of the palm grove. Looking at the mess of broken timber, he realized that a small twister must have come through low enough to strip the treetops. Spotting what looked like a familiar crooked magnolia, Brad worked his way through the splintered trees and branches, trying to pick up his usual trail. He stopped and peered through a titi thicket that had been stripped of its leaves. He noticed an elongated sinkhole that he hadn't seen before. It was small, maybe thirty feet wide by fifty to sixty feet long. Its cool dark waters were littered with this season's fresh green leaves and stained brown by the cypress knees lining one corner of the pool. He knew the tannic waters would be safe to sip from, and bracing on a cypress knee, he bent over to drink. It looked as delicious as iced tea but actually had a slightly musty taste.

He rose and looked around, making out a giant deadfall root a short distance away. The freshly exposed root mat of the fallen forest giant towered above him. Tapering off into the distance, over a hundred and twenty feet of the forest giant lay among the tangle of smaller trees that had come down with it. The bald cypress had been crippled by a small band of well-intentioned workers a few decades back when one of its major surface spreader roots was severed by a fire trail cut through the tract. The side of the tree that no longer had the benefit of its spreading feet took the full onslaught of the storm's fury, and the twister had been the final blow.

Towering over palms, pines, sweet gums, and magnolias, the patriarch had stood quietly through fire, flood, and dozens of earlier storms. It had provided perch and nest for countless families of raptors—eagles, hawks,

3

and ospreys. It stood sentinel as red men, black men, and white men hunted in its shade in one century or another. Oblivious to the passage of years as men counted them, it only grew more gnarled, lost some bark here and there to lightning, and dropped most of its branches save for the few in its upper reaches.

On that cool, dark night in May, winds had shifted through most of the compass points, loosening the giant's grip, especially on its vulnerable side. Unheard in the thrash of wind and lashing rain and the roar of the twister, the earth popped with the snapping of old wooden feet as the venerable tree began to tilt. Crack, groan, shudder, and then, adding to the violence of the storm, the giant fell. It took smaller trees with it, and unlike some trees that hang up in the arms of their brothers, it went all the way down, crushing younger trees in its path.

Great clods of earth, captured in the matrix of sinew and root, rose up, clinging to the root mat and leaving a considerable cavity behind. In the trailing hours of the storm, the pouring rain had found a new opening in the forest. The clods gripped in the tangle of cypress root lost soil to the torrential rains of the last half of the storm, and ran muddy into the hole left by the root ball. The small, newly formed pond would soon become a home for tadpoles, mosquitoes, and a mélange of aquatic plants. But for the day, it was just a muddy pool.

Trotting through the thin ferns toward the massive, earth-encrusted root, Brad glimpsed something sparkling blue in the tangle. At first, he thought it was a skink drying in the sun. But a bright shaft of metallic blue protruding from the muddy mess caught Brad's eye. He approached but stopped to look behind him; he again felt the presence of someone or something back there. Distracted, he tripped on a branch and fell headlong into the scrub, knocking himself temporarily unconscious.

Dazed by the blow to his forehead, the boy was seeing stars. Literally, he was seeing brilliant stars in a black field. To one side, streaked brilliant flashes of yellow, followed by staccato bursts of blue and green. Turning his mind's eye, he saw, in a distant corner of his field of vision, a planet—a ringed gas giant. His mind's eye seemed to pass with enormous speed through planetary space.

Chirring insects in his own space brought him closer to consciousness. He lay quiet, dazed, absorbed in visions of a black void punctuated by flashing colors. Above, a small leaf at the edge of the new clearing, weakened by a night of tearing winds and now dried by the warming sun, fell in gentle propeller fashion, landing on the tanned human cheek.

Startled awake, the boy rolled over with a groan, rubbing the swelling lump on his forehead. Rising to an elbow, he found the three-inch branch in the ferns that had knocked him senseless. Looking around, he saw that the faint bands of yellow light had a much steeper angle and had thinned as the moisture baked out of the morning air. Overhead wisps of condensing vapors seeped through the tree canopy and rose to feed the clouds that would form miles north. Again, he had the feeling that some creature was watching. From behind?

Sensing the lost time, he thought, *"Oh, crap! I'm going to be late!"* He brushed his knees clear of minor debris and looked back up at the base of the huge fallen tree. The tangle of root, partially rinsed, did not look quite right. He walked over to the edge of the muddy pool. A straight line was visible in the muddy root ball where only tangle and curve should be. There was a light-blue edge, metallic and shining. Brad reached for his belt knife to cut away at some of the mud. Forgetting his haste to get home, he scraped at the mud and root, occasionally washing the knife in the pool to clear his grip. The shining piece took on shape, only not one he could place. With it loose and muddy in his hands, he stooped to rinse it.

The metal piece was a little over a foot and a half long, not quite round, but not quite oval either. One end looked as if it had been ripped apart with great force, the other as if it were missing an attachment. And it was light—he had expected it to be heavier. Looking at the Timex on his wrist, he swore softly to himself, arranged his web belt, slipped the knife back into its sheath, and began to trot back home. He stopped, whirled, pulled his Instamatic from his day pack, and took a picture of the small hole in the root ball, and smiling, ran back up the trail toward home.

Below the forest floor, a once-proud intellect, tactician, warrior, and, of late, a historian of local human passage through the forest, slept. It lay completely unaware of any changes above except for the crashing thud that had reverberated through its bed of crushed limestone as the cypress giant fell. At the crash, a light briefly flashed green in the darkness below. A recorder readied itself to turn on and then lapsed to full off when no new stimuli trembled its sensors. The panel again went dark, passive, waiting. But there had been that one interruption of a new sentient being above.

~ ~ ~

With a slam of the screen door and a shout, Brad announced his arrival to dad and dog. "Dad? You home?"

"I'm back in the kitchen. Why're you late? Not much left of the morning."

"I'm late?" He feigned ignorance.

"Well, yeah. I thought we talked last week about your getting distracted and making us both late. We need to get on down to the beach before anyone beats us to the goods!" From a back room, a scruffy, mixed-breed dog with a strong tendency toward Labrador came in, tongue lolling and dripping, tail wagging furiously. Dusty was a little overweight, and his aging hips swayed as he wagged. His white-tinged cheeks pulled back in a toothy Labrador grin on seeing his pal.

Brad came into the kitchen to the smell of freshly ground coffee and biscuits and dropped to a knee to grab the dog's head and scratch his ear. The biscuits were the pop-out-of-the-roll-and-bake kind, but when hot and smothered with blackstrap molasses, they were his favorite. "Oh, man, Dad, biscuits! Thanks!"

"It's not like you deserve them," his dad said, folding a dish towel over the oven door handle. Whitcomb, "Whit," Hitchens, looked at his son as reproachfully as he could. "Grab a few for the ride, and we can talk about it on the way to the beach." He twirled an end of the dishtowel and threatened to pop the boy if he didn't comply.

"Can Dusty come with us?"

"What else? If he sees us head south, he'll follow us anyway." The 'beach' meant any one of a number of places where all kinds of interesting storm debris might have washed up. Occasionally, some Richie Rich would learn a hard lesson about storms and anchors, finding that the sandy bottom of Apalachee Bay did not hold as well as the cleats on his usual dock. Whit looked closer at his son, as the youngster tried to avoid showing his forehead, and called him over.

"Bradley Delaney Hitchens! Hold still. Let me get a look at your head. Did you forget to look up and get mugged by a tree?" He ran a thumb over Brad's forehead and across the rising welt.

"Ouch!" Brad ducked away from the prying hand. "Actually, I didn't look down and tripped. There's so much deadfall lying around, I smacked a branch on the way down."

"Hmm, arms? You know those long, dangly things hanging from your shoulders? They're useful when making landfall."

"Yeah, I know." And suddenly impatient, he said, "Can we go?"

~ ~ ~

Walking on one of the grass-lined beaches a few miles south of the Hitchens family homestead, father, son, and dog picked their way through small mounds of sea grass littered with the usual six-pack rings, plastic debris, crab trap floats, and miscellaneous bits of lumber. Stepping through the mess, Brad began to lay out a set of questions that had been troubling him since his rough wake-up in the forest.

"Dad, can I ask you something?"

"Sure, shoot, kiddo."

"You know how when a big tree comes down in the woods and it lifts a big pile of dirt?"

"Yeah, those dirt piles are all over out there; we talked about that a few years ago."

"Well, a big tree came down yesterday in the storm."

"Where? The big pine over by the Cathedral of the Palms?"

"No, it's a big cypress." Brad thought about the location. "It's maybe a coupla hundred yards north of the old pine."

"Damn, I know that one—or knew that one." In fact, Whit knew most of the big ones in the woods around his house in the coastal flatwoods. He was third generation, and the Hitchens surname was sprinkled around the county as a last name, middle name, maiden name, and first name, shortened to "Hitch." The family patriarch had moved to the county in the closing years of the nineteenth century. Counting on the courthouse fire in Ohio to erase his early troubles with the law, Joshua Hitchens started over as a teenager with little more than a desire to go straight and work. After a horrendous stint in France with Pershing's expeditionary forces, he had returned to the quiet backwoods and coastal flats that he had fallen in love with. His son, born Charles Bradley Hitchens, avoided the killing fields of World War II by servicing landing craft engines at Camp Gordon Johnson, an hour's drive away. The camp had been the semitropical training ground for Anzio, Normandy, and most of the landings throughout the Pacific theater. This experience led, shortly after the war's end, to his ownership of a boat-and-motor dealership on the coast of Florida south of Tallahassee and, eventually, a small fish camp.

Whit, named for his grandmother, Carrie Whitcomb, had opted for the sciences and after flunking anatomy, his first interest, had pursued geology. After Nam, he'd used a GI loan and developed a well-drilling company. His knowledge of the woods around his grandfather's home was encyclopedic. He did, in fact, know the big cypress. "It's down?"

"Yeah, it's down. It's humongous … or was."

"Too bad; that cypress was older than white people."

"What?"

"Well, except for maybe a few Spaniards, that tree was probably around when the Creeks or Seminoles ran the place. Way before Jackson, before Lafayette, Prince Murat, and the rest. Maybe next weekend, we can take a crosscut saw out there and get a cross section. We'd need to take the tractor with us to bring it back though."

"That would be cool, Dad." He thought back to the shiny object tangled in the root mat. "So if that tree has been there for … what, maybe three hundred years, or so …" he trailed off, lost in thought. Dusty, previously romping in the ankle-deep shallows terrorizing snow crabs, came wagging up to them and began a shake. Father and son automatically reprimanded, "Dusty, no!" as they turned their backs on the now-skulking dog.

Whit said, "Three hundred years? Yes, at least that long. We can check it out Saturday. But you know, some of the oldest of those big boys have been around five or six centuries."

Thinking of the implications, Brad walked on in silence, hoping to find something interesting in the debris. They slogged through knee-high piles of brown sea grass, heads down because of the uneven footing created by the blown sea grass lumped along the shore.

Glancing up, Whit noticed an unnatural green in the grass. "Brad, check this out!" Pulling aside a curtain of brush, they saw an upturned green fiberglass canoe.

"Wow, Dad! Can we keep it?"

"I suppose, rights of salvage and all, we could surely keep it." He looked at a length of quarter-inch cord tied to a milk bottle full of sand. "It's probably local folks, though. Tell you what, we'll take it for safekeeping and post a notice in the IGA grocery. If no one can describe it or its milk-bottle anchor, it's yours."

Brad was alongside it in the brush, running his hands over the smooth bottom. "It looks like it's not busted or anything."

"Let's turn it over and see if it's all here." Doing so, they noted one bent cross brace amidships but no other apparent damage. "Boy, looks like you might have yourself a decent canoe here." He rubbed his two-day growth of whiskers. "'Course, you'll need a paddle or two, and a safety cushion."

"No problem, I've got a little of my yard work money saved up."

"I thought you were going to save that for a good cause?"

"But, Dad, this is just too cool! What could be a better cause?" His dad was looking out across Apalachee Bay now, thinking about the storm. He pointed at the green headlands to the south along the west side of Apalachee Bay. "It could've come from down there, either Panacea or Bald Point. Or, for that matter, it might've come down the river and been blown up here. This little milk bottle full of dirt sure isn't much of an anchor." Looking back at the canoe, he continued, "Let's not spend anything on it until we let a few weeks go by."

They started walking again, not finding much and nothing as good as the canoe. Whit did pick up several crab trap floats with markings he recognized. They didn't cost much, but some of the crabbers he knew didn't have much and they would appreciate getting their floats back at least. Each float meant a lost trap somewhere out on the flats that wouldn't surface until the next full moon's low tide.

Brad's thoughts returned to the early morning find. The implications of the location of the piece of bright metal were coming back to him. Tomorrow, he thought, I'd better get back out there tomorrow.

"Dad, can I come back after the canoe this afternoon?"

"Sure, kiddo. Better get a paddle from the Williams, though. That's the easiest way to get it back. The tide should be high enough, too." He glanced over his shoulder at the pale crescent moon, high in the clear sky. "Full tide in the afternoon." He looked out at the quiet waters of the Gulf and up at the sky for cloud sign. "You can hope this on-shore wind holds out too."

"Why don't I just wade it around the shallows to the landing. I can use that kayak trailer to bring it back to the house!"

Wakulla Beach Road, 11:00 p.m.

The Hitchens homestead was mostly dark. A pulsing chorus of crickets, happy about the return of warm evenings, filled the night with primeval noise, while green neon flashes of the season's first lightning bugs punctuated the dark. From Bradley Hitchens's window, the mechanical rattle and hum of a window air conditioner masked most of the natural noises filling the woods outside the wood-frame house. Its galvanized roof snapped loudly to the random drop of cones from an old-growth pine too close to the house. The AC's vibrations hummed through the heavy timbers of the house, providing a slight trace of its sixty-cycle buzz to waves in the water glass on Brad's desk. Under the glow of his desk lamp, he examined the odd piece of metal he had pulled out of the root tangle. His oscillating fan provided brief moments of cool while he looked the piece over again. Dusty, curled in his usual spot beside Brad's bed, slept in profound peace, oblivious to his master's mental searching and frustration. A little under two feet long and a pale blue-green, the metal rod was light, rigid, and hard to break. Earlier, he had tried whacking it on the brick supports of the front porch. He had been rewarded with a stinging vibration in his arm while the metal rod remained unaffected.

His swing-arm desk lamp attracted its own set of night creatures. The bodies of gnats and moths that had ventured too close to the heat of the bulb littered his notepad. Above his head and the cone of light from the lamp, three model airplanes—a B-17, a P51 Mustang, and a deHaviland Mosquito bomber—swung in the pulsing breeze of the oscillating fan. A faded movie poster from *Bullitt* featured Steve McQueen behind a black Mustang. His bookshelf held matchbox cars, fishing lures, a pile of annual Hugo Award Sci-Fi anthologies, Cousteau's *The Silent World*, London's *White Fang*, a curled snakeskin waiting for a straw hat, two of last season's baseballs, an FSU football, and a jumbled set of the New World Book Encyclopedia. On a shelf by itself was an olive-drab model Bradley fighting vehicle with custom paint depicting his dad's unit. Almost everywhere, chaos seemed to have an edge on order, but his room was a comfortable, well-used haven for a generally introverted but self-sufficient boy.

The blue metal piece lay on top of the pile on his desk. Aside from this recent addition, the desk also held a pile of schoolbooks and the "A" and "E" volumes of the encyclopedia, one opened to "Alien," the other to "Extraterrestrial." Brad, tired from the day's efforts and too much thinking, fell asleep, chin on arm.

The dream came later, as the night fell silent just before dawn. Gyrating views of star fields and planets filled his head. He had the sensation of being chased by someone or something he couldn't visualize, but the overwhelming sense of danger could be read on his face and the twitching of muscles from ankle to cheek bore witness to the realistic images passing behind his closed eyes.

10

May 26, 1976
Wakulla Beach Road, 6:00 a.m.

Brad awoke in the early dawn—not at his desk, but in bed as usual—and drowsily became aware of his dad in the doorway and a throbbing headache.

"I see I didn't disturb your plans to get to school. Come on, there're only a few days left, and you've got the whole summer ahead of you!"

Yawning, he replied, "Isn't it over yet?"

Whit smiled, recalling the contests he and his wife had had urging Brad toward consciousness. "If I remember your schedule, you're off at noon today for teacher planning. I will never understand what teachers need to plan at the end of the school year!"

Brad rolled over and tried burying his head in the pillow, but that hurt the knot on his forehead. He mumbled through the feathered pillow. "All the tests are tested. What can they possibly have to do with us today?" As he remembered the late night at his desk, the predawn dream began to make sense. At first, there were Sioux Indians massing along stony ridgelines. Then he was being chased and scared to death by four aliens firing green energy rays from their ships. Rolling out of bed and stretching, he looked to see if the metal rod was still on the desk. Seeing it half hidden by the open "A" volume of the encyclopedia, he wondered if his dad had noticed it. He shut the heavy book. Its entry on alien life was useless. The extraterrestrial life entry in the "E" volume referred him back to aliens and alien cultures, which covered the indigenous cultures of South America and Asia. He rubbed the still-sore lump on his forehead and wondered about the headache near the base of his skull.

He sat down at the desk and in a few quick movements, placed the two encyclopedias on top of their cousins, put the few tools he'd had out back in a drawer full of tools his Dad had cast off, and hid the artifact under his mattress.

Entering the kitchen, he poured some juice and sat at the table. "Say, Dad?"

"Say, what?"

11

"Remember what I was sayin' yesterday 'bout that big cypress?

"Sure, we can go look at it tomorrow."

"About what I was saying about the root ball?"

"What about it?"

"If there was something in the dirt deep down in those roots, it would have to be pretty old, wouldn't it?"

Whit turned around to look his boy in the eyes. "What did you find?" He knew Brad's circumspect questioning held a much bigger question. As a geologist in karst country, Whit had become interested in artifacts from paleo-history and had donated quite a collection of his finds to the high school history department. He had even worked on a project with the state geologist a few years back. He knew that men had been on these shores for five or six thousand years and that their artifacts might be found almost anywhere.

Brad looked at the table and traced circles along the faded pattern on the Masonite surface. "Didn't say that I did find something."

His dad would have none of it. "Boy! Look at me. What did you find?"

"If this thing is really old, I can only think of one explanation, and it's just ..." he faltered, "... too weird!"

"One more time, Son, what did you find?"

"A piece of metal." He looked up at his father's serious face. "Can't be Spanish—least I don't think it is."

"Well, there were all kinds of explorers in these woods. Could even have been from the Civil War."

"No, Dad." He got up and went to retrieve the piece from under his mattress. As he left the room, he said, "It's not from here."

"What do you mean, 'not from here'?"

Brad came back into the kitchen holding the blue metal bar in his outstretched arms as if he were presenting a samurai sword. "This thing is not from here! Not this planet!"

Whit took the piece and examined it closely. It was as Brad had said. It was bluish, actually more of a teal, and colored as if from a dull powder coat, not polished, but not scratched. One end looked like it might take an addition of some kind, as if something else had been there. Although the thing was unfamiliar, it seemed unfinished in the same way that a socket wrench would look unfinished without a socket.

The other end was distressed—broken in fact, snapped off. Whit looked closely at the broken end. "It's not painted!"

12

"I know. The color goes straight through the metal." Whit Hitchens furrowed his brow. "Odd and odder." He turned it over a few times and then examined the broken end, saying, "It looks like there might be layers to this thing." He looked up at Brad. "Did you try to get this outer layer off?"

"Yeah, but I couldn't budge it. Heck, and what's weirder is that I couldn't even scratch it. I tried to cut off a piece last night with my coping saw. Not a mark." He stood and took it carefully back from his dad's grip. "And it's too light!" he said, hefting it as if he might be calibrating a weight. "Dad, I was going to tell you yesterday, but I wanted to look some stuff up." He thought of his fruitless search of the encyclopedia. "It seems like it's at least as light as aluminum, but it's too strong. I couldn't touch it with pliers or your vice. I whacked it on the brick steps, and all I did is hurt my hand. I'd say it's hard as nails, but I think it's harder."

Whit sat in his chair at the table and stared at the artifact. "You say you found this in the root ball? Where exactly was it?"

"I got pictures of where it was after I got it out. Something told me that this was way too unusual, 'specially since you said that the tree was hundreds of years old." He added, "'Course, I won't be able to get those pictures for a while. Maybe I can get 'em developed this weekend."

"Sure," said Whit, distracted by his study of the metal rod. "Where exactly was it in the root ball?"

"Pretty much under the tree; looking at the thing from the side, I guess it was about a little over a foot under the surface under one of the bigger roots."

"Hmmm ..." Whit pulled at the now-absent beard whose scrub was trying to reestablish a presence on his chin. "Maybe, maybe in years past, there was a burrow under the tree and somebody or some critter stuck this thing in the hole. The hole filled up, and it was underground."

Thinking for a moment, Brad said, "How 'bout if I take you out there so if we have to explain this to anyone, you can explain it. I don't think I want to talk to Channel Six about this thing. I don't mind being famous for finding it, but I think they'd listen to you, a geologist, before they'd listen to me. I can put this thing about where it was in the roots so you can see for yourself."

"I don't know; there's probably a good explanation for how it got where you found it. Besides, the forces of being yanked out of the ground were probably tremendous."

"Dad, come see for yourself, please?"

"All right, I need to go into the shop to see if everything's nailed down after the storm. Oh, and your aunt Susan needs some help clearing her yard. We did all right 'round here from all reports, but they lost power up in Tallahassee and there's branches down all over her yard." He pressed a hand on Brad's shoulder. "I'll go out and look with you this afternoon before the yellow flies rise, but I bet we'll figure this thing out. And tomorrow, we're going to town. I can drop you and a rake at Susan's house while I get some errands run."

~ ~ ~

That afternoon, standing as close as he could to see where Brad had reinserted the metal rod in the root mat, Whit examined the area immediately surrounding the disturbed soil around the rod. Taking a field knife and carefully clearing away loose material, he cleaned a smooth plane from the rod to what had been the surface of the root ball nearest the hole. "I don't like what I'm seeing here, Brad."

"What do you mean?" The comment seemed ominous, and the boy shivered slightly. He had that odd feeling again that something was behind him. Looking around, he decided everything appeared normal—if you considered the huge tree now turned sideways normal. Something seemed to be there that shouldn't be.

"There doesn't seem to be an old void that was filled with sediment," said Whit. He hummed quietly to himself as he poked root and scraped soils. "A burrow would have had a vegetal layer at its bottom that would have left a thin line of carbon from decayed organics even after years." At one point, he almost fell into the hole behind the root ball, which had drained, leaving a slick frosting of thin mud to dry and crack.

"Other than the mess you made when you pulled this out, the soils appear to be a typical depressional ring around the root ball of a fairly massive tree."

"De ... pressing ring?"

"Depressional," Whit repeated and then explained, "As a tree this size gains mass, it begins to compress the soils immediately under it. It's been pretty much disturbed by the tree fall, except here." He tapped at some of the roots immediately adjacent to the small cavity. "There appears to be no evidence here of an old animal burrow. There's mostly sand here, so there's no sediment layers." He poked gently at the area where the metal rod had been pulled from the root mat. "If a burrow or cavity had been here for this thing to have been hidden in, there would've been some evidence of extra carbon as that area filled back up with compost and soil."

"Okay, Dad, speaking as a geologist, how old do you think my piece of metal is?"

"Can't speak for the age of the metal, but it got wrapped up in those roots somewhere between three hundred and six hundred years ago." He turned, sighted down the length of the immense tree, and calmly folded the knife and put it and his hands in his pockets. Taking a few steps away from the massive root, he lined himself up with its former surface level. "It appears to have been about eighteen inches below the surface, so it's extremely unlikely that it was put there. Certainly no raccoon or possum pulled it into a nest." He mused for a minute, looking at the tree root mass in profile. "Gophers and foxes build burrows that deep, but they don't scavenge for bits of metal."

"So, now what?"

"Now we very carefully find out what the heck we have … er, you have here before we go calling Channel Six. I have an old friend at Florida State I can call down here to look at this root for a second opinion." He reached over the hole, retrieved the muddy relic, and wiped it on some ferns to clean off the bulk of the mud. "Or maybe I should first get a sample of it up to his lab. We probably ought to get a tarp over this thing to keep it from getting rained on. You say you have pictures of it when it was in the tree?"

"Yeah, the first thing came into my mind was it was from some alien, and I didn't want everyone to think I was nuts."

"Good thinking there, Son. There's a lot of squirrels that'll come out of the woods over this if you're right, and a lot of people will be mad as hell at both of us if we're wrong."

"For real?"

"Yes, for real. You remember the stories about the Wakulla Volcano?"

"Yes."

"It's geologically impossible, but its legend lives on; almost no one will admit to believing it, but some of the old-timers still think there is a volcano deep out in those woods when it's no more than swamp gas and morning steam." He began walking slowly back to the house. "You ever learn about the Piltdown man?"

"No … least I don't think so."

"In England, about just before the First World War, a great discovery was made in a gravel pit that seemed to indicate that a missing link between man and monkey had been found in England. It was an age embroiled in the debate between creationism and Darwinism, and there was outrage, press coverage, and international attention. The finders became famous and had some serious respect for a while in the scientific community. Their fame was sidelined by two world wars and a world economic collapse, but as things settled down in the fifties, the whole thing was exposed as a hoax."

"You mean it was a joke?"

"No … well, maybe it might have started as a joke, probably not. But it became 'fact' and was generally accepted until the truth came out. Unfortunately, one of the men who put up the hoax lived too long and was still around to bear the shame and humiliation forty years later. I guarantee you that at your age, you will be around to hear about it if this thing turns out to have a better explanation than we can come up with."

"What do we do next?"

"Get more proof and second and third opinions! Believe me, the government would be all over it if they thought you had a real alien artifact."

As they left the area, the sensor in the ground listened. After a while, it could no longer detect complex thought waves and went quiet. A blinking amber light dimmed and went out.

~ ~ ~

Bradley Hitchens got home from school and immediately tossed his backpack into a corner, changed into shorts and flops, and headed into the woods. School had been as boring as he'd expected. Big deal, sit and erase all the pencil marks you could find in your textbooks and turn them in. For most of the morning, they had been in homeroom comparing notes about storm damage. In the eastern part of the county, not too much had happened, so he told the story of the big cypress, omitting any mention of the artifact. Kids from the western parts of the county had less to tell: lightning had struck a camper down at the KOA campground; there was a lot of new sea grass on the beaches; and some scattered power outages. His tale about the big tree was the best of the morning, short of a galvanized roof that had peeled back from a friend's barn.

With storm damage on his mind, he trotted out to the path of the tornado and began to clear debris from his running trail. It had originally been his mother's running trail. She had passed on to Bradley her love of the great woods beyond their homestead and her love of running. She had liked to run in the morning. He often ran after school. His mother had taught him the names of many of the plants and how to discern the sometimes subtle differences between the four or five kinds of magnolias and the truly confusing variety of oaks, showing him which kinds could live with high water and which couldn't.

Whit and Lucy had moved into the family homestead when he returned from the army. She had always loved the woods from her early travels to the coast with her parents and from many trips to the area's sinkholes during her teens when skipping school with girlfriends. She'd gone into the family's woods and farther into the adjoining wildlife refuge properties, exploring and cutting her own walking trails though the rougher areas. Later, when she got the running bug, she had improved her trails in preference to running along the Coastal Highway or the often muddy road to Wakulla Beach. Lucy had shown Brad the running trail through refuge property when he was eight and had him running since he was ten.

Now, walking the narrow trail through a carpet of ferns, he tossed smaller branches into the brush and lifted the larger pieces aside. A clearing, newly visible at the edge of a titi thicket revealed access to a small sink. Obscuring deadfall had been tossed aside by the dying twister. Slipping through the opening, he made his way through the intertwined branching trunks and sat at the base of a big pine and looked around. Usually, if he sat still for a little while, the creatures that lived there full-time would begin to stir.

A woodpecker began its snare rat-a-tat on a dead pine a few hundred yards behind him. A thrush, being chased by an overhead hawk, flew down into the thick top of a cabbage palm. Something else, not far to his left, was slinking through the thin ground cover intent on surprising a beetle or caterpillar. He closed his eyes to get the bearings of these motions in his head and to better listen for any new sounds. It was the way his dad had told him to stop and "see" the forest with his ears and then locate what was making the sound. Whitcomb Hitchens added to his son's woods lore when recounting the long nights in the jungles of Vietnam. He had told Brad of the usefulness of the woodsman's skill of sound location while standing watch over his sleeping patrol mates when on deep recon.

Learning to identify plants and creatures had come later on morning and evening trips into the woods with bird and insect guides, tree pamphlets, and, in hunting season, an over-and-under 410 shotgun. Whit had trained him in the basics of hip shooting, which was especially useful with a shotgun and game birds. After bagging his first wild turkey, he realized that he did not care for the grisly result, hated the necessary cleaning, but had learned to love the gamey taste of the bird.

He knew he loved hamburgers way too much to be a vegetarian. He just thought he might wait a little longer to see if he would ever go hunting again. His mind drifted to some of the hikes he had taken in the Appalachian range with his dad and mom before she left them. He tried to picture her face, but actual memories were harder to pull up, and frozen images of her had to be placed into familiar scenery from the photographs on the family room wall. His thoughts of trails blended into a recent dream. What, two nights ago? Last week?

In that dream, his run down the woods trail had become a race and then morphed into a car chase as he imagined being in McQueen's black '68 Mustang, flying through the streets of San Francisco. Then he was driving, looking over his shoulder, sweating out a terrible outcome. Some fearful thing was chasing him. The scene went to night, and the dashboard of the Mustang became a control panel of the Millennium Falcon as Han Solo urged him to get all the power out of the ship that he could. "Come on, Brad! Get up to jump speed!" He dodged some space junk and tried not to think of the TIE fighter on their tail. Was it Darth Vader or one of the inept troopers? He startled awake to find the woods very quiet—no woodpecker, no thrush, nothing hopping in the ferns off to his left. His mouth was dry, his palms cold.

Brad stood quietly listening, feeling the "presence" of something behind him again. His problem of location compounded when he realized that no matter where he turned his head, the presence always seemed to be behind him. He felt as if something, something a little awful or weird, was trying to reach out for him. He looked carefully around the big pine— nothing. There were no rooting hogs, no fast-darting birds, nothing but more woods. The titi thicket was a little darker, as the upper canopy shade had shifted to darken it, and cabbage palms in the distance rattled their remaining fronds in the evening shore breeze. He felt silly, scared by his own daydream.

He started back to the house but diverted to the newly discovered sinkhole. Down inside its banks, the breeze did not ruffle the surface. Down there, water bugs raced aimlessly around pulling tiny wakes behind them, miniature motorboats on a glassy lake. He found a cypress knee to support his weight and leaned out over the dark water to look at his reflection in the shallow end of the elongated pool. The deep, brown, muddy bottom was broken only by a few lime-green leaves that had been blown in by the storm. His focus shifted from the bottom up to his reflection, which he stared at for just a few moments. With a slight wrench of his gut, he again had the feeling that something was behind him. He whirled around to look. Nothing! Here he was, almost fifteen years old and getting spooked in his own woods! Feeling ridiculous, he set out for home.

~ ~ ~

Brad called out when he entered the kitchen, "Anybody home?" Dad was not home. Of course, it would only have been his dad. His mother left when he was ten, only eight months after Whit came home from the army. He still didn't fully understand and might not ever, but his father had tried to explain that sometimes people get strange ideas in their heads. While Whit had been overseas, his mother had started having hallucinations. He had tried to reason with her, but she had gone off the deep end and left suddenly. Whit Hitchens had filed for a divorce three years later when he had had no word for two years. Later, when Brad was twelve, he learned that she was living in a small town outside of Las Vegas.

Before she had lost her center, Lucy Hitchens had been a junior high school teacher and had loved working with her kids, taking them to a next level of understanding. She got great joy from graduating each class of eighth-graders into high school, knowing that they could all fill in the bottom three rows of the periodic table, that they could all convert metric and English units, and that they could compare and contrast chloroplasts with mitochondria. She'd been a firm believer that every child should be versed in science and citizenship. All of her kids went to the ninth grade with "sirs" and "ma'ams" properly appended.

Brad did not remember the subtle changes that gradually overtook his mother's mental state. Nor could he recall when she started to fear something terrible was going on as she lost sleep and then energy and then confidence. He had not understood her paranoia or the reasons she would keep looking over her shoulder. He just knew that she had become less connected somehow, and he'd tried to please her even more. Then she was gone.

Brad walked through the silent house thinking of her. Her picture on the heavy cypress-beam mantle showed her holding his hand at an overlook in the Appalachians, both of them squinting into bright sunshine. Holding it with reverence, he stared at it and let the chain of memories carry him to their walks on the forest's many trails and to the time when he first noticed that she looked over her shoulder with something that looked like fear on her face. He sat suddenly on the edge of an overstuffed easy chair. He had first noticed it as they were leaving his woods—the area he had just left, the part of the trail where he had just had the weird feeling that something was behind him. In the heart of the titi surrounded sinkhole. He set the picture back on the mantle and ran upstairs to his room.

From under his mattress, he pulled out the blue-green metal rod. It was only a little shorter than it had been. Whit couldn't cut it with his hand hacksaws or his power tools, so they'd taken it into his shop and used a hydraulic press to shear off a half-inch piece to take to his old professor. Looking at the shiny end where the three-ton press had taken off a small sample from the stressed end, he again began to feel uneasy about where it might have come from. Was it Heinlein or Sagan who said: "There are billions of stars out there; many of them with planets, and there must certainly have been life on more than one of the planets." He had also said entire civilizations could grow, become technically advanced, and obliterate themselves before another intelligent species could discover them and make contact. *But, would we want to make contact?*

Looking around the room for inspiration, he found none and flopped onto his bed in an uneven mood. One of the things about being so far down the road from everything else was that friends weren't just up the road to play with. He had to make arrangements to go home on a bus with someone or just get by on his own as he had done most of his life.

He looked up at the eighteen-inch-long B-17 slowly spinning above him. Closing his eyes briefly, he drifted into a familiar fantasy of cruising across the Rhineland in a vast formation of B-17s, white contrails spewing out behind the planes. Between the thundering roar of the 160-plane formation and the giant white tails trailing behind, only a blind gunner could fail to get a range and send ack-ack up at them. He scanned the ground for a Messerschmitt coming up for a belly attack, their most vulnerable side. Here they came, the small fast fighters finding the formation only a few miles after the P-51 Mustangs had to return to England. The Krauts' fighters were no match for the fast, new P-51s, but they could chop up a bomber formation like rats on cheese.

He sighted in on a Messerschmitt 210 climbing up under the squad leader to his left. Rotating in his turret, he sighted above and ahead of the powerful twin-engine fighter bomber. This was no romantic duel of equals with exchanged salutes. He was a guardian of the fleet, which soon would have to face flak that probably would take out every fifteenth bomber, but first, they would have to fend off the fighters that would try to disrupt the bombers as they lined up their approach to Berlin. He saw the Me's tracers rising to meet the bomber's left wing as the stream of his own tracers began finally to intersect the cowling of the Me 210. Brad's fists clenched as he grasped the imaginary dual turret handles of his twin 50 calibers. The Kraut's engine exploded in a flaming ball, shearing off a wing. The Me's doomed crew was already getting ready to pop the canopy when his tracer line cut across the fuselage and the main fuel tank. The Me 210 disappeared in a fireball, but the damage to the squadron leader's B-17 was taking its toll. A thickening stream of black replaced the white contrail on the number-four engine.

Red-and-yellow flashes of flame spewed out of the number-four nacelle. Losing speed, the plane slowly dropped back and downward, jettisoning its load of incendiaries on a nameless village to shed weight. Once the doomed bomber got behind the formation, it would turn back and hope to at least get back across the Rhine. The crew was too far behind Axis lines to parachute out, but as the plane dropped farther, another Messerschmitt jumped it. It took an awful beating from the Kraut fighter until slowly, gracefully almost, its nose rose, wings flaring into the oncoming two-hundred-mile-per-hour wind. Then, with only one prop still powered, it rolled over on its back. Only one crewman jumped before it flashed into a silent ball of blackened flame and metal parts.

Suddenly, there was a loud banging on the fuselage! A row of bullet holes traced across the fuselage just over his head. Bam! Bam! Bam! And again, Bam! Bam! Bam! Bam!

"Brad! Get out!" He struggled to get out of the belly hatch, but his legs seemed to be tangled in something.

Chapter 2

The language of friendship is not words but meanings.
Henry David Thoreau

May 27, 1976
Wakulla Beach, 5:35 p.m.

Bam! Bam! Bam! His father was banging on his now-open door to his bedroom. "Bradley Delaney Hitchens! Last call, get up!"

"Yessir!" He popped awake, the brown bomber model still slowly turning on its thread above his bed. He felt foolish. His palms were wet. "Man, that was so real!" he said to himself. He popped up on his elbows. "Was I asleep?"

"I hope so! I thought you were possessed for a while there." Whit, looked down at his sandy-haired boy, smiling. "You hungry? I've got some oysters need shucking. You up to it?"

"Yessir, how many'd you get?"

"Bushel. But we don't have to do the whole bag. In fact, we can do it together. I'll put some corn on to boil and join you. We can fix up some cheese grits and sausage, too."

A few minutes later, he was in the back driveway, which was paved in a half-crushed-rock-and-half-crushed-shell mixture. The burlap bag of oysters was leaning up against his stool. The heavy, reinforced rubber glove on his left hand protected him from a repeat of the painful stab he had given himself last year when his shucking knife had slipped. His dad pulled up a lawn chair and sat beside him. He pulled an oyster out of the bag.

They sat in silence through a few oysters each, and soon, a dozen were ready for reading. A couple were taken iced and raw off the shell. "So, Brad, do you remember what you were dreaming about when I woke you up?"

"I was dreaming?"

"Yes, you were twitching and grasping at air like you were really hanging onto something with a death grip."

22

"Well, I think I musta fell asleep ..."

"Fallen asleep?"

"Yessir, I musta fallen asleep dreaming about the Memphis Belle. There's a dream I sometimes go to where I'm flying across Europe to bomb Berlin, and the whole flight is catchin' heck from the Krauts."

Whit chuckled softly. "Maybe you're watching too many of those old war movies?"

"No, sir, I just get to thinking about those guys, the brotherhood they had, and how they all had to depend on each other."

Whit sat thoughtful, wondering what it would have been like if Brad had siblings. As he shucked a new oyster and tossed its shell into their bucket, he asked, "Do you often have dreams of being in danger?"

"Umm, hmm, no, not really. I don't think so," Brad answered, tossing an empty shell into the bucket. "Why?"

"Oh, nothing, I suppose. Just hoping you don't get too caught up in a fantasy world and forget about real life and real problems."

"Problems? Like what?"

"Son, I'm just trying to be a good dad and look out for you. You're pretty self-sufficient, and you've had to be these last few years." He looked down at his son. "I'm real proud of you." He mussed Brad's sandy hair and patted him on the back.

They each shucked a few more. Whit Hitchens cracked open a big one and offered it to his son. "Here you go, kiddo." Brad eyed the huge oyster and smiled. "Not much better than a fresh Apalachicola Bay oyster only a few hours out of the water."

Brad lifted the shell to his lips and let the cool meat slide into his mouth. "Umm, thanks, Dad." He hesitated pulling the next shell out of the bag. "Dad?"

"Yes?"

"Back when Mom started getting, umm, strange, er, did she ever say what was bothrin' her?"

"Yeah, she did on some occasions, usually not." He paused, a frown on his brow. "Sometimes I'd catch her dreaming, and she'd be talking to someone, or herself. I don't know, but she started thinking she was losing it several months before she left. I couldn't make her go talk to anyone, and she didn't talk to me much by then."

"Why?"

"She was afraid she would be locked up, sent to Chattahoochee. Or drugged. She was scared."

"Of what?"

"I don't know, Bradley; I wish I did." He fumbled in the bag for a shell. Changing the uncomfortable subject, he said, "This can be the last one for tonight. The corn's probably done by now, and the oil's sure to be hot enough. Let's let Mom's memory rest, okay? Better to think of her in better times."

"Sure, Dad." Brad tossed his shucking knife into the oyster bag and picked the bag up. His mind was running on overdrive, but he tried to not to show it. Halfway up the stairs, he paused. "Dad, when I was in the woods today, I had a feeling; really spooky for just a second. Like somebody was behind me, trying to talk to me. There was no one there, but when I turned around to look, well, it made me think of how Mom used to do that."

Whit turned at the kitchen table to look back. His son, bag in hand, was framed in the open back door, his face wrinkled in worry. "Son, come here." He hugged his boy to him. It had been a long time since he had done that. Maybe, he thought, maybe I need to do this more.

"Son, it'll all be okay. It'll take time." He tried to think of a distraction. "Come on, let's get this dinner on, and maybe we can go in and rent a movie. School's out, right?"

"Near enough; can't think of a single reason to go tomorrow except I got to. Exams are over, books are turned in—what is there to do?"

"Get used to it, boy. There'll always be things you don't want to do, but you just have to do. Sometimes others set the schedule, and sometimes you just know you have to do something right or it won't get done." He tousled his son's hair affectionately. "Come on now, let's eat."

May 28, 1976
Wakulla Beach, Friday afternoon

Brad had not run his trail since the last trip had spooked him. He knew it was silly. But, he told himself, he could slack off a little, as summer had just started. If he was going to try out for track in the fall, he didn't need to start working on his endurance runs until August. In reality, he would come home and start reading and let it get too dark to go out. But this was a Friday,

24

and he wanted his woods back. He wanted to face his unreasoned fears, to "man up" as his dad would tell him.

He knew his dad had been a soldier in Vietnam and had faced far worse. He had rarely spoken to him about the army years, but he had heard him talking with another Nam vet on his drilling crew about it when they thought he was asleep. Those overheard conversations had started a whole new batch of daydreams, fantasies, and night terrors. Maybe that last experience in the woods was a flashback to those Nam dreams.

He trotted, arms loose at his side, Ranger-style, as his dad had taught him, through the section of planted pines into the wildlife refuge property, and soon found himself in the fern field. Dusty bounded ahead, seeking out smells left and right. Some low scrub, wild grasses, scorched palmetto, and millions of ferns spread out before him. Spotting the toppled cypress, he approached it.

They never had gotten around to covering the root ball with a tarp but rains had been light and the exposed dirt was unchanged. The hole in the ground left by the root ball was already sprouting growth, its shallow pool alive with water bugs lunching on mosquito larvae. He looked at the knife scrapings his dad had made and convinced himself that the soil over the artifact did not appear to be any different from the soil around it.

Dusty lapped at the small pool. Reaching for his canteen, Brad realized that he hadn't put on his web belt. That meant no water, no knife, no camera. Though thirsty, he didn't like the look of the puddle even though it didn't bother Dusty. He remembered the little sinkhole beyond the titi thicket. That was decent water, he recalled, if a little tannic. Pushing through the web of branches in the thicket, he thought he might need to bring a machete out next time to cut a little trail through. The water in the hole was dark, even at midday.

He leaned over the same cypress root to get a drink and saw his own reflection in the smooth, dark mirror. Sitting back and leaning on a cypress, he relaxed. Dusty curled up beside him and rested his nose on his leg. Soon, as the low whirring of insects and the last heat of the afternoon began to dull his senses, he was nearly asleep.

hell-o? The thought was tentative. Was it a thought?

"What?" Brad sat up, peering through the underbrush all around.

please not a-fraid. The thoughts forming on their own came in single syllables.

"Who is that? Who's there?" He stood up and twirled around looking for anyone who could sound so close.

friend ... glad you back ... friend.

"Where are you?" He could feel a cool sweat beading on his flushed forehead.

here ... with you ... here long time.

"Where are you? I'm leaving if you don't show yourself."

not go ... want talk ... talked before, you leave

"Last week?"

not know week ... be-fore I talk ... you leave

"Why are you hiding? Why won't you show yourself?"

not hide ... here can not see ... can only feel

"How long have you been here? Where are you from?"

here long time ... from far way ... long time be-fore I talk others

"Come on, this isn't funny. Where are you hiding?" This was beyond spooky. This must be another one of his fantasy dreams. He looked up into the sun, blinding his retinas with yellow spots and temporarily blurring his vision. He pinched hard on the web of skin between his left thumb and forefinger. "Ouch, not asleep."

not hide ... here long ... you come here be-fore

"Yes, I come here a lot." He realized that his eyes were closed, and he had not been talking out loud. *"Why can't I see you?"*

not see me ... not in this place ... of this place

"Of this place?" He'd opened his eyes and spoken aloud.

of this place long time ... other friend come be-fore ... we talk many time

"What other friend?"

my friend ... you friend ... friend Lu-cee

Lucy? Brad was stunned, a trickle of moisture ran down the small of his back. He braced to run like hell, but was also scanning three-sixty. There was nothing moving anywhere except the occasional leaf overhead.

"How did you get here?"

chased—lost ... fall here ... stay here

"Where did you come from?"

home far away ... make drop ... get lost

"But—" He wondered how to rephrase the question. *"Where were you before?"*

many places ... not here be-fore ... get lost come here

As he was trying to ask the question yet another way, he realized his though was answered, he had not spoken. Brad was silent for a moment, thinking. Either his mother was not crazy, or he was just as crazy as she was. She had felt a presence in these woods and had been seen talking to herself or some "imaginary friend." He felt the thoughts forming in his head again.

Yes ... you think talk, then, "you have star ... me have star ... not same star ... not know your name for star.

He thought, *What name you star?*

He asked aloud, "What is the name of your star?"

alal ... my star alal ... alal home

"This planet, umm, this satellite is called Earth. What is the name of your home world, or satellite? Does your home world have a name?"

world

"Yes, world, where we are now is a world that revolves around our star. Its name is Earth or Terra." He couldn't think of the name for earth in French. Le mondy or something?

erth ... same tera ... same ay-lohee

Alohee? Brad sent the thought back in verification of the unusual name.

There was a pause and then, *long time before ... other friend say ay-lo-hee*

Brad heard the word in his head in a singsong with the middle syllable accented. *Holy crap!* he thought. *That could be Seminole or Creek!*

what ho-lee ca-rap?

"Nothing, I forgot you could hear me think." Returning to his question, he did not notice the darkening sky and rustling trees. "What is the name of your world, the place you come from?"

Dzura ... long before lost ... before lost no world ... many stars many worlds

His mind was whirling. A space traveler? He felt the inquiry inside his head again.

you come be-fore ... come with other friend

"I came here before?" He hadn't spoken aloud.

come be-fore ... with other friend ... friend Lu-cee

"How long ago?" He was hunched over now, elbows on knees and hands on his forehead; he could feel his headache deepening. A memory came back to him with a flash of clarity. The picture painted itself clearly without sound, but with color and detail. He was sitting nearby on the other side of the pond, poking at the water with a stick while his mother sat where he was now for long intervals. He could clearly see her in a short-sleeve work shirt under his dad's cutoff overalls and her favorite navy-blue Keds.

Brad had become aware that his mother was not talking, but that she was conversing with something. She had been mumbling, talking to herself, but he had begun to hear the conversation. Then, grasping at the base of his neck from a sudden sharp headache, he had almost fallen into the pond. She had not noticed, and she usually noticed his every move.

you remember friend Lu-cee now? ... not see friend Lu-cee long time

The text in his head was getting better now and had lost its syllable-by-syllable cadence. Maybe it was he who was getting better at receiving the thoughts.

He said, "Yes, Lucy is my mother." A large ball of cold water hit him on the back of his head, followed by a rushing overhead. In unison, the treetops in the canopy began to thrash overhead as a cold downburst wave swept across the forest. He looked up and heard the rain approaching through the trees. The downdraft brought much colder air from the cloud tops. The temperature dropped quickly from a comfortable upper 70s to an uncomfortable lower 60s.

"I am called Brad by my friends." He simplified the thought. *"My name Brad. What are you called by friends on your worlds?"*

I am Ka-Litan ... my friend, your friend Lu-cee ... Lu-cee not come long time

Shivering, Brad stood up, waiting for the rain. The voice was talking about his mother. He was definitely not in one of his vivid fantasies; there was a cold front racing through the forest toward him, and he could feel the goose bumps beginning to rise on his arms and the back of his neck. Was it from the chill wind or the truth of this encounter with Ka-Litan? And what exactly was he encountering? At his knee, Dusty was whining and blinking at the falling rain. "Okay, buddy, we're leaving."

Trotting back toward the house, he thought about what had just happened. The basics of an eighth-grade English report last year had required that he explain who, what, why, when, and where. He only knew a name; he had no idea what, when, where, or why. *Or am I simply going bonkers like Mom?* A rush of white noise filled his ears as the wall of rain passed over him. He stood transfixed with the problem of insanity-induced hallucinations versus reality, experience versus delusion. He was now drenched; that was reality. Dusty shook water from his wet fur, breaking into his thoughts. He scratched the dog's head absently and trotted the few miles back to his house.

Deep Space 1

If your death shall, in its moment, preserve the Light's creation, Shine.
Unknown author from the time before Cho secession

3,156.22
High Dzuran Orbit, 21.2

"Where do you want to go?" asked the ship's computer, Jai.

"We should form up the squadron, head for the highest concentration of skeeters." Jai toned an affirmative and sent the order out to the other eight skeeters in Ka-Litan's fighter group. As Kā, or squad leader, Litan, fought to ignore the chaos on the planet below. From the rear seat, weapons officer Mritan, offered the distraction of an offensive systems readiness report. All was ready, but this was not going to be a good day.

Abruptly, a wave of horror, pain, and death emanated from the Dzuran surface as another asteroid impacted the northern ocean close to a nearly destroyed megalopolis. The twin planets of Erra and Dzura were embroiled in an uncivil war for mastery of the system. The Errans had learned that the added power of a steam explosion amplified the destructive blast of asteroid impacts. The incandescent fireball spreading from the center of the new crater roiled outward in boiling waves of red and black killing everything on the surface—blasted in turn by successive pressure, heat, and debris waves.

Litan, Mritan, and Jai, linked by psi were a formidable weapons platform. When combined in their nine-unit squadron, Squad Leader Ka-Litan was the offensive brain of a lethal and highly mobile fighting force. Litan's main goal was to find the other eight ships in his squadron, form up and get into a defensive position near one of the recently completed city ships. The Dzuran defense force built nine evacuation city ships from tour ships, freighters, and amalgams of cargo barges, anything that could be pressurized and fitted with a jump drive. Defended by a fleet of battle cruisers and destroyers, a small fraction of the home planet's population was saved from the barrage of space rocks. All had system jump capacity. Not all were well armed.

30

Erran leadership, aware that they could not win a war of numbers, evened the score by the most abhorrent method— systematic destruction of the sister planet Dzura. Their expertise in moving heavy masses from the mineral rich asteroid belt just outside the entwined orbits of Erra and Dzura led them to the tactic of simply bombarding the heavy industrial sectors on the home world. None of this was at the fore of Litan's thoughts as Jai's com-links had failed to locate all of his squadron. "Jai, location of S4 and S8?"

After a pause, the computer responded. "Munitions bay on Aelo; refitting and arming with heavy metals."

"Understood." He received a psi note from Mritan that they were good, which he confirmed over audio channels for the record. Litan, stressed but almost enjoying finally getting into the long awaited showdown, took a long calming breath. Breathing flaps on his canine snout flared. He linked with fleet command, received orders and commanded: "Jai. To all units: New staging location: Shift to Aelo—anterior nadir engarde formation and await orders from command."

Mritan, his best friend, crèche mate and crew mate, second in his class at fighter school, psi'd a calming note and said, "Friend Litan, we have done all we can do. Our squad will soon be ready, we trust you. By the Lights! We will have our revenge on these monsters. Errans will not win this day!"

"Thanks friend Mritan." Appreciative of the calming blend of psi current and closed channel audio, Litan throttled up and ordered his small ship to a point below the massive city ship in high, nearly synchronous orbit over what had been the Dzuran capital. He was thankful he could not see the fires burning beneath the cinder stained cloud surface.

~ ~ ~

The bombardment lasted for much longer than was necessary. It concluded when the Erran attackers could no longer distinguish surface features on the dying planet to choose targets. They loosed the four remaining asteroids from orbit to slowly fall where they might.

The Dzuran refugee fleet jumped though a half dozen systems in its attempt to escape their Erran pursuers. The final showdown occurred in the shadow of a ringed gas giant in a star system devoid of habitable planets eighty three parsecs, or about two hundred and eighty light years distant from a very promising system whose dominant intelligent culture would not consider the meaning of light years and complex cosmology for another four Dzuran centuries.

Chapter 3

*When a distinguished, but elderly scientist states that something is
possible, he is almost certainly right; when he states that something is
impossible, he is probably wrong.*
Arthur Clarke's First Law

May 31, 1976
Wakulla Beach, Monday morning

The unseasonably cool late spring felt wonderful to Whitcomb Hitchens as
he opened his venerable cypress-plank front door to sniff the dawn.
Weathered and scratched, it was the original door crafted by his grandfather
in the 1930s. The house had started as a two-room cracker cabin with a
corrugated tin roof and had been added to by his father in the 1950s when it
also got its first indoor plumbing. Whit built the second addition himself in
'73 to distract him from his residual war demons. More recently, he had
added new siding, extra bedrooms, and sheetrock. Standing at the top of the
front porch stairs, he called back into the house, "Bradley Delaney Hitchens,
get your backpack and come on! What is the problem this time?" He heard
a rustling and a small crash of something hitting the floor.

"Coming!"

"Now, boy!" He started toward his well-used F-250 and took some
time checking the contents of the toolbox. Allowing time for Bradley to
catch up, he smiled as his son and Dusty leaped the three steps to the ground
and headed to the passenger side at a run. Whit smiled as he thought, *Just
like puppies!* Dusty, by habit, jumped into the bed of the truck, and Brad
jumped up into the passenger seat. Dusty, he thought, was still pretty spry
for an old dog.

In the dark gray light of predawn, he rolled slowly out of the sand-
and-shell driveway and onto the graded road that ran from Wakulla Beach
to the Coastal Highway. Keeping his lights off, he slowed as he noted dark
shapes milling around a hundred yards ahead. Coming to a stop, he flashed

on the headlights to reveal a half dozen turkey hens, which quickly headed for the safety of the brush.

"Hot dang! We might not be able to wait for season to open this year." He looked over at Brad. "Let's get the guns down this evening and get them oiled up."

"Yeah, Dad." Brad peered over the dash at the last of the dis-appearing turkeys as the truck rolled slowly down the road. He suppressed his queasy reaction to the thought of having to clean a bird as large as a Florida wild turkey and tried to match his father's enthusiasm. "Wow! That's cool! How did you know they were here?"

"Saw the tracks last night when I took Dusty out to get the mail." They rode on in silence, headed north. As they joined the parade of office and service workers commuting to Tallahassee, traffic slowed.

Brad started uncertainly, "Dad, can I talk to you a minute?"

"Sure, what's up, bud?"

"Friday, I took a walk with Dusty. Back out to the big cypress."

"Okay ..." Whit trailed off, waiting for more.

"Well, it was not like before, not spooky. But very weird."

"Good, I guess," his voice seemed cautious, "not spooky is good."

"Dusty and me sat down a little ways off, by that little sinkhole I told you about, and kinda rested for a while. I started to get sleepy, and I guess I thought I was sleepin' and dreamin'. Anyhow, I started talking with something that seems to be living in the woods. Only I can't see it, and it says it can't be seen."

Whit looked over at his boy, who was picking at a fingernail. His eyebrows furrowed in worry above his nose. "You sure you weren't dreaming?" He patted his son's hands to stop the picking. "You know you get awful lost in those daydreams of yours."

"No, I'm sure ... least I'm pretty sure it wasn't a daydream. It started to rain, and I was still talking to him or it. It seems like it's talking inside my head. And it doesn't seem to matter whether I'm talking to it or thinking at it, it still seems to be talking to me and listening."

Whit was quiet for a while, thoughtful, and spoke softly, "Are you sure somebody wasn't pulling your leg?"

"No, Dad, there wasn't nobody there."

"Anybody—there wasn't anybody there."

"That's what I said, there wasn't anybody there."

The senior Hitchens furrowed his brow. "So who were you talking to? Are you starting to get imaginary friends?"

"Naw, Dad. It isn't like that. It's not like talking either. Maybe more like thinking out loud, only you can hear the answers inside your head."

Sunlight was flashing through the planted pines as they drove. An impatient Volvo sped around them to gain one position in line.

"Idiot. In a few minutes, we'll pull off and he could have had this spot without risking all our lives." He dropped back a little to maintain his preferred following distance. "So why isn't it like talking to this man who isn't there?"

"When I first started hearing the voice, I answered back, called out to whoever or whatever to come out where I could see him. Nothing showed itself. But I kept hearing the voice."

"Where did this 'voice' come from?"

Brad was picking at his finger again. He looked out the passenger window as nothing in particular passed by out of focus. "As I thought about it later, it was like coming from inside my head." He rubbed at his skull just behind his ears, remembering the headache that had come on after the conversation. "It was like I was remembering hearing, but after a while, I realized that I didn't have to talk out loud to talk back. Just had to think what I was going to say, and it talked back."

They approached the lineup where all traffic seemed to catch up to itself every morning approaching Tallahassee and slowed into the queue. "Brad, I need to tell you something, about Mom. You know she thought she was going crazy and couldn't stand herself because she was hearing voices." He looked at his son and rested his hand gently on his knee. "She was out in those same woods when she said she heard voices in her head."

"Yessir, that's why I didn't tell you Saturday when it happened. I was afraid you would think I was nuts too. I'm still not too sure what happened out there, but it didn't feel like I was daydreaming." He looked up at the taillights of the Volvo in front of them in the line. "When Mom was having her ... uh, spells ... when she was hearing voices, did she only hear them in the woods?"

"Hmm, I think so. At least at first and for quite a while. But just before she left, I'd catch her sitting on the edge of the bed, talking and crying softly." He let out a long sigh and then downshifted and turned into the parking lot. "By then, I don't know if she was talking to something or just talking to herself about it. She was really depressed and disturbed."

"Should I go see a shrink? Do you think this is something I could'a got from her?"

"I don't know, Brad; let's not do anything hasty. You've got a great imagination, and maybe our talking about it earlier triggered a dream about it." He looked down at his son, who was clearly upset.

"Let's not worry about it today. Let's get this sample of yours to the lab, and then we can get out the shotguns and get 'em ready for a turkey shoot!"

June 5, 1976
Tallahassee, 11:35 p.m.

David Duggars was beyond exhaustion and hope. As the sole occupant of Florida State University's geology lab, he was considering the slave labor aspect of being a teaching assistant. The last of the department's cleaning crew had come and gone without a curious glance. He thought his presence here was only a little more infrequent than the furniture's. He was spread out on one of the huge black worktables facing a very ordinary, yellow stained suspended ceiling punctuated occasionally by humming fluorescent lights. One set of lights in the corner flickered spasmodically, but he found that if he turned his head just right, he could ignore the irritation.

The air-conditioning, straining to keep up with Florida's heat, now seemed to have finally caught up with the daily temperature swings, and he ran his hands across his forearms to smooth out the goose bumps. He rolled over, sat up, fumbled on the table, and came up with the checklist. He had scribbled it with the intent of transcribing the list into a table of contents for the lab notebook he had started for Dr. Hill.

He grumbled to himself, "I don't know what to do next." He ran down his actions and options. "I've gone through the standard acid-base testing, check and check. Specific gravity? Check. It doesn't present any known crystalline structures under UV, IR, or visible. Check, check, check. Tests positive for carbon as a minor component, but is not reactive to flame. No loss of mass after prolonged heating. Check. Does not react to heating up to four thousand degrees other than turning white. Super check! Electrical conductivity is close to nil, but unusual reaction to magnetic fields above twelve thousand gauss. We'll need to check that further over at the physics lab."

Duggars sat up and grabbed the rough version of his lab notes. He wrote, "Conductivity increases with increasing gauss." He tapped his eraser tip on the table, pursing his lips. He wrote again, "Need to take sample to physics mag lab and test for conductivity vs. field strength." Scratching his hairline, he walked over to the windows. Set relatively high in the wall to allow work tables to be positioned under them, they permitted him to stand and gaze at the campus spread out below him. The student union was nearly empty, although he could hear parties going on up on fraternity row, or was that the multi-track blare of over two hundred blended stereos coming from the men's dorm out of sight to the right. He couldn't tell. With almost no school work left to do in the semester, there was nothing going on in the dorms but partying and packing.

What he could tell was that he was still upset and distracted by an earlier argument with his girlfriend. Actually, they'd only had three dates, but he had been hoping for some sense of exclusivity. He had apologized for not making a proffered movie night, which he had missed because Dr. Hill had promised a favor for an old student. Duggars thought this assay would only take a few minutes. It had looked like a small bit of aluminum with some teal-blue colorant somehow mixed into the alloy. Dr. Hill had become curious and wanted to know how the blue permeated the sample; usually such coloration was the result of anodized powder added to finished piecework. He'd have to work to convince Beverly that this investigation was both frustrating and compelling, more compelling than she was.

Dr. Hill's simple favor had become his "Mission Impossible." David only wished he could have declined and the sample had evaporated in a small, fizzy cloud of smoke like the television series' signature self-destructing mission tape. With the base beat of Lalo Schifrin's television soundtrack running through his head, he looked back at his list to see if he should go any further. *Damn, might as well shoot for the whole wad. If I put this off, he'll just have me do it on Monday. Or worse*, he thought, *he'll get someone else to do it.*

At twenty-four, Duggars might have been more self-assured. Dubbed "the Hermit" by his housemates, he really hoped to shed that persona and get a life going. He knew he was starting to wallow in what could become another bout of insecure self-examination, so he stood up, stretched, and grabbed the small bit of bluish "metal." At this point, he didn't know what he was examining. And what bothered him was that by now, after this series of preliminary testing, he should have figured it out. The more he tested, the

36

less he knew what he was working with and the further he got from an answer.

He shuffled down one flight into the musty sub-basement. The place was dusty and filled with shelves upon shelves of rock and core samples that exuded the dry, musty smell of a desert cave. He entered one of the only clean rooms in the basement, the closet-size space reserved for the new electron microscope. He turned it on, and as it warmed up with a whir of cooling fans and compressors, he prepared his small remaining sample. He wasn't sure what it would tell, having been bathed in acids and bases, heated beyond his expectations, and beat on in malleability testing. But it was worth a shot.

When Duggars first dialed in the image, he wondered if he had zoomed in on some other sample left on the scope's specimen stub. No, there was the bluish tint in the optical reticule, even under 400x magnification. *Let's go in a little further, and now centered, a lot further ...* "Whoa!" He sat back. Pulling the stub out of the retaining brackets, he looked to see what kind of other bit of dust was in the clip. Nothing visible. He hit it with a blast of compressed air and reinserted the sample in the scope's sample bracket. Settling his forehead back into the viewing scope, he again centered the sample and began to zoom in gradually, making sure it stayed centered at each successive zoom. As he approached maximum magnification, he tried to register what he was seeing. Slowly, the pattern emerged from chaos. There was a flash of recognition, followed by incredulity and an even deeper mystery. He was too tired for real excitement. He breathed slowly out and then slowly in. *Oh, my God!* He looked at his watch; it was both too late and too early to call just yet. "Damn!"

June 6, 1976
North of Tallahassee, 7:15 a.m.

Dr. Hill was unusual for a still-teaching senior college professor in that he was almost completely deaf. He had a fondness for symphonic music played at levels that made most humans cringe. At his favored listening volume, floors and windows shook. A graduate in chemistry from Gallaudet, he took a master's at Cornell and his PhD at Michigan State, which led to a hatred for icy winters and his ultimate decision to take a teaching post in the South. He was small framed and athletic, and most new acquaintances were astounded to discover the extent of his deafness, as his lip reading skills were so advanced. His disability did lead to difficulties for those who needed to make contact with him though.

As Sunday dawned warm and muggy, he returned from his walk to the end of the driveway for the morning paper to find his phone flashing. Looking at the readout, he saw that his TA, David Duggars, was calling. He plugged in the ear jack and took the call. "David, is everything all right?"

"Yes, sir. It's just that I've found something a little unusual about this little piece of aluminum you gave me to work on."

"Oh, David, you didn't work on that last night, did you? Wasn't there a big hoo-doo on campus last night?"

"Er, no, sir, graduation ceremonies were last week, so last night was pretty low key for me. I think dorm life has hit a new standard for post exam debauchery, but I managed to stay distracted most of the time. Anyway, sir, I had wanted to get this over with, and I didn't think it would take as long as it did."

"Did you find out how they managed to permeate the metal matrix with colorizer?"

"Well, no. Actually, it isn't aluminum … I think you had better come look at what I found."

"Now?"

"Umm, if it's not too much trouble, sometime today. You might want some time to think about this before the week gets busy. When did you say you would get back to your friend with an answer?"

"Oh, that's not a problem." He looked up at the face of the gravity clock in the foyer. "I can meet you in about an hour; let's say nine thirty. Go get some breakfast, and I'll see you in a bit."

~ ~ ~

Duggars heard softly shuffling footsteps echoing down the darkened tile hallway. He'd eaten a solitary breakfast at the student union, and his frame of mind was probably in the worst possible place. He hated being dumbfounded by this damn bit of foolishness. All he really wanted to do was show Dr. Hill what he had found and go to bed. With the squeak of a very old door and a rush of energy, Dr. Hill came into the lab wearing a V-neck sweater vest over a short-sleeve golf shirt. His glasses rode high on his nose, giving him an air of expectancy. "So how are we this morning, David?"

"Tired, sir, I …"

"You haven't been to bed?" He noticed the darkening circles under David's eyes. "Umm, no. I started doing some standard tests. You know, we

38

just figured it was aluminum at first, so I thought I would try to isolate some sort of high-temperature polymer or metalloid colorant that gave the sample the teal color. I tried physical deformation to get a cross section and realized right away that despite its light weight, it wasn't aluminum."

"No?"

"No, sir; its sheer strength is incredible."

Hill tweaked the level adjustment on his hearing and said, rubbing the stubble on his chin, "Hitchens mentioned that!"

Duggars continued, "I was expecting a specific gravity of somewhere around twenty-five hundred, but it came in closer to thirty-eight hundred. So, the sample is too heavy for aluminum, and too light for titanium. I went back to basics and started a whole train of tests, as if it were a total unknown. Acid wash, no resultant; same with extreme base. It isn't reactive in the normal test ranges even under a charge."

"What did you say the SG was?"

Duggars pulled out a small flip notepad from his breast pocket and thumbed through a few sheets. "Let's see, specific gravities; I got 3,759 and 3,772 kilograms per cubic meter. I did the second run because I didn't believe the first."

Hill merely put thumb and forefinger to his chin and stared. Duggars continued, "I tested for melting point and didn't find one in this lab. If I had access to an arc or acetylene, we might get there, but all I got was a cheery white glow with the oxy-butane torch."

"Could the SG be a result of the carbon impurity in the structure?" Hill asked. "And it's titanium after all?"

"No, sir, the signatures aren't right. If I had to guess, it probably has an atomic weight in the high nineties with mass compensated for by its loose crystalline structure."

"Structure?"

"A hint of crystalline structure under IR or UV bands. I just couldn't type it." He mumbled something about stress deformities and yawned. He rubbed at his eye sockets distractedly and then, as if remembering something, looked directly at his professor in earnest. "Where did you say your friend got his little nugget?"

"He's an old protégé, great student who came through this program. He had a lot of promise as a professional. He went to Nam and came back to open a well-drilling company. Too bad. Huge waste of talent and intellect."

"But where did he find this? It didn't come out of a well!"

"All he told me was that his son found this metallic rod in the woods under unusual circumstances and he wanted to find out what it might be made of. Where is our sample now?"

"Downstairs."

"SEM?"

"Yes, it's loaded, but we'll have to boot it up again. I don't trust the new main frame; it crashes unexpectedly and often."

They went down to the basement, powered up the scanning electron microscope and its controlling system and waited for the indicator panel array to go green. "I haven't moved anything. The sample is still in the bracket."

Hill rolled his chair up to the scope's optical spotting scope and looked at the sample under light at high magnification. He hummed a few phrases of a Chopin etude and moved over to the cathode ray viewer. He settled his head into the light shield and said,

"What do we have here?" Still humming, he adjusted the settings on the electron gun to higher power. "We have crystalline structure.

The matrix seems to be ... what? ... variable across the sample.

It's ..." He sat back, astonishment clearly lighting his face. "David, my boy!"

"Yeah, I thought you would like this. I really hated to call you this morning, but—"

"No, no, no. This is truly incredible." Hill was clearly excited. "Is it possible that this bit of metal was grown in place?"

Duggars said, "What do you mean?"

Peering intently at the output display, Hill continued, "This structure, this apparent crystalline matrix, seems to have been grown to a pre-determined shape." Hill looked down thoughtfully for a moment and then back at Duggars. "David, I purposely didn't tell you what the origin of this sample was, mostly just to test your analytics, but the little bit I gave you was taken by extreme force from a larger piece, about a half-meter-long rod, a little over nine millimeters in diameter. Hitchens said the donor end, the bit I gave you, was already deformed by stress trauma, but the other end was clearly a manufactured end that looked like some attachment had been ripped from it, also by great force." He stopped for emphasis.

"It appeared that the rod may have been sleeved, that is, it might have rotated or extended on an inner layer of a slightly smaller diameter. But what's important is the amorphous—no, not amorphous—umm, variable structure of the crystalline growth. From what I've seen, it appears that this structure is of a crystalline lattice. It's surreal." He looked up at Duggars, who was trying to take in what Hill was saying.

Hill tapped at the monitor, pointing to a detail on the screen, and continued. "At lower magnifications, there is this concentric line, suggestive of a shell or sleeve. The outer ring seems to have a different crystalline structure than the interior, and it's concentric! I've never seen that in a metallic lattice! The change to the interior structure is hard to describe because of the shear strains here and here." He pointed at striations running across the image on the screen. "But the interior also appears to have a radial/concentric lattice structure that perfectly matches the alignment of the shell. Incredible! I can't imagine its utility or its manufacture, and we still haven't identified the material, or what its purpose might have been—or who made it."

"Who? I mean, what it does is secondary at this point. Who could do this? Who has the capability?" Duggars said. He had been wondering for the past few hours who could have manufactured this, thing.

Hill responded. "Well, possibly NASA has something we don't know about yet; seems too sophisticated for the Russians." Smiling, the professor swiveled a full 360-degree rotation in the old wooden chair and stopped to look at David. "Perhaps one of NASA's advanced materials labs made some component for a very specialized use or environment." He swiveled back to the scope. "I haven't been in materials for a long time, though. Monday, I will make some calls, but let's get some data down so we can talk intelligently when we start calling. We also need to get this sample over to the particle accelerator to see what this is made of.

"First, though, I think I'll get a sample up to an old friend with a great metals shop in Detroit. He reverse engineers other people's work all the time." Hill scratched his chin thoughtfully.

"It seems to be doped with something in the matrix, but I don't know what the primary is," Duggars said. "And those black dots? I believe those are carbon inclusions, too. But I never saw a molecular structure like that before. We might send it down to the physics people and their accelerator. See if we can get a grip on the primary lattice material."

Hill caught David yawning through a grimace. "Yes, I agree; we don't want to let them in on our discovery unless we have to." He smiled at his sleepy assistant who appeared to be fading as he spoke.

"Go get some sleep; you've done great." Hill thought about the next few days. "Tell you what, David, you've already given up the better part of the weekend, why don't you take some time today, get some sleep. We can probably get some more time in on this in the next few days. By the time the piece gets mailed up to Detroit, we can type up the documentation of our— of your findings. We also need to get Hitchens on board before any attempt at going public."

With mixed feelings of success, vindication, and exhaustion, Duggars left his mentor adjusting the angle of the sample for another view. He could almost feel the pillow under his head as he trudged out of the building. As he made his way to his house, not far from campus, he had mental images of two satellites colliding in orbit and some ultra-secret exotic bit happening to end up in the woods in Florida.

He thought of the calculations he'd read about for the upcoming Skylab re-entry in a few weeks and the anticipated visible fireball. Then he thought, *Not all satellites move in the same direction! Many are polar orbits, and some are geosynchronous, but some are retrograde. What if one grazed another and the effective ground speed of a dislodged piece after impact was close to zero? It would simply fall nearly straight down. Lucky the damn piece of metal didn't start a fire. It's a damned odd way to get a sneak peek at Russian technology. Soon, we'll figure it out, and we may even have to sign a pile of confidentiality papers, but first, I'm going to bed.* He then smiled to himself, *I wonder where Beverly is?*

June 7, 1976
Fort Meade, Maryland, 0915 hours

Gloria Shefly was about to take her morning break when the bank of intercept filters she was monitoring beeped. One of the lights went green and began blinking. The hundred and seventy-nine other lights on the panel array remained dark. A phone surveillance operator in a third-floor cubicle in the National Security Agency's Directorate of Science and Technology, Gloria tapped the blinking green toggle and adjusted her earphones. Selecting the channel for record, she began to listen in earnest. Her expression subtly changed from interest to disbelief, then wonder and then back to disbelief. When the signal terminated, she rolled back in her chair, smiling peculiarly. She called up the "from" and "to" phone numbers, jotted them down, pulled the recorded cassette, and went to her supervisor's desk.

"Colonel Henderson?" She offered the cassette across his desk.

"What have you got, Gloria?" The young intel officer had aced every math class he had ever taken, and he had taken a lot of them. His PhD in advanced crypto-analysis had been financed by a grant from the CIA's tech scholarship program, and, as they had hoped, he rewarded the sponsorship with a six-year tour. He was fit and trim but did not have the advanced physical training of a typical field agent. His conditioning had more to do with a handball court than an obstacle course or running grueling miles in the Virginia foothills. His obvious intellect and academic standing had earned a rare direct commission as captain, and over the last ten years, he had quickly moved up the ranks through major to lieutenant colonel and head of the listening post and special advisor to the decrypt wing.

"Sir, it's kind of a bizarre one, a little hard to think about." She shrugged and grinned. "I'd like to see your reaction." Handing over her notes, she said, "The conversation is between a Doctor Hill in Florida, Florida State University, and a Jason Walters in Michigan. He's in structural metals research for GM, at a Detroit materials lab."

Henderson plugged the tape into his console and turned up the speakers. The conversation had apparently been in progress when the text screener started to record. The two listened:

Hill: … didn't quite believe it, either; that's why I've asked your lab to do an independent test array.

Walters: Harrison, I'm going to need at least a few cc's of material.

Hill: We've used or abused almost all I have for the moment. I'll have to get the original artifact or a small piece of it to you, and that won't be possible until tomorrow.

Walters: Tomorrow?

Hill: Yes, the original piece is south of here. An old student of mine lives down on the coast.

Walters: Beach house? Geologists must be doing better there than they do around here. He find oil or diamonds?

Hill: No, he lives in the woods in a cracker shack he inherited from his folks. He's third generation or so, pillar of his community. He asked for my confidentiality until we had some positive ID. I haven't even taken it over to the physics department until we verify. So, what else do you need?

43

Walters: Okay. From what you've told me so far, you have confirmed what Mr. Duggars has already determined. Also, to test the crystalline form you tried ... [The audio became garbled.]

Hill: Yes, and that's where it gets interesting. There is definitely a carbon structure of some sort entrained or formed and another material. We just don't know what it is.

Walters: Why not? I thought this would be fairly elemental for you guys.

Hill: Elemental, that's a good one, Harrison. Old chemistry 101 joke. From all I can tell so far, this stuff doesn't appear in our periodic table. But then, the sample size was so small, we really didn't have much to work with.

Walters: What do you mean? Not in our periodic table?

Hill: [Garbled] ... an atomic weight around 100 but we get spectroscopy results in the 50s.

Walters: That would make it pretty heavy, wouldn't it? Something between molybdenum and silver? You said this stuff was light, closer to titanium. Maybe it's some sort of isotope. Radioactive?

Hill: Yes, but at such a low level, it's either been irradiated, or it's pretty stable. The test results were pointing to a rare metal with impurities, but that must be wrong because it is simply too rare. It should be more radioactive; our problem is, we don't know why it's stable. We found that when ... [garbled] ... a heavy magnetic field. The few elements that are, are far too heavy to—

Walters: Magnetic? Interesting you should mention that. When we can get enough to work with we'll have to check out Duggars's mention of unusual magnetic properties.

Hill: I'll try to convince Hitchens how important it is to get a larger sample. He may not want to further chop up the artifact.

Walters: Well, if I was a sci ... [garbled] ... tell you that your blue artifact, or whatever it is, is not from here.

Hill: Do you mean what I think with, "not from here"?

Walters: What I said, not [garbled]... this planet, hell, not from this star system. Sagan is gonna love this!

44

[a low hiss becomes audible]

Walters: Do you hear that?

Hill: What?

Walters: Dead air, like there's another line open.

Hill: What do you mean?

Walters: Remember our old student housing? When we had a party line? A pop and then dead air, like someone else is on the line.

Hill: No. I don't hear anything.

Walters: Right, sorry. Forgot about your hearing. I'm not sure we should be talking on an open line.

Hill: Jason, you're being paranoid. This is some serious stuff. You should see the artifact.

Walters: If we get a leak before we can verify our conclusions, we will be drummed out of our respective departments before you can say "loss of tenure." When can you … [garbled] …

Hill: I will have to express mail it as soon as I can get another piece from Hitchens. I don't think he'd release the whole thing and I don't blame him. Should be able to get that to you Wednesday or Thursday.

Walters: I'll reserve some spectrometer time for Thursday night.

Hill: Okay. Say hello to Deb.

Walters: Yeah, sure.

Hill: You are still married to her, aren't you?

Walters: Yeah, but … [garbled]

Hill: Oh. Sorry, I'll call you when it's in the mail.

Colonel Henderson leaned back in his chair and slowly let air out through pursed lips.

Excited, Shefly asked, "What did you make of it?"

He responded with caution, hiding his piqued interest in a near monotone. "I only went as high as organic chemistry in undergrad, and that was a few years ago. Sounds like they have an exotic material that we need to find out about."

"Do you think they're overreacting about the not-from-this-planet stuff?" she asked.

"There must be an explanation, something from an orbital stray—hell, it's probably NASA and above my pay grade, not likely Russian,"

Henderson said. "I'll need to get this uphill as soon as possible."

"NASA? You really think so?"

"And see if you can find out who the guy is that lives on the coast in a 'cracker shack.' What was his name? Kitchens or something? Oh, and what the heck is a cracker shack, anyway?"

"Yes, sir, I'll get someone on it." She turned and started to go, but made a pirouette when she heard him puff out an exhale. "Yes?"

"Hell, it might even be something the Russians cooked up, but it'd be more like them to brag to the world if they ginned up a new mouse trap. Can you clean up this signal? I want to take this upstairs, but I want you to get it cleaned up first and type up the transcript for the file." He saw her shoulders actually droop with deflated excitement.

"Yes, sir. I'll see to it, sir." Facing him again, she said, "I think a 'cracker shack' is just a small cabin or house with a tin roof and a full front porch. Pretty humble homes, I think." She turned again on her high heels and left, hoping that he was watching her leave.

Henderson did in fact watch her leave, swearing she was struttin' her stuff on purpose, and then he swiveled around in his chair, scanned his bookshelves, and located the book that had popped into his mind: Robert Heinlein's *Stranger in a Strange Land*. The next word that popped into his mind was inevitable; *"Grok!"* He wondered if he did understand. "Dammit!" he said and swiveled back around as he picked up his receiver and jabbed at the dial.

June 7, 1976
MacDill AFB, 1130 hours

Air Force Special Operations Captain Sheldon Richards was in mid-call to the Pentagon, this morning's third cup of coffee cooling at his side, when a decrypt notice was laid on his desk by a nameless airman. Grunting audibly, he took the sheet and rotated it to read.

"Yes, sir, I just got the crib notes delivered as we're talking. Yes, sir, I understand. Let me see, yes, I have assets in north Florida we can mobilize; we have a unit up at Fort Rucker that can give us no fuss tactical support if need be and some troops here at MacDill who have just come back from night jungle ops training in Panama. I'll pick from the two and make up a

46

team." He scanned further down the thin, flimsy sheet. "Yes, sir, I understand. Small team, details on need-to-know only." He listened, irritated as vocal volume increased on the other end. "Yes, sir, no need-to-know on the ops end. Transparent positioning for security and deniability built into the methodology."

Richards's deeply tanned face reddened, evidence of thinly controlled building anger as he listened to the condescending general on the line. He raised his eyes to the ceiling as he fully comprehended the content and intent of the memo. This was not actually a decrypt, but it was on the same official incoming report form. He puckered his lips into a silent whistle as he began devising a tactical mission plan. "That's right, we should be able to mobilize by close of business today and be positioned for ops by tomorrow at the latest."

He gave an exasperated sigh, irritated at the mothering from the other end. Yes, he did know what a level-three confidential meant. He could only tell the team what they needed to know, their targets' identities, but not why they were targets or the identity of the two-star talking in his ear. They were to tell no one of this event, ever. The usual penalties for disclosure were jail, fines equal to twice your net worth, and loss of pension. Well, he thought, maybe congressional oversight in a closed panel briefing if it should come to that, but possibly not even then. Those bastards were notorious blabbermouths. No way those liberal bastards would ever condone rendition or removal of a citizen or worse. Captain Richards signed off with the two-star and grabbed a fast gulp of coffee.

Rereading the instructions, he memorized the two names on the cleanup list: Dr. Harrison Hill and his assistant, David Duggars. There was also a Whitcomb Hitchens down for background. He then crumpled the flimsy into a military-issue, five-inch-square glass ashtray, lit it, and watched it flash to smoking dust.

He went to his closet and removed a packed olive-drab overnight duffle and headed for the door. On his way through reception, he informed the Spec. 4 on duty that he would be out for a few days and to save all calls. An hour later, he was lifting off from MacDill AFB in an F-18C Hornet. At a leisurely, fuel-conscious two-hundred and fifty knots, he would be on the ground at the TLH commercial hub in a few hours. He could also do a low recon of the subject coastline and maybe even buzz one of the beaches for babes before picking up the new runway. Coming in from south to north, his would look like one of many flights that flew in from Tyndall AFB every day.

June 9, 1976
South of Tallahassee, 0515 hours

Richards checked his watch and then the mirror and saw that he was pressed, gig-line straight. He had replaced his uniform with blue jeans and a short-sleeve, light-blue work shirt with "Eugene" embroidered over the pocket. He pressed the artificial mustache against his upper lip and adjusted the fake hair and sideburns that extended just below his ears. Smiling at the reflection of his alter ego, he almost missed the two team members he had selected. Also wearing wigs and false facial hair, they almost made it past his car before he noticed they were his guys, Jenks and Lassiter. Jenks was trim and nimble. His skin tone, self-described as coffee with a splash of cream, set off intense black eyes. His blue-eyed companion was an overdeveloped gym rat with a Sergeant Rock chin line and a blue tattoo on his left bicep that was partially erased by scar tissue. Dressed down in skivvies, though, they could pass as citizens. Just not civilians you would mess with.

The team got into three rental vehicles, two Chevy Suburbans and a pickup, and headed north. Driving into the plantation hill country north of Tallahassee, they took positions on the capital city's Meridian Road. The narrow country road had virtually no shoulders and steep ditches or nearly vertical clay walls on both sides. It was covered by a dark canopy of ancient live oaks. Arriving in position, the team parked and waited for the target's car to pass the spotter car.

~ ~ ~

Dr. Hill, coffee mug and morning paper in hand, left his rural driveway at 9:10 a.m., long after Tallahassee's rush-hour traffic had withered to occasional shoppers and service vehicles. His late-model Buick had been easy to identify and isolate. He didn't notice one of the Suburbans and a pickup, pulling out of a side road into line behind him. Hill had been thinking about his promise to get another sample from Hitchens and put it in the mail to Michigan before day's end. He had been planning his trip to the coast and thinking about how it would impact his typical Tuesday schedule when two drivers took over his life. A little over a mile into his commute, Hill, taking

48

a sip of coffee, looked in his sideview mirror and noticed a pickup making an insane attempt to pass on this dangerous winding country road.

"What an idiot" He thought and began to slow down to ensure that the pickup could make the pass.

To his utter surprise, an oversized station wagon behind him sped up, its front bumper engaging his and pushing him forward. He hit his pedals, and the Buick's front brakes locked and began to smoke, losing traction as the car behind him overpowered his own car's brakes. Hill, terrified now, could not believe the events unfolding. His mug rolled to the carpet, spilling its amber liquid. The driver behind him was wearing dark Ray-Bans and a grim smile. "Kee-rist!" He shouted out loud. "This is malicious endangerment, and it's working!" Hill began to feel a searing pain in his chest as his pulse rose to dangerous levels.

As he struggled to steer, he realized he had to release the brakes to keep from being forced off the road. At his side window, he could only see the passenger door of the pickup beside him, and it wasn't passing. The damned fool was keeping pace with his car while the SUV behind him kept pushing from behind. At over sixty-five miles per hour now, the three vehicles were accelerating as they rounded another bend and began to climb toward a blind hilltop. Hill could only hope that an oncoming car would force the pickup to pass or drop back. Sixty-five and accelerating uphill, what the hell was going on? In a breathless panic now, he attempted to accelerate ahead of the vehicle that was actually on his bumper. The roar of the truck's motor, less than ten feet away, did not help his rapidly rising blood pressure. Hill could hear his heartbeat in his temples over the whine of his Buick, the throaty base of the pickup, and the irrelevant gentle tones of the classical music station.

"Christ Almighty!" he swore, focused with deadly intent on the lane ahead, praying for oncoming traffic of some kind. The three vehicles crested the hill, and as they entered a long, downhill run, their speeds increased. At over seventy-five miles per hour he again tried braking, trying to slow the maniac down. He didn't like the resulting swerve as his Buick rolled on its soft suspension. Hill's left arm began to tingle as the incipient heart attack began to rob its muscles of oxygen. The downgrade took them out of a cut bank section, and the top of the steep clay bank dropped to ground level. The roadway became a narrow, tree-lined asphalt path with steep embankments that sloped down to wetlands or water on both sides.

Finally, the SUV dropped back. The last thing Dr. Harrison Hill was ever aware of was the pickup truck's hard lane shift to the right. As it impacting Hill's car, the Buick's tires left pavement. The pickup gave a final shove to the right, and the Hill's car became momentarily airborne before its right headlight assembly impacted a large sweet gum at over eighty-five miles per hour. The Buick's engine compartment collapsed, and its rear end leapt to almost vertical. The vehicle rolled onto its left side, slid across the roadway, and careened down the opposite embankment. It slid to a stop on its roof, wheels spinning. His limp, unconscious body hung from its seat belt. White smoke began to drift from the wreck's engine compartment.

The pickup's driver, Lassiter, backed up to the wreck site, got out, and clambered down the slope. He felt Hill's throat for a pulse and then forced an ice pick into the fuel line. When enough gas had spilled onto the engine, he tossed in a wooden match. Then Lassiter in the pickup and Jenks in the chase vehicle drove a short distance before pulling into an abandoned convenience store parking lot where the third vehicle waited. The two drivers got into the sedan with Richards and made their report. The cigarette break and debriefing were completed in a few minutes. The small caravan proceeded north, passing the scene of the wreck and noting that flames were licking at the crumpled Buick. They were soon out of earshot and did not hear the loud whump that signaled the gas tank exploding. They could not return south along Meridian Road because they knew the roadway was blocked from the south by a freshly fallen tree. Forty-five minutes later, they were on the opposite side of the city settling into a breakfast buffet.

June 10, 1976
South of Tallahassee, 1415 hours.

Writing in a small spiral-bound notepad, Captain Richards was finishing up his after-action report on the morning operation that neutralized Professor Hill in as vague a language as could be used and still creditably serve as his report. He startled to the harsh ring of the desk phone in the motel room.

"This is Eugene Johnson." Richards enjoyed creating the anonymity of his field ops personas. The surnames he used often spanned half a column of fine print in the phone book of a medium-sized city. His aliases might be memorable, but they were by no means unique. "I have pen and paper at the ready; go ahead, sir."

50

He wrote with the receiver crooked under an ear and the pad on his knee. A detergent commercial played out on the motel's tiny color television. Moments later, he called the room numbers of his team and set a conference for 1530 hours. He was oblivious to his drab surroundings, the yellowing paint, the rust-stained sink, and cheap motel art. He had billeted in far worse in Columbia and Nicaragua. Most of the motel's other patrons rented by the night or by the hour. Its main attractions were dim outside lighting and a cash-only, no-questions-asked policy. He finished writing, sighed, and lay back for a catnap.

June 10, 1976
Crawfordville, FL, 3:30 p.m.

Whit Hitchens sat in the utilitarian office of Hitchens Pipe and Water Supply checking current billings and past-due accounts. The one pile he had yet to attack was the short stack of invoices for drilling equipment and two truckloads of recently delivered eight- and six-inch PVC pipe. A couple of blue flies buzzed at a windowpane. His cluttered office seemed seedier today than usual. He looked around at the accumulated dust, the piles of files that Lucy had kept organized, and fought overwhelming grief. It seemed that he had gotten used to increasing levels of disorder. Looking around the office at the business he had created, he moved some short stacks of paper and found a family picture taken several years back on their front steps.

Lucy's cousin's family had been over for the day. Lou Anne and Chase Chappell and their kids, Jamie and Connie, sat on one step with the Hitchens family behind them, all staring benignly at the camera. Whit looked at the smiling faces and thought of his son's pain at the loss of his mother. If only he had been able to talk to her, to share his own thoughts.

He had to believe in his son's statements the previous morning for two very important reasons. One, he understood his wife's struggle to retain sanity. Her early church upbringing made her believe that she had been communicating with demons. He had tried to humor her when she came to him with confessions of an unknowable possession. Toward the end, just before she left, she had told him how certain she was that the "friend" in the forest was real. He still greatly missed her presence in his life. When he suggested that perhaps she was dealing with angels, not demons, the laugh she gave in response held a nervous, terrified quality that had truly scared

51

him. Then one day, she had simply not been there when he came home from work. Gone. Suitcase gone. She had left a note on the table.

The second reason he had to believe Bradley's plea for help was that he also had been interviewed by the "friend." Two months after Lucy Hitchens left home, when pain began to replace his anger, he had gone walking on her favorite trail beyond the Cathedral of the Palms to what she called the "fern garden." It had been a bright spring morning without joy when he'd spotted the massive cypress he knew was near her "spot." He slipped, as she had, through her break in the interwoven stems of titi. Sitting on the bank, he had looked around at all she had described to him. At thirty and sixty feet above, the low canopy of palms and the higher canopy of longleaf pine provided shade for the titi thicket, which in turn shaded the ground around the spot so that little ground cover grew with any enthusiasm. Short grasses, lichen, and several varieties of ferns and fungi provided a musky scent to still days. The earth had smelled good there.

The thoughts had come as suggestions at first. He had thought he was imagining the conversations Lucy had related to him. The thoughts had congealed from a thin narrative to conversation. Then, as it had with so many visitors to the site in the past, a suggestion of a question received an answer.

yes, here now had formed unbidden in his back brain, not his ears. He had jumped to his feet, shaken. Then the unbidden thought had come, *My name Ka-Litan* The thoughts had formed as a picture on the rear lining of his skull. In his later memory of the brief encounter, he felt like he was seeing the thoughts form.

Frozen in place, he yelled in response, "Who the hell are you, Ka-li-tan?"

Li-tan friend Lu-cee ... Li-tan friend you ... you friend Lu-cee

Whit's will melted; his lifetime of reasonable and considered solutions to all problems, big and small, began to slide out from under him. He found himself moving. As fast as he could squeeze through the tangle of brush, he left the small sinkhole. Trotting, then running, he had felt an impossible, gut-wrenching horror that for whatever reason, something beyond reason, a person—no, a presence—had been talking with him, talking with thought; he hadn't actually heard anything. *"Freakin' damn!"*

Lucy had been experiencing something real. Terrifying and real. Sane people didn't have rational conversations with things that weren't there. That only happened in the scriptures and his kid's pulp science fiction. He had belittled her and not sought to understand or to truly listen. She had come to him, he now realized, out of fear for her sanity. He had failed her out of redneck machismo, and now she was gone, fearing that he could not be trusted to keep her out of the state mental hospital in Chattahoochee. Tears of pain had blended with the sweat of fear, and he'd soon found himself at the trail head along a country road. He'd turned back to the hog wire fence and doubled over, suddenly overcome by nausea. He had emptied his gut and continued to heave until his whole body ached.

Now, sitting in his office recalling the experience, his cowardly escape from the presence in the forest flooded back in all its painful, shameful reality. He picked up the phone and called for Dr. Hill. Just before the ringing bleeped into a message machine's voice, a tearful receptionist answered the phone. "Yes?" He heard a choking sob on the other end. "I mean, this is FSU Geology, may I help you?"

"Is Dr. Hill in?" Whit asked. In response, the person on the other end began to sob uncontrollably. There were some sounds of consoling voices audible over the crying receptionist. He heard a clumsy transfer of the handset and then a more controlled voice took over.

"FSU Geology, this is Jim Kenner, may I help you?"

"Dr. Kenner, this is Whit Hitchens, I took some of your classes several years back. Marine microorganisms?"

"Umm, yes, I remember. What can I do for you?"

"I was collaborating with Dr. Hill on a research project, a private matter. May I please talk to him if he's in?"

"Mr. Hitchens … er, Whit, I am afraid that won't be possible. Dr. Hill was killed in an accident on the way to work this morning."

"What? What in the world happened?"

"I'm afraid his car left the road on the way to work today, and he was … he was killed; there was a possible heart attack at the root of it. There was a history. I am so sorry, Mr. Hitchens. Perhaps after things settle out here, someone else can assist you."

"Is his Teaching Assistant at the department? I heard he had one of his best students working on a project that I have an interest in." He thought about his conversations with Professor Hill. "Dugan, or something like that?"

He heard some off-speaker conversation in the background and then, "That would probably be David Duggars. No one has seen him in here this morning. But I expect he will be in when he hears about Dr. Hill. This is going to be hard on him, as well."

Whit sat thinking about the call, about Lucy, about how good things had come to an end, and how he had let it happen. With a gasp of air, he felt the loss sweep over him again, and he put his head in his palms and wept.

Chapter 4

*There is no act of treachery or meanness of which a political party is
not capable; for in politics there is no honour.*

Benjamin Disraeli

June 10, 1976
Tallahassee, 1735 hours

Captain Richards stood across the street from the FSU geology building,
finally convinced that most of the day workers had gone. Phone intel had
indicated that the grad student would be working late to finish a project for
the recently deceased Dr. Hill. The kid would need a new major professor
but still had to complete a dozen tasks before picking up with a new PhD's
work assignments and a new lit review, not to mention trying to sell the new
prof on the soundness of his research project.

Well, Duggars, he thought, turns out you won't have to worry about
that new lit review after all. He smiled grimly under reflective Ray-Ban
aviator sunglasses and checked to see if his team was in position. Jenks and
Lassiter are good boys, he thought, but, damn, it seemed like Lassiter maybe
enjoys it too much. Maybe he should recommend him for CIA black ops; let
him take out his aggression on bad guys. He again studied the problem at
hand. The geology building's original main entrance was rarely used, as it
faced one of the busiest entrances to campus and had no vehicle access. The
well-used entrance on a lower level had been the de facto main entrance for
years, and since exams were over for the semester, it had seen only a few
exiting students, faculty, or staff.

Giving a barely visible hand gesture, he walked toward the lower
entrance. From two other locations nearby, Lassiter and Jenks entered at
thirty to forty-five-second intervals behind him. No one would notice two
casually dressed young men just a little over the average age of a college
student or the fortyish man with gray stubble, a short-sleeve work shirt, and
jeans. Richards's most noticeable visual identifier was an oversized, silver-
and-gold cowboy belt buckle designed to draw the eye away from his face.
Jenks sported a small afro, a distinguished goatee, a black V-neck sweater,

and a gold chain. Lassiter, somehow, loosened up frame and gait to look like a slightly intoxicated jock complete with faded sweatshirt that covered tattoos on his developed upper arms.

Quietly descending to the basement level, the three cleanup specialists found David Duggars concentrating on the scanning electron microscope, making notes and peering at the green CRT monitor. The monitor displayed a crystalline structure. The young grad student was intent on the view through a binocular viewing piece. A half inch long bit of blue-green metal was clamped under what appeared to be a plexiglass cover. Lassiter's gum shoe sneakers made no sound on the dusty tile floor as he approached.

One of Lassiter's hands pressed the cloth over Duggar's nose and mouth; the other grabbed the back of his target's neck and pressed him into it. Eyes bulging in panic, the grad student's last breath had been awful. Lassiter looked coldly into Duggar's last panic driven wide-eyed stare. He felt a little sorry as those eyes begged for understanding against all hope. Hope of escaping whatever would come next. Nothing was going to come next.

Down the hall, Richards had just loosened the wiring connection on an electrical outlet. Allowing his carefully planned short to scorch the Bakelite outlet housing to leave evidence of a loose contact, he then cracked the plastic cover leaving half of it on the floor. For good measure, he kicked the outlet box softly to deform the metal housing. Taking one of the many cardboard file boxes from the stack he had just moved, he lit a corner that would have been next to the outlet before putting the smoldering wooden match in his pocket. As he rebuilt the pile of cardboard and paper, white smoke began to rise up the wall behind the boxes followed by the flickering yellow of a growing column of flame.

The fire alarm would never be able to signal trouble in room B-32. Jenks had taken a paint-splattered ladder from a utility closet and installed dead batteries in the two Sentry fire alarms in the hallway's ceiling. Within minutes, flames licked up the stack of file boxes, reached for the plastic suspended ceiling in the file room, and began to develop some serious heat and caustic smoke. In only a few minutes, deadly fumes began to curl into the small room adjacent to the file room, and the SEM room. By the time the fire alarm in the hall would have reacted to the spreading smoke, David Duggars's limp body would already have breathed in the poisonous cloud filling the room down to the floor. At each end of the basement hallway, ancient soda-and-water fire extinguishers hung from brackets, totally inadequate to address the fire that was filling the hall with thick smoke. By the time sirens were heard approaching the building, the three young men were casually walking away in three different directions.

On his way out, Sergeant Jenks stopped, pointed toward the building, and commented to a stranger that someone should call security. Students had just begun to notice the trails of white smoke sifting out of the lower-level entrance as the last staff hurried out of the building. When the first truck squealed to a stop on the sidewalk, David Duggars was already dead from smoke inhalation. The news crew from Channel 6 followed right behind the firemen, assured that it would get some great action shots for the eleven o'clock news.

Richards, Jenks, and Lassiter, divested of false hair and makeup and in casual clothes, ate dinner alone, separately. Approaching their motel rooms at different times, they would not have been remembered together or as being in a group. With any luck, by tomorrow, they would get ID and location on their last target and could leave this dump.

June 11, 1976
Wakulla Beach

Whit Hitchens was busy in his pole barn when Brad's bike brakes announced his arrival. Whit had heard the rustle of bike tires over leaves and then the crash of the bike as it was allowed to fall against the front steps. A few moments later, his son bounced into view, smiling the infectious smile he had when the world was on its right axis.

"How are you doing, sport?"

"Fine, Dad. What're you doing out here?"

"Seeing if I can fix the riding mower without taking it into the shop." He was pawing through a metal box full of bolts and nuts of all sizes. After finding a nut that looked like a candidate, he compared it to the bolt on the workbench. It was tossed back into the box and he continued to search for the right size and threading.

"Say, Brad, I don't see the canoe anywhere around here. Weren't you going to bring it up to the house?"

"Yeah, Dad. I pulled it up into the bushes down by the old hotel. Can I borrow the truck?" He looked up at his dad hopefully.

"Not on your life. I told you, you can only drive it in the yard for now. Why don't you get the trailer rig I made for your bike and go fetch it. I've got to get this mower fixed, so I can start mowing the yard this year." Hitchens had built a little rig for his old kayak that consisted of a little bit of heavy electrical chase framing metal, some bolts, and two bicycle wheels. It attached to the carrier rack on the back of a bike and made the short trip down to the beach easier when he and Lucy wanted to go for a paddle. He had recently pulled it free from its weed pile, cleaned, refurbished, and oiled it. "I put air in the tires earlier. Since you found that canoe last weekend, I thought you might get some use out of it."

"You want me to go now?" The question had the air of a whine as he made an obvious stare at the low sun angle. Whit looked at his watch. "Yeah, I think so, sport; it'll be getting dark soon, so you might as well go after it."

"Can I help you with the mower?" He stood, a thinner, scaled-down version of his dad, hands in his pockets, hoping to share a little time with his tool mentor. His dad could fix almost anything if there were enough spare parts around. And very few parts got thrown away if they had a potential reuse.

Whit put the can down and looked thoughtfully at his son. "Just a second, though, there's something I need to tell you." He put down the bolt and sat on his metal stool. "I should have told you last night. I called Dr. Hill, my old professor yesterday afternoon, and—"

"What did he say?" Brad was clearly excited.

"He didn't. When I called the department, they said he had died yesterday morning on the way to work. Seems he was traveling too fast and lost control, might have run a tire off the shoulder and overcorrected or something. Anyway, he hit a tree and died on the spot. It was on the late-night news. Apparently, they said he may have had a heart attack." He watched the excitement flow out of Brad's face. "It might be a little while before we hear anything about the piece of metal you found."

Not knowing what to say, Brad finally offered, "Bummer for your friend!"

"Yeah, bummer! There's something else, too, and I don't want you to freak out on me or anything, but I need you to listen carefully."

"Uh, yeah, sure, Dad."

"You know all of that sci-fi stuff about Area 54 or 51 or wherever? If your idea is correct, there's people out there who would not want news of your metal rod to get out. Even if it would only spur debate and argument for another ten years, there are people, government people, who would go to extreme measures to keep it a secret; to claim that you need to be committed or put you away on drugs until you believe you are crazy."

Brad's mouth dropped open as he tried to let that sink in. "Really? You can't be serious."

"Well, Brad, there's something else. There was a fire at my old geology department yesterday afternoon. Dr. Hill's research assistant was killed by smoke inhalation." He paused, letting this fact sink in. "There is plenty of evidence that our government isn't always the guys in white hats. Due process sometimes only happens if someone catches them in the act." He watched the reaction on his son's face and saw he had clearly upset him.

"What I'm trying to tell you is this: If his wreck was not an accident, if that fire was not an accident, if they are not a coincidence; then we should be worried that they will figure out where the metal came from and come for you or me or both of us. It would be fairly easy for the black hats to check Dr. Hill's phone records and come looking for us." He paused and put his hand on his son's shoulder. He gave it a squeeze for emphasis. "I'm just saying that you should be careful, okay?"

"Okay, sure." Brad walked over to his bike and saw that the homemade kayak trailer had already been pulled out and was waiting for him. "Be back in a few minutes, Dad."

"Mark my words, boy!" Hitchens said. He watched as Brad attached the simple eyebolt connection to fix the lightweight trailer to the bike. He felt a surge of love and pride in his boy, his life. But he had an ominous sense of foreboding as the boy, bike, and trailer noisily made off toward Wakulla Beach. Dusty, always ready for adventure, bounded beside him, tongue flying.

~ ~ ~

The last of three incarnations of the Wakulla Beach Hotel had died in the hurricane of 1929. The storm-battered wreck had been shifted off its concrete foundation and then suffered scavenging, looting, rot, and, finally, demolition when it became public property. The hotel's front yard, now scrub grass, saltbush, and cabbage palm, was still a favorite launching spot for johnboats and other small flats boats. The "beach" was a narrow sandy strip flanked by salt grasses that spanned the intertidal zone. Just above high tide, palmetto and cabbage palm merged into a sparse pine forest. The two-rut road, which began as a wide, graded county road at the coastal highway, was a barely reassuring track by the time it approached the shoreline.

Generations of Floridians had launched from Wakulla Beach or seined the shallow waters for mullet, speckled trout, and shrimp in various seasons. The vast flats of grass-bedded bottoms between the Ochlockonee River estuary to the south and the Aucilla River to the east were the hatching grounds for a majority of the Gulf's incredible seafood harvest. Brad loved the whole area, and the beach was one of his favorite haunts. From the elders who came just to pass the hours and fish, he'd learned the different baits for different catches and seasons, how to fold and throw a cast net, how to replace a worn trailer tire with a couple of screwdrivers, and a lot of other valuable life lessons. One of the locals, Sunny Rogers, was sitting on his tailgate, sorting through a cooler half full of fresh-caught mullet. Some were food; some would be crab-trap bait.

Brad's curiosity soon found him out wading in the shallows of high tide. He only stopped when he heard the faint echo of a shotgun blast up by the highway. His first thought was turkey. "Hot dang!" he cried to Sunny. "Dad got us a turkey!" Sunny was over seventy and a frequent visitor to the area's many fishing spots. A well-known curmudgeon and skeptic, he was still Sunny to fourteen-going-on-fifteen-year-old Brad and everyone else the old man opened up to. He didn't open up to just anyone, but Sunny had been a friend to Whit's father, had seen the next two generations go through diapers, and had paternal affection for Brad as if he were family.

"Little early this year, ain't it?" Actually, it was several months early.

"Maybe a little, but Dad says come turkey season, they'll all disappear."

"Right he is, Swamp Boy. It's only a few months off, but the little bastards always seem to know." He scratched his rough chin and then winked at Brad. "You reckon that they can recognize orange hats and know when to get scarce?" The old man was tanned as dark as a hickory nut on his arms, legs, and neck. His deep wrinkles were forged by decades of exposure to sun, wind, and cold. His hands still had a formidable grip despite the deep scars and leather-thick pads.

"Don't know. Prob'ly." He grinned at the old man and winked back. "Maybe it's the camo gear. Bet if we went out in jeans and a T-shirt, they wouldn't pay us no never mind."

Sunny laughed a rich, deep laugh that infected Brad too. Stopping just after the laughing tears began to flow, he said, "Boy, you're gonna turn out all right, despite your dreamy ways."

Looking back to the west, Brad saw the sun was nearing the tops of the pines across the grass flats. "I better git home, Sunny. Hi to Maybelle for me, okay?"

Brad set off thinking how easy it was to peddle the canoe around on his Dad's invented trailer. Dusty, knowing the way, galloped ahead. He could get all over the place with this rig. Peddling on in the darkening shades of twilight, he was abruptly jolted out of his reverie by the sound of revving engines. A few hundred yards ahead, a black Suburban pulled out of his driveway and sped up to the coastal highway. Brad pulled over to the edge of the shallow roadside swale and waited. He didn't know anyone with a black Suburban. He heard another sharp report, small caliber, and felt a wave of fear wash over him. A few moments later, a second vehicle, a sedan that was harder to ID, also sped away. The manner of their exit, plowing curves in the graded sandy clay road, throwing dirt as they left, was extremely unusual for his dad's crowd.

He became aware of his heart thumping in his chest. The sudden exit of the two cars and the gunshot on top of his dad's warning just before he went to retrieve the canoe had him a little "freaked," as his dad would say. He pulled the bike and canoe under some roadside brush and crept through the underbrush. He took a shortcut to the backyard that he would not normally take at dusk. The house was dark except for one lamp's light coming from the living room. Normally, his dad would have been in the kitchen by now, working on dinner. He wouldn't have a recently shot turkey in the living room. Who'd been in the cars?

Looking around the backyard, he saw the riding mower was in the pole barn, but oddly, it was facing in. It was always parked facing out because the reverse gear pulley was shot. Maybe Dad had fixed it? As he approached the house through the brush, he heard Sunny's pickup heading for the highway. He thought of running after it and then thought he was probably just being too scared.

Bucking up his courage, he came up the back steps. "Dad?" No response. "Here, Dusty, come here, boy." No response. Entering by the back kitchen door, except for the darkness, everything seemed normal. Then he tripped over a drawer, and the rattle of dinnerware startled him. He stepped back and flicked on the overhead light. Looking around, he saw that most of the cabinets were open and drawers pulled out. The tumbled and shuffled contents of cabinets were strewn around. "Dad?" he called, then louder, "Dad!" No response. He was really frightened now. "Dad! Where are you?"

He stepped down the hall slowly; the hair on his neck stood on end. Every nerve told him not to walk any farther into the house until he found his dad. He flipped a switch. The hall light helped. Its glow added to the one lamp glowing in the living room. The living room was a shambles; cushions ripped open, the upholstery on the couch and the recliner ripped off. Motes of stuffing dust still floated in the air.

He could smell his sweat as he moved into the room. The stereo cabinet stood open, and all their albums had been tossed around. The search had been thorough; he could see the entire inside of any storage cabinet or cubby hole in the room. Even the old-fashioned built-in ironing board his grandfather had installed was ripped off the wall. *So where did the shotgun sound come from?* With this thought, he glanced sideways down the hall to the last addition, which held the two bedrooms and the bathroom. He could see miscellaneous debris lying in the doorways of these rooms. Dad's room at the end of the hall on the left showed a litter of feathers dusting the floor.

Brad willed himself to take a deep breath and slowly exhale to keep himself from shuddering. "Dad?" His call was softer now than his shouts from the kitchen, plaintive, questioning. He heard a soft moan and cuss words that seemed more like soft breathing than speech. He ran into his father's bedroom, turned on the light, and found Whit lying on the bed curled in a ball. His shirt, the quilt, and his hands were a mess of blood and feathers. "Brad, come here, Son." Brad reached for the phone. "No, don't worry with it; they ripped out the cord. Come closer."

"They? They who, Dad?"

"It's the Black Hats, like we were talking. I don't think they found your metal rod. They think I was hiding it. Things went from bad to worse when I reached for the shotgun." He gasped and choked, a thin line of blood formed on his lips. "I only wanted to warn them out of my house." He paused for a breath. "No warrant." He winced as he tried to move. "An EMS siren up to the highway scared 'em off or they'd still be here."

"Is it bad? How can I get help? I can run up to the highway and flag someone down."

"Probably no one would stop after dark. Anyway, I don't think I have much time. I need you to listen."

"Don't talk that way, Pop." His voice began to falter, and he struggled to keep it from cracking. "You're gonna be OK; I'll go get help."

Whit reached out, gripped his son's arm, and winced at the effort. "Listen, boy, at least listen to me first and then go."

Brad sat on the edge of the bed, felt the barrel of the shotgun under his thigh, and then stood up again. He grabbed his father's hand. "Okay, Dad, just take it easy."

"Brad, come closer." Whit's breath was becoming more labored, and short puffs of breath began to push dribbles of bubbling bloody saliva to the corners of his mouth. "Shit, I hate this!" He took a few more breaths. "I hate leaving you like this."

"You aren't leaving, Dad. Let me go get some help."

"Boy, please just listen for a second. I hate this, but listen carefully to me. I've been gut shot here. I saw gut shots in Nam. They got my stomach and probably a kidney and apparently a corner of my lung. I'm bleeding bad inside. I need you to be strong in the next few days. Things could get rough. If they report back that there was a kid's room in the house? Well, they may come back. They specifically asked for the sample of exotic metal; they know that it's blue and that it is extremely important." He panted a few times and held himself still. "They will be back for you and your room; you can't stay here."

Brad's moist eyes began to run, and he sniffed. Wiping his nose with his wrist, he cried plaintively, "Dad, where can I go? Aunt Susan's?"

"No, she's your mom's sister, too close a relative. I need you to go to Apalach and find her cousin Lou Anne Chappell and her family. You remember them? They were here coupla, three years ago. Her husband, Chase, has a shrimp boat there. Look for his boat on the docks; it's the *Lou Anne*." He coughed, and a thin line of blood began to ooze down his cheek. "They'll look after you. Tell Chase what happened, but don't tell him about that damn piece of metal. Bury it if you have to, or throw it in the creek, but don't ever give it to those bastards."

"Yes, sir. Let me go get some help. I'll wave someone over. I'm a kid; they'll help."

"Okay. Go quick," he said, coughing up more blood. "And, Brad, I love you, Son." A thin line of blood trickled from the corner of his mouth. Brad started to cry now; watching his dad in such distress was too much.

With a quick, "I love you, too!" he turned and ran out the front door. He made it almost to the driveway. Dusty's body was lying at the edge of the drive. Brad reconsidered whether to flag down a motorist or to return to his dad's side. Re-entering his dad's bedroom, he saw that Whit had fallen to the floor and a small stream of bloody bubbles was draining from his nose and mouth as his chest shook with jagged breaths. Brad cried out the universal cry of loss and anguish and crumpled beside his father. Whit looked up wearily at his son, knowing that he was near his end. He weakly clasped Brad's hand and tried to mouth something. The blood clogging his larynx made speech impossible. He closed his eyes with a wave of pain. Brad felt his dad's grip loosen. He saw the slump in his dad's frame as the rib cage expanded one last time, hitched, and then relaxed and sagged. He knew. Even as he got up to run for help, he knew.

Sniffling as he ran, he quickly made the few hundred yards up to the corner. For all the noise he heard at night from the highway, it was empty now save for some taillights heading north. Darkness and the buzzing of insects dominated the night. A few minutes later, a slight glow spread along the pines, coming from around the corner to the south. The first car passed by without slowing. The second one swerved a little, the driver surprised by the waving figure at the edge of the road. Then, miraculously, its brake lights flared bright red as it slowed. White backup lights momentarily burned his night-tuned eyes, but all that mattered to him was that the car was coming back.

The car belonged to an off-duty deputy sheriff, and in what seemed like no time, sirens began to fill the night. His father was still and gone when they returned to the house. In a matter of minutes, the house filled with strangers. For hours, green-uniformed deputies walked through the only home he had ever lived in, peering into all the empty cabinets, straightening a few chairs, taking dozens of photographs. A family services deputy talked to Brad most of the time. Holding his hand, asking questions, and taking notes, she made him feel a little better, but he began to get nervous and fidgety. He watched as his entire world was reduced to evidence. His whole world for the past few years had been his father, the fading memories of his mother, and this house. Now his dad would only be memories. With a shudder, he began to sob. As the young brunette officer tried to console him, he pushed her away.

"Can I just be alone for a minute? I need to sit here and wrap my head around this, okay?"

"Sure, honey, come find me if you need anything. You don't want to be in there right now." She left him alone and quietly pulled the door almost closed.

She cracked the door twenty minutes later and spoke into the darkened slot. "Bradley, your aunt Susan has been called; she'll be here in a thirty minutes. There was no reply, and when she looked in on him, the room was empty. She had not examined the room well enough while they were talking to note that a camper's backpack was missing, or that the sheets had been pulled out from under his mattress. She did see that his linen curtains billowed softly, letting the warm late spring night air into the room.

~ ~ ~

Brad hurriedly devised a simple plan as he peddled eastward along the coastal highway, exactly opposite from his intended target. It took only a few minutes to peddle the mile and a quarter to the Wakulla River bridge. He stashed the little bike trailer in deep palmetto inside the tree line and left his bike leaning against a bridge railing ready for law enforcement to find. The garnet-and-gold bike license plate emblazoned with BRADLEY hanging from under the seat would easily give the impression he was heading east and had hitched a ride. He found that the canoe livery at the base of the bridge had a weak storage door and spent little time breaking the hasp loose to get a paddle, life vest, and bailing bucket.

He wished he had taken the time to get some food before he left, but he couldn't have gone into the kitchen with all the deputies using it as a crime scene office. He paused in front of the snack machine on the porch of the rental office and considered busting its glass with the canoe paddle to get some provisions. He couldn't bring himself to do it. Prying four screws out of a rotten door and taking an overused paddle was one thing, but destroying the machine for a snack was too much. He pushed the canoe off from the bank and began to paddle.

~ ~ ~

In daylight, the Wakulla River is a natural beauty. Swag chains OF Spanish moss drape from overhanging branches. Turtles sunbathe on partially submerged branches. Mullet jump for bugs and for no particular reason on hot afternoons that breed laziness and contemplation of nature's finer creations. The river's clear, cold water swirls through the branches of drowned trees around and through long grassy beds on the brief trip to the Gulf.

At night, the river is forbidding; full of nocturnal animal cries, the underbrush rustles with the movements of unseen creatures. Swooping bats pass down the water-paved opening in the forest, scooping up mosquitoes, dragonflies, and anything else that rattles or buzzes as it flies.

Slapping his neck occasionally, Brad proved that there were many buzzing things out this night. He stuck to the middle of the river and hoped that moccasins only ventured into the river when warmed by the sun, that its cold waters would suck the energy out of snakes. At least, he had never heard of anyone being bitten by a moccasin at night. But his biggest fear was gators! Alligators had owned these swamps since before humans crossed into the Americas. If he ran up on a log in the dark and overturned, he would be in their element. He'd be fair game.

Brad struck out with confidence, hoping to put the first river bend just below the bridge behind him. As he added distance between his small craft and civilization, he heard rapidly approaching sirens. Blue and red flashes strobed the treetops overhead. The sirens kept going and faded, whooping into the distance. He knew the bike would be found in the morning by a passing motorist who would have heard the missing person report on the morning news. The find would lead the official search for the missing boy eastward toward Jacksonville, Gainesville, or Orlando. He smiled grimly as he thought of his picture on milk cartons all over Florida.

After leaving the yellow glow of the yard light at the canoe rental, darkness enveloped him. With the waning quarter moon not yet above the horizon, the darkness was nearly absolute. Only the stars provided light by which to anticipate the turns ahead. They could not tell him how to miss the thick mats of grass, and they barely illuminated the larger logs. If he strayed too close to a bank, damp leaves slapped his face. Although his dad had told him that bats would not attack or bite, their overhead swooping and chittering evaporated his last pretenses of bravery.

More than anything, he wanted to call out for his dad. His father, mentor, and best friend was dead. That reality was becoming solid and touchable. In the cold and dark, the tears began to flow. He stopped paddling and let the river's slow pulse carry him along. With the paddle lying across his knees, he shook with the evening chill and with sobs. Blinded by tears, he allowed helpless despair to take over. He drifted silent and alone, as alone as he had ever been.

When the sobbing stopped, he realized that he was really cold. He mentally reviewed the materials he had stowed in his hastily put together pack: a few changes of clothes and underwear, sandals, a sweater, and a light jacket. Besides clothes, he'd packed his field knife, compass, his savings passbook worth $182, canteen, camper's matches, insect repellent, and the few dollars and change he had in his allowance and work money can.

A clear June night on a cold-water river is no place to sit quietly in a T-shirt, like the one he'd put on in the afternoon. He reached into the pack for his windbreaker. After some determined paddling, he spotted the glow of lights ahead that meant he was getting closer to the small town of St. Marks. Consisting of an oil terminal, a power plant, three marinas, three seafood restaurants, and about a hundred homes, the small town had more character per person than the hundreds of identical suburban planned neighborhoods stamped along the Florida Peninsula. It was home port to oil barges, a few commercial shrimpers, and pleasure boats that ranged from million-dollar yachts that rarely moved to a small fleet of flat-bottomed rental rowboats.

The first sign of life as he approached was a small marina and fish camp. Seeing the beacon of its glowing fuel sign, he realized he had not eaten dinner. He was hungry, and he considered his possibilities. A pair of lights suspended near the waterline on the dock attracted a buzzing swarm of insects. A given percentage of these hit the water as fish food. For Brad, in his desperate need to not be seen, the bug-encrusted forty-watt bulbs seemed to light the world. He thought that he and his canoe must be lit up like a Christmas float against the darkness behind him. In truth, the world was asleep, and on a weeknight this early in the summer there would likely be no fishermen staying in the cabins. He drifted slowly up to the pilings and pulled himself, hand over hand, to a point between the two lights on the dock.

Working up his nerve, Brad quietly slipped out of the canoe and took slow, cautious steps toward the shoreline. As he stepped onto land, first one dog and then its neighbor began to bark; a shout in the dark shut them up. He slipped into the shadow of a pine and waited. From his cover, he saw that the bait shop was unlit. Only one truck was pulled up at the boat repair area, and it might have been left there. There were cars under the owners' house, but a flickering blue glow from the living room proved they were distracted.

He decided to go for it. A short sprint across the grass resulted in a few desultory woofs and not much else. The door to the bait shop was locked, but the small metal building enclosing the bait tanks was open. He spent an agonizing minute listening to the squeak of the door's spring as he slowly opened it with as much stealth is possible with an old steel spring and rusted hinges. Investigating inside, he found a box of cricket food, otherwise known as saltine crackers. He took a sleeve of the crackers in its wax paper wrapper and looked around. As he ate a few of these, he realized that the only other edibles in the shed were crickets, minnows, and worms. They were safe from his foraging.

The crescent moon was now climbing above the eastern horizon. He reasoned that it must be well past midnight, and looking west, he saw that the night sky beyond showed no stars. Clouds must be moving in, he thought. On the Florida coast, the weather changed fast, so he knew that he needed to get moving. As he crept into the canoe, the paddle slid off the edge of the dock hitting the wooden gunnel with a loud thunk that he thought must have been heard in the next county. Again, an excited chorus of barks was followed by a shout and a curse. Soon, the momentarily silenced buzzing of insects was back up to its previous background levels, and he pushed off letting the river carry him into the dark. A few hundred yards south of the fish camp, the Wakulla River joined the St. Marks, which wound another few miles south in an ever-widening estuary. Headwinds were bad news for canoes, and he hoped the night remained calm because he wanted to be well down the estuary before dawn.

In the narrow reaches of the Wakulla River upstream, virtually no breezes stirred the water. As he approached the old Spanish fort at the junction of the two rivers, he found a light but freshening breeze from the west, and he had to work to stay as close as he could to the west bank. He did not want to get out of the very short wind shadow of the high salt grasses lining the river bank. Soon he was well down the St. Marks and he let the bow point into a tuft of grass at river's edge. As the moon arced over into the western sky, the estuary was nearing full tide, balancing incoming tide against the flow of two joined rivers. It would soon start to ebb, helping him travel south. He layered another application of bug repellent on his hands, face, and neck and settled into the bottom of the canoe for a short rest.

In what felt like minutes, he awoke with a start, as a predawn fishing boat sped by, its wake tossing him around the bottom of the canoe. Though it was still early, he could tell there would be no sunrise. The wind had dislodged his canoe, and he had drifted across the channel and was now being slowly blown by a cool, light breeze toward the grass border of the eastern bank. This was not good. The quarter moon was gone; it had not set but had been covered by a thick blanket of cloud that let only a dim gray light down onto the river. He pulled out his Boy Scout compass and made sure of his impressions. At less than three feet off the water on a moonless night, all grassy banks looked alike. He would have to work across the wind to get back into the lee of the opposite bank. And soon, he would be approaching the various cuts and channels along the western shore that offered no wind protection.

Brad knew that there were several channels; some only tidal feeders and some that provided shortcuts behind the low, grassy islands. His dad had showed him several of these in their kayak. In the dark, he knew it would be hard to tell the difference. He decided to play it safe and stay out of the smaller channels. If he guessed wrong and the tide turned, he would have to haul out by foot, and some of these inlets had very thick bottom liners of tidal ooze. He did not want to face that. He had been knee deep in that smelly goo in sunshine and warm weather, and this day had neither. Bradley pressed on, a heavy ache returning way too soon to his shoulders. Without his watch and with no moon showing, he could only guess that it was an hour or so before full light.

Taking a break with the paddle across his knees, he pressed his thumb into the swelling flesh of his palms. He figured he was probably a few hours away from some serious blisters. In the brightening light, an eternity of paddling later, he took a compass sight line almost northwest of the St. Marks lighthouse, and he knew he had made an important waypoint. He could now make the turn west. This meant, though, that he had lost his windbreak and would have to pull into the wind. Fighting exhaustion and pain in his shoulders, he put his head down and just paddled. He had long since shoved the pack as far forward as it would go to lower the nose, and that had helped some. What he didn't expect was a grinding crunch that stopped him completely.

Prodding with the paddle, he realized that he had grounded on an oyster bar. Pushing harder than he thought would be necessary, he finally backed off the bar and pondered how far out he would have to go to get around it. Some of those bars ran for hundreds of yards. He stepped out onto the sharp-shelled bar, pulled the canoe across it, and got back in. Fine, now he had cold, wet feet to add to the sensations he could think about instead of the pain from the blisters on his left palm.

The smells of the tidal marsh are often overpowering to visitors to the coast. The overall first sense of rotting mud is replaced by the individual smells of salt, damp mud, and an occasional whiff of methane-laced decay. The melded scents change throughout the day and through the tide changes as the cycles endlessly turn. Brad had been aware of these for as long as he could recall. He and his family had fished, played, and simply enjoyed the estuary and the acres of tidal flats for years. What he had hoped to miss that morning was the damp, cool smell of an oncoming rain.

He smelled it first and then heard the soft hiss as an approaching shower passed along the grass beds before him. "Crap, can this get any worse?" He knew his windbreaker would soak through quickly. With the wind slacking slightly, his progress west was improving, but he was terribly tired, his arms ached, and he knew that the flats extended miles to the west before the shoreline turned south. If he kept traveling and the wind stayed out of the west, he realized he was going to need much more than a few saltine crackers to get anywhere. His ultimate target was Apalachicola, which was what? Thirty or forty miles to the west? The canoe, which had seemed like such a good idea late last night, was turning out to be less and less of a good idea as dawn turned to day.

The shower was brief but he stayed wet to the skin. The added weight of the soaked jacket made paddling even harder. Adding to his discomfort was the blister on his left palm and he avoided putting pressure on it. Discouraged but prodded by the sisters of desperation and necessity, he paddled on. Soon, a break in the misting rain revealed a familiar shoreline ahead. The wind had backed around to the northwest, and he had taken some cover in the small, grassy islands that formed the actual coastline in this part of Florida. Now he knew that he had about a mile and a half to paddle to get to a lee shore or he could just wait. Wait, he thought, for a little more warmth, sunshine, dry clothes. *Hell! I might as well wish for hot cheese grits, sausage, and scrambled eggs! Long as I'm wishing.* From the last shelter of a small bit of usually dry land, he focused on the wind and eyed the shoreline to the west as he tried to gauge which way to point to reach familiar grounds. With a deep sigh, he pushed off. Blisters were now beginning to grow on the finger pads of his right hand.

The on-again, off-again rain showers had finally ceased. The cloud cover broke into a ragged patchwork of gray puffs tinged in morning pink. The winds increased slightly in intensity and kept moving through the compass to almost due north. His early aiming point was slipping by, and he dug in with earnest. If he didn't make it to the headland at Live Oak Island, he might be driven south to Shell Point. This enclave of coastal development was largely inhabited by retirees from Tallahassee, wealthy boat owners, and retired snowbirds. It was a rare coastal community, in that it had very few rentals; most homes were just that, homes. A good many might be seasonal homes, but it was the kind of area where most folks knew their neighbors and recognized a stranger. It was the kind of area where if people looked out their window and saw him, they would, in their well-intentioned good-heartedness, call in the sheriff. Thinking these thoughts, he reassessed his aiming point and pulled harder.

The paddling became rhythmic and automatic; vague shapes took on more focus as the morning brightened. For some reason, he thought of the book they had read at the start of school. Hemingway's *The Old Man and the Sea* had been inspiring and depressing. The transition from rhapsodic joy when the big fish was hooked, to its long-fought death, and then the terrible loss to sharks paralleled his early escape plans. He began to see himself as the old man rowing, rowing, and rowing. He tried to distract himself with the story, but it was hard to translate the tropical sun for the rains he could see across the salt flats.

Brad's left hand had reddened. Except for a two-hour nap, he had paddled through the night, and it was increasingly sore and swollen. The blister on his palm had broken, and he had to avoid putting any pressure on it at all. So he was pulling by grasping the paddle end in the curl of his fingers. If he didn't reach shore soon, these would blister as well. *Serves me right, for stealing the danged paddle! This must be what Dad meant by instant karma!* He smiled grimly and pulled. Daylight brightened, and he saw activity on the shoreline in the distance. He realized it must be his old home port, Wakulla Beach, to the northwest. Soon, a small boat was being offloaded and pushed into the shallows. In a few minutes, he heard the pock, pock, pock of a small engine idling.

The surface of the bay had become gray and was developing a light chop—not high enough to splash into the canoe, but it did indicate that the breeze was growing. He was getting concerned. The small flat-bottomed boat pulled away from shore and paused from time to time as its owner pulled up a crab trap, emptied it, stuffed more bait in its bait bag, and threw it back in. The waterman worked his traps, and Bradley paddled in earnest; soon, the two small craft came within a few hundred yards of each other. As color came into the morning light, Brad could now make out who was working the boat. "Sunny!" he called. "Hey! Sunny, over here!"

The old fisherman tossed a crab trap over his bow, sat down, and looked. Soon, he turned around and gave a pull on the four-horse Johnson, and the little green johnboat wheeled around and started coming toward him. It powered down and pulled up alongside.

"Damn, if you ain't a fool, boy. Half the world is out looking for you. You know how many folks has been out combing the woods fer ya?"

"I had to get outta there, Sunny. The guys that killed my dad are likely to be coming after me!"

"You're talking crazy, boy. Why'd a bunch of no-counts who burgled your place want to come back and get you?"

"They wasn't burglars, Sunny. They were looking for sumpthin' that they didn't find. I think it's important, and they wanted to steal it. They killed Dad and made the thing look like an burglary."

"So how do you know this is true?"

"'Cause Dad told me who did it, and I have what they're lookin' for."

The old man sat back and pondered this. "Do tell."

"It's here in this backpack. I found it in the woods about a week ago, and it's been nothing but trouble since." He thought about the tidbit of advice from his dad, that sometimes you just have to do things that need to be done and resolved to somehow get the metal rod to someone he could trust. He could no longer trust the government.

"Is it worth dying for? You could just give it up." He looked at the disheveled boy next to him in the little green canoe, water-wise, woods-wise, but not yet wise to the world.

"It's a pretty unusual piece of metal. Dad sent a piece of it to a friend up at FSU for testing. That guy is dead, and he was a professor. His assistant is dead, both meant to look like accidents, but Dad said that those two accidents combined with the kind of metal it is makes it way too unlikely that these really was accidents." He looked at the pack. "Dad said they weren't killing to get; they were killing to cover up."

Sunny relaxed in his seat and ran his rough fingers through his stubble. "Bradley, how long you been out on the water in this little boat?"

"Since about ten o'clock last night." He began to shiver a little. "Put in at the canoe livery and been paddling ever since."

"Looks like you could use some help." He reached down under his seat and retrieved a thermos. "You drink coffee?"

"Well, no Sir, but if it's warm, I'll give it a shot."

Sunny unscrewed the cup and then the thermos stopper and poured some of the black, steaming liquid into the cup. "Coffee's still pretty hot, so take a little sip at first. Don't need to add a burnt lip to your miseries." Brad cautiously took one sip and then a longer drink. Then he grimaced.

Sunny laughed a short, barking laugh. "It ain't got no cream and sugar in it. Ain't no sissified brew." Brad took the rest of the cup in a gulp and handed it back.

"Thank you, Sunny; I think I better be getting on. And thanks for the coffee."

"Hold on there, boy. Where'd you plan on getting to?"

"Not sure I should tell you. Might be best for you if you don't know."

"Well, that might be and it might not be. Kinda depends on whether you trust me or don't. Don't it?"

"Yessir, I suppose you're right. It's just that, well, damn, there's already three people dead including Daddy, and I got no idea who's doing it 'cept maybe the dark side of the Feds." He started massaging the sore meat around the blisters on his palm and fingers. "I think it would be stupid to go to the Sheriff right now and explain everything."

"It is true that the law can sometimes be a hindrance to what oughta happen." Sunny poured a bit of coffee for himself and took a drink. "You like some help?" He looked around at the offshore drift they had taken in the last few minutes. "Fer sure, I'm gonna get you to shore."

"That'd be great, Sunny. I'd really appreciate that." He rubbed absently at the swelling white pads of blisters on his left hand.

"Go on now, get set up on the bow seat and I'll tie that thing off the back, and get you back to the beach'"

In minutes, Brad and Sunny were back on dry land at the landing on Wakulla Beach. Sunny had pulled the canoe back into the bushes where it had been stashed less than a day earlier. Sunny put his gnarled hand on the boy's shoulder. "Now lissen, Bradley, the roads will be getting busy pretty soon. People all over six counties gonna have an eye out for you; what do you say to some breakfast while we talk about your predicament?"

"Where?" He shouldered the pack and winced at the weight on his shoulder muscles. Since he had stopped paddling, they had begun to stiffen. "I can't go out to eat, and my house is a disaster area."

"Well, I thought we might just mosey on down to my place. I'll get you fed, and if there's no one at your place, you can do a better job of packing for wherever it is you were settin' out for. I wouldn't sit there too long, though. Bound to be some law back there checking for you." He grinned at the boy. "I guess you must be headin' west since you decoyed your bike up at the lower bridge. Accordin' to the radio, they got people out all over looking for you. Posted missing child reports all over, but they're focusing on south Florida."

Brad smiled. "Yeah, that was kinda the plan. I've got kin near Orlando, some of Mom and Aunt Sue's people. I thought I'd let them think

I hitchhiked outta here." His stomach growled audibly, and he rubbed at his belly.

After a pause, Sunny added, "Bradley, I've known your dad since he was a pup himself. Your mom too. If you don't want to go to the law, well, I guess that's the way we'll do it. I just shore hope it don't make things harder." He placed his hand softly on Brad's shoulder and gave it a reassuring squeeze. They put the jon boat back in the pickup and drove off the beach. As they slowly passed the Hitchenses' driveway, the noted yellow crime scene tape wrapped around the mailbox, and that there were no cars in the yard. Yet.

Chapter 5

No one can escape his destiny.
Plato

June 12, 1976
Medart, Florida, Mid-morning

Sunny's house was an aging mobile home, a doublewide on blocks. It was not one of the newer models with skirting of faux brick or stone. And it wasn't one of the old ones that looked like a refugee from a fifties' mobile home park with space-age styling in molded aluminum trim. It was a basic twenty-four-by-fifty-four-foot model with no eaves and little styling. It did have new vinyl skirting, real bricked steps, and a row of grown and trimmed azaleas planted along the front. The mowed yard looked like someone gave a hoot. Unusual for that part of Florida, it didn't have a loosely organized pile of everything ever thrown out somewhere in the back. Sunny had worked for the county for thirty-five years before they made him quit. After a lifetime on motor graders, bucket loaders, and backhoe trenchers, he'd done his time in the Florida retirement system and was now earning a retirement supplement supplying crab and mullet to the local fish houses. It was an easy enough occupation for a not-quite-elderly man who was still spry enough to work the flats in most weather—especially as he did not need the money and didn't have to work when he didn't feel up to it.

Bradley looked around as breakfast smells filled the house. For as bad as Sunny looked every time he had seen him down on the water, he kept a clean place. "Sunny, why is it I wouldn't 'spect you to live so good from the way you dress all the time? Between your shirts, your boat, and your truck, I figured you were dirt poor."

"My daddy said, long time ago, that things ain't always what they seem. Guess that would apply." He winked at Brad.

Checking out the room behind him, Brad decided it looked comfortable, if a little time-worn. "Say, where's Maybelle? She off somewhere?"

Sunny gave a grunt. "You might say that. She is off somewhere. Whatever it is, she went off to her great reward, as she liked to say, 'bout three years ago." He stopped stirring the grits for a second and drifted. "She's right over there on the wall." He nodded to a framed picture by the front door.

Brad thought for a second and said, "Usually, when I say 'bye,' I always tell you to say hi to Maybelle. How come you never said anything?"

Sunny just smiled at him. "And ever' time, I did. I'd walk in the door, tap the frame of that picture there, and say, 'Swamp Boy says hi.'" He resumed stirring. "She always was partial to you, always said if you'd had a brother, the two a you'd'a been dangerous." He looked over his shoulder at Brad. "I take it you weren't partial to that coffee; you want something else to drink?"

"Juice, if you have it; coffee's all right, if you don't. Only I'd rather a little cream in it if you got it."

"I got it. Keep it for Maybelle's cats." He started fixing the coffee and looked over at the boy. "You sure I can't get you where you're aiming for?" Then he looked over at the backpack. "You sure you want to keep whatever it is that's gettin' people killed?"

Brad followed his gaze, got up, and went over to the pack. He reached down into its depths and pulled out the blue metal rod. "This is the mystery metal." He handed it to Sunny, who hefted it and examined it. He looked at the shiny end where the hydraulic shear had taken a sample and the swaged end that looked like something ought to be attached.

"Feels like aluminum."

"Ever see aluminum that wasn't silver or gray?"

"Yeah, sure—blue, green, red. Lot of them new fishin' reels are all colors—gold too!"

Brad persisted, "If you scratch 'em, what color are they inside?"

Sunny looked thoughtful and examined the shiny teal green exposed at the newly sheared end. "Gray or silver." Then after a pause, he said, "Well, you got sumthin' here." He tried to bend it, looking like an aging superman trying to bend the bar of steel.

"Dad tried that, Sunny. We tried driving over it. It don't bend."

"Do tell ..." He handed the bar back. "So what else makes it so special?"

"Where it was found. Where I found it didn't make sense to me and got my dad curious, too. We were stumped 'cause we found it under a cypress root. Where it shouldn't'a been."

"How'd you get a look under a cypress? Last I heard, they weighed in at several ton."

"A big one blew over, and this was stuck under it, deep in the roots."

"That would make this thing ... hmm, real old. Reckon you got a mystery there, boy." He handed over a plate full of food—hot, greasy, and good as it gets. Ironically, it was the picture of the hot cheese grits, sausage, and scrambled eggs he'd prayed for a few hours ago as he paddled into dawn. And there were fresh butter biscuits as well. Sunny said, "Eat up, and we'll get you on your way."

~ ~ ~

The sun shining through rain-cleansed air had brought some heat back to the world along with its local curse, humidity. The Hitchenses' yard and house looked bright and cheerful. Spring perennials poked out of overgrown flower beds, vying for sunlight. Only the yellow crime-scene tape across the front porch steps told of the turmoil of the previous day. With Sunny's truck in the back and Whit's in its place in the barn, it was hard to believe that his entire life had changed. The back-door key was still under the piece of border rock lining a bed of lilies past their prime. Plate-sized sycamore leaves scratched softly as they brushed across the metal roof of the porch. Brad noticed a clump of aloe growing near the steps and thought about taking off a leaf to ease his blistered palm and fingers.

He passed through the wrecked kitchen and went down the hall to his room to get some more clothes. He sat on the bed and looked around. It seemed like years ago that the room had provided comfort and protection. Even when his mother had disappeared in the night, his father had been there for him, an umbrella in a storm of emotion.

He knew that finding safety in the familiarity of Aunt Susan's house in Tallahassee was impossible. If the black hats were really out to get their hands on the metal rod—"the artifact," his dad had called it—he was surely a target. The plastic bombers and fighters rotating slowly overhead seemed childish, as did his fantasies about life in the US Army Air Corps. His posters seemed old and pathetic.

He seemed older. Yet he was only a day older than yesterday, when he was a son. Now, somehow, he was older and parentless! The word was orphan. "Oh, my God! I am an orphan." A vision of a barracks for boy orphans from old black-and-white Mickey Rooney movies conjured itself up. "Not cool! I'm getting outta here." He crossed to the closet and began to look at clothing for a hot summer.

Chase? What was he, an uncle-in-law? Aunt's second cousin's husband, once removed by marriage? Hmm, maybe they weren't even related. Well, if that didn't work out, there was always the road. He reached for a waterproof rain jacket, a pile of T-shirts, more jeans, and a fistful each of underwear and socks. He pulled back the clothes in the far left of the closet to find last year's long-sleeve shirts. They were hopelessly too short this year. He went into his parents' room and stopped, shocked. The room seemed full of something real and tangible, something solid and familiar that he could not identify. At the same time, it was as empty as the space between four walls that was strewn with the debris of his parents' lives could be. That emptiness hit him full force; this was not an adventure. It was not an extension of one of his fantastic daydreams. He was alone now. He was alone in the world. Heavy pressure in his gut seemed to keep him from drawing air. His roving glance fell on the fallen folding gilt double frame holding the pictures of his grandparents. Even though its two smiling faces looked into the floorboards his grandfather had laid, Brad knew the faces he'd memorized.

He'd never known Grandma Hitchens. She'd gone before he was born, gone to cancer. Grandpa Hitchens had cherished him when he was small; he'd played with the three-foot-tall model of his father, taken him on walks in the woods, and bought him his first Zebco push-button casting reel. He had become an indispensable part of his life, an adjunct to his parents that made his life complete. Then he'd died. At five and a half, Brad had been too young to understand the phrase heart attack. The next spring, as his classmates at kindergarten made cut-out valentine paper hearts, he refused, confused about what hearts were and this celebration of something as deadly as a heart. His grandfather had been the first person he'd loved who had died. He took a deep breath to get his lungs working again, felt the rhythm, and realized that he was the end of the Hitchens line. Last male of the tribe. He felt responsible suddenly for something he did not yet understand. He tried not to think about the smell of dried blood coming from the mattress and floor on the other side of the bed.

He suppressed the tears gathering in his eyes, knelt, and opened the bottom drawer of his parents' dresser. With the drawer out, he felt into the back of the cabinet and retrieved an old cigar box. His mother had kept

78

household cash and some old photos of her sister and parents in the box. It was there. He counted forty-eight dollars and took the five photographs too. Moving to his father's closet, he pulled out a favorite blue denim shirt and a work sweater. Going back into his room, he glanced out the back window and saw something moving.

A black-clad figure in the yard was crouching low, running across from the pole barn. Another was running from the tree line. He froze. Shortly, loud voices were rising on the front porch. He overheard enough to know that Sunny was stalling the men. He hurriedly tossed the clothes in his backpack and passed it through the window. Pausing to hear that Sunny was losing the conversation, he jumped out after the pack and reached up to pull down the sash. He peeked around the corner of the front porch and saw three men surrounding Sunny.

"What do you mean, why am I here?" He stuffed his hands stubbornly in his overall pockets. "Whit is like family to me. Known him since he was fillin' diapers. Who the heck are you?"

"Not your problem, Mr. …?"

"Rogers, Oscar T. Rogers, most people just call me Sunny on account of ever'one knew my daddy called me Sunny and so they did too. Stuck with me since I was knee high to a toad." He eyed the tallest one. "And who might you be?"

"We're here to look out for the boy and check his effects. With the death of his father and him missing, there may have been an abduction."

"Abduction, you say? Would that make you the F-B-I?" He feigned an interest in the idea. "Naw, there's no one 'round here woulda taken any offense at Whit, too good a fella. Now his son, he mighta caused a ruckus at school from time to time, but he's mostly a quiet boy. And who are you, again?"

Captain Richards, not dropping a beat, said, "Michael Sanders, Detective Inspector Sanders, with the FBI's kidnapping unit." He pulled a black leather badge wallet out and flipped it open for Sunny to read. He flipped it shut again before anyone would have been able to read much more than the large FBI embossing. "You were saying about his son?"

"Yeah, Whit has a kid, Bradley, after Omar, the General." Sunny parsed the information out slowly, burning time. "Word is he got freaked by the sight of his dad 'n all. Hopin' he's over at a friend's house or up at the church."

"Where's this church?"

Sunny nodded his head back. "Up the road to'rd Tallyhassee. Big white thing on the left. Cain't miss it."

Richards made a note on his pad and looked up. "Now why is it you're still here?"

"Well, Whit's sister'd prob'ly get the house, but she won't want it flooded if one of the pipes leak, so I was going to turn off the water, clean up the mess those bastards made last night." He eyed the agent, looking for a reaction. "You know, sorta straighten things so it won't shock her so bad when she gets down here. And I was kinda hopin' that if the Hitchens boy was hiding in the woods, that he'd come on out if'n he saw my truck."

"Okay, Mr. Rogers." Richards pulled gently on Sunny's shoulder and guided him toward the porch steps. "Why don't you give us some time to do our job and you can come back in, say, an hour and button up the house?" They both moved down the stairs, Richards was smiling reassuringly. "This is still a crime scene. You'd probably want to check with the sheriff before you did any cleaning. If you give me your number, I'll be glad to pass it along to the sheriff's office."

Sunny didn't bite at the bait. "Reckon I'll just check with the deputies; I'm related to half of 'em anyways. Maybe I'll call them; see if they can give you any clues."

Outmaneuvered, Richards continued, "And, sir, if you know the phone number for his sister? What'd you say her name was?"

"Didn't say and don't know it, not the married name anyhows. Heard she's married and divorced. Guess I will wait for the sheriff to get through though, it being a crime scene an' all. 'Spose they'll be coming back today to finish their investigating." Walking away, he added for effect, "If the boy comes back, he should be able to tell you the aunt's phone number." Chuckling, he took one more glance over the house and grounds in his side mirror as he left and then simply drove away.

~ ~ ~

Brad had gone quietly and quickly; crossed the backyard, crouched in the brush behind the pole barn, and waited. In a few minutes, he'd seen Sunny come around the back of the house with one of the young men holding him by the shoulder hurrying him along. He'd seen Sunny had glanced at the nearly shut bedroom window and not reacted and watched as his pickup slowly eased around the house and out the driveway. It turned south toward the coast and disappeared. Brad tried to wave to get his attention, but once on the dirt road, the old man never turned his head back to the house.

Brad heard a crash of glass and then voices coming from the house. In a minute, his bedroom window was raised; a head looked out, and it slammed shut. Crashing sounds from the back of the house let him know his room was suffering the same fate as the rest of the house. The brush in which he had taken cover was not high enough for him to move much farther away without being seen. With no other choice but to wait out the destruction of his house, he tossed some branches and leaves over the duffle and got as small as he could behind a palmetto.

In less than an hour, he heard car doors slam and saw at least two of the men leaving in a black Chevy Suburban. He had to think. Had he heard two doors slam or three? Waiting was uncomfortable, and it was getting buggy. The sand gnats had found him. He could only hope that all three men were in the oversized station wagon. He got up and brushed himself off and was about to reenter the house when he heard a siren coming down the highway. He figured that Sunny had called the sheriff when he got home to flush out the Feds, so he headed back for the woods and, picking up his duffle, moved deeper into the underbrush.

As he walked, he realized that the deputies would soon notice that the burglars had been back. They would be there for a while, with more likely to come, and he couldn't get back into the house to pack food. His experience the previous night made him realize he would need food and water. He needed to get some rest, and he knew where to go. About two miles into the woods to the southwest was his haven, the titi thicket, and his new "friend."

The weather front that had soaked him only a few hours before now brought in warm, dry air and pristine blue skies. As he walked, he could almost feel the forest drying out. Woodpeckers busied themselves making their rows of holes in the many standing dead pines. In less than an hour, he arrived at the privacy of the pool behind the thicket. He used his pack for a pillow and, lying down, soon fell asleep to the soft rustling of leaves overhead. The scene began playing immediately.

Deep Space 2

Ka-Litan's Dzuran Coalition forces were falling back. Scouts had reported a second wave of Errans jumping into the red dwarf system where the Dzuran Coalition fleet had taken refuge. The system's low gamma emissions allowed longer maintenance work periods for a pilot outside of his own ship without having to dock in a maintenance hangar on the big long-jump ships. Ka-Litan had been outside his own fighter working on a yaw thruster when the Erran fighters popped through. Brief flashes of light were about a tri-sec away, just visible above the darkened rim of a gas planet that his battle group was using as a rally point.

With that much cold space between the groups, he was hoping to get his thruster problem fixed so he could get back into battle line. He did not want to sit out another skirmish. He found the problem: a piece of hull metal had been folded in around the thruster housing, preventing full swing on its gimbals. There was no way he could bend shield metal with hand tools, but he could cut it with his ion torch.

His battle group of nine heavy cruisers, three carriers, a city ship, three pulse-cannon destroyers, and a variety of lesser support units and miners, had been forced to fall back to this system in order to avoid total annihilation. The Erran attack had been brutal, forcing abandonment of one of their outer systems completely, leaving only a suicide battalion of skeeters and bombers to harass the Errans as they slowed down and dropped shields to jump. Apparently, those brave fighters had been successful because fewer enemy ships were dropping through than he would have expected. He hoped some of those fighters would be able to rejoin his group or jump to one of the home system worlds if they survived the deadly chain guns on the Erran cruisers.

Ka-Litan remembered the scan array for this system he'd downloaded before the jump. The ships were sheltered between a small methane-ammonia gas bag and its captured moon of light metallics. His indicators showed that a few of the miners were already down on the surface. He needed to restock on coolant halides and rail-gun munitions, but he would have to do that on a carrier when he got the chance. Crawling over the hull's hand holes, he pulled the small ion gun from its housing and waited for it to power up. Around him, a battle line of fighters was forming into a double V-formation.

The inner V would attempt to pinch off one of the main Erran battle wagons. The leading edges of the larger V would attract fire while a cruiser at the apex got fully powered up and in range. Soon, the space around this little gas bag would be littered with space junk and exotic biochems as ships and pilots disintegrated each other. Ka-Litan saw the amber indicator light on his gun blink and began to cut. In a few moments, he had cut the metal flap away, stowed the ion gun, and crawled into his cabin.

Clutching extendable hand grips outside his ship's hull made him feel especially vulnerable. The fleet was extremely short on personnel. The loss of a city ship in the surprise attack in the last system had wiped out two classes of flight crews that had just graduated, not to mention over a thousand support personnel, hundreds on breeder leave, and their extended family groups. The losses to personnel had also taken their toll on every aspect of defense—scavenging crews, crèche attendants, bio gardeners, everything.

Now he had lost his weapons officer, Jen-Mritan, who was piloting a new ship. He hoped they would both survive. He, Ka-Litan, was the pilot. His second officer, the weapons expert, Jen class, was a good friend. They and the little ship Jai had bonded almost immediately so that as soon as thought or need was expressed, the ship responded. They were a perfect triad. With Jen-Mritan gone, Ka-Litan and Jai had relinked their psi-bond to co-opt the Jen officer duties and share that decision-making role. Ka-Litan closed his eyes, shutting out the flickering lights and flashes overhead that meant death and dying. He felt the positive pressure in the hull come to normal, and he opened his eyes again to check the indicators to prove it. He had to wait a few seconds at pressure before he could loosen the helmet clamps, pull off the brain bucket, and get his peripheral vision back.

Jai was going through his power-up checklist as the first double V began to move in on a flanking Erran ship. A second formation was going for the adjacent ship, so the first would get no support. Fewer and fewer Errans were dropping in. That was the good news. The bad news arrived moments later when a brilliant green flash zipped by his right field of view. He was being shot at from behind. His rear screen indicated three Erran fin fighters closing in on his ship and the few others that had been held back for repairs. The bastards had split their jump to come in on two opposing sectors!

He accelerated at heart-stopping g's and pulled a sliding 180 so that his main guns were aimed at where he had just been. The simple fin fighters had good targeting computers, but their tacticians were generally stupid, only a little better than miner drones. On they came, with almost all their pulsed laser energy bouncing off his forward shields. He cross-haired the center fin, and as it filled the center screen, he evaporated it. Only little bits of stray metal were left. He pitched up slightly to target another and gave it a crippling blow. One of the ships to his left began to take damage as its pilot scrambled to get inside and power up. Immediately after the bubble closed, the skeeter exploded in a blinding yellow-green flash as the chem tanks and then the ion chamber exploded in turn.

The Lights will miss him, he had been a good pilot and excellent wing cover. Pitch down now, and target a third. Try a little reverse thruster, too. Put on a little show, and maintain targeting distance. Poof, another bug splashed into space dust. Errans were of the same genetic stock as his home world Dzurans. They'd migrated off planet so many generations ago their limbs had atrophied in low to no gravity environments. They'd developed an abnormally tall, abnormally skinny body type. Bugs.

By the Lights! Erran ships were ugly! His own skeeter was a sleek atmospheric effect ship with no permanently extended sensors. And it was powerful; a deadly weapons platform mounted on a responsive multi-drive propulsion system. It had the advantage of being able to make system jumps without the protective shield systems of a carrier. The little bubble at the nose for crew was a concession to the Dzuran designer's insistence on having piloted vessels capable of independent thought. In comparison to the Erran fighters, which were limited to vacuum or very low pressure operations, his craft was a beautiful blend of art and lethal function. He really loved the shock in his seat when his ship's main cannon fired off. At high forward speeds, it was a gas, but in reverse, wow! And to be able to watch the destruction was awesome. Usually, the fireballs zoomed by at high speed, and he couldn't record the results of a hit.

He could see that the carrier behind him was sending out another squadron of skeeters to take on this new threat. In a few major pulses, this second wave of in-dropping fin fighters was gone. With no new ones coming in, it seemed that the diversion had been only that. The Errans must have hoped to pull off more of the Coalition forces than they had. It appeared that fewer of their ships had jumped into this quadrant. As he approached the carrier to reform a group, he saw that the first two V attacks had been mostly successful. One big Erran cruiser was a red outgassing blister surrounded by a growing glowing cloud of bits of molten metal. Flaming jets of fuel had started the big hulk spinning, and it began a slow drop to the gas bag's frozen ice core. The second cruiser was nearly disabled but had not been breached

84

in any important ways, although it looked like its shields were down and it would soon be out of the fight. He received orders to form up on the right flank of a third V, and he hustled to get into formation.

The Errans did not have advanced shield systems. They could be taken down with brute force, but suddenly, there seemed to be so damn many of them. He got in line and waited. He spoke to his ship's computer, "Jai, report on structural and systems status."

He watched the other fighters lining up in the 3-D array screen while he listened to the onboard computer's readout. Then the order came over his com: "All units forward; concentrate on the last cruiser on their right flank. Another formation will be backing us up. Good luck and good shooting." Slowly at first and then at increasingly higher velocities, the formation moved toward the doomed target.

Chapter 6

The family is a haven in a heartless world.
Christopher Lasch

June 12, 1976
Behind Wakulla Beach Road, Late afternoon

Brad felt the pain in his back when he rolled over. As he came slowly awake, he realized it was not a branch poking him but a cramp in his shoulder. The long night of paddling was not so many hours in the past that his muscles could have recovered. He rolled onto the other elbow and tried to rotate his arm to relieve the muscle spasm. *Wow!* He thought. *That was a very cool dream. Hope I remember that one.* He had always meant to write down the essentials of his dreams, but usually, they were gone within a few moments. His stomach growled, and he remembered that he was hungry and soon began to forget what had been an exceptionally vivid dream. He found some edible berries and some greenbrier shoots. In late spring in the flatwoods, he often found long, fat runners of greenbrier, which, other than being a little bitter, were good for hunger pangs, but only for a little while.

He knew of a patch of blackberries closer to home that might still have fruit, but he needed to get back to the house for some real food. As he approached, there was a light singing of tires on the coastal highway, and at least one pickup rolled down the dirt road to the beach. There were no strange cars in the backyard, and he cautiously peered around front. No cars there either, and someone had retied the crime scene tape back in place. Returning to the back of the house, he got two milk crates and stacked them below his window. It was unlocked and he squirmed through.

Brad was instantly heartsick. His room had been overturned and then scrambled. There had been no reason to break the plastic models, but they had been trashed too: the B-17 was in several pieces. He could see a wing of the P-51 near the door. He swore aloud, "You mean sons a' bitches!" He shuffled through the debris, thankful that he had already packed his backpack. He went into the kitchen and fixed a sandwich and a glass of milk.

He found some Oreos and ate half a row of the little chocolate wonders. That demanded that he finish the last of the milk. He glanced at the stove clock and saw that it was 5:30. He thought, I can't afford to hang out; I need to get out of here!

He took stock of the pantry and determined that he should concentrate on canned food, but then he became undecided. Cans would be heavy. As he wondered what to do next, the night's exertions and the full stomach caught up to him. He wandered into his father's room, pulled the top mattress back onto the bed, found the quilt, and curled up in it. With the familiar scent of his father wrapped around him and in the comfort of the shelter of his own home, he fell deeply asleep, vaguely wondering if he could hide out there at home.

~ ~ ~

Brad woke with a start in full darkness in a state of near panic. He settled a little when he realized he was home, but his emotions boiled with memories and loss. His sense of comfort and calm usually felt at home turned to grief, and as he thought about the last twenty-four hours, to fear. He grabbed up a few things from the fridge and, leaving the door open for light, made a few more selections from the pantry for his pack, and went out to the truck in the barn. His dad's F-250 was a '71 work truck with the high side of a hundred thousand miles on the odometer. Heavy-duty, go-anywhere tires and four-wheel drive versatility had made it a good choice for Whit Hitchens and his well and pipe business, and he had never wanted to replace it. A new clutch and belts two years ago had convinced him to keep it and put the cost of a new truck into paying his crew well enough to slow down the inevitable turnover of semi-skilled labor. The heavy-duty Koenig truck box, when full of his usual menagerie of tools, brought the weight up to almost three thousand pounds. Although it got a hosing every Saturday after the workweek closed, it had never seen new wax.

Brad found his dad's key chain and removed two keys, the house, and the truck. Starting the truck, he remembered the conversation of what, only two evenings ago. "Not on your life," his dad had said. *Well, this **is** for my life.* He pulled out of the pole barn carefully. It was his barn now, as sole heir. So was this truck and the house and ten acres. He wondered if it would have to go into holding with his aunt as guardian until he was eighteen. Heck, he thought, edging onto Highway 98, I don't know what to expect of next week, much less three years from now. There was no traffic to be seen at this late hour. He was alone on the road. He got the feel of the wheel and gradually got his speed up to fifty-five.

Brad considered that maybe if he worked for Chase and got some money, he could get this side window fixed, and he would have a truck of his own for when he eventually got a license. Definitely, he'd have to fix the window soon. As he drove, a sharp wind was coming through on a roar of wind so loud that the radio was nearly useless.

Traffic on the Coastal Highway was sporadic at best; oncoming cars were rare. Now on the other side of the Ochlockonee River, there wasn't any traffic. But it was getting late; he found himself given over to yawns and had to stretch frequently to keep himself alert. Despite the discomfort, Brad was enjoying the solid feel of the ride when a movement in the dark caught his attention. What had appeared to be a driveway reflector in the distance seemed to move, to bob up and down. He let his foot pressure on the gas lighten up, and the truck began to slow down. The small red dot kept moving on the shoulder, and then the shape around the light began to reflect his headlights. He saw it was a doe. He took his foot completely off the gas.

As the big truck gradually slowed, Brad saw that the deer was hesitantly approaching the edge of the road. He was prepared for what might happen, and he began to reach for the brake pedal. At precisely the wrong moment, the deer bolted. Brad jabbed at the brake pedal, and it went to the floor. When nothing at all happened, he realized he had hit the clutch pedal and, as the deer began to accelerate in front of his lights, he finally pressed on the brakes.

He did not swerve. Whit had always made a point that it was better to kill a deer or even someone's dog than yourself. "Never, absolutely never, leave the road for some dumb animal," he had said, emphasizing the 'nevers' with a slap on his knee. "Better to repair a grill or headlight than wreck the car and get thrown through the windshield. Nobody's dog is worth it!" That lesson spelled doom for the whitetail trying to get across before the heavy Ford pickup broke its neck. Her shoulder took out the right headlight; her head slammed into the grill; and as the truck, now moving at less than thirty-five miles an hour, kept going, her body pulled around and her hips dented metal over the right front wheel well.

Heart and breathing stopped, he brought the truck to a stop centered in its lane. Despite the tender flesh on his palms, Brad had a death grip on the steering wheel and stared ahead into the single cone of light shining out of the remaining headlamp. After catching his breath, he looked into the rearview mirror and saw nothing but the red glow of brake lights. There were no headlights approaching, but he put on the emergency flashers and got out to look for the deer. In the pulsing red light, he saw the brown lump of hair about fifty yards back. He approached it slowly and saw that it was clearly very dead. It had a broken neck and possibly a broken spine; its legs were tangled as if some of them had been broken as well.

How could this day get to be any worse? *Jeez! What did I do to deserve this day?* Then he felt the gorge rising in his throat, triggered by the sight of the deer and the smell of warm blood and visceral fluids spreading on the pavement. He lurched over to the edge of the road and vomited up his meager dinner. Distracted by this, he was fully unaware that headlights were approaching. He only had time to look up in surprise as a car flashed by in the night, honking as it passed.

He took off his T-shirt and used it to wipe his mouth and nose clean. He threw the shirt into the back of the truck and put on a fresh one. It was actually his dad's denim shirt with the sleeves rolled up; he would not part with it for anything. It still smelled like him. And there was an odd smell coming from the shattered headlamp. The metal around that corner of the fender was smashed in. He could see where the deer's head had pushed in on the grill, and then he heard it. Over the night chorus of insects, he could hear hissing and then saw the water dripping from the radiator. "Dammit and to hell! Man, this sucks!" The string of epithets continued until he ran out of creativity and steam. Leaning closer, he took in the pungent smell of hot radiator fluid rising from the steaming puddle on the ground.

He was not usually profane. Although his father knew how to express his brief frustrations with a varied mixture of choice Southern epithets and foul army cursing, his mother had brought him up to polite manners and a sense of pride in himself that did not permit crude public displays. But this was not a particularly good day and he was tired and alone—and hunted, to boot. He really had been looking forward to getting to a safe haven by at least the next morning and letting someone else share his burden. His eyes started to water, and he fought the urge to let go completely. Sniffling and wiping his eyes on his sleeves, he got back in the truck.

"I wonder how far I can get on a leaking radiator?" He started the truck, eased into gear, and began to head down the highway. Taking stock of his progress, he saw he had just passed the side road to the Alligator Point Beach community and would be approaching a thinly developed section with private homes on large wooded lots that lined part of Alligator Bay. He had just about decided to turn around and reconnoiter the beach houses when he thought he might do better with one of the bay-front homes ahead. The needle on the temperature gauge had just passed the last "e" in temperature. Wisps of radiator steam were blowing from under the hood.

One car passed from the other direction, and he was alone on the highway again. He thought, If only I could trust the law to get help and not turn me in to the Feds. They'd turn me over to Aunt Susan, and then whoever it is that's after me would get all of us. His single headlight illuminated a set of reflectors on a handmade sign that gave the route number to a waterfront house and an engraved and gilded name: "Southern Sands." He was about to pull in when he saw a forestry road on the north side of the highway. He took that instead and drove off the pavement—far enough, he hoped, to keep the truck from being found for a while.

When he came to a stop, the truck's engine knocked a few times and stopped on its own. Dead. "Ahhh! Dad's truck is dead, and I killed it!" he cried out. A furious boiling sound was coming from the engine block, and he could see wisps of steam slipping from under the hood. He thought briefly about just curling up there in the woods, but he was determined to keep moving. What if he was found on the road in daylight? He could not imagine sneaking all the way to Apalachicola on foot.

The modest, elevated beach house had been spared the winds of last week's tropical storm and looked to be cleaned up and habitable. There were no cars parked under it that he could see. A hand-painted sign over the door, illuminated by a feeble yellow light, proclaimed: "Welcome to Southern Sands." There was some wreckage of a shed that had been knocked off its blocks by the storm's mild winds, but mostly, the grounds looked intact. Walking toward the narrow beach lining the bay, he was taken by the beauty of the calm, nearly mirrored surface with the moon riding high. The moon was a thin crescent in the midnight sky, but in the clear summer night air, it still provided a glorious reflection. The Milky Way spread clean and close overhead. Turning he found his favorite constellation, Orion, setting in the west.

He turned back to the house and began to look around. Under a tarp-covered trailer, he found a small catamaran sailboat. Pulling the tarp back, he found the sail bag tied to the mast. Everything he would need to sail it seemed to be in ready-to-go condition. The only obstacles to using the boat were the chain securing the trailer to one of the house's pilings, the thirty or so yards to the water. "Yes," he told himself, "I'm actually stealing this boat and finding a breeze to sail it."

First things first, he jogged across the highway and retrieved a bolt cutter from the back of the truck and in a few hard moments, had the chain cut. A half an hour of hard pulling moved the boat and trailer to the water's edge, where he turned the trailer around and pushed it in. He paused, winded, considering if there was any other way to get safely to Apalachicola. Nope. After going back to the truck for his backpack, he was finally ready to launch. The dark waters of Alligator Bay were a black mirror of the Milky Way's grandeur. Looking at the moon and glancing back to the east, he reckoned on a few hours before light, and who knew how long it would take to get a breeze up?

June 13, 1976
St. Teresa, Florida, Pre-dawn

Working carefully in the moonlight, Brad ran the sails' track slides into the sail track, hauled on the halyard, and brought the sail up to its full height. The logo high on the sail told him he was "borrowing" a Hobie 14 catamaran. No jib to worry with, there was only the single mainsail and it hung limp in the moonlight. Its normally bright rainbow-colored sail subdued in the thin light of the moon to bands of dark gray and black. He let the sail drop and secured it around the short boom. He found a short wooden paddle bungeed to the frame, loaded his packs onto the platform, and pushed off. After paddling a short distance with a lot of effort and pain in his still tender fingers, he experimented and found that he could make slow progress by pushing the tiller slowly back and forth using the two rudders as paddles. It was ungainly, and if anyone had seen him, it would have appeared a little comical. But then, he was banking on no one seeing him.

Within half an hour, he passed well out of sight of the boat owner's house and found a very slight breeze playing just off the surface of the water. It was coming out of the northwest and was perfect for a beam reach down the bay. And so he sailed, very slowly at first, into a long stretch of protected water that lay behind barrier islands. As day broke, he shared a reverie with Huck Finn. This wasn't a river, and his method of conveyance was considerably higher tech than a log raft, but on the catamaran's trampoline deck with his head on his backpack, he felt bonded to vagabonds everywhere. Serenity itself! He made a pre-dawn snack of another peanut-butter-and-jelly sandwich. The light breeze picked up enough to scratch small wavelets on the surface of the bay providing better tiller control as he glided southwesterly along the long reach of St. George Sound toward Apalachicola.

The morning light was glorious as it lit up the rainbow colors of the sail, and for the first time in a few days, in the swirl of water beneath him, Brad found some peace. He hoped that he could always find a way to stay near these waters and on boats. He and his dad had shared good times on the family's two-man homemade kayak. He had learned to sail with friends whose much wealthier parents had real seagoing boats, serious offshore vessels that could go out for a week and brave whatever weather the Gulf offered. The little Hobie Cat didn't even have a jib. Above his head, the sail began to flap. As he tried to trim it to maintain momentum, he found that he was heading southeast, away from his target. The winds shifted through the compass and shortly thereafter, died altogether.

After what seemed like too many hours later he was disappointed to look up and see the sun only nine o'clock high and what he thought was the Southern Sands still visible less than a mile and a half behind him; its white concrete piles shone in the morning sun. But by late morning, the off-shore wind was putting pressure on the Hobie's sail again, and the little boat began to move with a noticeable wake. The gurgling noises gave him a satisfying sense of progress down the miles long stretch toward safety.

Brad lay back on the plastic woven trampoline and luxuriated in the warmth of the sun on his face. Soon, he was able to take off his shirt and feel the glorious heat on his skin. By turning his head occasionally, he could keep track of his bearings and let the wind take him. He thought about telling his dad about how well he had managed when he got back home, and the totality of the last forty-eight hours came back to him. Dad was gone. He had seen it, been there, but the truth of it had not yet hit home. He had run off and no one would understand why. When there was a funeral, he'd miss it. He couldn't go.

He felt the coolness of a tear track down his cheek. He fought to control the heavy pounding in his chest. Visions came to him of his house in shambles, of his room torn to pieces, of his dad curled into a fetal position with one bloody hand extended over the edge of the bloodstained bed. The last thing he had said that awful night was, "I love you, Son." More tears flowed, and he began to sob. He wanted for just a minute to roll over the edge of the boat and sink, to let the cool salt water take him away.

That'd be stupid. His dad had always told him that suicide was stupid. Unless you were in horrible pain and terminally ill, there was no excuse for a suicide. There was always an option to just drive away, to change venues. Incongruously, he found the *Suicide Is Painless* theme song from M*A*S*H rolling in his mind. It had been one of his and his Dad's favorite shows. Although Korea was not his Dad's war, the show's subtext of military stupidity rang true.

He rolled over on his side and looked at the distant dark-green line of the mainland. The vegetation was punctuated at random by white, gray, pink, and yellow beach homes. Most of them had large, full-width windows facing the Gulf. Behind them, three large piles of white cotton stretched to the heavens surrounded by smaller popcorn clouds. Brad had always loved to sit and just watch the slow-motion roiling balls of steam push out of a cumulus's interior. The two largest of the row were massive for so early in the day. The recent rains were still cooking off the swamps inland, but then, he thought, the inland never dried out completely, even under fire-emergency-warning conditions. Glad for the distraction, he watched the cloud masses boiling in slow motion.

Brad was not aware of exactly when he fell asleep. The sun on his back combined with his exhaustion from the last two days' trauma and travels had taken him to a point where he could not resist the veil of sleep being pulled down over his troubles. The little boat sailed on. With the tiller lodged between his knees, the boat found its own point of sail; balanced on a light quartering breeze from the north, it made its way, more or less, southwest—a little too far south of west.

He startled awake as the rudders kicked up in the shallows. It thudded at first over surface lumps in the large shoal of sand that most conscientious boaters knew about and avoided. The Dog Island Shoal was, in fact, a former barrier island. Overcome in recent centuries, it was now a high-tide navigational hazard and a low-tide expanse of tidal sand. Looking around for bearings, he found the green line of the mainland was now very thin. He barely recognized that the small, white island beach to the west covered in trees and beach houses was Dog Island viewed from the end.

With a shudder, he realized that he had almost sailed outside the line. His dad had described a thin, dashed red line extending from Alligator Point in the east, southwesterly along the outer edges of the Dog Island Shoals,

Dog Island, Big and Little St. George Island, and finally, St. Vincent Island and Cape San Blas. It was not a ruler-straight line, but it separated offshore from inshore. He was grounding on the shoal that separated inshore from offshore, and he had almost missed that. Not that the little boat couldn't take mild swells in the true Gulf, the Gulf that lay a few hundred yards south, but Hobie Cats were notorious for tipping under a strong breeze. He knew that if he found himself in a such a breeze, a lumpy swell and no more ballast than his young body, his only defense would have been dropping the mainsail and riding out whatever came. Shaking his head at his own foolishness, Brad grabbed the nylon bowline and jumped off onto the shallow, sandy bottom. He could not steer with his rudders kicked up, and he couldn't lower them on the shoal.

He laughed at his near miss, pulled the head around to point shoreward, and began to drag the little craft into deeper water. He was surprised at the strength of the tidal current pushing mini–sand dunes across the surface of the shoal. This rising tide, he knew, would develop an eastward flow against his forward progress to the west. Finding knee-deep water, he pushed off and set a course again toward the center of the bay and his goal to the west. The white columns of storm clouds above Tate's Hell Swamp had grown larger; their darkening bottoms spoke of a rainy afternoon that would likely drift north and east if they followed pattern.

Brad had embarrassed himself in front of God and anybody who might have been watching by going aground on the shoals. It was bad enough that he had been dozing. At the same time, he was grateful that he grounded when he did and had not allowed his exhaustion to get himself blown into deeper Gulf waters. Older catamarans were known to come apart in steep swells, and he didn't need that complication in his life right now. Still, he did know that there were shallows that extended hundreds of yards offshore from both the barrier islands to his left and the mainland on his right. The channel markers anchored along the center of the inter-coastal waterway indicated enough depth for oceangoing barge traffic, and he resolved to keep them in mind as aiming points.

This was easier to resolve than to do, and he worked at rudder and sail to maintain a heading just south of westerly toward the next marker buoy. The morning sun climbed higher, warming the black trampoline, and soon, Brad had to take shade from the sail on the starboard trampoline rail. Getting comfortable and trying to maintain his bearings, he found that lying next to the rail and scanning below the boom allowed him to maintain distance from the offshore islands and their shallows and glance forward for the widely spaced navigation markers that indicated deep water. Inexplicably, the offshore breeze died again. He had been drifting with the little catamaran pointing in no particular direction for a short while when a long, low, deep rumble got his attention. This was not the occasional interruption of a fighter jet from Tyndall AFB to the west, but the ominous growl of cloud banks growing over the warming wetlands of Tate's Hell Swamp. He rolled over and uttered a quiet, "Oh, crap!"

The several individual thunderheads that had been forming over the swamp had pulled together by co-attraction, drawing on the same fuel: the sun-warmed waters of the swamp. Propping himself on his left elbow, he stared in wonder at the black tower of cloud boiling up over the mainland. Staccato flickers of lightning passed from ground to crown, flashing out into the anvil top as backlit hues in cerulean gray or, alternately, breaking out to stab the ground in white-hot flashes that blinked the eye. Gray-and-white masses boiling out of the central cloud columns testified to the dangerous up-and-down drafts transferring energy inside the cloud mass. As the three original cumulonimbus cells had joined, they had formed a small super cell, a steam engine with adequate energy to pierce the stratosphere and tap into the freezing temperatures five miles up.

The uninspired maxim that "what goes go up, must come down" was playing out in shades of gray before his eyes. Water vapor was hurled into the deep freeze of the upper atmosphere and then tumbled, turning to snow, ice, and, if you weren't lucky, hail. When the updrafts could no longer support the weight of the solidifying mess, it all came down—fast! The leading edge of this terrific downdraft became visible as it bottomed out. The cold air, laden with water vapor, blew out of the bottom of the cloud and spread across the surface of the land and across the bay. The condensing forward edge pushed a white wall of chilled fog with it in what mariners referred to as a white squall. Brad had heard of the effect but had only seen them from afar while out on the salt flats.

This one was coming his way. As he watched, the water surface immediately around him lay glassy, its softly undulating surface giving an imperfect mirror image of the towering black storm over the mainland. The reflection, too, flashed and flickered as white pulses of energy leapt from ground to cloud. Softly, his sail swerved on its gimbals, tightening the mainsheet. A few seconds later, the first ripples fanned the surface. This was only the harbinger. The real sailor-take-warning notice was already visible.

Whitecaps were building out from the coast as the gust hit the bay. Brad loosed the mainsheet to the boom so that it could swing wide when the gust came, and he was only a brief moment too soon. The sail filled and the boat bolted like a skittish mustang. His bare back felt the air temperature plummet to something in the fifties and wind speed jump from barely perceptible to, he guessed, more than fifteen, probably twenty knots. The little boat had no real mass in its hull and quickly responded. In a few breathless moments, he was gaining real speed. At first, he thought it would be great. As long as it lasted, he could ride this storm to Apalachicola. Then the hull under him gave an ominous bump. The windward hull lifted three feet out of the water, and he had a panicky urge to jump. But this was his lifeboat; he could not leave it, not here.

The catamaran sped up quickly to about fifteen knots or more. A single furrow of white foam laid out behind the one hull still in the water. He released the main sheet to drop the airborne hull. The twin rudders began to vibrate in a low rumble as they reached a velocity that neared the boat design's maximum speed. The once-glassy surface now angrily pulsed with greenish-gray, close-packed, steep-sided swells. The tops were beginning to curl and foam as their crests were whipped by the down blast. Brad pulled slightly into the wind and tried to reach over to release the mainsheet further. The sail couldn't spill enough wind, so he pulled further into the eye of the storm. Hull speed slowed, and finally, so did his heart rate. Wind was ripping at the trailing edge of the multicolored sail, creating a furious flapping, cracking racket overhead. He could no longer see any shoreline as mist and spume blew off the growing wave tops.

Unable to get his bearings, he could only suppose that the wind was still roaring south or something like it, and he attempted to crab westerly. Most centerboard sailboats have an option in these crises of hauling up the centerboard and literally slipping sideways or to leeward, essentially using leeway as a mitigating strategy to maintain a desired course without giving up too much sail area to an overpowering wind and without luffing the sail beyond a stall point. The twin knife-edged hulls on the Hobie Cat were permanent, and Brad's only option was to haul in the sail to let the wind work, gain some speed, and, when he felt he could no longer keep both hulls in the water, to let it out again to dump wind and hull speed.

Despite a light peppering of pea-sized hail, he found himself grinning. The boat was as responsive as a two-seater sports car. It could accelerate from almost nothing to scary fast in half a moment, and, with insignificant hull weight, it would stop in a few yards if he brought its nose up into the wind. But aside from his exhilaration, this was a truly perilous situation, and he was dealing with it! Dad would have been proud. The full implication of that past tense shook him, and he was angry, as furious as a human can be with a bad hand dealt from the deck of life. He took a full breath and screamed into the wind at the top of his lungs—a long, protracted primal scream that let more out than he had imagined. At times, it verged on the yeehaw of a rebel yell and then became a simple agonized wail. When he had no more energy, he simply held on, concentrated on the myriad balancing forces acting on his little ship, and sailed. He found he could tuck his toes under straps on the trampoline and haul his weight out to help counter balance the tremendous forces trying to capsize the boat.

He was committed to riding out the storm. Figuring worst-case scenarios, he decided he'd rather go aground on the lee shallows to windward than on the windward shoals to the south. As he planned his little cup-shaped maneuvers, he hoped he was edging closer to the mainland than the island. His clothes and backpack were soaked, and probably most of its contents were as wet as he was. He was physically drained. When he realized the hail had stopped, he looked up and let the rain beat on his face.

With no warning, the rudders both kicked up with a load bang. The nose came around to windward and nearly came about. He probably would have if he hadn't fallen off the trampoline when one of the hulls scraped bottom. He still held on to the mainsheet, but that was counterproductive. The wind still had a powerful grip on the sail, which was now pulling him off his feet. The boat no longer had his ballast to keep it on the sand. Running crazily after the boat, he tried to unwrap the line from his right hand to let everything go if he had to. It pulled him headlong into the shallow, shell-covered bottom before he finally let go. Untended, with no one steering, the boat would either capsize or it would pinwheel, hurtling down one side of a wind-driven ellipse only to point up automatically, stall, bear off, and repeat. He would have to keep up. Everything he had taken from the house was in the backpack lashed to the mast. When he finally caught the boat, it had grounded. Its sail was flapping less furiously, and there was almost no wave action over the flats. He wrapped the line around the mast and then around the forestay and sat down. Sitting, he was in neck-deep water, and as an anchor, he figured he was adequate as long as the wind didn't pick up again.

Closing his eyes, he let the elements play themselves out. Damn, he was cold! The downdraft had chilled him. He was shirtless, and the comparatively warm water of the bay was a relief; but he couldn't stay there. The bay waters weren't up to their midsummer bathwater temps yet, and if he stayed submerged, hypothermia was a danger. Sighing, he let his lungs totally empty. He forced all the breath out that he could and drew a long, full breath through his teeth. He repeated the action, totally ignorant of the benefits of hatha yoga, and cleared his mind to his central purpose. Survive!

He stood, stepped between the lead wires that supported the mast's forestay, and loosened the halyard. Although the wind was slackening, it was still running over ten miles an hour, and he had to jerk on the sail to drop it. He waited for the weather to calm. As the sky cleared, he could see the cross-bay bridge. He raised sail and aimed for the high point in the arch. He made good progress to and through the bridge, and with a freshening evening breeze, he headed for the next target, the high bridge crossing into Apalachicola seven miles to the west.

~ ~ ~

By dusk, his tiny boat was approaching the Gorrie Bridge that routed US 98 into Apalachicola. He thought about the possibilities of finding Chase and Lou Anne Chappell, finding a bed, and getting some real sleep. In twilight, he had been aiming at the red lights marking the channel on the bridge, but seeing a small boat trailer being backed into the river near the base of the bridge, he changed his mind. With the last of the evening breeze, he made the boat launch area at the base of the bridge and ran the boat ashore.

A flat-bottom oyster boat was being loaded onto a rusted trailer at the ramp nearby. He asked the oysterman where the shrimp boats parked, and the gruff waterman only laughed. "They park," he said accentuating the incorrect term, "all along there. 'Bout forty to fifty of 'em from that first one there on up to the mill pond. You looking for one in particular?"

"Yes, sir, it's the *Lou Anne.*"

"I haven't worked the big boats for a few years, but it used to tie up, just up the way there." He pointed at a jumble of pilings connected by a seemingly flimsy dock to a rusted metal shed. "If you find the courthouse and look to the river, it'll be right about there."

June 14, 1976
Apalachicola, Sunday Morning

Raucous caws of gulls fighting over scraps of fish heads woke Brad well after first light, but he did not stir. Sometime later though, a city crew mowing and trimming the grounds roused him. He had found reasonably dark, dry cover under the ramp of the bridge. The John Gorrie Bridge entered Apalachicola in a descending curve onto the main drag, Market Street. The vertical bulkhead at the base of the bridge and the broad cover of concrete under the ramp had provided shelter for hundreds of travelers over the years—some waiting for boats, some for a ride out of town, some merely waiting. Brad rose to a view of a concrete wall covered in semi-literate graffiti, crude and rude sketches painted or scratched into the concrete, a scattering of empty beer cans and bottles, and fast food litter.

He couldn't stand the thought of another peanut-butter-and-jelly sandwich, so he found a corner café and ate a good, hot breakfast before heading over to the waterfront. He scanned the boats nearby but couldn't see all the names. After a short walking survey, he still had not found the *Lou Anne*. He walked north along the riverfront checking the names on all the boats.

After a few blocks, he finally asked a man loading gear onto a boat that had tall outriggers draped in netting if the *Lou Anne* was in or out fishing. "Well, now," he said pointing south, "usually it's downriver a ways. Go down a block, and take a left, then you'll be on Water Street. Keep going until you see a big building looks like a courthouse. If she's in, she'll be across the street tied up. If she's out, she might be out a coupla days." The crewman asked, "So who's asking?"

"I'm family, kinda. I'm looking for Chase Chappell. You know him?"

"Yeah, sure, I know Chappell." He pronounced it to sound like 'chapel.' "Good captain. Old boat, but he does pretty good."

Brad thanked him and walked on past a half dozen boats, a few seafood restaurants, a hotel, and several fish wholesalers. He saw the courthouse on the right and looked to the left. He had to slip between two buildings to find docks with boats. A little more poking around and he found that the only access to the docks was through one of the fish houses. Asking inside, he found out that the seafood distributor allowed three boats to tie up, and one of them was the *Lou Anne*. Its berth was empty, but it was due in shortly. He found a vantage point on a piling at the end of the pier and watched river traffic. He almost missed her arrival distracted by the dance of seabirds. Eventually, the *Lou Anne* sidled carefully up to the moorings and tied off. For half an hour, the dock was busy as large plastic tubs of iced shrimp were hauled out onto the dock.

The unloading process wound down and the last man left on the boat began to hose it down. Brad was about to approach when a girl jumped up onto the wide side rail. The pretty, red-haired teenager greeted the crewman with a simple hello and began to help put things in their places. To Brad, it seemed there was an overly complicated array of ropes, cables, pulleys, and things he didn't know what to name suspended from two large metal booms.

When the two workers stopped and sat down in the cabin, he approached the boat cautiously. "Are you Chase? Chase Chappell?" He pronounced it "chapel" as he had heard earlier.

"Yeah, that's me. Only Chappell is pronounced with a soft c-h, like in chaperone, and who are you?"

"I'm Bradley Hitchens. I'm kind of a relative. I'm not actually sure what you'd call it. You all were over to my house in Wakulla a few years ago, before my mom, umm, when Mom, when Lucy was still there." He paused, embarrassed at having to say his mom had left. "Susan Delaney in Tallahassee is my aunt; she was my mom's sister." He scratched his ear as if in deep thought. "My mom is Lucy Hitchens. I really don't know if you remember. There's was a picture …" He added and then trailed off.

Chase chuckled softly, said, "Sure, I remember that visit, and if I remember correctly, Lou Anne's mother and Lucy's mother were half-sisters, same father or something. But with all the married names in between and a few divorces, I guess we're something a little closer than strangers. So what brings you to our fine city?"

The young girl climbed up the companionway, brushing something pink and sticky off her cutoff overalls. Brad was momentarily transfixed; she was a lot younger than Chase, and when she stopped and looked at him, he saw she was beautiful. He tried to get his mouth to work, but no sounds came out.

Filling the embarrassed silence, Chase volunteered the introductions. "Mr. Hitchens, meet Miss Chappell, my daughter, Connie."

The young girl came over and shook his hand, and they exchanged "Glad-to-meet-ya's."

"Connie," he continued, "this is Bradley Hitchens from Tallahassee."

"Oh, no, sir, I'm not from Tallahassee; I'm from Wakulla Beach, way south of Tallahassee." He was aware that around the Florida panhandle, Tallahassee was "different" somehow from all the rural areas surrounding it. Brad's eyes darted between the two of them; he now saw the resemblance between this pretty girl and the red-haired kid in the photograph from their visit to Wakulla Beach. He hadn't thought about what he was asking until he actually had to ask it. "My pop ... er, my dad, got shot a coupla days ago, and he said I should ask if you could put me up for a little while."

"Oh, man!" Connie looked horrified. "You're that boy!"

Brad blanched. His mouth opened and shut, said nothing.

"Calm down, Connie. Don't scare the boy," Chase said. He looked seriously at Brad. "Why is it you've run off over here? Why is it you're not with your mom, or up with your aunt Susan?"

Brad slowly told his story. He told them about the disappearance of his mother, the break-in, and his dad's death, of the search for something the killers thought might be valuable, almost everything that had gone on, including the possible link between the murder of Dr. Hill and his assistant and his dad's death. He told them almost everything except anything to do with the metal artifact in the backpack.

When he stopped and looked up at them, he found Chase examining him, pondering the options. Connie looked stricken. She said, "Dad, can we find some room, for a little while at least?" She had developed her mother's protective instincts, and this cute young boy could be her cause. "What about Jamie's room?"

"I suppose. We'd have to figure out how to arrange things, and, of course, we'll have to talk with your mother."

"I can be very useful. Dad taught me a lot about how to use his tools, and I even help him with carpentry and mechanic work and painting if I have to." He hoped he looked earnest but not too desperate.

"What about school? What grade were you in, boy?"

"Mr. Chappell, I just finished the ninth grade." He furrowed his brow in thought. "I don't think I can just come over here and get in school. Least, I can't come over here and be Brad Hitchens."

She looked at the tawny deep-tanned boy. "Ninth grade. So you're fifteen?"

"I turn fifteen in July, the eleventh."

"Bradley ... do you like Bradley or Brad, or do you have a nickname?"

"I like Brad."

"Okay, call me Chase, all right? Look, Brad, are you for certain that you're in danger?"

"I wish you could see how bad they broke everything in the house, looking for something that Dad didn't have." His voice broke slightly, and he swallowed the lump in his throat. "When Dad was dying, he was pretty badly shot, he made me sit and listen and not go for help. He made me listen as he told me to come look you up, 'cause you're family and especially 'cause you're not close family."

"That's true. Probably take a truckload of detectives to figure out the connection between the Hitchens and Chappells." He rubbed his hands on his grime-covered work pants. "Brad, you understand that I have to talk to Lou Anne, but I want you to know we'll figure out something for you. Okay?"

"Thanks, it wasn't easy getting here. And now that I think on it, I don't know what I'd do if you couldn't help."

"You carrying anything?" Connie asked.

"Excuse me?" Brad didn't understand the question. Was she asking if he had drugs?

"Do you have any stuff? You're standing here two days after a major lost-child search is announced, and all I see is sneakers, jeans, and you in a shirt that's too big." She sniffed, "and you smell like bay water."

"This is pretty much it. I have a backpack stowed down under the base of the bridge. I had to travel light."

Looking at Brad, Chase said, "You leave something lying around in this town for very long, and one of the dock rats'll relieve you of your burden." Chase asked his daughter, "Connie, I've got to finish tying things down here. You get the truck and get his stuff, and we'll carry him on over to the house and see what's what." He pressed his temples, just wondering what was next. As an afterthought, he called after her, "And drive careful, y'hear? You don't have your license yet!"

Yes, Sir!" she exclaimed, turning for the parking lot before her dad could change his mind.

Following quickly behind, Brad started. "Connie, can I tell you something?"

Connie looked sideways at him. "Is it something you couldn't tell my dad?"

"Kind of," he answered. "I stole a boat to get over here. I'm not proud of it, but I was desperate." She looked over at him, appraising him, but didn't say anything quite yet; he was too cute to fit her impression of a truant. In less than a minute, they had pulled up under the channel bridge. Connie looked out over the assemblage of power- and sailboats, from little runabouts to yachts and flat-bottomed houseboats. "Which one did you take?"

He smiled and pointed far left of where she had been looking and at the Hobie 14 tied up to a branch. It was dwarfed by the concrete supports of the Highway 98 bridge. Connie couldn't stop the chortle that erupted. "That?" she clapped a hand over her mount to stop her laughter. "I mean, you came in that?"

"Yeah," Brad answered, a mixture of embarrassment and pride trying to sort itself out.

"Well, actually, I'm impressed that you got all the way here in that little thing."

"Yeah … and, well, I didn't take it all the way. I had to borrow a truck, too."

Connie turned to look at him with furrowed brows and a dimple that hinted at a smile. He looked into her pretty green eyes. He thought, She's got a way of looking right into you that makes you feel like you're connected to a lie detector. He realized he never wanted to lie to her. "It was my dad's, but I hit a deer and busted the radiator over near Alligator Point. Technically, I'd have inherited it."

"Bradley Hitchens," she said, "you just get interestinger and interestinger." She added, "Heck, I'm almost sixteen, and I don't even have my license yet, and you, you're fourteen and drove your dad's truck and survived hittin' a deer?"

"Actually, I'm almost fifteen, and it was a pretty small deer, but big enough to hole the radiator." He looked back at her and gestured to the dash of the Dodge pickup they were sitting in.

She grinned at him, held a shared stare, nodded. "Yeah, right, I guess having a license might not be all that necessary when escaping from bad guys."

Brad looked over at the little boat. The bright trademark rainbow colored sail lay spread out, flapping on the trampoline deck. "Connie, I need to figure out how to tell those people where their boat is. I think the house was called Southern Sands."

"I wouldn't worry about it," Connie said, seemingly unconcerned. "Dad knows people who know people. Our sheriff can call their sheriff, and the owners will get their boat back."

Thinking about it, she added, "I guess it's a good thing you knew how to sail!"

He allowed a thin grin, born from a deserved portion of newfound pride. "Let's just say I can sail better today than I could this time yesterday." She nodded in understanding.

"… and Connie?"

"Yeah?"

"Thanks."

June 15, 1976
Tallahassee, 1330 Hours

Captain Richards was waiting on the phone call from Fort Meade. His earlier call had only gotten a message on a machine, and he had waited in the shabby, cramped motel room for the callback. His two special ops agents had gone to the county courthouse to search records. When it rang, he started and grabbed for the receiver.

"Richards here."

"Jenks here, Sir. We may have found something."

"What have you got?" Richards sat up on the edge of his bed.

"Hitchens's wife had a sister who still lives in town." Jenks reported.

"I thought Hitchens was single, divorced, or separated."

"Not officially, Sir. Seems she ran off, left him and the kid. We can do some more digging down there in the community. They have a decent microfiche index at the Wakulla Times, and we can see if there was some wife-beating or something. Hitchens is a Nam vet. He could have been a beater."

"That's news in itself; I don't feel so bad about bagging the cretin if he was." He had his notepad on his knee and was writing down, 'possible wife beater.'

"So what about this sister-in-law?"

"She works here in town as some sort of executive assistant at the state offices."

"Governor's office?"

"No, sir, one of the agencies. We're tracking that down to verify her work schedule and location."

"Fine, find out where she lives and get over there during working hours, just not anytime near lunch. I've got to clear the phone; I'm still waiting on Langley."

104

He stood up, pulled curtains aside, and scanned left and right through the room's filthy windows. He scratched and stretched, wishing he had a second large cup of coffee to go at the breakfast buffet. The phone rang again.

"What is it this time?"

A slightly offended female voice advised him to stay on the line for General Saxon, and after a pause, he heard, "Richards, you there?"

"Yessir, I appreciate your call back. Our primaries have been accomplished."

"Good job, Captain. I knew you'd be capable of getting this done."

"Yes, sir, thank you." He thought, You bastard. You trained me and my squad to do whatever was necessary for whatever reason you could justify as national security, send me out to do the country's dirty work, and then go eat bagels and jam with the silver-plated congressmen on the hill. He said, "I don't think they're going to be connected, sir. One was an auto accident, one a freak electrical fire we can blame on some cheap aluminum wiring, and the other was a B-and-E with a homicide."

The silence on Saxon's end made Richards pensive. "Sir?"

"You're saying they're dead?" There was an uneasy sense of disbelief in the two-star general's voice.

"Sir, yes, sir. Removed as directed. I haven't seen any buzz in the local press connecting the two incidents in Leon County together or to the B-and-E in Wakulla County." He listened as he heard muffled off-phone conversation at the Maryland end of the line.

"Removed?" The general's voice was more direct now, more in control.

"Yes, sir. I no longer have the flimsy of the orders that came in on the two in Tallahassee, but they were clear on removal. Terribly sorry about the third one, he was supposed to be an interview. We didn't plan on having a shotgun pulled on us."

After a short pause, Saxon continued in a mocking tone, "Sorry about the third one! Jesus Christ Henderson!" Richards heard a muffled comment not meant for him. "… damned second amendment has every third house in this country armed to the windowsills." Then more clearly addressed to him. "Just be sure that your after-action says you were drawn on and in mortal danger." There was a pause on the line, more muffled conversations, and, "So when can you clean up down there?"

"Working on that right now, sir. At the Wakulla site, that target had a kid. From the condition of the room, he lives at home or in shared custody. Don't know which yet. He seems to have run away, headed east, we think. No sign of a wife; we're checking on whether they were separated or what. He's a Nam vet, may have been violent. At this point, we don't know what the family status is. Lassiter and Jenks are at the Leon County Courthouse now and have found the principal has a sister-in-law in town. We're planning nonlethal measures from here out to see what gives with the family."

"Richards," Saxon cut in. "It is imperative that you find and collect the artifact. As your orders indicated, that was your primary objective, not the elimination of a few overly curious citizens. You are authorized to do whatever is necessary, short of further murder and mayhem, to get that thing out to Dreamland for comparison." Saxon paused, recognizing a slip. "Just find the damned thing. Stay on top of the search for the kid. How far could he get, anyway?" There was a brief silence on the line, and Saxon came back. "Richards, listen. I just took a crap load of abuse over the dead geologist. The two researchers were into genuine science. That was unavoidable. But the well driller? Discretion, man. I'm only going to say this once. You have got to control your team, or you won't have one. We clear?"

General Saxon covered the receiver with his palm and spoke for a few moments with others in his office. He came back to say only that he expected that Richards could wrap this up in a few days and to check in when he was ready to come in. Richards lay back on the bed, hands behind his head. He was careful to separate his emotions from his job, but he thought he could like the kid who had that room. Hell, he had even built some of those models himself. And the Bullitt poster ... For the first time in his career, Richards felt like he was seriously screwing with the American dream.

In Maryland, Saxon looked across his desk at his junior liaison officer in Air Force intelligence and quietly mouthed, "Goddamned Rangers are all cowboys. This mission's gone FUBAR!"

June 15, 1976
Apalachicola, Dinnertime

Lou Anne Chappell was a buxom, freckled redhead with a natural smile and bright-blue eyes. Her forty-hour job was assistant manager of the County's Health Department. She also managed a late dinner shift at a seafood restaurant out on the beach and was studying for her real estate license by correspondence when she could. On weekends, she helped at a beach rental agency. She planned to cash in on the real estate explosion on St. George Island. Over dinner, the family discussion had gone well for Brad. The big uncertainty for the short term was what to do about getting him enrolled in school next fall. A cover story for his presence had to be built.

Brad felt comfortable at the table with the three Chappells. Their house was a large, wood-frame two story with gingerbread trim on a small city lot with a well-kept yard. It had come down to Chase just as Whit Hitchens's house had come to him. Like most houses in a seaside town, it was a little overdue for paint, but otherwise, it was weather tight, and comfortable.

Lou Anne asked, "Bradley, what do you want to do about school? We have a while to think about it, but come September, we need a plan."

"Miss Lou Anne, I like school enough. I'd like to go, but what kind of story we could come up with, I don't know. If it's like Wakulla County, everybody in town knows practically everybody else. It'd be hard to just sneak me in here."

"You may be right. Let's sleep on it for now. Say, Chase? Are you going out tomorrow?"

"I've got the crew scheduled to come in before first light, and we'll take the tide out in the morning." He suddenly got the question from the suppressed smile on Lou Anne's mouth. "Brad, would you like to go out with the crew and me tomorrow morning?"

"Sure! Heck yeah!"

June 16, 1976
Offshore, Southeast of Apalachicola

Bradley Delaney Hitchens, approaching fifteen years of age, started the shrimper phase of his life early on a hot summer day. The three previous years of getting to know his father better had not been overshadowed by his mother's disappearance. He had come to know and appreciate his father's drive to succeed at his homegrown business. He had learned a great deal of life's lessons about respect and become as self-assured as a young teen can be without descending into arrogance. When Brad stepped over the low stern rail and onto the *Lou Anne*'s deck that morning, he entered into an education in hard work, low wages, and interdependence with a team of coworkers.

The *Lou Anne*'s diesels purred smoothly on fresh oil as she passed through the Sike's cut, the man-made channel sliced through St. George Island, and motored into the softly rolling swells of the Gulf.

Guthrie was crew boss, first mate, and substitute captain when Chase wasn't on board. Guthrie was simply Guthrie; no one ever offered whether this was a first or last name. Bradley never did ask; it didn't seem necessary. Guthrie was in his mid-thirties to mid forties; it was hard to tell by looking. He was of medium height and broad in the shoulder. His coppery, leathery skin had been aged by the sun and wind to look more like that of a man in his fifties. Slow to speak, but sure in his opinion, he was a good leader for a crew on which every man knew his job. He had a silver-flecked beard that made scraggly look good.

Jeffie was a heavy lifter and had the physique to prove it. He was an ice loader, skinner, and peeler, a careful winch man, and, on trips lasting more than twenty-four hours, the cook. The man could do wonders on a simple gas grill producing anything from Louisiana gumbo with black beans and yellow rice to fried gator tails or crawfish étouffée, and the usual seafood entrees, fried, blackened, broiled, or whatever his fancy told him. His deep black color set off a wide line of white teeth whenever his good-natured smile shone.

The lowest man on the seniority list, Mike, was a skinny nineteen-year-old, who had just signed on the previous summer. His brief attempt at Gulf Community College had informed him and his instructors that he had to be outdoors. He wasn't yet a committed offshore fisherman, but he had learned most of the skills required to take any position on the boat whether it was dropping nets, dragging, or hauling, and because of his position as low man, he made sure the work areas and coolers were cleaned up to the level required by fisheries inspectors.

After a long day out with little to show for the spent diesel fuel, they began hitting shrimp toward sundown and dragged the bed in earnest until three in the morning. With the crew exhausted, they lay at anchor until dawn before returning to port. Brad sat in a semicircle with most of the crew arranged around the short stern rail surrounding the afterdeck.

"Swamp Boy?" Guthrie asked. "Why did you say you were called Swamp Boy? You wrassle alligators?"

"No, sir," Brad answered. "I got lost out there for a few days last year." He looked around at the faces of the crew. "Actually, not lost, just sort of stuck. Everybody else thought I was lost. I guess I got famous."

"Stuck?" Mike asked. "What do you mean 'stuck'?"

"I was checking out some of the little islands out on the salt flats. Arrowheads and spearheads and stuff are all over out there. Anyway, I was crossing one of those little drainage cricks that run through the saw grass, and when I jumped across, my tennis shoe got stuck in the mud and root mats down deep in the muck. I tried to reach down and get it back, but I couldn't reach deep enough in the mud to grab it without sticking my face in the muck. That stuff really stinks!"

He looked around at the guys. Chase had tied off the wheel and was listening from the doorway to the pilothouse. Brad continued, "So there I am, miles from the nearest road, with one bare foot and one tennis shoe, and it's getting dark. I started to hobble back, but almost immediately cut the bare foot on a shell."

"Damn, son!" Jeffie said. "What'd you do, crawl?"

"Naw, I stayed put and figured Dad would put out a search. They'd find my bike at the end of one of the forest roads leading down toward the flats. I'd probably be there a day or two at most, and I could find swamp food to eat." Seeing furrowed brows, he added, "You know, shoots, berries, crawdads, and I could smear myself with swamp muck to keep off the bugs."

Guthrie swore softly and tossed a cigarette butt overboard. Brad continued with his story. "Second morning, I'm sitting out there on the edge of the bank, way out on the grassy flats, a coupla hundred yards from where I got stuck, and realized I could get myself out. Mostly 'cause I was tired of chasing down crawdads on one foot." He spit over the rail for effect and went on. "So I hopped back to the ditch where I lost my shoe and tried to reach my foot down to the sneaker. By sitting all the way down in the muck at low tide, I was able to get my foot back into the sneaker."

Mike was staring wide eyed, picturing the image. "Was it hot out there? Warm enough for gators to be frisky?"

"Heck, yeah! Two of 'em had been looking around and sniffing out my tracks, but I spent the night in a tree. So anyhow, I've got my foot as far down that hole as I think I can get it, and I'm getting my toes in there. And then the strangest thing happened."

Mike went for the bait. "What?"

"Somethin' started pulling on my leg. I mean it was like quicksand with a personality!" He heard a low chuckle from Chase up in the doorway, but he kept going, extending his right leg and shaking it and pulling on his thigh like there was a contest for the leg. "I was really, really scared now.

109

My leg is now stuck in muck and is being pulled in, and it's about an hour past low tide. Water's backing into the creek and soon will be up to the top of the bank." Mike was all ears, captivated. "I'm wondering whether I'm going to be able to keep my head above water." He looked back at Mike with all the intensity he could muster. "I swear something was pulling me deeper and deeper." He paused for effect.

Mike waited politely at first and then asked, "So what happened?"

"Well, I didn't know what was pulling my leg." He paused and locked eyes with Mike. "The problem with something pulling your leg is this. Well, like right now, for instance, I might be pulling your leg right now and it's just so hard to tell." He looked back at Mike in all innocence.

"What?" Mike looked perplexed. Guthrie grinned and cussed.

Jeffie started to laugh and moan at the same time. Chase uttered a mild profanity and went back into the pilothouse. Mike finally got the joke and that it was on him. A look of gullible surprise, embarrassment, and then a cracking smile passed in succession across his face, and he began to guffaw in abandon. "Damn, boy, don't you understand? You're the new guy; we're supposed to pull the jokes on you."

June 16, 1976
Tallahassee, 0600 Hours

Sergeants Lassiter and Jenks had stopped going to their favorite Denny's because the waitresses had begun to recognize them and would offer their regular orders at breakfast. One of them seemed to have developed an interest in Jenks. Familiarity with the locals was not in their best interests. Looking over a menu at a nearby Waffle House, they tried to keep their voices low despite the loud Sunday morning crowd. Lassiter was consulting his notepad. Captain Richards, having made a predawn flight from Maryland for this meeting, was pushing a wedge of pancake slices into his mouth.

Lassiter began his report. "Captain Richards, the sister, Susan Delaney, is single, divorced, and has a modest single-family house out near Lake Jackson. It's a decent lower-middle neighborhood, but she keeps a clean house. She's been divorced for years; it was uncontested. No kids. Don't know from the pictures and personal effects in the house if she was close to her sister or the kid. There are some boxes of family photos, no real idea who they are. No family Bible showing relations." He flipped through the pages on the small pad, looking for anything really useful. "Umm, she's an assistant to a division director for the Department of Education and has been with them for five years, her first job out with an MS in education administration from Eckerd College. Nothing found from a direct search of the premises on Friday afternoon when she was at work and again yesterday afternoon when she went out shopping."

"Surveillance of that excursion revealed no purchases that would indicate the missing boy is in residence. Most purchases were in preparation for services for her brother-in-law Whitcomb Hitchens. Traces on her calls and tapping indicate that she's been preoccupied with the search for Hitchens's son Bradley and the burial services she supervised last week."

"Okay. What have you dug up on relations or friends? This kid can't have just disappeared."

"Well, he's become a ghost. We've been monitoring the sheriff's dispatch band, and the search is still concentrated in East, Central, and South Florida. There's also an army of volunteers canvassing the woods. This is based on an abandoned bike a few miles east of their residence the night after the intervention. We have no new leads of our own, but they do have confirmation that it was the boy's bike. There is also the dis-appearance of Whit Hitchens's truck late Thursday or possibly Friday morning. Could be a local took advantage of the situation. No shortage of lowlifes down there. The truck hasn't been spotted at any of the local relatives' residences we checked."

"So, what's your best educated guess about the boy? Any reason to think he has any idea of why we're even looking for him?"

"Only that reference in the calls between Hitchens and Dr. Hill." Lassiter looked at some papers in his case file. Flipping down to the oldest papers, "Here we go. It seems Hitchens mentioned that his son found the artifact in the woods." He looked up at Richards. "If I was to spend the next weeks of my life searching for him, I'd think he's out hiding in the woods. The kid is smart, probably smart enough to fool the sheriff's dogs last week. The kid is a straight-arrow student, and he's been raised in those woods. My guess is he's in the sticks. We can hope that the search teams and the hounds will pick up a trace." There was silence at the table as all three men paused to work on their breakfast.

"Okay," Richards said, chewing. "So, we need to maintain focus down by the homestead. Jenks, I want you to monitor both Leon and Wakulla County's Sheriff's dispatches to make sure we stay on top of their leads.

Lassiter, dress nice and get to know the aunt; keep your eyes open for lines of sight that the kid might watch from a remote location." As an afterthought, he added, "Might be good to stake out the mortuary."

Lassiter sagged perceptibly. "Sir, Hitchens has already been buried."

"Oh, right!" Richards continued, "I'll check with Sig-Int when I get back to see if the bug on the phones has pulled anything up." He stretched and yawned.

Richards stabbed a piece of country fried steak from his plate, swirled it in over easy egg yolk, and began chewing. Through the thick mass of meat in his mouth, he continued, "If we don't find something in the next few days, you're going to demob and return to your respective bases." He swallowed and pointed a fork. "Jenks, you will be on standby since you are closest at Eglin. For the time being, let's try to not let this kid slip out of the net. He's got to know where the artifact is, and obtaining that object is our primary mission."

He unfolded a flimsy with his left hand while he poked at another piece of steak. "I quote: 'The service of your country demands that the allegations or assumptions hinted at in earlier telecommunications be verified or proved groundless. In spite of the unfortunate loss of three primary subjects, every effort must be made to locate and secure the original artifact and any samples that may be available.'" He looked up at Lassiter and fixed his gaze. "Sergeant Lassiter, it took a whole heap of frosting to cover up the mess you made out of that Hitchens screw-up, so try not to let me down, son. Let's be sure that we don't miss any possible leads." He pushed the last piece of steak in his mouth and mumbled, "Any suggestions?"

Jenks slid his plate with the half-eaten meal away, swallowed the last of his juice, and offered, "We left the geology lab too soon, I think, but that damn fire just took off, and the ceiling tiles really started to lay down some smoke. There may have been another sample on the machine that Duggars was using when we took him down. Although we retrieved his notebook and it was useful, it was not conclusive, and frankly, it was hard to believe. They still had not taken the thing to the particle accelerator for testing. And if the fire department got to the fire quickly enough, there may be a floppy disc in the machine that would leave trails or even allow someone to get a handle on the chemistry of the sample."

"Good idea, Martin." Richards looked over at Lassiter. "How about it, Larry? You have any thoughts?"

Lassiter finished a gulp of coffee, looked thoughtful, and said, "I'd been thinking, and we know that—or rather, there is a report of an artifact that is about a half-meter long. We have what was left of that small sample, most of which has been used in destructive testing, and we know that there was an intent to send another piece of the original for testing. We don't know for certain, but time lines suggest that the second sample wasn't prepared yet." He set the cup down.

"There's a good chance that if we get into Hitchens's shop or check out his workbench at the house, we may find filings or shavings of the material that we could send in for analysis."

"Great!" Richards sat back wiping his mouth with a paper napkin. He leaned back while a server with two coffeepots asked if they wanted refills. She topped off the three cups at the table and moved on. "Okay, Larry, I want you to pursue those two trains as you can. Martin, we still need to maintain access to the sheriff's dispatch tapes, and we still need to monitor the aunt's house here in Tallahassee. I'm flying out to JPL this morning to see if there are any recorded orbital collisions over or near North Florida airspace that could have resulted in exotic metals falling out of the sky." A few minutes later, they had paid and dispersed into their separate vehicles.

~ ~ ~

Sergeant Jenks was reviewing a tape recording of the dispatch operator at the Wakulla County Sheriff's Office. As he listened, he noted the license plate of an abandoned Ford F-250 reported to the west of the Hitchenses' homestead. With a whoop, he stood up, knocking his chair back. The records secretary helping him yelped in alarm and stood up staring, hands on her cheeks. Martin Jenks cried out in excitement, "Hot damn, Charlotte! We got a hit!"

June 16, 1976
Apalachicola Docks, 8:30 p.m.

One of the results of the Saturday night family meeting was the decision that Brad would eat, maintain a closet, and spend family TV time if he wanted to at the Chappell house a few blocks from the waterfront. He would inherit a used bike from Connie's older brother, who was in Marine boot camp at Parris Island. He could sleep in the limited crew quarters in the stern of the *Lou Anne* behind the ice locker. He would also provide security for the family business and the two other boats that shared that dock.

The working waterfront slowed down for the evening. Lights winked on, first at the restaurants and then a few other lights from working boats. On the high bridge over the river, the red center lane flasher turned on at dusk. It had been an exciting first night out on the Gulf, and the crew was a good bunch of guys. Having been accustomed to small boats and inland waters most of his life, he was exhilarated by the power of the twin diesels on the *Lou Anne* and the live feel of even small swells in the Gulf. He had watched as the twin winches raised the booms high enough to bring the net's side doors out of the water and collapse the net. As the wriggling, squirming mass spilled out onto the deck, he was amazed at the variety. Somehow, he had expected it would be just shrimp.

He was soon shown how to sort, tossing out the sea slugs, rocks, starfish, veggies, and other unmarketable dregs that got in the net when the drag chains scraped the bottom. He knew he would later learn the names of the various critters, but for now, he was tired. A nearly full moon was rising, bathing the warehouses, loading docks, and moored trawlers in a full but colorless light. He had been sitting in the dark on the forward deck leaning up against the sloped face of the cabin trunk, deciding between another coat of bug repellent or simply going to sleep. Squeaking bicycle brakes nearby brought him to wakeful alert.

Connie hopped off her balloon-tire Schwinn and stepped onto the stern rail. Brad was groggily getting to his feet at the moment. The sudden lurch made him lose his footing, and he fell chin-first to the deck. "Oww!" Lying there, momentarily stunned by the pain, he heard and then saw Connie's powder blue sneakers approach.

"Here, let me give you a hand."

"I can get it." With a suppressed groan, Brad got up, reddening. He was glad for the darkness; the blush was a reaction to both the approach of Chase's pretty daughter and his embarrassing clumsiness. "I must look like a real landlubber."

Trying not to laugh, Connie said, "No, really, I am sorry; I didn't mean to knock you off your balance." She sat down on the forward cabin trunk and motioned to a spot nearby. Brad sat too, rubbing his chin. "How was your first trip out? I hear you didn't go overboard."

He said, "Won't be the first time in history a pretty girl knocks a guy off his feet." He immediately regretted sounding so brash. He followed up with, "Nah, still dry. Tell the truth, it was pretty cool."

He became animated and made himself keep his hands off his chin even though it still throbbed. "At first, it seemed like we were going to have a bad run, then the tide turned or the moon rose or something, and it seemed like the place just filled up with shrimp." He tried to get a good look at Connie in the dark, but the moonlight was filtering through some high-altitude clouds. He continued, "Man, I couldn't believe the amount of shrimp and critters came out of the net the first time Jeffie hauled the rig in. And we barely had time to clean out that haul and wash down the deck before we hauled in again. And the phosphorescence, Wow!"

Connie said, "Yeah, it's like magic sometimes. It's totally awesome when you can get those hauls on a sunny afternoon in July. Air temperature is just right, skies are beautiful, swells are flat, just like magic—food from the ocean by the ton. It sure beats farming. It's a helluva lot harder in December in deep winter swells, with the air just above freezing."

"Well, I really liked the trip, but I don't know if this is supposed to be a career change or if I'm going to get an identity that I can go to school with next year. I'm not sure what to do about that."

"I think Mom's working on that for you. Reason I came down here is to tell you they found your dad's truck today. Six o'clock news was full of it, 'Missing boy may have gone west!' They found the deer, the bits of fur in the grill, and put together the rest." She explained the news feature said they had reversed the direction of the primary search. "The keys in the ignition have 'em thinking that you probably hitched a ride to who knows where." She shoulder-bumped him gently. "They also mentioned that a sailboat in the area had been reported missing. The talking heads are all over the map with ideas."

"Dang, they could be comin' here."

"Daddy said there's not much chance, with too many married women in the family tree and a divorce or two confusing things."

"These are not stupid bad guys, Connie. They could even be special ops or something. Maybe I should keep moving; they don't seem to mind killing people. You and your folks have been real good to me, and I don't want anyone else hurt."

"Well, thanks, but where'd you go and with what? Even if you still had the truck, you wouldn't git far with no money."

"I got money," he said defensively.

"How much? I mean, not meaning to pry, I just figure you ain't had time to go to a bank is all."

"I got over a hundred dollars still."

"Yeah, and even taking the bus, you might get as far as Houston. And the other side of Houston just gets hotter and drier every mile for the next thousand miles."

"Well, maybe I could go south? With summer vacation and all, I could look like a tourist."

"A homeless tourist? Know anybody in South Florida?"

"No," he answered, sounding beaten. "No, I don't. Mom had some relatives somewhere near Lake Something. I never met 'em."

"Daddy says you should stay here and stay low. People 'round here know everybody, and they'll talk or they won't; can't be helped. But you should probably stay on the boat for now." She dug into her purse and handed him a small box.

He held up the box to the rays of the nearest streetlight and saw the flowing letters of Clairol.

"Hair color?"

"Yeah." She giggled. "Your days as a blond are over!"

Brad looked at the ruddy glowing strands haloing the dark silhouette of Connie's hair. Her face was invisible with only her eyes picking up pinpricks of light from the surrounding waterfront. "What grade are you in?"

"Going into the eleventh grade; the high school's just down there," she said, pointing generally west, "it's a pretty good school, I guess."

"Wish I could go. So, you're sixteen?"

"Not any time soon, next April. I started early. It was cheaper than paying for pre-school."

He scratched his stubble. "Say what day is this? I've lost track." He gestured in the dark. "With all that's happened, and all…"

"she held her watch up to the light of the nearest streetlight and squinted. "Today's the sixteenth."

"Wow. My birthday is in about a week. "I'll be fifteen on the 22nd!" He turned looked out across the water, east. "But I don't know if I can even go to school. The Feds are going to be all over the place like rats."

"Yeah? Most kids I know would love a good reason not go to school. You a brainiac?"

"Hah!" He let out a short burst of air, turning back to her. "Me, no. I ain't no brainiac; I just always loved learning new stuff. I used to hate the dad-burned reading list, because I wanted to read other books instead." He rubbed at his throbbing chin. "I get mostly Bs, some As, with occasional Cs.

They put me ahead to the sixth grade from fourth on account of my reading, but it didn't last. I'm a chronic underachiever, according to most of my teachers."

"What do you read? When you're not on the reading list?"

"War stories, spy stories, a little science fiction, and I had just started my second Hemingway. How 'bout you? Are you smart?"

"I do all right—As and Bs. I just want to figure out what I'm going to do after school. I have no idea what to do after high school."

"College?"

"Prob'ly. I don't know. I know I don't want to just get pregnant and raise fishermen. I want to see more of the world—you know, Europe, the rest of this county." She slapped at a mosquito and wiped the blood spot from her wrist. "I am so tired of bugs. I wouldn't mind someplace that didn't have mosquitoes."

"You could join the Air Force and ask for Greenland. I don't think they have mosquitoes."

She laughed at this and stood up to leave. "I gotta split. Things to do, places to be."

"There any way you could get me some books to read? Not much happening here, and I wouldn't mind something to help kill the time."

"I'll see if Mom can help. She's connected too." She turned to go. "See ya later." Connie paused and placed a hand gently on his shoulder; she gave it a small, reassuring squeeze and left. Brad watched her go. Even in the dark, her thin, agile body looked great in the backlight of the distant streetlights. When she turned a corner, he went down to his bunk and tried to catch up on several nights in a row of lost sleep. He knew he had to turn his body clock back so he was awake and alert in the daytime and could get to sleep at night.

The dream started in familiar fashion: he was being pursued. He seemed to be on an endless country road. Pine trees lined the shoulders, and straight-line dirt roads offered a poor alternative to the pavement he was on. He was running at first, trying not to trip as he glanced over his shoulder at … what? Then he was on a bike. Whenever he looked over his shoulder, a pursuer always seemed to be a quarter mile back and gaining. The pain in his legs was real; his breaths became labored as the unknown shadowy form followed. In a flash, he was in his dad's truck and the trees disappeared in darkness. The F-250's all-terrain tires sang on the pavement, and the motor was revving much too fast. Headlights in the rearview mirror seemed to be

117

nearing. His speedometer needle rattled near the white line at ninety miles per hour, but the lights behind never left him. He was sweating and restless; his dreams paralleled his life. He was prey. He was being pursued.

Deep Space 3

Ka-Litan was plunging through the wreckage field of the exploded Erran cruiser his V formation had just destroyed. It was a help that his skeeter craft was small, much smaller than many of the pieces of hull tumbling around him. At least the gun emplacements on this cruiser were out of commission. He was maneuvering around a large hunk of glowing metal when a green blast of energy erupted from below and walked in his direction. A plasma beam had locked on the former thruster housing beside him but would soon be recalibrated to him. He hit the thrusters and tried to slip into the shadow of the scrap metal. A glance at his array told him that he had no friendlies in the area and there were at least two Erran fin fighters below him.

There was too much debris around his little craft for headlong acceleration. A blip in his ears and a red flash on the array showed him that one of the pursuers was gone. The other fin fighter doggedly pursued him out of the cloud of metal. He veered sharply left and then tried a sliding reverse turn to allow himself to put his main guns on the problem. He lost momentum in the turn, and the fin fighter approached rapidly. He could see the helmet of the enemy pilot in the instrument glow of its cockpit lights just as his targeting computer acquired the closing fighter. It was all timing now; the fin fighter's plasma cannon was beginning to glow, indicating Litan's ship was about to take a lethal hit. Litan expressed the thought, Hang on, Jai, wait, wait! He pressed the chain gun's burst button, and six slugs of plutonium-hardened iron tipped with HE heads slammed into the left engine cowling of the fighter. It spun out of control, its plasma beam gyrating wildly. The frantic pilot inside couldn't release his trigger, and the beam quickly lost intensity and faded. Litan hit his second button, and a stream of negative energy particles cut into the fin fighter's pressurized hull.

Litan returned his attention to getting back into formation and the protection of numbers. His V formation was reforming on the other side of the wreckage field, and he felt vulnerable and alone out here. The next Erran cruiser in the formation had a cloud of fin fighters protecting it, and three of them peeled off to attack. Those three were not going to go after his formation; they were coming for him. They became a much more dangerous threat than the debris field between his ship and the safety of numbers. He punched the boosters and sped into the field of twisted metal. As his velocity increased, the chance that he would impact a large chunk that could overpower his collision shield increased exponentially.

He turned right and then left, taking crazy chances by sliding between colliding chunks of hull frame. One of the pursuers wasn't as good a pilot and impacted a major structural frame head-on. His craft simply stopped and popped, a small lump of twisted refined metal attached to a scorched large piece of the Erran battle cruiser. The two others were trying to catch up and had a good chance of doing so. "Come on, Jai, help me out here." The computer only bleeped. Litan and his pursuers emerged from the debris field at high speed into an ongoing mop-up skirmish between two friendlies and three fin fighters. He aimed at one of the three, fired, and kept going, unable to vector off his speed. As he passed, his target exploded. He had taken one of the Errans out but added two to the uneven skirmish going on.

With the safety of a developing claw formation only a few minutes away, he turned back to help even the odds. He looked at his power reserves and knew he couldn't stay long and expend so much of his fuel on high-speed maneuvers. Another fin fighter found itself in the crossfire and exploded in a cloud of flame. The odds were getting better. The two friendlies were dodging green wands of destructive energy and had moved into wing-on-wing to share shields. A blast of green flared on their invisible shield bubble, and Ka-Litan took aim on its source. Closing and tracking, he kept firing at his enemy until the little craft simply disappeared as pulverized junk. His anger was getting the better of him. He needed to preserve ammunition for live fighters.

He slid into bottom gunner position below the wing-on-wing fighters above him and studied the array. The right wing pilot, leader in this formation, took control of the three fighters, and they began to move as a unit toward the safety of the nearly completed claw. The two remaining fin fighters, angered by the losses their forces were taking, followed them toward the trap. The claw formation was hard to detect when the ships were blacked out with passive sensors and shields deployed. Thirty-six fighters positioned in a hemispherical array were all pointed toward the center like a huge, destructive lens. Ka-Litan's retreating group aimed for the center of the bowl and slowed, allowing the two chasing fin fighters to spring the trap. The lead ship of the claw sent out its signal to the invisible rim of the bowl formed by thirty-six Coalition skeeters. As one, they opened up on the group of fin fighters, all of whom were quickly vaporized.

Orders came over his head gear for all fighters at less than 30 percent power to return to command base. Catching a deep breath, he glanced over at the shrinking line of Erran cruisers and knew his day was not over.

Chapter 7

How inappropriate to call this planet Earth when it is clearly ocean.
Arthur C. Clarke

June 16, 1976
Apalachicola Docks, Midnight

The wake of a passing boat rocked Brad awake. He hadn't been sleeping deeply, and he had to take a leak. He went to the head and then looked out on the sleeping town through a porthole. He grabbed a T-shirt, now tinged with seafood smells. The quiet streets of the night were interrupted only by the darting shadows of the feral cats that thrived in any seafood town. He approached the only intersection in town with a light, a flashing light. In the calm, he heard the approach of a vehicle coming off the bridge. Its lights first illuminated the concrete barrier as it rounded the turn and then the roadway; eventually, it came into view. He watched cautiously and slowly slid into the shadows of a storefront.

Recognition! With growing apprehension and then relief, he watched as a black Chevrolet Suburban slowed for the intersection, turned left, and accelerated west. When there was no longer any part of the red glow of the departing taillights and he could hear no moving traffic, Brad slipped back to the dock and into his bunk. He wondered if boats had addresses and if they did, what his address was. The phrase 'lost boy' drifted into his thoughts. He was a lost boy, a lost boy who did not want to be found. He rubbed at his chin, feeling the lump growing under his stubble. Had it only been three weeks since he first saw the blue glint of the artifact and fell on a log? He felt the top of his forehead; that lump on his head had hurt too.

June–September 1976
Apalachicola

Brad's new life developed a pattern. The *Lou Anne*'s newest crew member was a live-aboard. He moved a few essentials into his berth, and he, Connie, and the namesake Lou Anne herself made the plywood bunk behind the ice locker a little more comfortable, if not larger. Screens and a fan were installed to make the evenings more bearable, and later in the summer, a camper-sized window AC proved more than enough to air-condition the small area below deck.

Brad got faster at sorting and was becoming a skilled head man, flicking the heads off the large and jumbo shrimp with both thumbs in two-handed competition with Mike. Although Mike was five years older and out of high school, he was the closest in age, and they became friends. Brad could sense that Mike was not the sharpest knife in the drawer, but he had tool smarts and was a competent woodworker. He offered to let Brad work on some of the minor wood repairs that came up. As they talked, Brad learned that Mike had met Chase on a construction crew. Chase had not always been a shrimper, but like many in the community, had been close to it, had often avoided it, but had worked as the occasional crewman to fill a berth and make some money when construction was down.

After working on St. George Island building three-story sand castles for rich retirees and investors from all over the country, Chase had finally had enough of the searing heat, sudden rains, and vicious yellow flies that flew out of the dunes whenever the coastal winds dropped. When finished, the beach houses were air-conditioned, and as cool and dark as you wanted to make them. For the nine to twelve months they were under construction, the sand castles were uncooled, unheated, and toward the end, even unventilated. With savings and a small VA business loan, he had bought a forty-three-foot hard-chine V-hull shrimper with curved front wheelhouse, a small galley, and a decent enough ice maker to ensure the catch stayed frozen. He had personally rigged an auxilliary chiller to augment the nine inches of Styrofoam insulation so that ice loaded actually got colder as they went out. The shrimper's rounded bridge and the clipper bowsprit made her one of the more elegant members of the fleet.

Just before school started after Labor Day, Lou Anne Chappell had come up with what appeared to be an official birth certificate from South Carolina. If he chose to accept it, he would be William Bradley Williams. He could still go by Brad. As he stood looking at the yellow slip of paper, he asked, "Why William Bradley Williams?"

"Good question. I had thought about Johnny Johnson, but you didn't look like a Johnny or Jack to me. Or Jim Smith, I had that going for a while." She handed him a two-inch-thick Tallahassee phone book. It included listings of most of the coastal and rural communities in the area. "Look up Bill Williams."

Brad cracked open the large book and flipped pages until he got to the W's. Then he let out a long, "Oooooooh!" He looked up at her and grinned, "There's a boatload of Williamses in here.

"Exactly, so do you want to still go by Brad?"

"Do you think it's safe?"

Connie added, "You still look like a Brad to me, always will. Bill's not so different from Brad, I guess, but you should go have a look in the mirror and see if you could pull off a Bill."

"I guess you're right." He walked over to the large mirror hanging over the fireplace and stared at himself for a minute. Turning around, he announced, "I'm a Bradley; I was named after General Omar Nelson Bradley, and that meant something to Dad. He was in the armored infantry in Nam when I was a little kid, and, well, that's a piece of me."

Lou Anne said, "That's as good as any reason I could think of to decide. But for the time being, until you get beyond eighteen and can go do a name change on your own, you just have to remember you're not Bradley Delaney Hitchens. You're going to be Brad Williams in public. There's a lot of Delaney in you," she said holding his chin and turning his face left and right, "and a lot of Hitchens, too." She looked like she was about to say something else, and he noticed a little moisture rimming her eyes.

Abruptly, she turned around and picked up a medium-size packing box from the table and turning back, presented it to him. "I met with your Aunt Susan last night at a restaurant up in Bristol. She's glad to hear you're doing well. She went all the way over to Hardeeville, South Carolina, to a get a blank birth certificate. I don't want to know how!" She handed over the box. "And she also brought these."

He took the box from her. "They're clothes from the house. Mostly summer stuff, 'cause she thought you'd be grown out of the rest by winter." He looked into the box of neatly folded clothes. He could feel his chest heave with emotion as he saw bits of his former self. His two favorite baseball caps, one green-and-yellow John Deere hat, and a dark-red FSU Seminoles hat were on the top of the pile. "There's another box in the car filled with some of the stuff from your room. She said most of your old models were broken, but she did preserve one for you and some of your books as well— and a few things of your father's too, and some family pictures. We can keep these things safe in the house here, until we can do something about a room."

Brad appeared lost in thought for a moment and looked up. "Why South Carolina?"

Lou Anne smiled. "Your aunt Sue is a smart one. You remember she works with one of the way-higher-ups at the Department of Education?"

"Yes, Ma'am." His eyes were saucered wide in question.

She beamed back at him. "Well, she's got connections with connections. It seems like the Hardeeville Middle School in South Carolina burnt down last May. They don't seem to have any records on their eighth-grade class."

Brad digested this and moved on. "You think I can move in?" He faltered, then, "Heck, it's not like everybody on the docks doesn't know I'm living on that boat anyhow."

"Well, soon, you will officially be William Bradley Williams, a cousin of Connie's whose parents were killed. That's kind of the story I'd been using at church and the grocery store whenever the nosey Nells asked." She hugged him close to her. "And you can start school next week." She gave him another squeeze. "She also said she very much missed you, but understood why you weren't at the service. She sends her love and wishes it was safe to come see you."

Connie asked, "Why can't we clear out the stuff from Jamie's room? I don't imagine the Marines are going to turn him loose any time soon."

Her mother looked at her with a disapproving frown, softened, and said, "I guess I'd wanted to keep it there for him, except for my sewing machine, but ..." Her voice trailed off. "Brad, are you willing to help Connie and me box up all of Jamie's things?"

"Sure!"

~ ~ ~

By New Year's, Brad Williams had become a new younger sibling of sorts. Fresh paint and a few of his own things on the shelves brought his own touch to the room. On a Christmas season shopping trip to Panama City, he had even found a replacement Bullitt poster for his wall. His resettlement was complete when for Christmas, Connie gave him a replacement model replica of a Bradley fighting vehicle.

March 26, 1977
Apalachicola

124

On one of the first warm Saturdays in March, Connie joined the crew of the *Lou Anne* for what would hopefully be a cruising overnighter. Brad and Connie took their usual positions on the foredeck against the forward bulkhead of the cabin trunk. She looked over and stared at him until he noticed. He would try not to notice, but he couldn't help noting that she was staring at his profile.

He turned abruptly toward her, startling her. "What?" Brad had grown accustomed to her beauty. She was a sixteen year old in good health, had survived the early and mid-teens without serious acne, and had impeccable skin. She did use some of her mother's lotions and potions, but these had been second nature to her in keeping the sun damage to a minimum. On most days, he just accepted that his new "sister" was gorgeous. He knew her to be intelligent, insightful, and resourceful. Her beauty was second now to her wit and sense of enthusiasm for new things. And he had seen her dark side at 5:30 in the morning when almost nobody looks good. But still, the staring habit unnerved him as did her habit of getting within inches of him to talk. It was as if their conversations were secret and confidential, but it was possibly just early farsightedness.

He had made some friends in school and didn't feel so much like an outsider nerd anymore. Working the shrimp boat all summer and on weekends after school started had earned him some points with the locals. He thought of himself as a grateful outsider, glad to be taken in, but still aware of his lack of status as a true son or brother.

Connie finally said, "I was just noticing your blond roots are growing out again. You're gonna need another hair-dye job. I can help you with it when we get back tomorrow."

"Okay, if you want." He kept looking at the approaching cut in the island.

"Brad?" she said quietly from two inches away.

"What?" he said again, faking irritation.

"Could you make me understand better why you think the FBI is looking for you? And why you think you're in danger from them. Aren't the FBI the good guys?"

Brad breathed in heavily and let out a long sigh. The familiar rumble of the twin diesels pushed them steadily onward toward the cut. Bob Sikes Cut was an armored channel through St. George Island. The island's presence made the Port of Apalachicola possible because it sheltered the coastal town and the estuary from all but the worst of Florida's fall storms.

The cut also allowed a huge flow of tidal currents to pass through at enough velocity that the channel washed itself clean twice a day.

As the *Lou Anne* lined up on the channel markers, he began slowly. He asked her to reserve judgment until he had told the whole story. He told her about the find in the woods and his father's assessment, as a geologist, that it had been there since the tree had been very young. He explained carefully the conclusion that the artifact, because of its position beneath the huge ancient tree, must logically predate modern metals like aluminum. He described his father's puzzled expression when they had gone into the shop to cut off a sample for his professor and the newly cut material was the same blue-green on the inside as it was everywhere else. He told her about its incredible strength and how his dad had thought that it could prove that there was an alien visitation to this planet probably more than a few hundred years earlier.

She had listened intently, but, as if she hadn't heard Brad's revelations, Connie pointed at some people fishing off the rocks as they approached the jetties on both sides of the cut. The granite rock jetties extended at least a hundred yards past the shoreline on the ocean side of the island, encouraging the scouring action of the tidal flow. Ahead, another shrimper was struggling to come in against the ebb and was not making much more than two knots over ground. Heading out, the *Lou Anne* was making just enough speed on water to maintain steerage in the roiling current, around eight knots over ground. There was plenty of room to pass, and both captains were more than aware of each other's presence. The cut was at best about a hundred yards wide and with outriggers, the two trawlers needed passing room. River-brown eddies played with all boats in the middle of the cut and even the *Lou Anne*'s forty-five tons had a habit of skipping around unpredictably.

Suddenly, curses fouler than any he had ever heard before from Chase erupted from the cabin behind them. A tall, fiberglass flying bridge sport fisherman, throwing a white bow wave, was heading into the cut at close to twenty knots. It slowed unexpectedly as it got into the main surge of the ebbing tide, throwing forward a four-foot bow wave. His intention of passing the slower shrimp boat looked more and more unlikely. "Son of a bitch!" Chase hit his air horns in warning, echoed a few seconds later by the incoming *Carla*, a forty-footer that usually moored upriver from the *Lou Anne*. Incredibly, the tall pleasure boat came speeding on; its captain hit his own dual tone air horns and waved back from his high bridge. He had not understood that Chase was waving him back, telling him to slow down. Both shrimpers moved to the outside of the channel to let the idiot through, as it became rapidly obvious that there would be three hulls abreast in a channel designed for two.

Brad and Connie were already bracing against the short bow rail as the fiberglass boat blew past. "Damned fool." Chase hit his throttles hard for steerage and waved a threatening fist at the red-faced captain of the sport fisherman. Six or seven passengers on the cruiser were all on the stern deck drinking, oblivious to any dangers until the air horns began to sound. Their combined weight at the stern increased the boat's wake. That wake soon slapped into the *Lou Anne*. The boat shuddered as it was washed to the right by the sport fisher's bow wave. Although there was a clear three or four feet of water between hull and rock at the surface, the crossing waves threw the starboard edge of the *Lou Anne* against a submerged three-ton mass of Georgia granite. Chase felt the hard thump as the hull bounced on the rock.

Brad looked back at the retreating *Boys' Toys* as its captain sheepishly made apologetic gestures from his flying bridge. It did not slow down. Chase was already on the radio, reporting the idiot to the Coast Guard station. Boating under the influence was against the law in Florida and perhaps the fool should know about it. Guthrie and Jeffie both leaped into the hold and began moving boxes and gear out of the way to look at the starboard chine.

The *Lou Anne* was a V-hull square-framed boat with one-inch plywood sheathing over the original one-and-a-half-inch bottom planking. Above the chine, the sharp break between almost vertical sides and the V-hull bottom, the hull's original planking had been sanded and layered in fiberglass roving. The plywood bottom sheathing was lined with blown fiberglass of extra layers of roving laid along the hard edges of the chine. Chase had stripped the interior to bare wood and impregnated all exposed surfaces with resin. The operation had made him ill for weeks from vapors, but he had never regretted the great investment in material to waterproof and strengthen the hull. Guthrie came topside and reported that there was a very slight leak, nothing more than drips. Chase responded in colorful "French" and swore that the owner of *Boys' Toys* would pay for the haul-out and repairs. The crew's anger over the idiot in the plastic boat subsided; the afternoon became warm, and soon, the *Lou Anne* was a working boat.

During one of the long passes with the nets extended, there was little to do but wait, and Brad motioned for Connie to follow him below. From behind the rattling chiller's compressor, Brad pulled the artifact out and showed it to her. They moved to his bunk and sat. She looked at it, turning it slowly in her hands. "This is what all the commotion is about? It looks like a broken piece of ... of I don't know what."

"That's just it. It is probably a piece of space junk, just happened to fall out of the sky in Wakulla County too long ago to be conveniently explained."

"Why don't you just turn it in?" Her puzzled expression amplified the question. Why wouldn't he give it over to authorities and let it ride? Brad looked exasperated—not with her for not understanding so much as his inability to express why it had become important to him.

"Connie, there's more." He picked at his fingers absentmindedly. "There's a whole new wrinkle that I have only shared with Dad. Now he can't back me up."

"Well, what, for heaven's sake? Jeez, Brad, there are people looking to kill you."

"Yeah, and that, I think, is why I'm telling you this. Something happens to me, and everything is erased, just like they want."

"They, who? Who is they?" She softly put her hand on his shoulder and peered directly into his eyes. "Who is trying to keep this quiet?"

He explained to her about the US Air Force Blue Book, the closure of the Blue Book project in 1969, and the steadfast denial of anything that might indicate that there ever was a valid report of sightings of extraterrestrials or aliens or their craft anywhere or at any time. He recounted that a very large number of individuals—he didn't know how many, but hundreds—had seen, photographed, videotaped, and sound-recorded suspected flights of vehicles that made maneuvers absolutely impossible by known aircraft.

Connie let him go on and began to look sympathetic, like the boy was becoming delusional and possibly paranoid. He caught her absently looking through a porthole at the wave tops and said, "What part of this aren't you following?" He handed her the light blue-green rod. "Six months ago, I found this in a very unlikely spot. What we first thought was aluminum can't be cut by any saw Dad owns." He showed her the sheared-off end. "We used a three-ton hydraulic punch at Dad's shop to cut off less than a half inch of this thing, and it damn near broke his press. A piece of rebar this big would have cut at about half the pressure on his machine. This piece didn't budge until his gauges redlined then, bam! It released and sheared off. That piece was sent to a lab in Tallahassee, where the lab assistant got so freaked out that he called his professor at eight on a Sunday morning.

By Sunday afternoon, they had called Dad to see if they could get a bigger sample to send to an industrial lab in Detroit for atomic alloy analysis. Before we could get around to the other sample, both of them were dead.

"Two days later, Dad talked to me right after he got shot. He told me to hide and stay hid. He actually suggested coming here." Brad still had an ace up his sleeve, but he didn't need to tell her about the "voice" in the forest that had driven his mother to the edge of insanity.

Connie at least sounded sympathetic, if not sold. "I don't know what to say. I'm sorry, but I had always thought there was some strange mob hit out on your family. People around here used to make a lot of side money making midnight runs out into the Gulf to meet with boats coming up from Mexico or Nicaragua. I didn't want to say, but it sounded like your dad might've gotten messed up with that crowd."

"I almost wish it was that simple, Con. Say I go to the cops? If I go to the cops, I can guarantee that those black hat guys will be down for a visit and an interview and everything will be all nicey-nice until they find a way to make me look like an idiot, or make me crazy, or look like I'm crazy, or wish I was crazy." His voice had been rising with pent-up emotion.

"Hey, hey, calm down. You're family now; you're safe."

He slipped the rod back behind the plywood box covering the chiller. "I'm sorry. Guess I got away from myself there. I haven't talked to anyone but my imagination about this for months, and I—"

"Don't worry about it," she said, tapping him on the back. "What are big sisters for?" She leaned over and kissed him on the forehead. He felt the warmth and the moisture of the light kiss, which made it difficult to feel like a little brother. She added, "If I'm good for anything, I can keep a secret as bond."

They heard the diesels winding down as the boat turned into the wind. From above, "Hey, kids! Come on up!" Within a few minutes, they were squatting on upturned five-gallon buckets sorting shrimp and tossing heads and trash over the side. Brad smiled to himself; in the light breeze he could still feel the moisture of Connie's kiss on his forehead. The trawler worked the bed until it wasn't worth the diesel. Jeffie had stoked his stove and was putting on cobia fillets as a small pot of oil sizzled with hush puppies and fries. Another pot was bringing green beans and ham hocks to perfection.

Brad had finished his wash-down duties on the work deck and gone forward to join Connie as she viewed the sun's glorious last efforts. Small, puffy, purple popcorn clouds were backlit pink. A high layer of stratus above them still glowed orange to yellow. It was a true painter's sky. A light westerly breeze was winding down for the day, and the low swells were glassing over.

"So, what are you thinking?" he asked, sitting on the cabin roof beside her.

"I was just thinking about the damned idiot in the yacht."

"Yeah, he was pretty stupid. He damned near didn't make it."

"We damned near didn't make it. We got a pretty good whack on the rocks. Some folks have more money than sense." She picked a paint chip off the gunnel and flicked it over the side. Looking up at him with a wry smile, she said, "You know, next week, I get my license and I have to take my driving test in a five-hundred-dollar junk mobile. That guy probably spent over fifty thousand on that boat, and he probably charges it off his taxes."

"You're getting your license?"

"Yup!" She grinned broadly. "My birthday is Friday, and Mom's taking me to the DMV after she clears the lunch crowd out of the restaurant."

"Well, ain't you gonna be something?" He gave her an elbow punch. "Won't have time for a lowly tenth-grader."

She returned the elbow punch and knocked him off the cabin to the deck. "You're right; I won't," she said, looking straight ahead into the sunset and trying to contain the grin. "Come on, get back up here." She waited for him to settle in beside her again. "I was also thinking that if you ever wanted to go back to your house again to look around, see if there's anything else you might want to collect, I could take you."

Brad sat for a while thinking about that possibility.

"Con, I would. I really would. I don't know if there's anything there or not. Aunt Susan may have cleaned everything out. But I do have to get there, if nothing else, to say good-bye to the place. When I left, I was in a hurry—either the black hats or the deputies might have come back at any minute."

"Next week, I'm sixteen, street legal, and I bet we can come up with some excuse for slipping away for a few hours."

~ ~ ~

Connie, born Brianna Constance Chappell, at the edge of sixteen, was at the cusp of womanhood. She had grown to nearly her full height and was

130

filling out in all the right places, her body no longer stringy and too thin. Strong-willed and pretty, she knew how to camouflage her intelligence around boys. And she knew that she was not destined for a career in real estate in a touristy fishing town. Panama City, fifty miles west, was known as the "Redneck Riviera" and held zero attraction for her. St. George Island, with its high-priced beach rentals, was barely on the world's radar. She wanted to go to college and get out for good. Her own good looks got in the way of what might have been a normal life. She hated being seen as only pretty, and now her body was developing in a way that made it near impossible for a boy to look her in the eyes. She was aware that her singular beauty gave her advantages, made her the "popular" girl everyone wanted as a friend. It also was a disadvantage. She was the girl that all the boys wanted for only one reason.

She had her mother's green eyes, freckles, and red hair, which was more wavy than curly. Her English-Scottish bloodline gave her light skin that freckled or burned instead of tanning. Her French bloodline gave her a proud stature. She was developing her mother's full figure but with added height from her father's side. With only a little training in poise, she could be a runway model at eighteen, but she was no primping beauty. She had spent her life on boats and had played softball for the last two years on the Lady Seahawks. She was athletic and self-assured. With her girlfriends, she was playful. With boys, she was mostly confused. In an earlier century, she might have been married off by sixteen. She was at that dangerous age when teenage urges collide with church ideology and a firm moral upbringing.

For uncomplicated male company, she had treasured her older brother Jamie. She appreciated his counsel, protection, and friendship. He had lettered in football and basketball but had passed up athletic scholarship offers at Auburn, Tallahassee, and Gainesville to enlist in the Marine Corps. The GI bill could help pay for college when the time came. Jamie wanted to see the world first.

Now Brad had come into her life as a substitute brother, and she was the older sister. He had been quiet, enigmatic, and complex. His self-confident bravado was a veneer covering a fifteen-year-old mired in mystery. The story of his mother's disappearance and his father's murder was horrible, and his bravery was endearing. He had taken up a hermit's existence on the *Lou Anne* with gratitude and had warmed her parents' hearts quickly with his willing assistance in all tasks. He rarely opened up about the past, so his candid and sincere discussion about his "artifact" and the three deaths that he saw as convincing evidence of his being in danger was unusual. One thing was sure, he was a very likeable kid and needed a friend. It helped that he was easy to talk to; he was also not at all hard to look at.

March 27, 1977
Gulf of Mexico, 3:30 a.m.

There are a number of ways that a boat can sink in a dead-calm sea. There are also a number of ways to prevent that from happening. On this night, a number of things went wrong that made the sinking of the *Lou Anne* inevitable. The minor bump with the Sikes Cut's stone works had not presented any major leaks. The small trickle could be taken care of easily by two automatic pumps that each handled over fifteen gallons per minute.

Invisible below the waterline, however, one of the planks on the starboard side three frames from the stern had sustained the worst of the impact of wooden boat against granite rock. It had cracked and splintered and been stove in with only the fragile layer of fiberglass cladding preventing it from letting in forty gallons a minute. The broken plank was located behind a built-in Styrofoam-lined cold locker and would never again be seen.

Many noises became so commonplace on board that they are barely heard or noticed. They could be caused by a number of things, from the straining of the hull against its anchor line, to wind blowing through the rigging, or the slapping of cables and lines against the outriggers. Depending on the load, they also could be the result of small waves slapping against the hull and, at random intervals, the small whirring buzz and splash of a bilge pump sending a small stream of water overboard. On this calm night, as the *Lou Anne* slowly gyrated about her hundred feet of anchor line, all of these noises, except the wind in the rigging, provided comfort for the weary.

Brad was in his usual berth under the stern. Connie, at Chase's insistence, was in the forepeak, in a small berth made up parallel to the bulkhead that closed off the smelly rope locker from humans. Mike made his bunk on the work table that doubled as the mess table. Chase slept in his bunk in the cockpit—the top of his tool locker. Jeffie and Guthrie, unless it was bitter cold or wet, liked to sleep under the stars. On this first warm evening out for the season, they were on deck in sleeping bags. All talk stopped long before midnight. A hard day's work, a full meal, and, for some,

132

two or three Budweisers made for sound sleep. Except for snoring on deck, all was quiet as the boat swung slowly on her anchor line.

One of the most insidious enemies of mariners around the world is corrosion. Seawater eats molecules of metal every second of every minute that it is exposed. Corrosion is even more effective at consuming metals when the metal is even occasionally exposed to air. In the trawler's last hours above water, the copper wires providing power to the bilge pumps, which had been corroding since the moment they were installed, finally passed their last few thousand electrons to the pump. The automatic float switch swung on its pivot as water level in the bilge slowly rose until the contacts closed. The resulting current, provided by four twelve-volt marine batteries, fried the last few strands of the corroding copper wire to the pump. Since this happened underwater, under floorboards, it went unnoticed.

The primary cause for the loss of the *Lou Anne*, of course, was the broken side planking. After all, the other second most dangerous enemy to mariners is wood rot. If the sides of the hull had the same new cladding as the bottom, she might never have sunk. Decades of water-soaked life had reduced its structural strength below the level required to fend the boat off the rocks. Leaning inboard against the cold locker, a portion of this broken plank had left behind the thin membrane of the fiberglass lining. This lining had been given a fatal blow that took just a little more time and pressure to fail.

The last ingredient in the scenario for failure this last evening was the calm sea itself. Chase was a careful man and a good captain. His initial concern for his boat had been eased by the report from his trusted crew. The weather report for the evening, unseasonably warm and calm, allowed his caution to drop just far enough. A ship in swells has a characteristic roll. Anyone who has spent ten working years on one vessel will feel the ocean through the hull and read sea conditions through the boat's response. If there had been a rolling swell, the *Lou Anne*'s increasing load of bilge water might have been noticed as the heavier boat's wallowing would have alerted any one of the crew. On a calm sea, this potential warning went unnoticed.

~ ~ ~

Sometime after midnight, with captain and crew asleep, the thin shell of fiberglass failed. As the scored line in the fiberglass fabric began to widen and open, strand after strand of glass fiber failed under the strain, and the thin barrier slowly opened like a zipper. Instead of the trickle reported earlier, gallons of seawater per minute began to pour into the bilge from behind the cover of the cold locker. By 4:30, the air space under the bilge had filled and water began to edge over the lowest floor boards amidships. Without drama, the impending loss of the boat became more and more of a certainty. By 5:30 a.m., the loss was unavoidable.

Jeffie, oldest of the crew, got up to relieve himself over the side. Jeffie had been crew for most of the nine years that Chase had owned the boat. He had helped with the original refit and painting and had signed on as paid crew a year later. He knew this boat. Even by moonlight, he knew something was wrong. With only a fourth of her ice lockers full of shrimp, the boat was too low in the water. The water was approaching the scuppers, openings in the low bulwarks that were designed to let water out.

He immediately thought of the thump as the shrimper passed through Sikes Cut that morning. He jumped down the companionway into calf-deep water. His first reaction was an unintelligible, frightened cry. Then he shouted, "All hands! All hands! Get up now!" He turned and climbed the companionway and then the short ladder to the captain's cabin. "Boss, we've got water, a lot of it!"

Chase was sitting up alert in his bunk as Jeffie's head poked into the cabin. A second later, he was in action. One hand flicked on several switches, and the boat was flooded in light.

"Jeff, how much? How bad is it?"

"About a foot above the floorboards; that's about two feet deep in the hold. We have about one and a half foot of freeboard before we're flooding the scuppers."

"What about the bilge pump?" His eyes went to the instrument panel whose switch indicated that the pump was engaged though no current was returning to the panel light.

"I'll check it out," said Jeffie; he turned and was gone.

As Chase jumped into the lower cabin, he shouted, "Mike, Connie, Brad, get out!" He heard a sleepy soprano complaint forward. "Let's go, girl, I need you topside now!"

Chase was down in the flooding hold in seconds. In the thin glow of the twelve-volt cabin lights, he felt under water for a familiar hasp near the small galley fridge. Chase had to see if he could revive the bilge pump. While he was groping in the elbow-deep water, trying to loosen the much-trodden hasp to the bilge hatch, he heard the diesels fire up. Overhead, he heard Guthrie call out to Mike to cut the anchor line. The diesels had minimal time to warm before the gear box ground and he felt the surge of power. With an extra two tons of water sloshing below, it was not the lurch that he might have felt. This time, the boat pitched back as water surged astern. The exhausts usually discharged just a few inches below the waterline to muffle the exhaust noise; now the tone of the exhaust bubbling up from more than a foot underwater was frightening. The mass of water in the bilge reversed course and surged to the bow, bringing the *Lou Anne*'s head down.

Connie heard the altered muffling of the exhaust and finally stirred out of her sleep and stepped out of her bunk into seawater. She recoiled in a near panic, drawing her legs back up on the bunk. As she looked at the inconceivable swirl of water in the cabin, she fixed on the debris floating out of the lower cubbyholes, and the enormity of what was happening sank in. In cold terror, she climbed through the forward deck hatch and ran back to get to the cockpit ladder. She entered the cockpit to find her father on the radio. Over the strangled roar of the diesels, she listened, stunned, as Chase made his distress call to all boats.

"Mayday! Mayday! Mayday! This is the Lou Anne. Our position is approximately fifteen miles south so'west of the cut and ten miles due west of the Air Force tower. We are taking on water and are making for little St. George or the cut if we can make it. Again, we are shipping water and are making for land."

He repeated this three times and then added that the situation was worsening, with Jeffie's report that the bilge pump was disabled. The *Lou Anne*, with all her night-fishing lights ablaze, was a very bright spot in a very dark ocean. Her last great purpose was to be a waypoint for others to track. Soon, Chase had raised the Coast Guard station and was trying to give them the best fix he could on his location. He gave them his sighted bearing to the lighted number-one marker at the head of the channel leading toward the cut. He did not have radar and could only give an approximate distance. He hoped that someone else on the water was awake. He was not going to give up on his boat, his office, his livelihood. When the Coast Guard dispatch took over the search for aid, Chase called down for Brad. In a moment, Brad had joined Chase and Connie in the small cabin.

Chase put his broad hands on their shoulders and said, "You two stay here for now. Connie, stay on the air and be ready to talk with the Coast Guard. Brad, hold a course at twenty-five degrees. If we have any current at all, that might change. In about ten minutes, if we are afloat, you should be able to see the marker light."

In the blinding glare of the working lights, it was hard to see anything else, but three miles to the east, another shrimper lit up in a blaze of lights. Two minutes later, another, two and a half miles south, lit up. These three ships in the night broke the glassy undulating Gulf's waters as they made best possible speed on intercept courses.

Brad, hand on the wheel, looked intensely at Connie. She was sitting on Chase's bedroll, crying, radio handset in hand. She sobbed quietly with slightly shaking shoulders, tears streaming onto her shirt. "Bradley?" She shuddered as she inhaled and began to shiver. "Did you see how much water there was?"

"We have about a foot in the lower cabin. Where did it come from?"

"I don't know." Her shivering grew worse. "Bradley, I'm scared." She almost never called him Bradley.

"Me too, but you know what? We're going to make it."

"How do you know?"

"Because your dad won't let anything happen to you." He looked ahead and at the compass to make sure he was on course and then back at Connie. "And I won't, either."

She stood and pointed behind them. "Look!" Another brightly lit trawler was visible behind them. "Someone's coming!" The radio popped and crackled with static. "Lou Anne, this is Swamp Fox, do you read me?"

Connie jumped. She gripped the mike and said very clearly, "Swamp Fox, this is Lou Anne. What's your twenty? Over."

Again, the speaker rasped, "Lou Anne, this is Swamp Fox, do you have your ears on? Can you read me?"

Connie looked mystified. Then realization dawned. She keyed the mike and heard the pop over the speakers as she hit the button a few times. Keeping the button down, she replied, "Yes, Swamp Fox, this is Lou Anne. I hear you loud and clear. What's your twenty? Over."

Then, "Connie, that you?" A short pause, "This is Ferrell, I'm coming up behind you. What's your condition?"

"We're taking on water, a lot of water! Dad and the guys are below trying to figure out where the water's coming in, but we are still taking on water. We are making for the number-one marker. Over."

"Forget the 'over,' sweetie, you're among friends. How much water's in the bilge?"

136

"Bilge, hell!" Connie blurted. "It's knee-deep over the floor boards."

Ferrell broke in calmly, "Just keep her going, honey. The cavalry's on its way."

"Say again?" She was listening as intently as she could, but between static and Ferrell's thick Cajun accent, she found it hard to follow.

"The Johnnie Bee is a little closer, hon. He's coming in on your starboard beam. You should be able to see his lights."

Brad pointed to their right. "Got 'em!"

"Ferrell, we can see both of you; please hurry!"

"Don't worry, missy, were paddlin' as fast as we can."

Connie had to smile at Ferrell's humor. "Mr. Ferrell, I got some things to do, but keep your ears on, okay?"

Brad pushed down the wheel lock and reached overhead for some faded life preservers. "Connie, are there more of these?"

"Yes," she answered, standing and lifting the locker lid. A few more jackets were inside. Brad pulled them out and tossed them down to the rear deck. He looked at the white water foaming behind the transom. It was a lot closer to the rail than it should have been. He was thankful that the diesel was running and that they had electricity to keep her work lights blazing. Shouts that were unintelligible over the diesel came from the lower cabin. Connie said, "Brad, there's a life raft on the roof if we need it."

"I know, but it's military surplus, and I'd want to make sure we all had life jackets if we had to spend five minutes in that thing." He was peering into the darkness, searching for the green flasher on the number-one buoy marking the entrance to the cut. He saw that Connie's face reflected her fear: peaked eyebrows, pursed lips, and dilated pupils. He said, "Please put that jacket on. It'll make me feel better." Connie's eyes took on new worry as the knowledge seeped in that they might not make it and the life raft she had always taken for granted might be useless. They were slowing as the lost buoyancy sucked the boat deeper into the Gulf. Usually capable of twelve to fourteen knots, *Lou Anne* was down to seven knots and getting noticeably top-heavy.

Standing there, Connie suddenly realized that Brad was a little taller than she was. When had that happened? He stood, feet wide, both hands on the wheel, intent on making the straightest possible line toward the channel marker. She wiped the tears from her eyes and looked aft. When she finished the straps on her life vest, she slipped one over Brad's shoulders and helped him with the straps while he held the course. He could now make out the pulsing flash of the navigation marker at the outer gate to the channel through Sikes Cut. Brad began to think they might make it. The *Swamp Fox* was gaining on them, and to starboard, the *Johnnie Bee* was about a mile away and closing in.

Connie put her arm on Brad's shoulder, mostly needing to hold someone. He turned to her, and they locked eyes. He put his left arm around her shoulders and hugged her close. "Connie, I've got you covered. We will get out of this, I promise." His arms around her gave her more comfort and ease than she'd expected. Then, the engine stopped, and in the silence that followed, they could clearly hear more eloquent cursing from below. The *Lou Anne* was so low in the water that her way slowed to nil almost immediately. The hull's stern lifted a little and swung to port as water sloshed forward, causing a lean that very nearly precipitated capsize.

The men crawled out of the lower cabin and climbed immediately overhead to begin loosening the life raft from its clamps. They were disheartened to discover that the clamps had been painted over years ago and again more recently. Jeffie jumped to the rear deck and then splashed back into the cold water below. A minute later, he returned with a pry bar and the hard case of the raft came loose. The rolled-up emergency craft was pitched off the roof to the rear deck as water began washing through scuppers meant to drain water. Mike found the emergency T-handle and pulled. Immediately, the air canister began to whine, and the canvas inflatable unfurled.

In the cabin, Brad bent over the binnacle housing the compass and sighted the flashing green of the number-one channel marker at the cut. "Connie, here's a pen; write down thirty-one degrees to the number-one marker." Then, killing the cabin lights, he found and sighted the abandoned lighthouse on Cape St. George. Even with the beacon forever dimmed, it was a white strip of moonlight in the dark. "Okay, we've got 323 degrees to the lighthouse. Now, get thee the hell out of here!" He pulled the binnacle box from its clips and joined everyone on the rear deck. The deck was now awash in seawater, which was flowing freely through the scuppers. The whine of air filling the raft lost energy and faded to a low whistle.

The surreal quiet that followed the inflation of the raft was unsettling. In the eerie stillness, they all heard the clicking below as circuit breakers tripped. First, the cabin lights flickered and died. Shortly afterward, the overhead brights that illuminated the rear-deck work area dimmed to a hot yellow glow and then faded to black. Lights on the horizon gave proof to the fact of the two rescue vessels approaching too slowly. Both were too far away to provide the comfort of their engine noise. Captain, crew, and kids gathered on the rear deck, tightening and adjusting their life vests. Chase was careful that Connie's straps were tight and came over to check on Brad. "You did good at the wheel, boy."

"Thank you, sir. I'm sorry." He handed the compass, an expensive stainless-steel and brass oil-filled compass with binnacle and lamp box, to Chase, who looked up, grateful. Brad looked at the approaching lights of the Swamp Fox and the Johnnie Bee and wondered who would get to them first. He realized that Chase was talking to him.

"Sorry, about what? You didn't do anything wrong."

Brad said, "I just seem to bring bad luck with me."

"Don't be ridiculous, boy; bad things happen to good people. That's all. If I catch up to the owner of that sport fisherman, some more bad things are going to happen to him." Chase turned and climbed back up to the captain's cabin. He rummaged for his ship's papers and a few odds and ends. Funny, there was not that much there that he wanted to take or that he had to take. He spun and jumped back down to the working deck.

Cold water splashing on his sneakers made him look down at the dark water sloshing on the rear deck. Chase had ordered Guthrie and Jeffie to the bow to raise the scuppers at the stern, but in a few minutes, despite this last attempt to trim the boat's weight forward, water was again washing across the deck and began sloshing into the cabin. Then the work lights went out. "All right, everybody," Chase called out. "Abandon ship!"

Mike and Chase muscled the inflated raft over the stern rail, which was now impossibly close to the surface. Mike grabbed the two pieces of one of the paddles and fitted them together before carefully stepping in. His foot went through the canvas bottom, and he yelled out in surprise. He grabbed at the hard canvas tube and checked his fall, pulled his leg out and slid to the far end of the raft.

"Kids, you're next, come on." Brad pushed Connie to the stern rail, and together, he and Chase lowered her slowly onto the aged raft's canvas bottom. Chase locked eyes with Brad as they helped her down, and in that momentary glance, each felt the other's protective instinct for her. One by one, the rest of the crew joined them. Sitting like sardines packed in seawater, they appreciated that rescue was less than half an hour away.

Using the light plastic paddles, they pulled away from the doomed boat. In the primal darkness, only the low rays of the moon lit the Lou Anne's last moments afloat. As it lost buoyancy, the steel upper structure and booms became too much for the filling hull to support. It started as a slow lean to starboard. It had been down by the stern, and as the waterline reached the open door of the cabin, the lean became a roll, and slowly, the *Lou Anne* settled deeply onto its side. The quiet of the night was broken as equipment crashed inside and air pockets found vents and crevices to blow, shrieking momentarily until their complaints were swallowed in bubbling foam. The *Lou Anne*'s last sounds were a groan and one final splash as the port outrigger boom slapped into the Gulf. A white boil on the surface was soon all that could be seen. They stared as bits of trash, Styrofoam cups, small boxes, and a cooler popped to the surface.

Brad thought of the scene at the end of that Titanic movie when the crying stopped and the survivors looked out over the floating wreckage. Brilliant stars lent their weak light to the bits of trash. Only a glow on the horizon advertised the location of Apalachicola on the other side of the island. Brad estimated that it was probably only a few miles away. Off to the east, beach houses sparkled in the darkness.

Although the day before had been unseasonably warm, the reality of an early spring night on the Gulf was that the air near the surface was only marginally warmer than the still-chilly water, and everyone had been soaked getting into the raft. They sat in silence and shivered, listening as the chuffing sound of approaching boats slowly grew louder. Connie snuggled into her dad's shoulder, but her left hand reached and found Brad's. He took her hand in both of his and held on like he would not let go. Cracking with emotion, Jeffie's deep resonant bass broke their quiet. His first few lines of "Amazing Grace" filled the night; by the first chorus, all were singing, and some were choking back tears.

Chapter 8

Life is a succession of crises and moments when we have to rediscover
who we are and what we really want.

Jean Vanier

March 27, 1977
Apalachicola, 6:45 a.m.

The pier and adjacent street were crowded by an early morning assembly
alerted by ambulance sirens and hurried phone calls. As the Johnnie Bee
pulled up to the city dock, a press camera flashed, strobing into still-life
scenes the activity on boat and shore. Yellow, red, and blue flashers on the
different response vehicles lit the downtown waterfront in staccato glare.
Family members found each other and exchanged tearful embraces. Not
every boat lost in the Gulf fleet gives up its crew, and the crowd's relief
bordered on celebration. The *Lou Anne*'s crew members were wrapped in
Mylar space blankets, given coffee, and whisked off to the community
hospital a few blocks away for heated blankets and monitoring. Minor
abrasions earned in the scramble to find and plug the leak or revive the bilge
pumps were cleaned and dressed, and by nine o'clock, the Chappells were
in their driveway.

~ ~ ~

The following week was surreal. For Chase, the stable life of hard
work and routine had ended abruptly, seemingly forever. An owner/captain
has the advantage of not being a slave to the commercial world of eight-to-
five bureaucracy or ten-to-ten retail, but there is servitude to the tides, the
moon, the cycles of the ocean harvest, and the requirements of boat repair.
Chase thought that this life was over and spent the week lining up contract
work on the island. Although Lou Anne and Chase rarely fought, the week
had been tense, punctuated too often by flaring tempers. Fortunately for
everybody, life began to look up Thursday afternoon when Ferrell called.

Although Ferrell Boykin owned three boats, only the Swamp Fox was
working at the time. One of the others had a good set of diesels and drive
train, but a fire-damaged hull that was just barely afloat. The other was an
overhauled hull with rebuilt superstructure and trawler works, but no power,
chiller, or fuel systems. Between the two, a working boat could be rigged.

Swapping out the mechanics, rigging the nets, and running it through working trials would take a good six weeks, and then it would need a captain and crew.

After several hours of wrangling details and nearly a case of beer, it was decided that Chase and his crew would do the yard work on Ferrell's clock. Chase would then work the boat with his crew, and Ferrell would take a piece of the cut at ten percent as rent-to-own. This arrangement would continue until Ferrell had his price for the boat that would soon be rechristened the *Lou Anne II*.

March 30, 1977
SIGINT, Fort Meade, Maryland, 0630 Hours

Captain Richards saw the clipping file come across his desk as one of hundreds of possible leads that someone thought might be of interest. One of the hundreds of gleaners in the Signals Intelligence, or Sig-Int branch, had picked up on it from the Pensacola paper that had run the story. In addition, a roomful of media experts, assigned to about three dozen different cases, monitored TV and newspaper clips for eight to ten hours a day in the thirteen areas of interest around the country. The Sunday-morning Pensacola News Journal had run a photo and caption circled with a wallet-size reproduction of Bradley Williams's eighth-grade class picture clipped to it. A handwritten sticky note stapled to the Xerox of the paper clipping read: "??Missing Bradley from next county over??" The picture showed six wet, cold people, rescued from the Gulf, now standing on a public pier surrounded by smiling onlookers.

The caption said: "SHRIMPER LOU ANNE LOST AT SEA: Captain and crew all safe after early morning rescue." The text began, "Captain Johnson and the Johnnie Bee bring shrimper crew home to safety after suspenseful midnight rescue."

Richards pulled a loupe from his side top drawer. Holding the small magnifier down on the desk over the newspaper, he scanned the photo and whistled softly. The half tone newspaper depiction of the survivors showed the boy's head at less than half an inch high. But if he squinted at it and blurred the dots just right, it did sort of look like the kid. He was named Bradley Williams, but Bradley was one of the yuppie names du jour. There were almost as many Bradleys out there as freaking Jennifers. He grabbed the phone's handset and jabbed at a number. "Get me photo analysis and who was that team leader we scrambled to Florida last fall? … Yeah, yeah, right. Get me Sergeant Jenks on the line as soon as you can track him down."

April 2, 1977
Apalachicola

By Friday, life had begun to look hopeful again, and Connie thought that was the best sixteenth birthday present she could have asked for. The colorfully wrapped presents contained the usual pre-agreed upon clothes, some costume jewelry, a bookshelf stereo with AM-FM, and a cassette player. This was to be the cool present, because almost no one had one yet in Apalachicola. The two cassettes also in the present were Journey and Toto. Brad gave her two books, one a find on his limited budget, the other from his worn collection. Larry Niven's *Ringworld* and Vonnegut's *Slaughterhouse Five*. She had studied Vonnegut in high school English and read *Cat's Cradle*, but her eyebrows furrowed and then rose at the Larry Niven cover. Brad knew that she was a sci-fi ignoramus, but he thought she could use the inspiration. His inscription was simply, "There are other worlds than Apalachicola. Happy 16th Birthday." Inside the Vonnegut cover, he wrote, "There is no drinking water in San Lorenzo. Beware of Ice 9. Happy 16th Birthday, Sis." It looked as though the "Sis" had been partially erased, smudged, and rewritten. All things considered, it was a good birthday, topped off by a trip to the Department of Motor Vehicles to present her driver's ed certificate, take her written and driving tests, and come home with a brand-new driver's license.

That evening after dinner, a knock on the door announced Sam Faircloth, a senior Connie had mentioned a couple of times. He had a single white rose from the IGA grocery and a birthday card. She went out to the sidewalk where they talked until after dark. Brad, trying not to be too nosy, feeling angry and confused, stole furtive glances from his darkened second-floor room. He was nominally an adopted younger brother to Connie, but he had begun to feel the stirrings that every fifteen-year-old has to go through. He knew his feelings were inappropriate, but there they were. And down on the sidewalk, there was Connie with a guy almost three years older than he was. He was two months shy of his sixteenth birthday, and Sam was a senior with a football letter jacket.

He turned away from the window and lay back on his bed. He missed the plastic airplanes he had painstakingly painted, and he missed the noises that had surrounded his home in the woods. This town was no metropolis, but it was big enough and civilized enough not to experience the chirring waves of crickets or cicadas in the Wakulla woods that made Bradley feel so at home. Feeling way too insignificant to ever be important as anything more than a fill-in for Connie's older brother, he rolled over to the wall and waited for sleep. Sometime later, he heard Connie's familiar skip up the stairs, and the squeak of the far banister as she pulled herself around the last turn at the top and the steps. The sounds stopped outside his room.

There was a pause in her steps. What was she thinking? What was he thinking? Then a short burst of three light taps on his door and he heard the latch turn. "You awake?" she whispered through the a thin crack of an opening.

"Yeah." He rolled over toward the door, feigning sleepiness. "What's up?"

"I was just talking with Sam and telling him about the other night, about the *Lou Anne* sinking and … and how scared I was for all of us." Unselfconsciously, she sat on the end of his bed. "It hit home as I was talking with Sam how careful you were that I was all right." She paused a moment, thinking of her next words. "I just wanted to tell you thanks, so, thank you." She put a hand on his knee and gave it a light pat.

"Well, sure, I mean, don't worry about it, I mean …"

"No, stop. I mean it, Brad. It's the little things that make people like people and little things that keep them apart. When you first got here, I mostly just missed Jamie. But, you, you're not anything like Jamie. I no longer feel like this is Jamie's room." She paused, waving her hand absently at the darkened walls. "Anyway, thanks for looking out for me out there and trying to make me feel safer than we were. I felt less scared because of you, and I had just realized it." She sat in the dark trying to make out his features but could only see the outline of his head. Before the silence could get too embarrassing for either of them, she was up and heading for the door.

"Con?"

She stopped at the doorway and turned. "Yes?" After a pause, he said, "Thanks."

April 5, 1977
Two Mile, Florida, Noon

Family and crew congregated at Two Mile, an area aptly named because it was two miles down the road, west of downtown Apalachicola. Looking over Ferrell's two boats that were separated by several hundred feet, the men were judging whether to move the two hulks closer together and use the booms to transfer the equipment or to borrow a jack lift to move major parts or to incorporate parts of several other ideas that came up. While their conversation became further involved, Connie approached her father and asked if she and Brad could go out to the island. Chase agreed with some reluctance and on the condition that she call when she got there and before she left.

This was, of course, her ruse for them to get away long enough to go all the way to Wakulla Beach. It wasn't like there was significant traffic to negotiate; it was just a lot farther away and in the next county. Although she had been driving on her learner's permit for a year, neither she nor Brad figured that Chase would let her drive that far away her first week after getting her license. With as little delay as possible, they were gone. On the way out of town, crossing over the high point of the river bridge, Connie let out a "whoopee" and held a nearly nonstop grin for the next several miles. As they passed through the various speed zones, she was careful to stay within one or two miles an hour of the posted limit. A little over half an hour east, they approached the area where Brad had abandoned the F-250. As they slowed, he read the named driveways leading to bay-front houses.

Finally, they came to Southern Sands, and he motioned for her to pull over. She eased to the shoulder in the gravel drive to the house. Looking through the wooden pilings, he saw the little Hobie Cat chained to the building's columns. Across the highway, the two-rut forest access road was overgrown and empty. The F-250 was gone. "Okay, let's go. It probably got towed to an impound lot." Several miles up the road, they crossed into Wakulla County and called from a pay phone outside a motel. Brad heard her apologizing to her dad for calling late and explaining that they had gone all the way to the end of the island's paved road and remembered that she had to call and had then driven all the way back up to one of the few convenience stores to call. A few "All rights" and "Okays" later, and they were back on the blacktop.

As they approached Wakulla Beach Road, he directed her to take a right down the road and pass the driveway to his house slowly. The yard was covered in last winter's leaves, and the place looked as if it had not been visited for a few months. As they eased by, the familiar Koenig truck box was visible in the pole barn. "Connie, the truck is back!"

"That's great, I guess."

"Yeah, it's great. It's nose in."

"And that means?"

"That means it was driven in. If it still had a blown motor, it would have been backed in by a wrecker, or just left in the yard."

"Do you want to back up and go to the house?"

"Let's go down to the beach first."

"There's a beach here? Who'd have guessed it?" They were deep in pine woods.

"Duh, it's called Wakulla Beach Road. It ain't much, but it's the only beach I knew for a long time. I never knew waves could get over a foot high for a long time." He laughed at a memory. "I thought beaches had grass and stuff; I don't remember seeing a sand dune until I was six."

Two pickups were parked at the landing when they approached. One belonged to Sunny Rogers, and the other, he didn't recognize. They pulled up beside the two trucks and scanned the area for signs of fishermen. Only one set of recent launching scars showed on the landing, so Brad figured that Sunny and someone were out on the flats together. He led Connie over to the old hotel where they could at least sit on the steps. Looking out across the grassy shoreline, she said, "Yeah, this is really some beach you got here."

"We like it. We don't get wave action, sure, but there's a million fish out there just waiting to come home for dinner." The shallows extended in front of them, and in the distance, the St. Marks light pulsed on schedule. He thought about his aborted escape by canoe almost a year ago. He flexed his shoulders as if he could still feel the ache he had felt that next day.

"Hey, look, a boat!"

Out on the flats, a small, olive-drab johnboat could be seen approaching from around one of the arms of land the protected a small shallow embayment. They walked down to the beach and watched the boat putt-putting slowly to the landing. When Sunny Rogers caught sight of the two, he erupted in a string of down-home epithets. He gunned the little boat and lifted the motor in a practiced movement that drove the nose up onto the sand.

"Dink, look who sprung up outta the swamp." He shook Brad's hand. "I see you been better'n most at hiding." Then he gave Connie a brief up-and-down once-over. "And you been better'n most at finding."

"Sunny, this is my, umm, sister, Connie." He saw the perplexed look on Sunny's face. "She's Chase Chappell's daughter over in Apalach."

Without skipping a beat, Sunny replied, "Never heard of him." But, smiling, he took her hand, "But ah sure am glad to meet you, Miss Connie." He bowed in mock honor, kissed the hand lightly, and turned to introduce his fishing partner.

Dink was introduced to Brad and Connie, and histories were exchanged. Brad finally got around to asking Sunny for any news about the house. Sunny looked at Connie and then at Brad, who offered, "She's cool, Sunny. She's just like a sister to me." Noticing Sunny's hesitation, he added, "One I can trust with secrets."

Sunny, for his part, looked back at Connie. "Missy, I reckon if he says you're okay, then you must be a goodern. Miss Connie, I've knowed Brad since his daddy brought him down here in diapers." He winked. "Never had to change one of 'em, though." He paused to think and then turned to spit brown chaw juice through his teeth. "While we're at it, Dink's cool too. You can share whatever you gotta share, we got our own history too."

"Swamp Boy, seeing how you were so intent to light outta here back last year, you being here is a surprise. But there have been some doings up at the house for sure. First, the sheriffs looked over ever'thing real good. You know there used to be some dope come in on this beach back in the day. They had to check to make sure there wasn't anything to do with any dopers goin' on. They had dogs all over the place, back to the barn and all over the old fields that's growed up now. They's finally convinced that your daddy wasn't in the drug business."

Brad was indignant. "My daddy never did any of that stuff. He wouldn't have; I heard him yellin' at the TV too much about it. He hated the stuff. Said it got too many of his buddies killed in Nam."

Sunny put a hand out to hush Brad. "Now, what did I just say? The sheriff looked all over; they had to check to rule out that crowd and didn't find nothin'." He smiled knowingly. "Rumor was that there was somethin' hidden on the property." He gave a silent huffing laugh. "Sure wasn't no buried treasure. Deputies with metal detectors run all over the grounds and around your woods. Then those guys from the Feds came back down. Says they was helping on account of you were missing and coulda been abducted. I didn't let on at all about you or what your daddy told you."

"Did they have a big, black Chevy station wagon?"

"Yes, they did, the same Suburban with darked-out winders. Looked like they was some kind of ex-military, 'cause they didn't wear any suits and all of 'em looked like they could run the hunerd-yard dash in record time. Not the same ones came to the porch that day. Looked way too fit and trim to be FBI. I seen them FBI boys before, and they're soft." Sunny swished his tongue behind his teeth and spit again. "'Course, that was a whole other story to tell you sometime. These new boys, they was all through your house a bunch of times. Then nothin'. Come the Fourth of July, and your Aunt Sue was down here and began carting up boxes and cleaning winders. I thought she was going to be putting it up for sale, but there ain't been a sign up."

Brad asked, "Did you talk to her?"

"Now, Brad, did you ever know me to let an opportunity to gossip slip like that? 'Course I did. Even helped clean up the yard a little to supplement my retirement plan. Helped her get the storage shed squared away."

"How was she?" Connie asked. "What did she think about what happened last year?"

Sunny rubbed at his chin, as though pulling on his whiskers would help conjure up the memory. "Well, Miss Connie, seems she was pretty well broken up about it. She said she had barely gotten over Miss Lucy leaving and was getting used to the fact that Whit ..." He shifted his gaze to Brad and said, "Your dad, that is, that he hadn't got his wife the help she needed. Now that Lucy had run off and not been heard of for so long, she had talked to Whit a time or two about how you were being raised, and then he got shot and, well, she was pretty broke up, to tell the truth."

Connie asked, "Have you noticed anybody at the house lately? In the past few weeks?"

"No, Miss Connie, least I can't speak about ever'day, cause I'm not here ever'day, but I don't think I seen anybody black, white, or otherwise in that drive since late summer, 'cept just your Aunt Sue from time to time."

Brad asked, "Was there anyone else here after I left?"

"No, well, just a deputy. Deputy Jarvis and some new partner of his, I don't know. They was there, but I think they was just checkin' to see if it was still buttoned up. Oh, and your daddy's truck showed up coupla months ago. One day, it was back like it had never been gone. I almost checked in,

148

but there was no heat from your stacks. The AC runs some now it's summer, so I guess your aunt's gonna keep the place in the family."

Brad looked over at the man who had been introduced as Dink. "Sir, have you noticed anything back up the road, anything unusual in the past six months?" Dink was a small, wiry, black man in his late fifties. His coal-black eyes seemed to have a perpetual twinkle like those of the kind of man who has a hard time having a bad day.

"No, son, and I wouldn't've; I'm not from here." His accent told the truth of it. "I visit with Sunny from time to time, but not as much lately. I drive long-haul trucks. Occasionally, I get over east, and if I can work in some extra time, I'll talk Sunny into taking me fishing." He shook his head and grinned. "There's nothing like fresh flounder or mullet from this bay." He cleared his throat and coughed. "Sunny told me a little 'bout your mom and dad as we were coming in. It's a tough row, son. Keep 'er straight."

Brad thanked him and Sunny for their help and walked with Connie back to her car. They pulled the car close behind the house, and Brad looked for the key rock. It was back where it had been, beside the lowest porch step on the left. They entered cautiously. The lack of any musty odor seemed to indicate that the place had been looked in on regularly. Most of the furniture was there. The kitchen was stocked with plates, cutlery, and a basic cookware set. The fridge was off, and the doors stood ajar to ward off mold. With only some generic pictures on the wall, it looked like it could be readily rented as a furnished house, or rented by the weekend as a fisherman's retreat. Whit's collection of rods and reels stood waiting in a wall rack. The old tackle box stood at the ready on the floor below them.

Brad went down the hall into his parents' bedroom and was shocked to see a folding, double four-by-six photo frame with a picture of his mom and dad. Next to it on the dresser was the family photo from five years ago taken at the Sears photography center.

"So, it doesn't look like it's for sale," Connie said. "Looks like she might have come down and visited now and then."

"Yeah, just it's been cleaned up and all." He went over to the master closet and rolled back the sliding doors. There was a pile of blankets and linens on the shelf, some rough woods clothing on hangers, and a pair of small hiking boots on the floor. "Looks like Aunt Susan does visit regularly, at least regular enough to keep hiking clothes on hand."

Connie wandered out and down the hall and asked, "Was this your room?" Brad walked in behind her and stopped short, gaping. His posters were taped together and back on the wall; the bed had been made, and clothes that he had left behind were pressed and hung in the closet or folded in drawers. The contents of his shelves were back on remounted shelving. Nothing was in the same place, but he was able to find everything that hadn't been broken. This was his room. His breath caught as his emotions rose; he found himself breathing rapidly and shallowly, and for a few seconds, he saw dancing dots, the kind you would see just before you fainted. He took several deep breaths and through watering eyes, looked through a window into his former life. He felt he could call out for his dad and get an answer from the backyard.

Connie noticed his distress and put a protective arm around him. He folded into her arms for comfort, for security, for the closeness of a hug that he had not realized he could miss so much. She returned the gentle squeeze and stroked the back of his head softly. Abruptly, he pulled away, wiping his eyes on his sleeves. He sensed that as he pulled away she was holding on to the embrace. "I'm sorry, Con. I was really unprepared for this. I could have taken a bare, empty room or even a cleaned-out room with just my furniture like the living room and Dad's room." His breathing shook one last time. "I just wasn't prepared for my room."

"That's all right, Brad. Take it easy. Breathe slow. It must have been a heck of a shock to see it all here."

"I mean, look! She even got the pieces of the P-51 together and hung it back up." He looked into his closet. "It's like she expected that I would come back here to stay."

"How could that happen? I mean, even if you found out you were safe, you couldn't live here alone. Your dad did die here   w   , didn't he?"

He looked at her strangely. "Yes! He died. I was looking at him! I watched him go. I know he's dead!" His voice grew increasingly strident with each pulsed phrase.

"Sorry, sorry, sorry!" Her face melted in apology. "I didn't mean anything by that. I'm just as puzzled as you as to why she'd put your room back like this."

"Maybe it's a signal to me that if I came back, she wasn't going to sell the place. It's my birthright. I'm the only Hitchens heir, and it's the house my grandfather built. Maybe she's just letting me know she'll take care of it until I can move in."

"That's real sweet of her, if that's true."

150

"Well, heck, I'll be sixteen in June, and then in two more years, I could own it outright. That," he emphasized, "would be really cool!" From the bedroom window, he could see Lou Anne's Honda and behind it the Ford under the pole barn. "Come on, let's see what's left in the toolshed."

The four-bay pole barn had been constructed with three open bays. One was the truck's parking spot; another housed the riding mower. It used to house Lucy's Toyota, but Whit had been unable to continue to see it empty. A third bay was an open-air work area with a heavy-duty table and lockable storage underneath for pry bars, pulleys, splitting wedges, and other tools that could stand weather. The fourth bay was enclosed and watertight. It had a rough plywood floor and shelving and had been used as onsite storage for large items that couldn't be stored in an old house with limited closets. Mostly, it had contained coolers; beach chairs; seasonal decorations for Christmas, Easter, and Halloween; and the miscellaneous junk that seemed to collect around a typical American family over time. The door to the shed was shut, with a Master lock on it.

Brad went to the truck door and found it locked. The passenger-side window had been repaired. On the other side, Connie pulled at the handle on the passenger's side, even though the lock button appeared to be down. She grimaced and shook her head at Brad through the two side windows. He walked around to the tailgate and let down the heavy industrial gate. The Koenig truck bed was a tool man's special. Whit Hitchens had also installed a five-inch, heavy-duty vice, a pipe clamp for threading pipe in the field, three pipe or conduit benders under one fender box, two padlocked side box compartments on each side, and the main tool box behind the cab, which was unlocked! He knelt in front of it and released the two clamps and the locking hasp and lifted.

Inside, among the tools, mud residue, heavy oil smells, gas cans, quarts of 40W oil, and other useful items, was another key rock like the one by the back steps. This, Brad knew, was a new one. He slid the top open to find two keys. One fit the truck; he could see that immediately. The other had the word "Master" pressed into the brass, and he looked up at the storage room door. He looked over at Connie, who was smiling from over the side of the truck bed. "Whoohoo!" he said softly. "Keys to the city."

At the storage room door, he took a deep breath and inserted the key. It turned. Slipping the padlock out of the hasp, he pulled the door and stepped back. Neatly stacked on one entire set of shelves was a new row of small mover's boxes. He looked at the neat black lettering on each box: "Pictures." "Curtains." "Linens." "Glasses."

"Holy crap," he said smiling. "All those boxes that Sunny saw being packed up? Here they are!" He took down and opened one labeled "Books." He lifted the lid and found the contents had been set into heavy contractor's plastic sheeting, wrapped, taped, and then covered. "Damn! Do I ever owe Aunt Susan big-time!"

He sat at the doorway on the edge of the plywood floor and looked back across the backyard at the house. Connie said, "I think she's saving it all for you, Brad. It looks like she's been very thorough at trying to preserve all of your things and taking care of all of your family stuff so that you can go through it sometime in the future and use it when and if you can."

He was silent for a moment, looking at the house. Connie sat down beside him and leaning lightly against his shoulder, said, "It's a nice house. You can kinda tell where the original was and what's the add-on. But, really, it's a nice house." He wondered how he could get a message to Aunt Sue that he was fine, and then he realized that it was easy and he should have done it long ago. Sunny knew Aunt Sue and he could at least get word to her. Maybe he should even try to get up to town to visit and thank her. His thoughts drifted back to the house.

"It'll need paint in a few years, and I remember Dad saying it was going to need a new roof. But, hell, it made it through Hurricane Jake all right." He looked over at Connie whose face was again just inches from his. He almost jumped back but didn't. He wanted to ask her if she was serious about the guy from last night—what was his name, Sam? Yeah, Sam Faircloth.

"What's on your mind?" she asked, a one-sided grin pulling a dimple on one cheek. She had been thinking about the possibilities of setting up housekeeping in a country house like this.

"I was thinking," he said and stalled, not really wanting to bring up Sam. "Remember when I told you about finding the 'alien' artifact?" He made quote marks in the air as he said alien.

"Yeah?" she answered slowly, as if pulling out a further explanation.

"I'd like to take you to look at the place, so you can know for yourself, to understand for yourself." Elbows on his knees, he placed his palms together, fingertips to fingertips, and lowered his nose to his index fingers. "I know when you listened to that whole thing, you believed maybe a half of what I said, and probably only the part about Mom and Dad being dead. The rest of it, well, you looked like you were just trying to be polite."

"Of course I was trying to be polite. I mean, not that I wasn't trying to believe. But, really, space aliens?"

Brad replied, "That's what I thought you thought. It's very hard to accept because it's so … so weird." He looked at her again to see that she was still very close. "Have you ever heard of Occam's razor?" She shook her head no. "Basically, it's a decision tool that says the simplest explanation is usually correct. It kind of goes along with one of Sherlock Holmes's ideas that if you eliminate all other possibilities, then the one that you have left is probably right."

"You read a lot for a ninth-grader."

"I lived alone out here in the boonies." He waved his hand at the surrounding woods. "There's one channel on the TV, and there's a library full of books. I guess I probably do read a bunch compared to most." She followed his glance to the boxes full of books. They covered everything from history and biography to science fiction and detective novels.

"Would you go for a walk to that place in the woods?" she asked. "We can drive part of the way."

~ ~ ~

He wasn't used to that option, but they took her car part of the way and walked in from another direction. The forest understory was bright green with early spring growth. In sunny spots, bloody dock leaves were opening deep green with crimson veins. White lilies sprouted, seemingly at random. In the shade, light-green ferns were unfurling from slender, furry stalks. Connie was full of wonder at the unfolding beauty all around. "Wow, this place is really neat!" She stroked a laurel shrub as she walked past it.

"Careful—some of the stuff out here can make you itch." She quickly pulled in her hands. "Don't worry; the poison ivy is still low to the ground—that is, unless it's growing up a tree." She put her hands in her pockets. Twenty minutes later, they were approaching what he had begun to think of as Ka-Litan's woods. He stopped and pointed at a large brown mass about a hundred feet ahead.

"Look, do you see that big cypress root ball ahead?" She pulled up behind him and followed the pointing finger with her gaze. "That is the tree that started it all." He left the trail, walking through the season's newly budding ferns. When they got close, he noted that there had been some weather erosion of the dirt clinging to the roots, but he could still see the depression in the ground where the rod had been pulled out and pointed at it. He showed her where his father had slowly and carefully cut away at layers of dirt on the stump to create a profile in the soil.

He then showed her the other side of the root mat where the forest giant lay out a hundred and twenty feet ahead. The lower trunk was gray and gnarled and had begun to grow moss in some areas. In some of the woody cracks, fan fungi spread like miniature staircases. "This fell in the storm last spring; possibly a funnel cloud found this guy standing up higher than all the palms and pines and took it down. Either way, I used to get out in these woods about twice a month or more, and right after the storm, it was down. Dad said that there's a good chance this tree was between three hundred and fifty and five hundred years old."

She looked at him, absorbing everything he had said before and just now. "So your problem is: how did that piece of metal get there in those roots?"

"Yes, that's exactly the problem." He looked over at the thicket. The branches were full of budding new leaves, but still looked a little spare with straggling reddened leaves left over from the previous season. He started to walk over and looked back to see if she was following. Connie was picking her way through the underbrush. He smiled at her careful steps and realized she was avoiding poisonous plants she couldn't see. "Con? There isn't anything poisonous around here. I used to come here a lot."

She looked up at him with a look that betrayed her uneasiness. "Where are we going now?"

"There's one last thing to show you." He started winding his way through the branches and looked back to see her following. Her easy athleticism was fun to watch. In every other pretty girl he had ever encountered, there was always a prissy, haughty, super-feminine mode that was more than repulsive enough to negate any of their physical attractions. Part of this negativity was his insecurity in the face of that beauty. He had always felt too much of a dork to approach most girls, especially a very attractive girl. Connie was just so natural that he often forgot how the rest of the world saw her. As she slid through and around the intertwining branches, he watched in awe of her easy athleticism.

"What?" she asked.

"Whaddyamean, what?"

"You were staring."

"No." He had been staring, hard not to. "I was just making sure you didn't slip in there and lose one of your tennies."

He stepped in behind her. There wasn't a lot of room on the bank. They stood a little over a foot apart. "Okay, then, so where are we?"

He sat at the base of the big pine. Motioned for her to sit beside him. "This is one of my favorite spots. I just wanted to share it with you." He waved his hand around the little sinkhole and at the nearly impenetrable wall of undergrowth on the other side. "I remember now that this was a favorite private spot for my mom."

hello, B-rad, a familiar voice said in his head.

He was startled and tried not to show it. He almost spoke aloud and then simply thought, *Hello, friend, I am back. I have a new friend with me.*

I feel new friend ... happy B-rad return ... happy B-rad bring friend

Can you talk to new friend? He framed the question silently.

yes, I talk to ... both ... is right 'both'?

Connie got a disturbed look on her face and then started to scan the clearing, a worried furrow wrinkling her forehead. "What? Did you say something?"

"No. Uh, Connie?"

hello, friend Ka-nee ... my name Ka-Litan ... you name Ka-nee.

"What's that?" Connie had whirled and stared at him wide-eyed. "Brad, what's that?" Her voice betrayed surprise and, possibly, a little panic.

"Wait, Ka-Litan!" He moved closer to Connie and got her to sit down at the edge of the pool. "Connie, I am not sure how, if it's really been here for centuries, but I think some memory of my visitor is in this place." She looked frightened; her eyes were wide, brows raised, and mouth grim.

"You mean your alien has a ghost?"

"Please, try to accept what you're hearing." He took her head in his hands and pleaded, "This is how I know." He placed his thumbs gently on her eyebrows and pulled down, closing her lids, "Just listen."

"How you know what?" And then in a whisper, she added, "Listen to what?"

"How I know that Mom wasn't crazy, unless I'm crazy too. It'll come from just behind you. It'll feel like someone over your shoulder."

hello ... friend B-rad name Ka-nee ... Ka-nee friend B-rad The last phrase had a hint of question.

"Yes," she answered involuntarily. She moved her fingers to the base of her skull and then moved her hands to cover her mouth.

"Oh, my God!" Her eyes widened and moistened. "William Bradley Williams, who, umm, what are we talking to?"

I think his name is Ka-Litan.

Yes ... title name Ka-Litan ... Ka is pilot.

A short pause followed. Ka-Litan often expressed his thoughts in groups of three.

Li name my creche ... Tan my child name ... all name is Ka-Litan

Brad said aloud to both of them, "My two good friends, Connie and Ka-Litan." Connie began to get up as if to leave. "Connie, please! This is important."

"Brad, I'm scared and want to go." Her eyes revealed the truth of this.

"There's nothing to be afraid of." He stood to talk to her, eye to eye. "It's a presence, nothing more. I don't pretend to understand it, but he's just here when I come here and we can talk. Well, I don't really have to talk out loud."

"Yeah?" Connie said to the trees, looking around for a source of the voice. "So, Ka-Litan, how long have you been here?"

long time ... not know ... need star. A pause then. *need star locate*

"That makes sense, Connie. He can't tell time without seeing the stars."

"Doesn't he have a clock?"

"His clock, if he has one, would be different from ours."

"Why?" Then she got it. She smiled that gorgeous one-sided smile that he loved to have directed at him. She made large circles with her pointed right finger. "His own sun and planet would have a different year and day. He would have gone to space with his people's time as an origin for their clocks."

"Very good, girl," Brad said.

yes ... need star locate ... not know time this place

Connie looked at the pond. "Do you think he's in here?" She pointed at the pool.

"I don't know; he doesn't seem to know either."

"I'm not sure how I know this, but I think he ... it is down in there. Ka-Litan, this is Connie. Are you underground?"

not know underground ... no star field ... only liquid ... liquid and ... I not know

"I think we call it dirt," Connie said. "Too bad he can't tell where he is." Suddenly, she looked at her watch and inhaled sharply. "Oh no, it's getting late. Brad, we're supposed to be home before dark, and I'm supposed to call home before I leave."

"Okay, let's go." He looked at the pool. "Ka-Litan, Connie and I have to go. We will be back to visit."

With brief thoughts of good-byes, they worked their way through the thicket and headed back to the car. They were supposed to have gone to St. George Island. Talking about where they were and how to time the call back, they first thought that they should call from the coastal town of Carrabelle. Driving time from there was about the same as coming from the state park end of St. George Island.

"Connie, we can't do that."

"Why? It's about the same time when you figure the slow speed limit on the island."

"Connie, you're a redhead with white freckly skin. If we had spent these last three or four hours on the beach, you'd be pink or blistered by now. If we try to stick to the lie, they will figure out we're lying and your folks have been too good for me to start lying to them."

"Wasn't going to your place lying to them? You were standing there when I said we were going to the island."

"Yeah, and that didn't feel right. If we tell 'em the truth, they just might be sympathetic, but if we try to stick to the beach story, we'll be in trouble for hiding it, and your mother might never trust me again."

A puzzled look crossed her face, she didn't understand.

Incredulously, he continued, "Have you looked in the mirror lately, Connie?"

"Yeah," she answered, looking at her eyes in the rearview mirror, not getting the point.

"Con, surely you must not be so dense as to not know how pretty you are. Your dad thinks every guy out there wants a piece of you. I can't afford to let them think ... to let them think for a second, that we are, well, doing it or doing anything like it."

"Doing it? You and me?" Her disbelief was so full of "ick" that he pulled back from her.

Brad felt a sting to his ego. He steadied his voice and said, "I know you don't think of me that way, but it might not be so inconceivable to your mom and dad if we show up with a totally unbelievable lie and try to stick with it. Listen, I'll take the blame. We'll just say that while we were going to the beach after the first phone call I talked you into going back to my house. Then we can tell them what we found at the house and don't have to keep that a secret too."

She paused for just a moment. "If we're going to do that, we might as well come completely clean. It will be far simpler to say that I asked if you could bring me here to the house."

"You're right; we should also square up for the first phone call too."

~ ~ ~

In Carrabelle, the phone call did not go as planned. Nervously, they fed quarters into the change slot in the phone booth and made the call home. They were bravely expecting to come clean about their plan to go to Wakulla, but the conversation took an early detour. Lou Anne seemed anxious for Brad and asked if he was all right. "Yes, Mom. He's right here. He's fine. I'm fine. I need to tell you something."

"Just a minute, Connie," her mother interrupted. "Tell Brad that there was a strange man here today asking around about him. Good-looking young black man. He was looking for the Bradley that was saved last weekend. He said he wanted to do a story about him."

"Who was he?" Connie asked. "Where did he come from?"

"Just a man; said he was a reporter."

Brad had been listening in with his head up against Connie's and against the receiver. "Was he in a big, black station wagon?"

"Why, yes, it was a Suburban, black with tinted glass. It had Florida plates. Have you seen it before?"

Brad swore silently and then answered, "Yes, last year. Just after Dad was killed and again, a week later, passing through Apalachicola."

"Oh, Brad. Don't come home yet. That guy's eatin' dinner down at the corner café, said he'd like to come back after dinner to get your story. Let me talk to Chase and figure out what to do."

Connie looked at Brad. "Can you think of any place to go?"

"Only one place I can think of; back to Wakulla."

Listening over the receiver, Lou Anne said, "Brad, I don't think you should go back to your house."

"No, ma'am, I have something else in mind. I don't think I should say over the phone."

He took the receiver from Connie and hung it up. Connie said, "Well? Where?"

"Sunny's house."

Chapter 9

Every new beginning comes from some other beginning's end.
Seneca

April 7, 1977
Apalachicola

Sergeant Jenks had drawn the short straw for the assignment. Captain Richards had been banished to overseas assignments. Having survived a near court-martial for the triple murders in Florida, he was permanently assigned to hunting bad guys in El Salvador, Nicaragua, Columbia, or wherever the War on Drugs took him. He might never get another stateside assignment which was fine with Martin Jenks. Jenks had priors on the case, as did Larry Lassiter. However, Lassiter was on paternity leave trying to be a normal person and help around a house turned on its end by a new arrival. Jenks had just finished an exercise in team planning at the B-Team underground lair in the desert.

Although some who knew of its existence thought the unit nickname derived from old Blue Book Project days, the B-Team moniker derived from their unit's building ID at the almost-secret facility. A little known branch of AFOSI, the Air Force Office of Special Investigations, the B-Team spent "discretionary" branch funding dispelling rumors and discrediting sightings of anything smacking of alien origin, and unlike the Blue Book, the B-Team did not prepare elaborate reports for anyone not in the need-to-know loop.

Jenks's briefing for this assignment was simple. He had read the file on the way in to TLH in the backseat of a fast mover from the Nevada desert. He was to see if the rescued boy in the photograph was the same missing boy from the incomplete October mission. If so, he was to take control of the "subject" and bring "it" in for psychotropic reprogramming. As he reread the jacket, he felt a surge of bile as he got to the third objective. The first two takedowns had been easy enough—simple enough operationally, well-executed, and the resulting mess cleaned up. The press, local cops, and arson investigators had picked up on all the right cues. Only problem was,

Richards had focused special ops training, not B-Team training. His interpretation of "removal" was fatal. The B-Team's use of the term meant psych-cleansing. Not only were the three "takedowns" unnecessary, but top brass had freaked, fearing the deaths would somehow get back to a military op targeting civilians.

The general had shipped Richards to a permanent post at the Panama Jungle School from which he could be assigned to projects in South America. The Hitchens interview had gone badly. Who would have guessed that the son of a bitch had a shotgun hidden in the couch? Damn, Lassiter was such a bastard. "Shoot first and live to talk about it," was his motto. They had not gotten much information from the elder Hitchens and had never actually seen his boy. The mother was an apparent runaway, and they had only the snapshots they took from the house. As for the artifact, the house, barn, vehicles, and grounds had been thoroughly searched with no trace or hint. Fingerprints and some family artifacts had been taken, but a trace on the family had gone nowhere.

Jenks still remembered hanging around for days in a bucket truck in the aunt's Tallahassee neighborhood posing as a telephone repair crewman. Breaking into her house hadn't technically even been a B-and-E. How do you break into a house that isn't even locked? Damned civilians, what do they expect? Happily, she only had guard cats and not guard dogs, but again, no intel from her house and none from her phone tap. Even using the family Bible to try to get close to relatives had led down thirteen blind alleys. Susan Delaney had been married twice and had been one of four sisters, two much older and one a year younger. She hadn't seen the two older sisters in decades because of a divorce in the family before the younger sisters were born. That was the problem with sisters; the extended family trees were hard to trace, especially after a few divorces and name changes.

If the kid was with a relative, he could be anywhere. If he weren't, he was just another American runaway. He could be in almost any city in the country. Jenks would have wagered a steak dinner on a Southern city. Most Southern boys didn't do winter. Hell, he could be down on South Beach being pimped out by some scar-faced bad-ass or, more likely, dead. This one lead, from the boat sinking, was the only thing to break on the case in months.

His plan was clear: simple surveillance and inconspicuous query of neighbors to determine if the "Brad Williams" boy was actually Bradley Hitchens. The kid in the photo was supposed to have been adopted from a

160

cousin's family from South Carolina, but that chain of paper didn't bear scrutiny in South Carolina's vital records. And Jenks hadn't been able to lay close eyes on the kid yet. His orders had been explicit: psychoactive drug interview with an amnesiac cocktail, find out where the artifact was, and release. But he couldn't grab what he couldn't see. Parked under an overhanging tree three blocks down the street from the Chappell house, he finally saw the little Honda pull in just before dark. He had gone down the two blocks to the corner and turned, pausing to see only one female, a cute redhead, bouncing up the steps. *Damn! Still no kid!* He thought. *Tomorrow he would have to ditch the agency car and get something less obvious.* He would miss the expansive interior of the Suburban. *Maybe a pickup would be good to blend in down here?*

Every second vehicle around here was a pickup truck, ranging from new and shiny ones to rust buckets. He wondered how long he would be able to pull off being inconspicuous in a town where everyone knew everyone's business. He had already been invited to join two different churches by people in the street.

~ ~ ~

Connie returned home, hoping that she would not have to get into any conversations about where she'd been. The emergency had thrown off any of their calculations of travel times. If her parents asked about her lack of suntan or sunburn, she would say they had gone on the trails at the state park because she hadn't brought her sunscreen lotion. She'd had time to think about the afternoon on the way back and reflected often that Brad would someday own that house. It really was a cute little house. She also reflected on his comment that her parents might be thinking they had been doing "it" or doing something improper for siblings. How had he phrased that? He had gotten embarrassed and flushed immediately. She had felt color spreading down from her temples, too. Brad was cute and fit, but he was like a little brother. Well, not actually, but still, he was not even sixteen! Did he think about her that way? Had she thought about him that way? She had to admit she had when he left the shower sometimes with just a towel wrapped around his skinny waist.

Lying in bed that evening, knowing that Brad was not down the hall made her feel a little lonely, like she might be about to lose another brother and a friend—no, it was not like losing a brother. Tears began to pool around the edges of her eyes and eventually one or two ran to the pillow before she rolled over and buried her head in it. What had he come to mean to her? Was he an adopted stepbrother, a boyfriend, or simply a friend? Whatever, he had become a very good friend and confidant that she was going to miss.

"Friend," that was what Ka-Litan had kept saying. How did he learn to talk? How did he talk into her head? Brad had said that sometimes he didn't even talk out loud. Were they talking between themselves without her hearing? Could they do that? Her thoughts went on in widening loops of questions until it became clear. She believed. She believed that unless Brad had all along been capable of telepathy and had waltzed her all the way into that secluded little clearing to try it out, then something else was there. Where? She knew that someday soon, she would be going back.

~ ~ ~

Sunny was in his element and was waxing grandiloquent in his woodsy fashion. He was one of the best fishing guides in three counties. He'd been on the coastal flats, up the rivers, and in and among the freshwater swamps and lakes neighboring the Apalachee Bay for over seventy-five years. He had seined for mullet when it was profitable. He had seined for anything when mullet wasn't profitable until Florida's seine fishing regulations had finally put that enterprise out of business. He had been married twice and widowed twice. His unflappable, outgoing disposition made him a friend to most who met him, if they could live with the nickname he gave them. He'd really gotten on the wrong side of a county manager a few years back by dubbing him Boss Frog. The man was obese and had a croaking voice and apparently no sense of humor. Sunny still flirted with the widow ladies at church, but as he liked to say, there wasn't no bait on the hook.

He had been recounting how high the water had gotten back in 1929, how it had rained for two weeks and how the bottomlands had filled up with water, then the ponds overfilled, and then the big storm hit. "Wasn't a whole hurricane," he said, "but it don't matter if it blows hard enough and long enough." After weeks of rain filled all the creeks and ditches, the no-name storm had driven a wall of water into the coast that moved houses off their foundations. Rivers all over three states jumped their banks, flooding downtowns and farmlands. Tornadoes tore big swaths through the forest. The storm peeled off tin roofs and made miles and miles of country roads impassable. His descriptive powers were awe-inspiring.

Brad almost forgot about his reentry into homelessness. As the conversation drifted back to more mundane matters, he got to know more about Sunny's fishing buddy, Dink. The nickname was Sunny's. If he liked you, he almost immediately came up with a nickname or brand, and you were stuck with it. Brad had always been Swamp Boy. "Dink" had just come to Sunny's mind when they first met. Sunny couldn't remember how Richard Helms had become Dink, but it stuck. Sunny had been hired out from a bait store's guide service when Dink had two days to kill before getting a good westbound load. For the last few years since that trip, Dink had found ways to schedule dead time on the east coast a few times a year. He had been unsure at first about hiring a deep-woods redneck as a guide, but he soon found that the old waterman didn't have a racist bone in his body.

Brad asked, "Mr. Helms, should I call you Dink or Richard or Mr. Helms?"

"Swamp Boy, you can call me Dink if you like; if that makes you feel silly, you can call me Richard, just don't call me early on Sunday morning." He laughed at his own joke. Dink was dark-skinned, with a flashing smile that matched the bright whites of his eyes. At a little over five foot nine and a soaking wet 145 pounds, he was as wiry as a welterweight. Brad didn't doubt that he was as fit.

"Umm, Dink, where are you going on your next run west?"

"Day after tomorrow, early morning, I've got a load of kiln-dried cypress going to a woodworks in San Diego." He added, "I have to pick it up first light over near Bristol, then I'm off."

"Is there any way I could catch a ride part way?"

"Where do you want to go, Swamp Boy? Do you have people in Louisiana or Texas?"

"Actually, in Nevada."

Sunny whistled softly. "Why'd you want to go way out there, son?" He spit into a cup. "Tain't nothin' out there for a Southern boy like you. You figuring on disappearing in the big city? They must have a bunch of Bill Williams out there. But you could do that in St. Pete or Jax." He stuck his thumb in the air. "Mebbe hitch a ride home, now and again."

"I need to at least try. I think maybe my mom's in Nevada ... or was."

"Your mom? I thought she'd gone ... excuse me, I thought she'd gone off a little crazy."

"She heard things," Brad said and paused. "She was afraid people would put her away."

"She heard things?" Dink looked genuinely concerned. "Voices in her head?"

"Yes, but after she'd gone, about six months later, she sent a postcard from Las Vegas. A few months later, she sent a Christmas card. All she wrote was, "I love you, Brad," and "Merry Christmas." I got another one the following year postmarked Indian Springs, Nevada. It had a Santa sitting in a folding chair next to a cactus with colored lights on it."

Dink said, "That's just north of Vegas, if I remember. But it's a long, hot walk from I-10. About three hundred miles north."

"If you took me as far as you could, where would that be?"

"Phoenix."

"Then, I'd like a lift to Phoenix, if you can. Are there any rules against it?" Brad looked at him in all earnest. "Any rules from the trucking company?"

"Well, let's see, depending on who's pissed off at the time. I could be arrested for kidnapping or transporting a minor across state lines for whatever they think my perversion might be, or simply contributing to the delinquency of a minor. I guess that it'd be somewhere between ten years and life." He poked a thumb in the air behind him. "That bobtail tractor out there is all mine. I haul as an independent trucker. That's how I can take vacations out here and get fat on mullet." He smiled at Brad and patted his twenty-six-inch waist. "So, I set my rules, and if Sunny will vouch for you, then I guess I can put up with you. Only you'll have to stay out of sight till we get into Texas."

Brad looked puzzled. "Why Texas?"

Dink put his mahogany-dark forearm beside Brad's tanned forearm. "I don't really want to explain why I have an underage white boy in the back of my cab as long as I'm driving through the Southland."

The details and the agreements were all figured out over a few beers and a Coke. Sometime before midnight, the two crusty adults were wrapping up their store of tall tales, and Brad was asleep on the couch.

April, 1977
Wakulla to Las Vegas

Usually, Brad would have slept in until daylight began to invade his room or his dad called for him. This morning, and maybe it was due to sleeping on an old couch, he was awake and ready to go at six. It was only when he got his shoes on and was rubbing the sleep out of his eyes and the front door opened that he heard the diesel purring outside. Dink greeted him with a good natured, "Good morning."

"Good morning to you, too," Brad got up and looked out at the huge Freightliner humming outside. The Cummins 350 was warmed up, its hum sending thrumming vibrations to his coffee cup on the counter. It was now apparent to Brad that he had been the last to wake up. Sunny came up the stairs behind Dink and saw Brad looking at the big rig.

"You sure you want to take off like this now? There ain't no knowin' if your mom's dead or alive from what I hear."

"I don't think I stand much of a chance around here, if they've already tracked me down to the Chappells'. I really hate to leave them like this, but I think if I stay around, it just puts them in danger." He rubbed his belly, feeling an opening void to be filled. "Sunny, thanks for your hospitality, but is there any chance of a piece of toast or something before we go?"

The trucker offered that there was breakfast available on the way to pick up his load and they should get moving. Brad looked around the mobile home's surprisingly large living room, feeling like he was finally leaving. He had only been to Sunny's twice, and both times it had been a safe haven. After a quiet moment in which no one had spoken, Brad said, "Well, Sunny, I guess I should be leaving if Dink will put up with me."

Dink put his hand on his shoulder. "Well, hell yes, boy. Can't think when's the last time I had company in the cab to talk to. Making the long run along I-10, I've seen so many of the same things over and over, it starts to get old. Truckers like to let on that we like the solitude—you know, the old warriors of the open road bit—but company's a good change now and again."

Dink picked up his thermos, which obviously had been ready and warm on the counter for a while. Brad realized he must be able to sleep through just about anything, if he had missed the brewing coffee and the truck starting up thirty feet from the door.

In a few minutes, Brad's small bag of belongings from the house was tossed up into the floor of the cab and the bobtail tractor pulled out of the yard. By 7:30, they were across the river and in a new time zone, backed up to a fifty-four-foot trailer stacked almost to the stenciled weight limit with dried cypress, some old growth southern yellow pine, and a few other exotics. By the end of summer, most of it would be furniture or office paneling. For now, it was just another load that needed to get to the other side of the country.

That morning, pulling westward through the hills of the Florida Panhandle, Brad enjoyed the very different view of traffic from ten feet up. Cars seemed to be almost in the way. He realized how stupid most drivers were around trucks. Dink explained the realities of cross-country hauling to him, and some of the narrow escapes he'd had with the driving public. One time, a passenger car had been rear-ended by another car and had swerved sideways into his lane. The poor driver's response had been to put on the brakes, and he skidded sideways and the Freightliner just pushed it along with the passenger door jammed into the huge chrome bumper until the whole thing came to a stop. By then, there weren't any tires left on the sedan to drive away on.

On another occasion, one of his tires blew on a hot August afternoon, a retread failed on one of the double tires on his trailer. The eight-foot-long slab of thick rubber peeled off like apple skin and rolled into the next lane where it laid out on the hood and windshield of an MG Midget sports car. The terrified driver had almost killed himself driving off the road. On one pass over the high Sierras west of Tahoe, he had nearly died when his rig lost hydraulic brake pressure to the van he was towing, and if there had not been an emergency run-off ramp he would have been forced off a cliff or into one. The stories of the road rolled out, and it was clear that Richard Helms, a.k.a. Dink, was enjoying the company. But he found it hard to engage the kid in talk about his situation. He had learned some of the details the previous night; however, there were whole sections of the story that he just missed or didn't understand—especially why the boy thought the government or spies of some kind were out to get him. Dink decided to let that come out when it would, if it would.

Lunch found them at a truck stop just west of Mobile. By dinner, they were in western Louisiana and hoped to make the Orange River and Texas by dark. "When you drive west, do you have favorite stops?" Brad asked.

"Yeah, I got a coupla places I like to stop in on. When you do it so often, you get to know some of the workers at the truck stops and they remember you, at least by face, to know you're a regular. It makes it more familiar than being just another lonely trucker eating alone, or even worse, getting caught up in a table full of other long-haulers needing to get a day's worth of talking out over one dinner. Most of the stories you hear seem to be recycled. I could swear I've heard the same escapades from more than one fella.

"If we leave early enough, I'd like to make the other side of Houston before shutting down for the night. Not only is the traffic worse than driving through molasses, but the folks over in Richmond County on t'other side of Houston are much friendlier. Houston's okay, I suppose, but you'd think no one there knew everything in that big, shiny city was delivered by a truck. Craziest damned drivers in the South. Way worse than Atlanta or Miami.

"After Houston, it's pretty much an all-day haul to El Paso. At the end of that run, I usually call ahead and get some tune-up time before I hit the desert. There is a whole lot of nothing at all west of El Paso. Now tonight, we probably won't even make the Texas line. I'm tired and ..." He looked over at Brad, who was asleep, his head pressed against the window glass, mouth agape. He let out a small chuckle and smiled to himself. Well, kid, he thought. *Get your rest, 'cause the desert is going be a whole nother world for you.*

Brad's sleep was restless. He had dozed off with images of little silver, red, and white sedans zooming by and RVs trying to pass one another at three miles an hour below the speed limit, causing half-mile long backups. As the dreams began, he was in the driver's seat, following a long line of vehicles. The cars and trucks ahead began to hover, to move in directions that were possible only in a dream state. The scenery began to dissolve around his peripheral vision and went dark.

Deep Space 4

The fighters were lining up in battle line to execute a fade-and-flank maneuver. It was a classic draw fake that had worked in 2-D and 3-D battlefields throughout the centuries and throughout the universe. The last round of sorties had taken out a significant number of the Erran forces, and if no additional reinforcements popped through this battle group, the fighters had a great chance of pulling a victory out of a desperate situation. Although they had been outnumbered by heavy ships, their main advantage had been that the Coalition forces were in-system first and were able to react to the dropping or down-phasing undeployed Errans. The Errans had still not learned to drop in formation or in unison. But after a series of jumps and battles, they now had strength in numbers. For this sortie, Ka-Litan's battle squadron of twenty-seven skeeters was to take a long, elliptical course and come in to attack one of the last two Erran heavy cruisers in enfilade. They would be exposed, but the concentrated fire of nine triad units would be deadly.

The Dzuran Coalition's battle group would form up out of mutual range of the Erran line in an obvious deployment for a final mop-up attack. As they closed, they expected that the Erran fighter forces would skirmish along the front, leaving the rear guard of the cruisers unprotected. By the time the larger vehicles were bouncing energy beams off each other's forward shields, the squadrons of skeeters would move flank en masse to take out the cruisers' main thruster plants. Ka-Litan monitored the chatter over the com systems and was pleased that all was proceeding as planned. He and his psi partner, Jai, were leading a platoon of nine skeeters in three triads that would combine their rail guns on a single array of pulse thrusters. Arranged in overlapping shield threes, in triad formation, they were able to share and hence amplify their effective shield strength. The deadly triad was hanging back, waiting for the signal to close. If they moved prematurely into position behind the neutrino thrusters as the massive engines powered up, his platoon would be atomized. There wouldn't be enough left to scoop into a factory ship for recycling. As he watched the engagement develop on his near-space display, a series of flashes in real space caught his attention.

The familiar static discharge of Erran ships dropping through the phase barrier lit up the backdrop of the battle scene. He watched as light and heavy cruisers, two carriers, and three battle stations dropped through. This was a tragedy of unbelievable proportions. Surely, the Coalition's heavy

168

ships were aware of the field disturbances behind them and would react soon. As these thoughts formed, the center two ships were executing a spin to react to the rear threat when one of them began to sprout bright green lines indicating a directed blast of lasers trying to break through its shield bubble. Suddenly, the beams coalesced and brightened, and the ship exploded in a flash that hurt his eyes. He had just lost two thousand fleet-mates, and the remaining number of Coalition individuals was considerably smaller. The crump of the ship's explosion had come over his ear patches as a hundred distinct cries. Ripping metal and the sound of crashes blended into a long, horrifying, high-pitched complaint as the ships around him felt the losses of crèche mates. His group got their orders amid the chaos and began to move in on the cruiser. As they approached the outer range of the rail guns, his group's pilots initiated the designed strike on the cruiser's thruster. Initially, the skeeters' concentrated fire flared into energy on the shield line, but the cruiser's force shield was weakening steadily. That much mass converging into a concentrated point soon breached the thinning energy wall, and they were eating away at structural metal that gave the thruster lateral stability. They couldn't destroy the thruster, but they could make it unusable for maneuvers.

Suddenly, the cruiser's main engines glowed and ramped up to full power. The ship was trying to maneuver but had not realized that not all of its controls were functional—either that, or it was maliciously turning on the attacking skeeters to blast them. It didn't matter; the wave of energized plasma from a starboard thruster washed toward Ka-Litan's group in a deadly hot wave of incomplete matter. The large ship began to roll as if not in complete control. Ka-Litan gave the order to disperse just before one of the triad formations was toasted. Three of this group's fighters flashed momentarily as the superheated subatomic matter wave ate their weaker components and then the hull skin. He fired off one more command into his mouthpiece to disperse and regroup at their carrier. His rail gun was nearly depleted, and he hadn't been docked long enough last time to fully energize his own lasers. He had to get back to the carrier *Te-eh Ha* to be more than marginally effective at anything. He set a course similar to the one he had taken to get into position in the first place: a long ellipse that kept him out of range of anything but pulsed lasers. He figured that the Errans wouldn't waste that much long-range energy on a lowly skeeter. As he sped away, Ka-Litan had no idea where the two remaining skeeters were. "Jai! Where are Ka-Mitan and Ka-Potan? Didn't they make it out with us?"

The sometimes feisty shipboard computer scanned all the recognizable signatures in the maelstrom of com signals, energy flashes, and high-energy explosions. "Ka, remainder of crèche not found. One ship, Mitan, is an intact tumbler. No reading on Potan unit."

Ka-Litan had felt as much. An unimaginable emptiness drained his being. He had to make a conscious effort to remain alert. Every receptor cried for immersion. He was aware of the flashing lights on his sensors and the real flashing energy exchanges outside his cockpit. *Concentrate!* He told himself others before him had moved on without crèche and had become Leaders of Mark. Maybe that was his destiny? Watching the battle major through his port screens, he watched the last of the remaining cruisers targeted by the original battle plan leave this universe in a belch of hot-blue fire. The cruiser took on a sickening, spiraling roll as it outgassed through huge holes in its side. That was supposed to have been it. They would have won the day, except for the troubling issue of the new arrivals.

The Coalition battle line was now in a shambles as they began to turn their attention to the new threat massing behind them. The city ships and carriers, which had been rear guard, were now dangerously on the front. As he watched, a city ship, his crèche home, jumped, leaving behind a tiny dot of antimatter that sizzled and sparked in the positive universe. The two carriers were scrambling to get out of the way of the heavy cruisers on both sides. A carrier was now being targeted by multiple green flares from a growing number of Erran cruisers. The strategy was basically similar to what the skeeters had just been applying to the plumbing on the business end of that cruiser's thruster. The cruisers were just much bigger and significantly more powerful, and they were now targeting his carrier. Even if he had wanted to, he couldn't intercede in any meaningful way. He could only watch as the *Te-eh Ha*'s shields began to heat with the strain. Engineers were working on safe and predictable inner-system jumps, but that seemed unattainable now with the home worlds in shambles and two of the Coalition partners' systems under attack.

Resembling a soap bubble lit by an aurora, the shield of the carrier under attack flashed beautifully, moving along the spectrum from infrared to ultraviolet as it absorbed the power of the Errans' focused hadron attack. Then the swirling colors brightened from orange to yellow and then white. He knew the end was near if an Erran cruiser couldn't be taken out of the fight. He made a correction to put himself on a collision course with the nearest cruiser's laser lens in the fastest possible time. He punched in the chemical kicker engine and felt himself being slammed into his couch. Accelerating forward at body-flattening pressures, he began to pass through his own lines. Flying past his own carrier into the newly arranged front lines, he saw the overheating shields of his carrier begin to falter. It shuddered, began to shrink, and finally disappeared.

The command bridge took seven focused Erran-pulsed hadron beams for about three blinks and then exploded. The beams stayed focused on the crippled ship until they bored through at least six decks. He could even see bodies being ejected into the heartless cold of deep-space vacuum. He was beyond anger. His crèche was gone; his carrier was gone. All of his energies were concentrated on the Erran cruiser's magnetic lens. If he threw the entire mass of his skeeter into the hot ring of energy, the sudden inclusion of matter into the energy beam would blow the lens, leaving the cruiser without its primary weapon. One less Erran laser to act in concert on the individuals of his fleet. His chemical thrusters automatically stopped at 10 percent charge, but he had accelerated to crazy fast. He was closing on his own death and the elimination of a hated enemy when the ship flashed before him and disappeared in a fireball. His own momentum would have carried him into the maelstrom, but the blast wave of expanding gasses deflected him.

Jai squealed in an excited burst of damage control data. "Okay, Jai, we'll take a time-out for full-system status. Do we still have full maneuver?" Lights on his control systems flashed blue in the affirmative; beeps in ascending tones accompanied the lights. He set a course for a long turn to take them around the back side of the Erran formation. He mapped the arrangement in Jai's holo banks and kept moving. He needed to get the information back to command and control. It could take a while. He was almost a full half-quadrant away from his rear lines, and he had only a little chemical boost left. "Jai, do we have anything to burn to get home sooner?" An orange light came on accompanied by a discordant harmonic burst. That was a "No!"

Litan settled in for the ride back and began to check subsystems with Jai. He needed to be at full ops if there were to be any more engagements. He thought back to his recent promotion to Ka, squadron leader. He never imagined that his command would so soon be decimated and he would have opted for a suicide dive into a heavily defended Erran battlewagon.

Jai began loading redundant systems, and they decided on best work-arounds for the damaged systems. Ka-Litan hoped there were additional Coalition forces due to drop soon to assist and that they didn't drop into what used to be rear lines. He took time to look at the ringed gas planet around which they orbited. It was beautiful, its frozen methane clouds locked into perpetual storms over a blue gas layer below. He longed to run in to pick up chemical fuel, but he had to get back to command and control to report on the Erran rear guard. A steady, harmonic vibration began to pulse in his ears. As his velocity took him farther around the back of the Erran position, flank right, he sensed darkness beyond bearing as his distance from other Coalition individuals increased.

Chapter 10

When trouble thickens around us, still will she cling to us, and endeavor by her kind precepts and counsels to dissipate the clouds of darkness, and cause peace to return to our hearts.
Washington Irving

April10, 1977
Western Louisiana

Brad was coming out of the dream, trying to make sense of his surroundings. He suddenly jolted awake in the dark. They were rolling through the Louisiana flats just east of the Orange River. Traffic had thinned, and only a few pairs of taillights were ahead of them. The glowing lights of the Lake Charles refineries lit the night sky ahead. "Welcome to oil country, Swamp Boy."

"Where are we, Dink?" He still had visions of high-energy blasters and disintegrating ships in his thoughts.

"Almost to Texas. Lake Charles is just ahead. We cross a river, and we're in Texas."

"The Mississippi?"

Dink laughed out loud. "Son, you've been out for a long time. Must have been some stimulating dreams."

Brad stretched himself awake and looked around. "I missed the Mississippi? Dang it."

"You're just in time to cross the mighty Orange River, the boundary of Louisiana and Texas."

"I thought that was the Mississippi."

"No. If you ever get back in school, pay attention in geography class. Now truckers, we not only have our geography embedded in our genes, we also memorize travel times, the menus at a hundred different truck stops, and who has the best apple cobbler, the best coffee, and the cleanest showers."

"How long did it take to learn all that?"

"Only thirty or so years. You hungry yet?"

"Yeah, I could eat a cow."

The Freightliner blasted across the Orange River Bridge, her yellow show lights ablaze along running board and fenders. "Welcome to Texas, boy. You are in it, barely. When we clear this weigh station, keep an eye out for the Dorman Road exit. I know a nice little trucker's haven where they can cook you that cow." The cherry-red cab glistened under overhead intersection lights, its dual-exhaust stacks growling as Dink geared down on the ramp to the exit. Brad's excitement was infectious. He had always felt like a trespasser when he and his dad had pulled into a truck stop. Now he was going in as the real deal, or at least, as a friend of the real deal.

At the truck stop's restaurant, a good-natured, dark-skinned waitress, with "Phyllis" embroidered on her blouse, strolled up and smiled at them. "Well, hey now, Richard. Haven't seen you in a coupla months. How's it rollin'?"

"Doin' fine, Phyl. What's special tonight?" Brad was impressed by the familiarity. Maybe Dink really was a legend on this highway, as he had been reported to be by both Sunny and Dink himself over last night's dinner.

"Hell, Rich, ain't nothing special around here, 'cept maybe me and Angie." She nodded her head back to a petite blonde about half her age waiting another table nearby. "So, you going to introduce me to your protégé?" She pronounced it "pro-toe-jay." Brad noticed that a twang had entered Dink's voice that had not been there around Sunny.

Dink nodded across the table at Brad and said, "This is Swamp Boy, known by his closer relations as Brad Williams. He's on his way to Nevada to look for his mother."

"Ooh wee, child! Did he say you're lookin' for your mama? Lord be with you."

"Yes, ma'am. She's near Vegas, I think."

"Son, don't pay me too much mind." She leaned in closer. "But you better have better than 'think' going for you 'cause we get any closer to summer, that desert is about to get too hot for trottin'." She took out her pad and prepared to take their order. "You just be careful as you can be, ya hear me?"

"Yes, ma'am."

Dink smiled up at their waitress, "Phyl, put that away and bring us two pulled pork plates with fired pickles and fries, and a Coke for him and a draft Bud for me. And if you got it, make it an iced mug."

Phyllis said she had it and walked off toward the kitchen. Brad noticed the trucker checking out her rear as she walked off with a little bit of sway in her hips. "Dink, I guess you know the ladies all up and down I-10."

He smiled and wiped his stubbly chin. "I guess I do know a bunch, but it's by name mostly. If you're friendly to people, they're friendly back. It never did any good to go through life being a hard-ass when there's good people all over this country just want to get along." He sipped at his ice water and wiped his lips. "You had any practice with girls yet?"

"No, sir. I mean, there's been a few that I've been sweet on, but ..." he said, a little color beginning to show on his cheeks, "well, I've never done it."

Dink laughed softly. "Give it time, Swamp Boy. Give it time. Don't you think that Miss Connie might be a little sweet on you?"

"Connie? Heck, no. She's a year older'n me, and besides, I know that she's got boyfriends at school. And now that she's sixteen, she'll get to start dating and such." He threw up both hands with a shrug. "And besides, she's a sister, sort of."

"What in creation is a 'sort of' sister? Either you is or you ain't."

"Well, her family is cousins to my family, and they took me in when Daddy died."

"So you don't have any real relation except going back a couple of generations, it sounds like." He leaned in close to talk quietly. "That girl is sweet on you, and I wouldn't've thought it sisterly sweet."

"Why do you—"

Dink cut him off. "I saw the way she was looking at you when we were deciding what to do and it became clear to her that you weren't going back home. You were pretty intent on Sunny and his advice. But she was tearing up and trying desperately not to. Then, when you two said your little good-bye in the yard? That was no sisterly hug."

"But I'm too young for her." Brad said a little defensively.

"Listen, son, a year or two may seem like a lot when you're fifteen, but it ain't squat when you get, say, over twenty. True, lots of girls do date guys older by a couple of years, and I'll bet that not one of their fathers approves." He winked. "It's mostly because us guys don't wise up, or grow up, as fast."

"Well, damn. This sucks." He was trying to digest the big 'what if' of Connie maybe liking him 'that way.'

"Life sucks, son. You just gotta take a little bit of control and go after what you want. 'Specially since you are off to find your future. At your age, you're going to have to scrap for what you need. Be polite when you can, assertive when you have to, and downright pushy if the situation calls for it. Remember; don't live your life like there's a score card. This is not a dress rehearsal!"

"Huh?"

"Just go after what you want if it isn't already somebody else's. And treat everybody with as much respect as you'd want back."

Brad thought about that and realized it was as good an expression of the Golden Rule as he'd heard. *What can I do about Connie from Nevada?* He shook his head in open-mouthed frustration. "She's back home with all her friends, and I will just fade into a long-ago memory."

"That's what you *can* control. Don't disappear. Keep in touch. Send her a postcard. Write her letters."

"Oh, fine, so I write her a postcard: 'Dear Connie (and Mr. FBI or NSA), we're in Texas, hope to be in El Paso this time tomorrow and in Nevada in two days. I'll let you all know where I'm staying when I get settled in. Love, Brad.'"

"Well, sort of, except why not just take on another persona that she will know is you. Sign it 'Your Pen Pal,' and pick a name; either something that could be a nickname or whatever. Tell you what, I'll pick you up a Texas postcard when we check out, and you can send your first one from here!"

~ ~ ~

That night in the motel room, as Brad waited for sleep, he focused on those last few minutes in the yard with Connie. He had pretty much made up his mind that he had to move on and had tried to convince her that he was endangering her and her parents. She had thrown up several arguments for his staying in Apalachicola or Wakulla or Tallahassee, but he had locked in his reasons for going, even though her pleading was tearing at his heart. Lying in the dark in a dank motel that smelled too much like an overworked air conditioner, he wondered if he was making a terrible mistake, if he was leaving for selfish reasons or taking too much on. Was he leaving to be gallant?

Was he really breaking her heart? Had she ever given him a reason to think he wasn't just a stand-in brother for Jamie? He thought about the dozens of different times when they had been just talking out on the porch and he would realize that her face was only inches away and she was staring at him. He remembered how she often sat with her fingertips gently nudged up against his thigh or even with thighs touching. She was never overt but certainly not reserved. Was that just sibling intimacy? He'd never had a brother or sister.

Hell, was this the right thing to do? He thought of her in a robe, walking down the hall, water still dripping from her red curls. Damn, she was beautiful. And boy, had her figure improved over the last several months he had lived in Apalachicola!

What a fool!

He was heading off across the country with a few hundred dollars in his pocket, looking for a missing person whom he had not heard from for two and a half years. This was a fool's errand, and despite the advice of a crazy old man, he was about to go hiking around the desert as summer approached. Well, he'd just be careful. He'd find out what he could. If he couldn't find her, he sure as hell wouldn't stay in the desert. He'd come back and take his chances that the black hats had given up on him. Maybe he could live in the woods and use his old house as a home base. But, then, he was still officially a missing person. He hadn't seen his face on a milk carton yet, but he also didn't have any parents looking for him, either. He fell asleep feeling a little more than sorry for himself.

~ ~ ~

The next two days were filled with the wonder that comes from seeing new places and having unexpected new experiences. East Texas was boring in its enormity, with vast green pastures and rice fields punctuated by horse-head oil well pumps bobbing up and down. Trees and greenery began to thin out west of Houston, which according to plan, they traversed unimpeded by rush-hour traffic. The few trees that seemed to remain in West Texas were down in the washes. Only scrub seemed to survive in the open. The horizon unfurled ahead as they moved westward. Interstate 10 was only a barbed-wire ribbon across a landscape that was as foreign to him as it was beautiful. And he was seeing it at its best. Winter snow melt was fueling an extravagance of blossoms. When he remarked on the pallet of yellow and orange flowers, Dink told him he was too early for the real show in May when a thousand acres of bluebells were in bloom. The approach to El Paso near the end of the day revealed vistas that he had never expected to see— arid landscapes that he had seen only in the National Geographic collection his mom had kept.

El Paso was their overnight stop. Brad was excited to know that Mexico was just down the hill. The motel Dink picked was actually in the eastern suburb community of Sparks, so in the morning, Brad would be able to see El Paso proper. The next day, they left with the rising sun in their rearview mirror. Brad was impressed by the huge wire-wrapped fence on the American side of the river and appalled by the expanse of slums on the other side. Soon, they were in the desert again headed for Las Cruces. He had thought that nothing could be drier and less inviting than West Texas until they got deeper into the sun-bleached expanses of New Mexico's plains. By late morning, a large lump of rock began to rise on the horizon, and an hour later they finally passed a mountain that Dink called El Capitan. Dink pulled off the road in the ghost town of Stein to take a break and get a shot of coffee from the thermos. After they each ate an apple, they were on the road again, heading for Brad's last stop.

By early afternoon, they made Casa Grande. The sun baked town was relatively cool for early April, and they walked downtown to get Mexican food for lunch. Dink found the Greyhound station and bought Brad a ticket for Las Vegas. It would leave at nine the next morning and make a number of local stops on the way. They took a room in the Hacienda Blanca hotel.

Dink was determined to give Brad his best shot and warned him about doing anything crazy his first day out, like trying to hitchhike to Vegas. They took in a movie and walked the town before heading back to the hotel. On the way back, they found a discount clothing store where Dink bought Brad a pair of jeans; two pairs of socks; a small, soft-frame backpack to replace the ungainly duffle; and, most important, a pair of boots. They were not Tony Lamas, but durable hard-toe cowboy corral boots with finger straps to help pull them on and an imperceptible ledge on the heel to help kick them off. Dink told him to wear them from there on to break them in.

At the hotel, a rack of tourist pamphlets and Las Vegas hotel and casino brochures leaned on a wall beside the stairwell. One of the offerings caught his eye: a black-and-white, cheaply produced flyer advertised the Space Invader Museum and Bookstore in Indian Springs, Nevada. He took it and put it in his pocket.

At breakfast, Dink told Brad he'd probably be returning east in three to four days and gave him a phone number to try in two days. If that failed, he was to use his CB call sign at a truck stop. He gave Brad a hundred dollars in twenties that Sunny had sent, just in case he couldn't talk Brad out of his mission. It wasn't as if he hadn't tried. While driving that morning, Dink had proposed that Brad stay on through the drive to San Diego and they could spend a day together in Las Vegas looking for his mom. By the end of the discussion, Brad had convinced him of his "sense" that his mom was alive and that if he was willing to come back through Vegas in a few days, Brad would join him for a return to Florida.

April 12, 1977
Las Vegas, Nevada

On a fine, clear, not-quite-hot April afternoon, Bradley Delaney Hitchens, a.k.a. William (Bill) Bradley Williams, a.k.a. Swamp Boy, stepped out of the Greyhound bus station in Las Vegas and stared in awe up the strip. Even though it was not dark yet, the flashing lights of Main Street were mesmerizing. He followed the running flashers through their intricate patterns and gawked at the display as so many thousands of first-time visitors had done. Walking north, he entered the tallest hotel he could find downtown and went directly to the lobby. Taking the elevator to the fortieth floor, he found a city-view restaurant that had not yet begun to fill for dinner.

"Excuse me, mister," he said, approaching a busboy who was cleaning tables. The guy didn't look much older than Brad.

He had been trained to be polite to the guests, so without looking up, the young man, wanting to sound cooler than a busboy, answered, "What can I do for you?" Then seeing Brad, he said, "Que pasa, my man. What's up?"

Brad pulled out the pamphlet. "Do you know how far it is to Indian Springs?"

"Never heard of it. Is that an attraction?" The busboy wiped his hands on his apron and tried to look thoughtful and then asked, "Is that in a hotel, or is it an amusement thing?"

"No," Brad said. "It's a town, I think." He showed the young worker his pamphlet.

"Oh, jeez, you going to look for flying saucers?" He almost sneered as he said, "Can't help you." Then he noticed the backpack and the fatigue in Brad's eyes. "Say, you on the road? You a runaway?"

"No, I'm not a runaway," Brad said, irritated that he had been seen through so quickly. "I'm looking for a relative."

"Aliens abduct your mommy?" he asked, a smirk on his face. The table polished and set, the busboy moved his work tub to the next table in

179

line and began to replace the salt and pepper shakers. He looked up, bothered. "You need something else from me?"

Brad wasn't sure what to do next. He was taken aback at the shift from obligatory politeness to sneering disdain. He glanced out of the darkened bronze windows as the sun moved closer to the horizon. He looked down at the pamphlet again and asked the busboy, "Do you know which of those highways is Route 95?"

"Look, kid, do I look like a tourist guide? I clean tables. I've been in this crappy town for six weeks, and I don't know a damn thing about it. I put in my hours, and I make my money. You need to go find someone who has a higher give-a-damn quotient."

Irritated but swallowing the bile forming, Brad went over to the window and looked across the sparkling lights below and the long avenues that spread out toward the edges of the city. This place was big. He realized that he was not going to be able to walk to the edge of town and hitchhike.

At the concierge desk, he asked about a taxi to Indian Springs and found it would take most of his money. There was, however, a UFO tour that left the Sands every morning at 10:00am that would bring him back by 2:30 in the afternoon. The man actually winked at him. *Was that a come-on?*

South Main Street was coming alive with bright lights and pedestrians. Maybe, he thought, people just don't come out until after the sun goes down. He wandered for a little while, trying to look like just an average tourist, found the pedestrian mall on Jacinto Street, and gawked. He saw a storefront McDonald's and went in. Even being an urban storefront McDonald's with no parking and definitely no drive-through, it was at least a familiar setting. After a cheap dinner of burgers and a shake, he continued a walking tour of downtown. He decided he couldn't afford anything on the strip and turned west.

Eventually, he saw what looked like a cheap motel. The Starlight was a no-tell motel. It looked like a place that gamblers stayed when they were trying to save bus money for a ride home but planned to try the slots just one more time. The lobby looked like it could never be called clean. Even sanitized, it would look grubby.

The attendant, sitting behind a scratched counter, overweight and smelling of alcohol and sweat, was not helpful. Brad pleaded with her to rent him a room for the night, telling her that his high school tour bus had left without him and he needed a place to stay while his parents came to get him from El Paso. And, no, he didn't have any ID other than an out of state learner's permit; why would a fifteen-year-old have any other ID?

She was finally convinced when he put a twenty-dollar bill down for the sixteen-dollar tab. He went over to a rack of postcards in a revolving display and found that he didn't like any of them. He finally picked one because it was bigger than the rest and gave him more room to write. Taking his key down to room 212, he decided that going it alone in his own woods was one thing, but after a good look and a sniff test, he did not like this big, overlit city.

He lay down to sleep that night, thinking about his dad and how he had always been there when the memories of Mom had gotten too dim, too fast. He thought about how they had loved to go out together in the kayak, casting for trout, redfish, or stripers in the tidal flats and of their hikes through the back trails of the wildlife refuge. He began to think again about Connie, how he missed having her to talk to, having someone who also believed in the invisible spaceman in the woods. He remembered the postcard and got up to write. Suddenly, it seemed like too large a space to fill. After overanalyzing what to say for so long that all creativity dried up, he simply wrote:

"Connie, we finally got to Nevada today. I miss Florida already. Wish we had not had to move away. This city sucks, your friend, Willa. P.S. Let's try to stay pen pals at least. I'll let you know what our address is when we get settled."

In bed again, hoping for sleep, he thought of tomorrow. He would finally be in the last place he knew his mother had been. Was there any chance that she was still in this part of the country? Why should she be? If she really thought she was crazy, why hang around in the desert? It was a dangerous place, unforgiving. Maybe she wandered off into the desert and coyotes got her. Dink said that coyotes were making a comeback. Alone and miserable, he finally fell asleep with tear tracks drying on his cheeks.

April 13, 1977
Las Vegas, Nevada, 8:15 a.m.

The cool Spring Wednesday morning had the scrubbed blue-sky look of a day that would soon get hot. Brad was not used to fifty-degree overnight temperature changes. The Sands Hotel's 11:00 a.m. UFO tour bus was late by a few minutes, but it seemed the stragglers kept showing up; running as if the bus was waiting just for them. It finally pulled away only twenty-five minutes late and headed northwest of Las Vegas, laying down a black diesel smoke screen behind it. Brad was not sure why he had expected the drive away from the city to be different from the drive toward it, but he had. A comment overheard a row behind him summed up his thoughts, "Same desert; different day." The monotony of scrub and cactus with interchangeable barren mountains on the horizon would have been numbing to the non-aficionado if the bus hadn't pulled off so quickly. They were there. It had taken longer to get out of Las Vegas than it had to get thirty miles up the road to Indian Springs.

His fellow travelers filed into a rough semicircle around a guide who materialized to show them around. The small, thin guide in an open-collar pink shirt that showcased an oversized crucifix on a hairless chest had a hard time sounding interested in his job but managed to point out the casino, drugstore, and the Space Invader Museum. Brad spotted a dilapidated convenience store across the highway, slipped around the back of the bus, and left the crowd. The aging 7-Eleven had the usual layout and offerings. One difference was the presence of a whole aisle of cheap plastic figures and books on various kinds of aliens, Area 51, Roswell, and related topics. Some of the books were cheap knockoffs of other more-researched volumes, and there were some in comic-book format and an array of monthly magazines. He picked up a copy of Aliens Among Us and went to the checkout. At the counter, he asked, "Sir, is there a place around here sells cards?"

"Postcards?" The attendant turned to point at a revolving rack near the door.

"Yes, sir, actually, I received a Christmas card from here a few years back and wondered where it came from." He checked out the rack, spinning it slowly as he scanned the offerings.

The attendant asked, "Was it bought here or sent from here?"

Brad realized he didn't know. "I don't guess I know; it was postmarked here, though. I remember that." He put the magazine on the counter. "I guess this would be it. Oh, and one of those bottles of water."

Crossing back to the other side of the highway, he listened for and then watched a military four-engine turboprop transport bank and descend toward a runway and then land not too very far north. Wow, he thought, could Area 51 be that close? He trotted over to the casino where he had seen some of the tour bus's tourists entering. Many of his fellow UFO enthusiasts seemed to have slipped off to play the slot machines, but he spotted the tour guide talking to a pretty, darkhaired hostess at the information stand.

"Excuse me, you're the tour guide, right?"

"Yeah, that's me." The young man winked and grinned at the hostess.

"How far is it to Area 51? I just saw an airplane land a few blocks away."

"That would be because there's an Air Force base just a few blocks away. As for Area 51, it's a bit farther. Actually, it's a lot farther." He looked over at the girl as if she could help.

She offered, "You can't get there from here, except by plane. The main gate in is east. You go to Caliente, Nevada, and then take the highway through the mountains. But it doesn't matter anyway."

"Why?" Brad asked, not understanding.

The guide interjected. "Because no one gets in! Don't know if anyone has ever gotten in, 'cept for top-secret Air Force types, and I suppose a few space aliens." He laughed at his own poor joke. The young woman rolled her eyes with a slight shake of her head as though she had heard all his bad jokes before.

"Is there a map for Area 51?"

"You don't want to spend your money on a map of the place, 'cause it won't show up, and believe me, kid, you won't get in. People with better equipment than a pair of boots and a backpack have tried. There's motion sensors and cameras with night vision monitoring the place. Soon as soon they felt your footsteps, you'd be under arrest."

"Damn!"

"Yeah and damn is right, 'cause if they arrest you, it ain't like they take you inside to talk about the weather. There's not really a fence, but there is a guard shack that's manned twenty-four-seven and a whole lotta nothin' to see." He paused for breath. "The crazy few that's come prepared for getting around the checkpoint overland all come back. They don't get close enough to see a thing. Security brings 'em here to Creech Air Force Base, wastes a lot of their time, and turns 'em loose hungry and pissed off."

The hostess, a pretty brunette dressed in a very short black skirt and top with a revealing neckline, said, "Are you with your parents? Some of your group is in the casino, where you can't go without an adult, and the rest are over in the restaurant."

"I guess I'll go over to the restaurant then and wait." He had turned and started to leave when he came back to the guide. "What ever happened to the UFO tour? Is that all there is?"

The guide motioned toward the door and said, "There's a bookstore with some exhibits down the street beside the gas station. Not much to see, but since they asked, I directed some of the people on your bus over to it. Most people come out for a few minutes away from the casinos in town and end up gambling anyway when they get here. If you go, watch the time 'cause the bus'll leave at two o'clock whether you're on it or not."

Brad thanked him and left. The Space Invaders Bookstore, a sun-bleached purple, looked like any other building that had its stucco painted over ten years before. The fading varied over the surface, and the corners appeared to have been sandblasted. In some areas, paint flakes were trying to escape the building in patches. The bright-yellow door had a small sign next to it that advised "TWA's, please watch your head." A row of symbols below it was the apparent translation should any tall white alien visit the store.

Brad was startled by the ringing bell over his head when he opened the door but kept moving. Welcomed in by the cool air-conditioning, he saw a few people, including a pair of young Japanese men, looking over the book racks. He knew that they were on his bus, so he determined to keep an eye on them. There were more books here on the subject than he thought were possible. Area 51 had a large section, but there were also books on the Bermuda Triangle; the Nazca desert images in Peru; and dancing lights over Illinois, Washington, China, Mexico, and France—almost everywhere you could think of. He had no idea.

Most of the books were priced at more than he could afford. One book whose writer he recognized, Eric Von Daniken, had a special markdown sticker on it, so he picked it up. A tabloid shouted news about a tell-all by someone named Bob Lazar. A new special section for the movie Close Encounters offered memorabilia and collectible junk as well as soundtracks. He wanted to look for something else, but most of it seemed, well, fake! He knew what he did about Ka-Litan and his conversations by the little pool. He knew that the piece of metal now lying at the bottom of the Gulf of Mexico was unusual in place and material; he knew with no uncertainty that a presence of some kind was near his home in Florida and that occasionally he could feel it seeking him out and feeding him thoughts, images, and dreams. But he also figured that most of the stuff in this store was crap.

Some of the tourists were seated on a small bench watching a TV with a looped documentary on alien abductions and jerky shots of white dots that could have been almost anything from Jiffy Pop pans to birthday balloons but were solemnly being reported on as alien spaceships. He could watch this for only so long. Hell, it even looked like it had been faked.

Browsing, he saw a revolving rack of assorted cards. He spun the rack looking for a postcard for Connie. He picked one of a Gila monster on a rock and gave the rack another turn hoping for other options when he found three cheesy desert Christmas scenes. One card depicted a Santa sitting in a lawn chair next to a decorated saguaro cactus. He pulled it from the rack and crossed over to the counter where an elderly attendant was carefully watching the remainder of the tour bus stragglers in his store. As he got to the counter, he heard the doorbell ring twice as the Japanese men headed out the door, each with a bag of books. He looked around and saw that one other couple from the tour was still in the store.

He paid for the *Chariots of the Gods* and the Gila monster postcard and asked about the Christmas card. "Mister, this card looks kinda old; do you sell many of these?"

"No, young fella. Matter of fact, I don't. Seeing how it's getting on summer, I might not sell another one for a while." He winked in a friendly way that made it clear the wink last night had not been intended the same way. The attendant had thick white eyebrows that came together when he peered intently. He was now peering at Brad, bringing the shaggy brows together into one long, undulating fuzzy caterpillar. "You want to add that to the book, you can go ahead and have it." He smiled, revealing yellowing teeth with one missing on the top row.

"No, sir. Actually, I got one just like this two or three years ago, probably from this store."

"Ain't that something, do tell." The old man's accent was becoming recognizable as being from the southwest. Dink had told him it came from squinting against the glare of light from sunbaked dirt. Too many years in the desert. Knitting his brows again, the man asked, "How do you know it come from this store?" He turned his head slightly to favor a good ear.

"Well, it had a postmark from Indian Springs." Then he added, "It was from my mother." He was here! She had been here. This was the time to start asking questions. He pulled a folded photograph from his shirt pocket and carefully opened it up. At the sight of his family posed for the photograph, he got a lump in his throat, but he managed to speak after clearing a swallow reflex. "Would you happen to remember if you saw this lady in the store? I know it was a while ago, but well, I'm trying to find her."

The old man took the photo and held it close; he raised his head trying to get the best magnification out of his bifocals and then gave up and pulled out a hand magnifier from a drawer and peered into the picture. He worked his lips over gums as if trying to gin up some memory from the past. He looked at Brad and then the picture. "This your mom, huh? I can see the family resemblance." Brad nodded, unwilling to speak in case his voice broke with the emotions boiling in his chest. Finally, the clerk laid it back down on the counter. "Sonny boy, I'm sorry. I have a hard time remembering last Wednesday, much less someone from two or three years ago."

"I was kind of afraid of that. Thanks a lot, though. Is there someplace around here that folks would stay for a little while? A bed-and-breakfast, or a little motel?"

"Nawp, shore ain't. Most of the newbies we get stay on with the casino for a while. And they got a special section out back of the casino where some of the employees crash after a long shift, but nothin' perm'nent." He looked down as if remembering. "Oh, yeah, we got a motel. Pretty much a dump, though." He looked Brad up and down. "You probably wouldn't want to stay at it."

"Hmm, thanks, mister." Brad made for the door.

"Son?" The furry eyebrows were now raised. "If'n you got a bedroll, it'll be cool after about nine o'clock; otherwise, you might want to avoid the heat." Looking back into the store, Brad realized that he was the only customer left. Had he not heard the door ringer while he was talking to the clerk? *Had he been that completely focused?* Then he heard the diesel of the bus revving up as it ran through first gear. It was now a few minutes past two o'clock, and the outdoor heat was intense. He broke into a sprint, wishing that he had on his sneakers rather than the boots, but it would not have made any real difference at this distance. From a block away, he saw the bus swing out into the highway and head away from him, back to Las Vegas. He let the sprint wind down to a winded trot and then slowed to a walk, took three more steps, and stopped completely. As he watched, the long line of black diesel exhaust trailing behind the bus hung in the still air. Shortly, the cloud drifted away, and there was no bus and no sound of a bus.

At least, he reflected, he was not in a ghost town. This place was civilized. It had an Air Force base, even if the people there were not too friendly. It had a motel next to the casino, and he saw a likely place for some

Mexican food later. For now, he had to get out of the heat. He knelt and put his new book into his backpack and retrieved the water bottle he'd bought when he first got off the bus. Taking a pull, he quickly drank half of it. Seeing this, he realized that he was in a different world. He might have to learn how to drink to conserve water and dress to conserve sweat. Should he get a cowboy hat?

Moving more slowly now, he headed back to the casino parking lot looking for some sign of a schedule for the shuttle to the Sands Hotel. He found none, but remembered the cute girl at the hostess station in the casino. He found himself holding his hands over his eyes to block the glare of the afternoon sun. The heat on his shoulders was more like the heat he would have felt with a mild, early-season sunburn, and this was through a shirt! If this was April, what was August like here?

Entering the casino, he saw that no one was at the hostess stand. He knew that he was not supposed to be in the gaming room, but he went to the entry threshold and looked in. Immediately, a uniformed guard came over to intercept him. "Boy, I'm sorry, but you can't come in here. Do you know where your parents are?"

"Not exactly," he answered truthfully. "Is there someplace I can wait on them?"

"Sure," the guard said, pointing through an arcade area full of slot machines to a restaurant. "You can go in there and wait on them. If they don't show for a while, I'll come in and check on you, and we can page them." He tried to look reassuring, like this happened a lot. "Don't worry; when they've had some fun in there, they'll remember and come looking. Happens all the time," he offered, giving Brad a reassuring pat on the back as he herded him toward the restaurant/fast-food area with electric arcade games and a few pinball machines.

Brad sat down, ordered the buffet, and then took advantage of it as only a growing teenager can: steak, fried chicken, chicken fried steak, fried clams, onion rings, garlic mashed potatoes, peas and limas, something green and mushy called Southern-styled greens—which missed the mark completely—and, for luck, a boiled egg and some overdone cornbread. When he put this away, he went back to the line for a slice of cherry pie and some peach cobbler and laid a scoop of vanilla ice cream on both. Finally sated, he sat back in his booth. He pulled the book out of his pack and opened it.

When the waitress, whose name tag read "Sherri", came to clear the table, she looked at the title, smirked a little, and shook her head.

She'd seen her share of the UFO crazies over her years in Indian Springs. "You gonna be here for a while, hon?"

"If it's okay; Dad's in the casino," he lied. He hoped to stay long enough for it to get dark and cooler outside.

"How about if you move over to the reception lobby. You'll find some chairs in there you could use where no one's trying to make a profit. The manager's gonna want me to turn tables in here. Do you mind, hon?"

"No, sure." He folded his book closed and thinking about his mission, took another shot at the search. He pulled the photograph out of his pocket. "Is there any chance you've seen this lady around here?" It might have been a while ago, but he got the feeling she'd been there for a while.

Sherri took the photograph and pursed her lips in concentration. She looked down at the boy and then at the photograph. "This here your mom?"

Same reaction as the store clerk, he thought. "Yes, ma'am."

She looked at the photograph again and back at Brad. "Did you say your dad was in the casino?"

He lied automatically, "Umm, yeah." He averted his eyes slightly and then looked back up at Sherri. "He might be on a winning streak; I don't want to mess with that."

Sherri had raised three teenagers and could spot a lying teen a mile away in the fog. "Okay, that's probably a good idea. You wouldn't want to mess with a winning streak. That's for sure, hon."

Brad relocated to the reception lobby. There were several couches in a line against the wall ready for the early losers to wait for their buses while the winners filled out their allotted time on the machines and at the tables. He went to the door and looked out. As he approached, the automatic opener did its job, opening and beckoning him outside. As he walked through the door, a blast of afternoon heat nearly stopped his heart. He went back inside and settled into one of the couches. He had just gotten involved in the first chapter of his book when he heard a voice and heels approaching.

"Well, hey there." He looked up and saw the pretty hostess returning to her station. With a sincere frown, she said, "Why are you here? Did you miss the bus?" She sat next to him on the couch; she was a natural at making people comfortable. Her name tag labeled her as Marina. She had light-olive skin, deep-brown eyes, and shiny black hair swept tightly back into a long ponytail. Her jaunty uniform cap was pinned at an angle into the silky hair.

188

He saw that she was really pretty up close. The closer she was, the better she looked.

"Yeah, I was looking for you earlier to find out if there was an afternoon shuttle to the Sands." He looked into a face full of concern. "Is it okay if I sit here until the next one comes?"

"Well, first the bad news." She gritted her teeth and sucked air in through them, her eyes apologizing in advance. "There's only one shuttle a day from the Sands, and, as you know, it's gone."

"There's good news?" His mouth then took off before his brain could engage. "Are you going to put me up for the night?"

Her laughter was genuine and hearty. She was still smiling through her laughter-moistened eyes when she got to the good news. "Good try, champ. I think you are the youngest hit I've taken. Thanks for trying. Don't lose that gung-ho spirit. No, the good news is that more buses from other hotels in the city come out after it cools down. That'll be after eight or so. I'll talk to one of the drivers and get you a slot on a bus with some room. Even if they're full, it's a short trip, and I'm sure someone will fit you in."

"That's great," he looked at her name tag. "Marina. That's an odd name for around here."

"Oh, really? Why do you say that?"

"A marina is where you park boats. There's not enough water around here to float a boat for a hundred miles."

"Wrong and wronger," she said and smiled, revealing dazzling teeth. "First, I am Hispanic, and Marina is a Latinized name for 'from the sea.' My people are from the sea, fishing people from Spain. It's also Slavic for the same thing, go figure. And, yes, you can park boats in a marina around here. Just the other side of Vegas is a pretty huge lake with several marinas. So, that's me, Marina. Anna Marina Martinez de Goya de Torrevieja." She extended a hand. As she rolled out the family name, the first sense of a Hispanic accent appeared briefly with rich, rolling R's. "And you are?"

"Umm," he replied, taken off guard, "Brad, Bradley Hitch … umm, William Bradley Williams." He took her hand; it was warm and firm and gave a good shake. She looked at him a little oddly. Had she caught the misstep with his name?

"So that's Bill Bradley Williams; I can tell who you're named after."

Brad's smile was back intact. "No, ma'am. It's really for Omar Nelson Bradley, the general."

She pursed her mouth, corrected, and said. "Okay then, Mr. Bill Bradley Williams, you're safe here for the time being." She looked up and around, and seeing no one was near the concierge stand, she decided she had a minute. "So what brings you to Indian Springs?"

Brad looked down at the toes of his new but scuffed boots. His shoulders sagged. Without looking up, he added, "I'm here trying to find my mom." Brad pulled out the photo again. He felt it was probably useless, but what the heck? "Is there any chance that you might have seen this lady around here; it might have been a few years ago." He handed the folded photo to her. Marina looked at the three figures in the black-and-white photo, saw the four-year jump in Brad's age, and took in the importance of the picture.

Then she took in a sharp pull of breath and slowly exhaled. "This is your family?"

"Yes, that's my mom and dad, back home."

"Your mom is very pretty."

He looked up from the photo to Marina's gaze. "Thanks. Have you seen her?" Mom may have been pretty, he thought, but this lady is something!

"Actually, there's a chance," she said, looking at the photo again. "How old is this picture?"

"About six years ago. I was ten, and I'll be sixteen this summer." He added, I got a post card from her from here, Indian Springs, a coupla years ago."

"I see. Let me ask around." She stood up, still holding the photograph. "Do you mind if I take this and get a copy made? I can get the face blown up so you don't have to keep using this original."

"Uh, yeah, sure. Thanks!" Brad watched as she walked away. She was gorgeous from a distance too. But did he just get a hint that maybe she had seen his mother and could remember seeing her? When Marina didn't return right away, he settled into the couch to wait. He tried to get back into chapter 1, but he kept thinking about that pause. Was it possible? With softly clicking heels, she came back holding several sheets of bond with the enlarged picture of Lucy Hitchens.

"Brad, or is it Bill?"

"I go by Brad, usually. Too many Bill Williams out there."

"Brad, I need you to sit here for sure; don't go anywhere because I think I have good news for you. I found a ride back to Vegas for you." Seeing his face fall, she asked, "What's wrong? Isn't that good news?"

Brad realized that his hopes had spiked for almost no reason. There were too many reasons to count why she had seemed to see something in the picture. "No, Miss De La, umm, Marina, that's great." He began to fold, to lose his bravado. Indian Springs had been his shot; he had asked maybe four people with no hits, and soon, he'd be going back to a very large city to look for signs of one person who disappeared well over three years ago. "When is that ride coming? I'd like to go to some other places and ask if anyone has seen her." On the last phrase, he extended the small pile of pictures.

Marina said that he had a couple of hours and cautioned him against the heat. "It'll cool down fast as soon as the sun's gone, but please be careful out there." He agreed and went back out reluctantly into the heat.

Scanning the businesses in view, he headed over to the Indian Springs motel. A hot white glare reflected off stucco walls. He knew his next purchases would be sunglasses and a hat. He wasn't sure if he could talk himself into a cowboy hat or not. He was afraid he'd look and feel ridiculous in a cowboy hat.

The manager at the hotel scrutinized the photo of his mother and shook his head. Apologizing, he asked some of the hired help. A gift shop next door produced a disinterested shrug from an acne-scarred teen behind the counter and a customer seemed a little too concerned about him. Brad figured he would have to refine his questioning style. Or maybe, some people were just creeps. He bypassed a propane company next door and looked down the street. There was an entrance to the Air Force base, what looked like a subdivision, and then more desert. Across the street, he saw only the 7-Eleven and a liquor store. He debated the liquor store and decided to go for it. He sensed that this was a highway you could cross without looking. With absolute silence filling the highway in both directions, he trotted back across to check out the liquor store.

This last chance for Indian Springs was also a bust. Both the counter and stock clerks looked at the photo but didn't recognize the woman in it. He returned to the casino to ask a few more employees before the ride back to Las Vegas. Marina saw him come through the revolving door and came over to meet him. "Brad, I have an idea that might be better than sitting out here. That ride I lined up will be here about seven, and you can sit back in the offices while you wait. Would that be all right with you?"

Brad thought about the boneheaded idea he'd had of coming across the country to follow a postcard and a picture. How many people went missing each year? How many went homeless, and how many homeless survived two or three years? "Thanks, Marina. Maybe that's best." He followed her to a rear reception area that was used for business visitors to the casino, found a comfortable armchair, and settled in to get back into the first chapter of his book. It seemed useless. The more Von Daniken he read, the harder it was to focus. Something like despair or defeat or humiliation began to overwhelm his ability to concentrate. He shut the book and covered his face with it. He seriously thought about posting his mom's picture with the police and the highway patrol and then planning what his next big idea might look like.

Probably, he should call Dink to see when he could get a ride back east. Even if the Air Force guy did find him, he'd just say he threw the damn thing in the Gulf that first night in disgust. He was sure he'd be welcome back with Chase, Lou Anne, and Connie. Hmmm. Connie.

There was a light knock on the wall at the entry to the room. "Brad? I'd like you to meet the lady that's going to give you a ride back."

He looked up, his watery eyes making it hard to see. "Thanks, Marina." He got up and wiped his eyes on his sleeve. Then he heard it.

"Bradley, honey?" The voice! "Bradley, baby. It's me!" His heartbeat thudded in his temples as he tried to clear his vision. Suddenly, he was engulfed in her arms. The smell, the strength of the hug, every nuance told him he was in his mother's arms. Then he could no longer see as his eyes filled. He tried a few times to pull away, to man the situation. Her grasp was too strong, and she was crying too. "I'm so sorry, baby. I am so sorry. I don't know how …" She choked. "I don't know if you can ever forgive me."

Together, they felt the rush of connection flow between mother and son—the eleven-year-old, now almost sixteen, grown in a few years to his mother's height; the mother stooped in sorrow, clutching her lost boy to her chest. Marina quietly backed away from the room. Choking back her own tears, she turned and walked down the hall.

PART 2

Six Years Later

Chapter 11

But if the while I think on thee, dear friend, All losses are restored and
sorrows end.
William Shakespeare

December 22, 1984
Phoenix, Sky Harbor Airport, 7:15 a.m.

Brad was running toward his gate at the end of the terminal when he heard the metallic overhead speakers announcing the last call for his flight. He cursed the distance he'd run from his beater car to the terminal and tried to speed up from sprint to dead run. It was harder than he'd have thought with only a gym bag carry-on, but avoiding the travelers with broken luggage, women with infants papoosed in body carriers, and others seeming to be in stall mode between their connecting flights was challenging. Spotting the gate number, he ran up to the empty counter and slapped down his ticket.

The brightly uniformed agent looked at it with something close to a disapproving frown, read the pertinent flight and seat information, and looked up. "Well, we're glad you could make it, Mr. Hitchens. We were about to button up the gate." She motioned for him to enter the ramp, and he felt for the first time in an hour that he was actually going to make his flight. Looking down the aisle as he passed a pair of stewardesses at the entrance, he saw the confusion of passengers wrestling with their carry-on luggage and backpacks. Several, he saw, were hindered by oversized ski apparel. In contrast, he was dressed for a North Florida winter in a sweater and windbreaker.

Later, as the plane lifted above a layer of thin, gray winter clouds, he shifted to pull his gym bag from the small place reserved for his feet and, exploring its depths, found a rubber-band-bound pack of correspondence. The letters and cards from Connie were sorted chronologically from the first postcard from Apalachicola through the letters from college in North Carolina to the last letter on top again from Apalachicola. Musing over the collected histories, he took the first card from the bottom and read:

195

4/26/77 Hi Willa, it is so terrible that you had to leave with your family so close to the end of the school year. The place will not be the same without you. I think about the times we would sit and talk from dusk to dark and only come in when the bugs got too thick. Haha! Luv ya, Connie.

He smiled at the memories. The bugs could get thick, usually a lot earlier than dark, but it took a while to get to the point where sitting with his pretty "older sister" wasn't worth the welts. That took until dark. Pursing his lips with inner questioning, he wondered why she had been willing to put up with the buzzing onslaught to sit out on the dock with him that long. He pulled another piece from near the bottom of the pile. A letter from more difficult times.

10/17/79 Hi Willa. Me again. I got your letter last week and remembered that it was the second one to come in since I wrote you last. Sorry. It's been a really hectic time getting fully moved into my dorm and life here in Chapel Hill. The town is beautiful, and you should see the colors in the trees! Wow! I know I'm only a freshman, but it feels so cool to be a college student. Apalach seems like worlds away. Classes are easy, so far. I imagine they'll get harder when I get past all the 101 level stuff. I hope your high school studies are going well. You must have had a lot of adjustments to make going out there like you did. Glad to hear your mom is doing fine. No news from home to report on, except that Jamie got transferred to Camp Lejeune, which is only a short drive from here. Well, I got to get to class. Luv ya, Connie.

Short and sweet, he thought. Well, short anyway. She had always been to the point, and her letters had been far from nourishing. She'd even rubbed in the difference between her college and his high school. Feelings he'd always repressed for what he thought were logical reasons, age difference being the most obvious, had never been encouraged in her brief notes back. The landscape below his window was a frothy white carpet furrowed at several-mile intervals by minor variations in pressure from below or above. The rolling waves of white reminded him of the rolling swells on the Gulf. God, it would be good to get back home again.

His mother had moved back months ago for a change of job and life. He'd missed her, but her visits to Tempe and his visits to Las Vegas were too infrequent to justify a family reason for staying out West when she had had enough. Home again! And Hitchens again. They had agreed that even if the home front was still under sporadic surveillance, there would be no point in having an alias. So a simple courthouse proceeding and a trip to the motor vehicles department would be all that would be needed to regain his heritage.

He examined the pack of letters and cards he'd brought back to give to Connie. He rolled it over and over, glancing occasionally out the port at the passing clouds. A voice interrupted his reverie from the aisle seat next to him. His fellow traveler was a middle-aged woman in business dress.

"Pardon me if I interfere, but I couldn't help noticing you looking at all those letters. Are those love letters?"

He stopped turning the pile over. He looked over at her. She was attractive, for an older woman approaching, what, fifty? Certainly, she would not be considered matronly; maybe classy was better. "No, ma'am, it's a pen pal. A good friend, I guess."

"Pen pal, hmmm. That's nice. I had a pen pal when I was your age; she moved to New York with her family, and I had to stay home in the sticks. I always thought she had moved on to a more glamorous place."

"That's kind of the same thing, only I moved away." He twisted the stack in his hands again. "Then she moved away too; seems like it got hard on the friendship, with less in common to talk about."

She nodded in understanding. "It looks like it lasted quite a while."

"Maybe longer than it might have. Sometimes I thought I was sending off one last letter, although I never quite got around to saying good-bye." He continued; confessions were a lot easier to a stranger than to someone who knew your past. "I went to high school. She went to college. Then I went to a different college and she's gone on to grad school."

"Life is a continuum," she said. "But it's episodic. You change. People change. Situations change, but friendship …" She patted his stack of letters. "Friendships can survive all of that, but you have to keep investing in them." She was silent for a time as they both listened to the whine of the jets outside. Then she added, "It looks like you must've made some continued deposits."

Brad jerked in a silent laugh. "Yes, ma'am. I guess I did. To continue your metaphor, I sometimes thought it was like throwing good money after bad, but there just was always something about it."

She reached beyond the narrow armrest that defined their own personal space in the row and patted his hand. "I hope it was worth it for you. If nothing else, remember that the journey is often more important than the destination."

He pulled Connie's last letter from the top and removed it from its envelope, considering. After a pause and a long exhalation, he slipped it back onto the stack and bound the pile with the band. The last letter had been full of joy at news of his visit. But this was the holidays. There was no point in giving in to unjustified hopes when so much time had passed.

After a time, he put the letters back in the pack and pulled out a book. The silence seemed to close a curtain between them that had temporarily dropped. He looked over at the woman seated beside him, and she met his glance.

"Are you going to be OK?" she asked, tenderness and understanding in her voice.

"Thanks. Quite all right."

She looked away at something happening down the aisle that caught her attention. The snack cart was coming their way, finally. He thought he noted a film of moisture lining her eye. She blinked rapidly and whisked her cheek with the back of her hand, and it was gone.

"You OK?" he asked.

"Yes, fine." She said, almost too softly to hear.

December 22, 1984
South of Tallahassee, 9:30 p.m.

Connie Chappell's Honda Civic sped down the Crawfordville Highway toward the coast from Tallahassee. Brad sat with his long legs folded uncomfortably under the dash, but he had ceased noticing that he didn't fit. He kept staring sidelong at Connie's face in the orange light of the dashboard's instrument panel. Some raucous garage band noise was playing over the university's student radio station. She turned to him and said, "Sorry you don't fit in my car. You look like a praying mantis, legs and arms all folded up." She gave him a quick side long glance. "Who would a guessed you'd grow so tall?"

It had been a long flight, his mind preoccupied with thoughts of this reunion with Connie, the "sister" who had been the object of his thoughts for a very long time. Instead of what he wanted to say, he blurted out irritably, "Connie, for God's sake! What do you hear in music like that?"

"This one isn't so bad. There are some real door bangers on here sometimes." She punched down the volume a few notches and looked over at the new and improved Brad. He was tall! She could hardly believe the

198

young man who had replaced the boy who'd left a few years ago. He had been just a tad taller before his fifteenth birthday. Now, at twenty-one, he looked like a refugee from someone's basketball pickup team. As winter set in, he had started to lose the sunbaked tan, but his hours outdoors had given him a toughened look, making him appear much older than his years. "Honestly, Brad, there's often some very pretty stuff on this station that you won't hear on any of the top-forty or hard-rock stations. This is still a backwater part of the world when you leave the edges of the campus."

"I suppose you're right; I just hope this Seattle sound doesn't last very long, it makes me afraid of what'll come next." He suddenly remembered something and pulled a small plastic statuette from his carry-on gym bag. "Merry early Christmas." The four-inch-tall image of a Spielberg-styled alien was dressed in a Hopi pattern poncho tied at the waist with a piece of hemp cord. She looked up from the statuette to Brad. He said, "I customized it with the clothing." He fiddled with the little belt, straightening the miniature bow. "This would be an ant person, female." He gave a short little puff of a laugh. "A man's poncho would probably be white. That is, if there was any connection with Hopi dressing styles and the clothing of the ancient visitors."

"Are you saying ancient because you don't know if there have been any recent visitors?"

"Yeah, I guess so. At least the Hopi aren't telling anyone if they're still coming." He looked out the window at the passing town's dimmed lights. Many of the stores were lit only by red and green strings of Christmas lights. Nothing was open after 10:00 p.m. in this part of the world. "Doesn't look like much has changed here."

"No, not here. But you have. I can't believe looking at you, Brad."

"What?" he asked, feigning surprise and knowing the reason. He shrank a little in the seat, but with so little padding on the Honda's cushion, he wasn't successful in achieving much. His knees pressed into the dash.

"You've grown so tall, and so handsome!" She tried not to let the last out, but it came of its own force, not quite whispered.

"Con?" He pointed ahead to the county courthouse. "Pull into that parking lot for a second." She did as he said and pulled into a poorly lit, empty parking place near the courthouse annex. Before she could react, he reached his left arm behind her head and pulled her to him. He placed his right hand on her cheek and slowly but deliberately pulled her close. Turning slightly, he gave her a long, gentle kiss. He would have immediately let go if there were any resistance, but there was none. Instead, he felt her breathe in long and slow through her nose as they pressed together in the tiny car. Both of them felt expanded, by breath, by each other, by something eternal and something they'd dared not name in the years of off-and-on correspondence. In a moment, he felt her tongue push gently between his lips, and they shifted in their seats to allow the kiss to linger. Brad felt his head swim. He had dated a few times at his Nevada high school and had a few relationships at Arizona State, but this was Connie! She had been the object of his dreams and fantasies since they'd met over seven years earlier.

He pulled back. Connie was breathing harder and couldn't, or wouldn't, break his gaze. "Con, I have dreamt of that kiss for too many years." He realized that his own breathing was audible. "I hope you don't take that the wrong way. It was very hard to be your 'brother' in Apalach, and it always felt strange and dishonest to be your friend 'Willa.' Being a pen pal for so long has felt really weird, and it kept near the surface a lot of feelings I had a long time ago. You've graduated, and I still have grad school to get through. I don't want to tie you down. I don't want to inhibit your choices." He paused, catching his breath, and held a finger up for more time. "I need to get this out, and it's not coming out as I had rehearsed on the plane." After a moment, his breathing slowed. "You should know how I feel is all," he finally said. "And it's probably ridiculous, but I feel like I love you." He saw no change in Connie's eyes except maybe a little softening, but a small upturn in one side of her mouth was turning into one of her trademark lopsided grins.

"Brad—" she started.

"No, please, wait. I had to say that; if I'm way outta line, if I'm your favorite little brother, if you still have a thing for Denny, or your editor in Chapel Hill, I understand." He couldn't stop his mouth from making words. "I've probably been stoking a fire on my own for too long, and maybe I should have been a realist, but—"

"Brad," she said, again trying to cut in.

He blundered on, "If I am being childish, just—"

"Bradley, hush!" He stopped talking. She pulled his head down to hers and kissed him again. After a few minutes, they stopped for air. Headlights coming down the county road beside them lit up their car, revealing a light fogging on the windows.

He took a long, deep breath as the car passed. "We should go. Are you sure that Mom would be up? It's almost midnight."

Connie let out a long breath, blowing it out through puckered lips.

She caught her breath and replied, "You know she turned into a night owl at the casinos. I'd be surprised if she was asleep."

"You didn't tell her when the flight was?"

"I didn't actually tell her I really was coming." They continued on in a strangely uncomfortable silence, leaving the county seat behind. She placed her hand gently on his knee. Brad felt the pressure through his jeans as a physical connection. He placed his own hand on hers and grasped her fingers in his. As they rolled through the last few miles in darkness lit only by the dashboard, he was wondering what would happen next. After the avalanche of his pent-up feelings, misgivings, hopes, and doubts, he wasn't sure what to say. Connie made the left turn onto Wakulla Beach Road and rolled to a stop short of his driveway.

She turned in her seat to face him. "Brad, I don't for a minute regret what just happened." She put a forefinger to his lips to shush him as he began to talk. "I have wondered about us for at least as long as you have. Every time Denny kissed me, I thought about you—well, almost every time. And whenever I watched the *Lou Anne II* heading out, I thought of you. I think I became reluctant to write more because it almost hurt to just talk about nothing, family, etc. Anything but us." He was staring at her mouth. She kissed him quickly and said, "I don't know if this is a mistake or not." She smiled her best lopsided grin, with her right cheek pulled back. "It doesn't feel like a mistake right now!" She put the Civic in gear and drove the short distance down the road and into the Hitchenses' driveway.

As the car rolled into the front parking area, the porch lights came on. Lights had been visible from the back of the house, probably the kitchen. As their footfalls on the porch began to be felt in the wood frame house, there was a movement in the hall. Brad peered through the sidelight beside the door and saw that it had been covered with a plastic coating that made it impossible to see in. A shape moved in the backlit interior darkness. It approached the door slowly, and the deadbolt turned.

Brad turned the knob and pulled it open. "Mom?"

"Oh, for heaven's sake, boy!" She relaxed her grip on an aluminum baseball bat. "You scared the bejeezus out of me!" She saw Connie standing behind him, grinning fiercely. "You scallywags! Get in here. Both of you come on in; you're letting all the heat out."

Hugs were exchanged all around, and they settled into the living room. Lucy Hitchens insisted on some hot chocolate and asked Brad to get a fire started. He saw that she had fat lighter and logs in the wood rack and soon had a small fire crackling. Connie settled into a couch cushion with the holiday edition of Southern Living. Brad followed his mother into the kitchen to help with the hot chocolate and, coming up from behind her, gave her a hug.

"It's good to be home." He almost said something about it being too bad that Dad wasn't there and checked himself. "I'm glad we surprised you."

Lucy Hitchens turned from the pan of heating milk. "You said you wouldn't be able to make it home this Christmas." She scowled unconvincingly. "You ought to be whipped, scaring your poor mother like that." Seeing him up close, she noticed that he was a good eight inches taller than she was, and she noticed the little red smear around his mouth. She peered closer and rubbed at the light film of lipstick. Her eyes opened wide, and she hissed playfully, "Bradley Delaney Hitchens! What have you ...?" She looked over her shoulder toward the living room door. "You and Connie?" she whispered. Connie sank a little lower into the couch cushions and flushed red.

Brad smiled, embarrassed. "Yeah, we were sort of glad to see each other again.

"Well, I guess. Isn't she supposed to be like a sister?"

He jammed his hands in his pockets. "That's for the Feds, Mom."

"But she's family!" It was hard for her to keep her voice down.

"Yeah, Mom, but she's a cousin about four and a half times removed." Brad looked toward the living room. Grinning sheepishly, he said, "Besides, I really like her. I have since forever."

Lucy looked up at him and said in a serious tone he hadn't heard in a years, "Boy! Can I trust you to behave if I offer her to stay the night? It's too late to send her home to Apalach."

"Yeah. Yes, ma'am, of course."

Lucy heard the milk begin to simmer and turned to stir the steaming liquid. Swiping her thumb over the last of the lipstick smear, she said, "Well, it sure looks like she likes you, too." She moved the pot toward the three waiting mugs and poured the hot milk. "Here, Bradley, grab two of these mugs and take one to your *sister.*"

December 23, 1984
Wakulla Beach, Into the Woods

202

The next morning, Brad, yawning, started a pot of coffee and turned to check the fridge for breakfast possibilities. Standing at the open door, he looked through the back windows into the gray light of predawn. His father's F-250 was still in its place under the pole barn! Forgetting breakfast, he bolted to the backyard to check out the truck. The screen door closed with a loud smack as he leapt down the stairs and crossed the yard. The white roof, light-blue hood, and most other horizontal surfaces were discolored by terra cotta silt deposited by hundreds of clouds of dust rolling off the graded road to Wakulla Beach. Cemented into place by subsequent cycles of dew and drying, the scale looked permanent. Brad spit on the door near the driver's side window and rubbed it. He was rewarded with a spot of smeared mud over good paint. Checking the tires, he discovered all but the right rear had good pressure but looked like they were beginning to suffer from dry rot. He heard the spring on the back door screech and looked up to see his mother smiling from the porch.

She called to him, "Come on in, Brad. I'll make up a batch of biscuits. I've got a fresh bottle of molasses and plenty of eggs for frying."

Connie came into the kitchen, combing her wavy red hair back into a clump that she secured with a double turn of a hair band, and sat down at the table. Brad thought, *man, she really looks great with no makeup.*

Lucy came over with cups and a coffeepot. "Children, coffee, anyone?" There were nods and grunts in response. Looking at Brad, she added. "Behave yourself last night?"

"Yes, Mom," he answered, with a roll of the eyes that took him back six or seven years. He looked over at Connie for support.

"Yes, ma'am! Absolutely, Mrs. Hitchens, er, Williams. You've raised a perfect gentleman."

Turning to Connie, Lucy said, "That's okay, Con. We're Hitchens again; seems proper for hereabouts."

Brad noted that some of her Southernisms, missing when they were living out West, were returning. "Mom," Brad said, "thanks for keeping the truck. It means a lot to me. It may have saved my life by getting me outta here."

"No, problem, really. It just sits there. I look at it, and it still just sits there. I've been reluctant to even get into the cab. I still feel Whit's presence in the driver's seat. I feel like I can smell him there."

"Well, thanks, anyway. Is there any chance that I could take it back to school with me? It would give me a chance to get around on my own and never take a bus or cab again."

"That, my love, is why it's still here." She stooped to pull an iron flat pan from the base drawer of the stove. In a fluid motion, she pulled open a kitchen junk drawer, found the ring with two Ford keys on it, tossed them to Bradley, and still turning, set the pan on the stove. "I would have sold it last summer when I came back but thought you ought to have first option. With that huge tool bed on the back, it's definitely not a girly truck." She straightened the pan on the stove and turned on the gas. "That's your truck now. And really, if you want to thank someone, you'd need to thank your Aunt Sue and Sunny for getting it back home and fixed." She looked over her shoulder at him. "We can go up to the courthouse before you leave and put it in your name."

"I don't know what to say." Brad raised empty palms wide.

"Say, 'Thanks, Mom, that's a great thing you did for me.'"

"Thanks, Mom, that's a great thing you did for me," he parroted.

Connie laughed. "You two are a riot together. I should'a guessed."

Lucy raised an eyebrow at her. "You ain't seen nothin', guurl," she drawled through thin lips in an exaggerated Southwestern accent. "Seriously, Bradley, you really ought to thank your Aunt Sue for getting everything set up here at the house, taking care of the truck, packing away everything. She and Sunny buttoned up the place while we were, mmm, incognito? Undercover? Whatever you'd call it—not home!" She wiped her flour-dusted hands on her denim apron. "I can't believe I almost fell into a permanent life in Las Vegas of all places."

Brad said, "The place isn't half bad if you can get out of the city. The high desert is actually a different kind of pretty."

"Yeah, but that city was built for people whose morals are no tighter than an unzipped body suit—drunks and eloping honeymooners."

Connie pitched in, "Don't forget divorcees."

"Right, and drunk divorcees looking for some strange."

Brad asked innocently, "Strange what?" In response, Lucy threw a dish towel at him. They all laughed.

Digging into his plate of eggs and biscuits, Brad asked, "Mom, have you ever thought of going back down into the woods to talk or listen to whoever's there?"

She whirled on him with a flash of something in her eyes that he didn't like.

Connie saw a dark, troubled moment and said, "Ka-Litan. His name's Ka-Litan."

Lucy looked at her. "Now don't you start, too."

Connie retreated to the back of her chair. "Yes, ma'am."

"Mom," Brad cut in. "She's right, the voice in the woods is a personality. Its, his name is … Ka-Li-Tan."

Lucy put her hands to her ears and turned away. "Yes, I know. He's some kind of space pilot from an intergalactic war, and he needs help." She slowly turned to face them both. "And if only God would speak to me someday that clearly and distinctly and tell me he was going to take me into his heart, I'd gladly walk off into the ocean or whatever he told me to do." She took a deep breath. Exhaling, she turned back around to face the stove and then spun back to them. Pointing a spatula at the window, she said, "You two can do what you want out there, but I'm not sure I want to hear about him anymore. I ruined your childhood and my marriage and did probably the most foolish, stupid, idiotic thing I've ever done because of that damned voice in the woods."

She leaned back against the stove, sagging, and with her face hidden by her hands, she said, "Bradley, I went through this years ago? That 'thing' drove me to the far edge of sanity. If your dad had ever gone to hear it with me just once, if he'd had the strength to admit or to tell me that maybe I wasn't loony—if he had gone to listen, maybe I could have stayed and lived with the dreams and the voices."

"Mom, all that is behind us." He opened his arms wide, their arc encompassing the three of them. "We have all heard him or her or it or whatever. Connie and I heard it at the same time. Talked with it and had a three-way conversation. What does that tell you? Does it tell you that we are all crazy? Could you have done anything about Dad? No. He was in the wrong place at the right time."

He stood up to face his mother. She responded by hugging him. He was the taller one now, and he hugged her close and bent to speak softly into her ear. "You aren't crazy, Mom. And you couldn't have saved Dad or prevented those bastards from chasing me all over creation. None of this is your fault. Dad died telling me to get the hell out of here and go hide. If he had heard it, I'm sure he would have protected you too. Maybe he was too boneheaded. He loved you. I heard him crying at times when he thought no one would hear. But all that is past. There is a future."

He looked at Connie. "Maybe we'll go back out there, maybe not. I don't know that I can believe in ghosts from space. I do know your alien encounter self-help group in Vegas was made up of mostly kooks and groupies for the few writers who were profiting as supposed experts on Area 51 and Roswell. But so what? We know what we know! Who knows? Maybe there are other Ka-Litans out there that didn't crash and are running around scaring people. I know that you aren't crazy, Mom; Connie's not crazy, and I'm not crazy." He looked back at Connie. "I'm not crazy, right?"

Connie smirked. "Well, maybe a little, but there's no accounting for some people. Maybe that desert water had something in it."

Brad said, "Mom, please. I won't ask you again if you don't want to go back out there, but I won't sneak around, and Connie and me—"

"I," Lucy corrected. "Connie and I."

"Okay, Connie and I will be going back out there, and we shouldn't have to hide or sneak, when you know what the real deal is. Okay?"

Lucy took a deep breath and answered, "Okay." She opened her arms to welcome them both into them. They plunged into a family hug, and Lucy sighed. "You two just be careful, ya hear?"

~ ~ ~

Connie set out for home at midmorning, leaving Brad to clean the mud off his truck. Lucy had a short list of handyman chores around the house, so he drove north toward Crawfordville to find a car wash, a hardware store, and the best price on a set of tires. With the Ace place behind him and new rubber under the truck, he had planned to take the worst of the dirt off with the power wand at a do-it-yourself wash bay. If the day got up into the fifties, he'd finish the job in the backyard. As he pulled into the bay, he noticed the cars around him and immediately behind him. Nothing unusual, so maybe he was being paranoid. Maybe Mom had been right; maybe he really was no longer a "person of interest."

Heading home, he again noted the cars behind him. He pulled off in front of a small strip center and noticed that a small white pickup about three vehicles behind had pulled off at the lumber store across the street. The driver didn't get out of the cab and seemed to search in the glove compartment. The white pickup had also been parked across from the tire store. He immediately pulled back into the traffic and saw the pickup turn onto the highway again about three to four vehicles back. Coincidence or paranoia? There's a simple test for that, he thought.

As he neared the coastal highway, he pulled into a gas station and got out as if to fill up. The white pickup went through the intersection but pulled off into an adjacent lot about three stores down. Not a coincidence and not paranoia!

He acted as if he'd forgotten his wallet and drove home where he waited for a minute on the porch as the white pickup passed his driveway and headed toward the beach. All he could see inside was a dark profile, aviator glasses, and a baseball cap. He waved in a neighborly fashion and then went in and shared that they were under surveillance again.

Finding his mother in the laundry room he told her about being tailed and described the truck to her. "Brad, do you think they know it's you? Are you sure it's you that's being followed or just the residents of this house?" She reached up and cupped his face in her palms. "You really don't look like the youngster who left here seven years ago."

"I don't know, Mom. Just be aware of that white Toyota pickup, and don't go anywhere isolated like the refuge or down to the beach unless you know someone else is down there." He pointed out the window as the white pickup drove past.

Lucy looked at her son with pride. He was as protective as his father. "Honey, I don't go much of anywhere."

"Would you call the sheriff and see if you can get a deputy to look in from time to time? If you see that truck again, call the 911 dispatch immediately."

"Yes, sweetie, and thanks for worrying over me."

"I do worry, Mom. I spent about six, seven months trying hard to stay hid. We spent the last seven years in another life. Last spring, you decided we were safe, and I dropped my guard. Now that we're back here, or maybe it's 'cause I'm back here, the bastards are back and tailing us." He gave a long sigh of frustration. "At least they don't seem to want to make us go away. Sometimes I wish they'd just come up and knock on the door!"

~ ~ ~

Brad made a sandwich for his walk, put on his canteen belt, and prepared to go on a hike. He checked that there were no eyes on him from either the coastal highway, which was visible in winter, or the beach road. Satisfied, he headed into the woods to find that his trail was gone. Any sign of it was overgrown with vegetation. He knew enough trees to make his way in and thought maybe it was just as well if he let the place stay overgrown. If he and Connie could find the spot, there was no reason to sling blade the undergrowth or blaze trees to mark the way.

Forty-five minutes later, he saw the landmark cypress trunk and its immense tangle of roots. For an overcast December afternoon, it was unusually light in the forest. There was only a thin winter canopy, and he was glad for the bright light. As he approached the titi thicket, he reached out through his thoughts to his friend.

"Hello, Ka-Litan, I am Brad." He looked around as if there were something to be seen that would reveal the source of the voice. "I have come back to visit."

welcome, B-rad ... bring friend Ka-nee?

Brad stopped halfway through a tight bend in the thicket and tried to place the voice. Was it heard or felt? Did it come from inside his temples? Where did he feel it? "No, Connie is not here today."

He wondered what else he could learn?

learn much with Ka-nee ... like talk to Ka-nee ... Ka-nee come again?

"Yes, she will probably come again to talk to you. Connie likes to talk to Ka-Litan, too."

B-rad gone long time ... Ka-Litan learn time here ... find radio and learn to read radio

"Radio—you can listen to radio?" Brad thought this was pretty profound. Radio implied a physical receiver of some kind.

radio not always ... not hear radio some time ... B-rad?

"Yes?" Although there was only a slight inflection in the voice, this last did sound like a question.

is light ... is dark ... B-rad see sun named sol

Yes, it is light out; the sun is ..." He thought about how to express it. "Our star is about fifteen degrees past zenith." Then, silently, he added, "Do you know zenith?"

yes, maximum altitude ... height above observer

"Very good, Ka-Litan." He smiled at this degree of possible conversation. Maybe he could finally get somewhere. "Ka-Litan learn much."

all Ka good navigator ... ship computer good too

"Is your ship nearby?"

There was a pause. *yes* A longer pause. *ship near*

"Where?" He scanned around him for any bumps in the terrain that would have indicated a crater mound. "Where is your ship?"

Jai close ... not know word ...   Again, a pause.   ... below

"Below what?"

below B-rad

Brad jumped up. He had been sitting at the edge of the pool casually watching some silver-sided minnows flitting under the few floating leaves and half wondering how minnows found isolated pools like this. Connie had been right!

"Below me?" He suddenly saw the sinkhole in a new light. It was long, narrow, and shallow at the south end, much deeper at the north end. He had always thought that it was a result of a collapsed cavern below ground.

yes ... Litan ship Jai below B-rad

"Is Ka-Litan's ship named Jay?"

Litan ship computer name Jai. The was a slight difference in the pronunciation, and Brad played with it on his tongue a few times.

"I see. You said you now have time. How did you understand our time?"

Ka-nee help Litan understand ... day one, Ka-nee say, three, two, one, mark one ... day two, Ka-nee say three, two, one, mark two ... mark one ... mark two ... one day

Brad thought that was very easily done and silently congratulated Connie for figuring it out. "Litan, there are 365.25 days in one solar year. Did you understand that from Connie?"

Ka-nee tell Litan, 365 days   A pause.   ... is wrong?

"Yes, a better calculation is 365.25 days."

There was a brief pause, and Brad wondered what kind of computer his friend had on board. The answer came quickly, *earth year is .8995 Dzuran Coalition standard year*

As soon as Brad could form his next question, the answer came.

standard Dzuran Coalition year is 406.2 earth days

Brad considered this. It seemed reasonable that that period would be in a sweet spot around a star, neither too hot nor too cold. Now that he knew this, the next question was obvious.

"Litan, how long have you been on this planet? How long since you dropped or crashed here?"

After a brief pause, *Ka-Litan drop in this system and fall on earth 428 years, 25 days, 2 hours*

This seemed incredible. He thought, "How has he stayed alive all these years?"

Litan rest ... rest right word ... not talk, not think, rest

Brad got the gist of his thoughts. "Yes, rest is the right word." He thought, *"Stasis?"*

stasis? The question came immediately.

"Yes, stasis is long, long rest." There was no response.

He looked at the pond with an interest in its less-than-random shape. Behind him was the shallow hole left by the root ball of the fallen cypress. It lined up with the hole in the long axis of the elongated pool at his feet. This was the shallow end, covered in titi that grew around the shallow slopes at the shallow end. As the sides of the pool steepened, vegetation changed to mosses and water-loving grasses. He looked back at the base of the tree. If a spaceship made a shallow dive into the ground, a piece could have broken off a hundred or so yards away on a long-dead tree or as it began to plow into the soil.

He wished his dad were there to check out his developing theory. If a shallow trench had been dug by the impact, it might have been partially filled by now with organic matter and who knew what. The pool did gradually deepen to a significant depth away from the thicket. He didn't know how deep it was at the other end. There was a midden beyond the deep end that he had always assumed was one of the hundreds of shell-and-shard middens along the coast.

His dad had told him that Apalachee and later Seminole Indian middens were all over the Florida flatwoods, and there were some huge ones up in Leon and Jefferson Counties where the big settlements were. The ones used for dry camp sites in the flatwoods usually had flat tops littered with shell, flat, fire-baked pieces of limestone or marl, broken pottery shards, and the occasional protected and preserved piece of fire-hardened stone. They had often found evidence of trade goods, cutting chips, blades, and arrow tips that had come down from the hard rock country of North Georgia in exchange for salted seafood. The midden here was just like so many others. Then opening his mind to what it might have looked like before, he wondered if the Indian occupants had flattened the top of an impact mound to make it more useable or if that shape weren't man-made, but a remnant of dirt thrown up by the shallow impact of Ka-Litan's ship.

They were all in a row. Now that he looked at it as a set of unnatural shapes, he realized that the location of the broken metal under the cypress was almost due south. It was at one end of a line with the elongated trench of the increasingly deep pool in the middle leading to the midden to the north of the deep end.

What if it was not a midden? Brad could almost hear his dad's voice giving the history lesson. If this were a flattened structure instead, a refuge from high water, it would be different structurally. He would have to learn more about this subject and return. Maybe he could figure out how to fit in his electives coursework about the Indians of the Southeastern United States in the anthropology department, as well as a get a Masters in metallurgy?

"Actually," he mused, "there's no real need to find out about the middens. I just need to find out more about Litan, how big the ship was, how deep it went." And, he realized, to get the artifact back, he'd have to get certified as a diver. Well, he'd better get busy!

The thought came from below.

not know deep. And in what Brad had learned was a questioning tone, he added, *Litan deep?*

"Yes, friend, Litan, you are a deep soul." Brad looked into the darker waters of the deep end of the pool. *Somewhere down there, if my dreams have been sent by him, was a spaceship, a small maneuverable fighter.* And if his dreams were any measure of his dawning reality, it would have low or depleted reserves of chemical fuel boosters and any amount of possible damage to its guidance systems. For all he knew, there might be additional missing pieces, other than the one he had found.

"Ka-Litan?" He cast the thought into the pool.

yes, B-rad

"Are you a memory? Are you real? What are you?"

Litan is Ka ... Dzura warrior leader ... Dzura warriors fight Erran warriors ... Ka-Litan fall on earth in fight with Erran He added, *Ka-Litan rest long time here ... Ka-Litan here long time*

Bradley looked up at a string of clouds sliding in from the west that were likely to curtain the bright winter sky in cold, slate gray. "I must go now. I will come back soon."

I will talk you ... send talk you

Brad barely noticed the unusual phrasing as he turned to go. He had to leave soon if the clouds were going to bring rain.

Chapter 12

If you confront anyone who has lied with the truth, he will usually admit it—often out of sheer surprise. It is only necessary to guess right to produce your effect.

Agatha Christie

December 25-27, 1984
Apalachicola

The clouds brought rain, a cold drizzle that lasted through Christmas. He had shared a brief but warm Christmas morning of gifts and laughter with Lucy and his Aunt Susan and enjoyed never before heard stories of two young girls growing up in 1950s Tallahassee. In a post leftover turkey-and-sweet-potato-pie slump, he spent the mid-afternoon packing and checking the truck for his trip back to school. Finding it hard to say good-bye on the phone, he told Connie that he'd drop in on his way back to Arizona to spend a day or two with the Chappells. When he thought about what was important, he decided he could afford to miss a day in his last semester at Arizona State. He'd rather spend a day with Connie and his adopted family.

~ ~ ~

Master Sergeant Jenks was having a bad day. He'd been called on the third day of his two-week liberty and told to pack his travel kit and head back down to Florida. They assured him that he could take his two weeks back in Montana when this mini-tour finished. The only good thing that could possibly come from the assignment was the occasional seafood dinner. Usually, he dined on prepackaged food from a gas station or fast food with, maybe, one decent meal per assignment. There was not much fresh ocean fish in Montana.

So far, the only bright spot had been checking in on the boy's girlfriend. Jesus, was she hot! He usually went for mocha, but this freckled redheaded girl had a body that could make him consider changing brands. How did this kid get that lucky? He must have some kind of mojo working. He thought of his last girlfriend and their ski trip to Jackson Hole. His mind

212

drifted to the white powder he knew was covering the Bitterroot slopes near his home in Montana. He was taking one of his favorite black diamond runs down a steep, narrow access road flanked by jutting boulders or sheer drops into snow-packed spruce. It was a high-contrast world of snowy whites shaded in cerulean blue-grey against dark-green spruce, damp rocks, and bright, high-altitude blue sky. The access road opened onto a sloped meadow that in summer served as a mountain bike terrain field and in winter, a freestyle jump heaven. Yawning, he shook his head back into the present.

In Florida, it had been overcast or raining for three days but only cold enough to warrant a sweater or windbreaker. To blend in with his environment, he had rented a white Ford Taurus, which he kept dirty, its interior made to look lived in. He thought his predecessor had been made but wasn't sure. From the surveillance agent's description, the Hitchens boy's dodge and drive maneuvers a few days ago had been amateurish, so he'd traded the Toyota truck in for an old pea-green Nova. His mark hadn't seemed to notice the tail, but he wasn't sure, so he'd traded the Nova in for the Taurus. Jenks had taken over the Taurus. Its white hood was a surrogate snow field spread out before him as he tried to fight boredom. Motion in his zone shook him out of his trance—off the powder run and back to the Florida flatwoods. The partially rusted, blue-and-white F-250 with the big work box was entering the road. It could only be an easier mark to tail if he drove a yellow school bus. Jenks let a buffer of three cars go by and pulled into line. Brad was headed west. Jenks figured he was off to his girlfriend's house.

He began to lose some buffer between the Taurus and the truck ahead as cars pulled off. Finally, Jenks dropped back so far that he lost sight of the truck and had to look down side roads to make sure the truck hadn't pulled off. Then, catching sight of the target, he'd let another buffer vehicle pull in front of him and remained two or three cars back. The F-250 was behind a small Japanese import that he couldn't get a fix on from his distance. His mark didn't seem to want to pass.

The short train of vehicles rolled across the Ochlockonee River bridge into the next county. The F-250 was three vehicles in front of him, and there were no side roads of any importance through the area. From the oncoming lane, a center console sport fisherman being towed by a dual-wheel Dodge caught his attention. Nice rig! He admired the rig in his rearview mirror, and when he looked ahead again, the F-250 was gone. What the hell! here did that little shit go? Glancing to his right, he saw a swirl of dust filling one of the pine canyons created by a forest access road. The timber companies constructed the roads usually at half-mile intervals if the wetlands permitted it. They usually were cut as straight as the section lines, property lines, or sinkholes allowed.

There was no reason for a vehicle to be on any of these roads in this crappy weather. He pulled around and edged past the road from the other direction. There was a fresh, two-rut trail marked in the thin lining of the timber-access road. He circled around again and edged in, thought about it, and paused. Why would the little creep drive off into these woods? Maybe he just needed to piss. He backed out onto the road and drove to the next convenience store. Twenty minutes later, the two-toned F-250 passed, still headed west. Again, Jenks got in line, three vehicles back.

He followed his mark, Bradley or William or Willa or whatever he might be called now, through the next two small towns. Despite its name, the coastal highway was seldom in sight of water. Now it was right on the water. Nearly calm bay waters spread out to his left protected by barrier islands from the slightly more agitated Gulf. He noted undeveloped land of palmetto, pine, and scrub punctuated by isolated homes on his right as he sped by. If there were more than a hundred feet to water, a bay-front house filled the space, with every other one sporting a boat trailer. A car braked and pulled out of the line ahead, leaving one car between the Taurus and the pickup. Blinkers and all, the Ford pickup turned onto a paved county road heading north. Was he testing again? He slowed to widen the gap and made the right turn.

He was alarmed to see that he was approaching a sheriff's office to the right, but the mark didn't slow and kept going. Jenks hadn't checked out this roadway and was unsure of where it might lead. Was it a shortcut to Apalachicola? Was the kid taking him on a wild goose chase? Now, he was tailing a half-mile back with no buffer and the kid wasn't even doing the speed limit. If he was made, he was made, and there was no fixing it. The arrow-straight county road took a sharp left and crossed a tidal creek. As the truck went into the turn, Jenks saw blue smoke pouring from its exhaust as it sped away. The road took a correcting sharp turn to the right, and the truck was not in sight. How the hell had he done that? Was there a boat launch back at the bridge? Where did he pull around? He saw an access road ahead on the left and decided to turn around.

~ ~ ~

Brad, cautious as ever, had noticed a possible tail as he'd passed through the small fishing village of Carrabelle on the way to Apalachicola. A couple of jigs and jogs and he'd confirmed it. Almost to Apalach, he took the county road turn off to Bristol to see if the Taurus would follow. Moments later, his heart rate jumped when the white Ford Taurus made the turn behind him. No matter how slowly he drove, the car hung back. This was it. Confrontation!

He'd thought about it for years in Arizona. Who were these sons of bitches? Were they the same guys who had killed his dad? The same team who had killed Professor Hill and his assistant? He took a sharp left off the road, pulled in about a hundred yards, and turned the truck so that it faced the highway. Nervously, he took his 410 shotgun from behind the seat. He crouched behind the open driver's door and waited. Despite the chilly afternoon, sweat instantly filled his armpits. The acrid smell of fear was all he noticed as his vision tunneled down to the end of the two-rut sand road. Please, please, please be a civilian! Please keep driving; don't pull in.

Almost as soon as he had the thought, the Taurus pulled in. Anger took over his fear, and bile rose in his throat as he moved out from behind the truck door. Striding forward with the barrels pointed down, Bradley closed half the distance between the vehicles, raised the barrels, pulled the first trigger, and blew out the Ford's radiator. He had one more shot without reloading. He continued forward at a fast walk with the black holes of the double barrels pointed at the face of the young black agent in the driver's seat. "Hands up, you son of a bitch!" he shouted. "If I don't see hands in one second, you won't have to wonder how long it will take me to reload this mini-cannon."

"Wait! Don't shoot!" Jenks's hands were in the air. He didn't trust Southern rednecks any more than he trusted the secessionist skinheads back home. Damn! How did this get so wrong so fast? He had to blame himself for underestimating this young man whom he had still thought of as a kid. This was no kid walking up to the door. He began to wonder if he would live to see 1985 and the snow-covered ski trails back home again. This idiot kid, this easy mark, was about to make gator bait out of his short career. "Look, kid, my hands are up. For Christ's sake, don't shoot that thing."

"Don't worry, secret agent man, it's only bird shot. It might not even kill you. It could, at the very least, remove your face and any chance of seeing home again, so don't think you've got me painted into any comfortable picture." He couldn't believe his own ferocity. *Whose voice was this? What was he doing?*

Brad approached the Taurus slowly, unlatched the car door, and stepped to the side, leaving ample room for the door to swing free. He used all the control he had to keep his voice firm, low, and threatening. "Okay, Mr. Secret Agent, slowly open the door and step out; I want to see two hands above your shoulders at all times. Understood?"

Jenks was well and truly pissed with himself. He had allowed the kid to take control of the situation. He hadn't expected him to be armed, and, above all, he remembered the damned shotgun from the kid's farmhouse. "Understood! Take it easy! Please?" He tried to sound genuinely scared and submissive; he didn't have to try hard. He slowly got out of the Taurus and into a fine, drizzling morning rain.

"If I disappear, there will be no place in the world for you to hide," Jenks said. He thought what kind of bluff might get him out of this pile of stink he'd stepped into. "If I don't call in," he looked up at his watch, "in three hours, I'm considered MIA, and you are moved from surveillance and report to removal and cleanup. You don't want cleanup, 'cause it usually means that more than just you are included in the cleanup detail."

"So that's why Dr. Hill and his TA were killed?" Brad's anger was boiling in his voice now. "Who was collateral for whom?" He was shouting now. "Was Dad on their list, or were they on his list?" He had to think to let his finger rest on the side of the trigger guard so he wouldn't actually kill this SOB. "What is it about a little bit of mystery metal that makes my government, our government, want to make people disappear? This isn't Chile or Venezuela of some other banana fucking republic! This is the God Blessed US of A!" He was just about vented and needed to think. "Get down on your knees!" When Jenks hesitated, he shouted, "Get down, now."

"Listen, kid, Brad, you are not on anyone's cleanup list, but that will change if I don't call in." He slowly dropped to one knee and then the other. He looked up at the kid. Hitchens's face was transformed. It was like he'd taken a pill and was turning into the hulk or something. His rage was palpable. Dribbles of rain ran down the transformed face.

Now, Master Sergeant Jenks, undercover for the Air Force Office of Special Investigations, was beyond worried; he was scared. He could die any minute now.

The angry kid behind the double barrels shouted again. "Now down on your butt, you Blue Book son of a bitch!"

"Bradley, there are things you probably have learned about the Blue Book report, pop culture, bad sci-fi, and who knows what, that are only hints of what might be going down." He was trying to think about what he could say and what he shouldn't tell even to, or especially to, his own executioner. Just keep him talking and maybe I can survive the afternoon. "Listen, I don't know much about the op that resulted in your dad's death."

"He didn't die, sumbitch! He was murdered! Dying is something you're supposed to do after a long, happy life. I watched his last breath. I sat while his hand got cold and limp." Bradley suppressed a sob. "I was fourteen years old. I hid in the damned trees while the sheriff's deputies muddled around looking for signs of burglary, but my dad told me it was a hit. He was shot because of that goddamned piece of metal." He paused to breathe. "Right? He died for a piece of metal? He couldn't tell you where it was hidden, so you shot him?"

Distancing himself from the reality of that night gone bad, Jenks said, "The report said he was shot because he reached for a gun." He almost had said "that gun," looking up its barrels. That would have gotten him killed. "The report says the team thought they were about to be shot with a shotgun and one of them fired." He looked up at the kid's face. It was now red, veins bulging in his neck. Jenks knew he didn't have long before the kid stressed out and he would be over.

Jenks reached deep to put on a show of calm. "What would it take for you to step back a few paces and let me talk to you about what my team is supposed to do and what may have gone wrong." He used the most soothing tone he could muster under gunpoint. "Can I talk to you a minute? Wouldn't you want to know what's behind all of this? Even if you do end up killing me, at least you'd know." The misting rain was thin, but he was now getting chilled. This is not how I want to die, he thought.

The two black holes of the shotgun's barrel lowered slightly, Brad's breathing slowly calmed, and he said, "With both hands up, sit Indian style, cross-legged. No fast moves. I'm going to step back here a bit, and we can talk." He added for effect, "Then I'll decide if you get to walk away or get digested by the last of the dinosaurs. These river gators would probably find your bleeding, not-quite-dead body in a matter of a few minutes. There's a big bull gator that lives under that bridge back there, so let's not get clever." He smiled as he finished the image. "Did you know that they don't kill you by biting? They drag you under until you drown. Then they'll stuff you under a log and protect your corpse while it gets ripe enough to eat."

217

Jenks swallowed hard and tried to think about what he could say and what might get him killed. He collected his thoughts, ignored the light drizzle, and began to talk.

~ ~ ~

Connie was standing on the curb talking with a girlfriend in front of one of the many gift shops when she saw the blue-and-white pickup coming down the bridge ramp. She jumped up and ran across the street to the northbound side. As the truck rolled up to the intersection, with every appearance of making the unobstructed left turn, she jumped out to the edge of the traffic lane and stuck out her thumb. At the last minute, Brad saw her, recognized her, and left four black skid marks on the pavement.

Grinning, she jumped into the cab. He looked bad and smelled worse. "Brad, are you all right? What's happened?" Her eyes widened in fear. "Is your mother okay?"

"In a minute." Brad slipped the truck into gear and pulled ahead to the end of Market Street. The new marina at the end of the road had replaced haphazard anchorages for a dozen or so boats with new dockage for the forty or more of the shrimper fleet. He saw the *Lou Anne II* tied up near the harbormaster's house. He turned off the truck and exhaled. The truck gave a few knocks before stalling, and he took another deep breath and let it out slowly, like his friend the Hopi medicine man had shown him. Doing so seemed to release the last of the shaking terrors that had followed him into town.

Three hours ago, he had left his house for the forty-five-minute drive to Apalachicola, been prey, turned hunter, become a captor, and almost murdered a special agent in the service of his own country. He wasn't sure where to start. He could not keep this in. He didn't want to keep it in. Trying to control his breathing, he slowly began to tell Connie all that had just happened and all that he had just learned about his watchers. He hoped that in doing so, he would be documenting the event for another set of ears and not putting her on a list of collateral dangers. He had to believe that Jenks would not be so stupid as to continue to follow him here. After all, he'd admitted he was going back to school in Arizona, and then too, he'd have to get the radiator in that Taurus replaced.

When the marina's overhead dock lights came on, he realized that it was almost dark, and that he was finally at ease. As he came to the end of the story, he looked over into Connie's eyes and saw concern, empathy, shared pain, and what? "Connie, as I was getting ready to leave the house earlier, I was—I don't know—stalling. I was undecided about going back to Arizona, transferring to Chapel Hill, or staying here. I—I don't know—" He took in her face; it was beautiful. Maybe he really was in love. Maybe he was foolish for even doubting it. Her lips were full and pink even in the acid light of the parking lot. The dozen or so most prominent freckles on either side of her nose were a little subdued, and her eyes lost their deep green-blue in this light.

Her elfin ears poked through the hastily pulled back hair, trying to get loose from an inadequate elastic band, and strands hung in thin curls around her temples. "God, please let me remember forever how you look right now!" She simply beamed back at him, dimples deepening

"Are you still OK with me spending a day or two with you and the folks before I go?" he asked. Tears began to well at the corners of her eyes, and a drop ran down her left cheek. He dabbed it with his cuff and leaned in to kiss the wet track below her eye.

She pressed into him, and they kissed, long and hard. Hugging, caressing, he explored all the shapes he had kept in memory or imagination. His hands ran up the knots of her spine under the heavy knit sweater and stopped at the unfamiliar construction of her bra clasp. He touched it clumsily, trying to figure out how it worked. Connie reached back, and in a second, it was loose. She did something approaching magic with it, and the contraption was off; she was still in the sweater, grinning impishly. In ten minutes, the truck was steamed over in the cool afternoon air, and in thirty minutes, it stopped moving on its springs. An hour later, properly composed, they went home to her house. A two-day stopover was just enough of a visit to let him pay respects and catch up properly before heading back to Tempe for his last semester.

December 29-30, 1984
On the Road

Late in the morning, two days after his encounter at gunpoint with Jenks and his heady session with Connie, Brad made it to Mobile. Hundreds of conflicting images flooded in, vying for attention. He could close his eyes and still see the man on his knees through the fore and aft sights on the shotgun. Was he really Air Force Special Ops? Images of Jenks were displaced regularly with thoughts of his passionate explorations with

Connie. How could the fates have conspired to have him stare down his fears and face up to his ultimate desires in one short afternoon?

The miles flew by, and he was surprised when he crossed the Alabama line into Louisiana. The overwhelming flood and ebb of emotion was so much better than any of the fantastic dreams he'd had since the last kiss. It was hard to tell if Chase and Lou Anne had been able to tell that there was any difference in them. He thought they knew that something had happened, but neither of them said anything.

Mississippi's southern stub went by so fast that he'd gotten the cruel impression that he was making great time. Then beyond Slidell, the extreme boredom of western Louisiana set in. Miles on end of elevated roadway through the Atchafalaya Basin led Bradley to pull off at the Flying J exit in Orange, Texas, to see if Phyllis was working. He remembered a lot about the trip west with Dink and his big, cherry-red rig. Phyllis was not on duty that night, so he ate his meal quietly and watched the interactions between drivers, waitresses, and the dazed and exhausted tourists.

He spent the second day of the trip in Texas heading west. From the Orange River to the Rio Grande at El Paso, Texas, was a full day of decreasing greenery and a return to the desert landscapes he had learned to appreciate. The streaked, cerulean winter clouds could not compare to the stacked cumulus giants against a deep-blue summer sky. On most trips through the desert, playing with the geometry of the cloud structures in his mind helped him get across the endless empty miles. His back and backside were sore; he hadn't appreciated how old the suspension in the F-250 was. Finally, El Paso's lights appeared on the horizon as a pale-gray glow before he rounded a bend and the glaring lights of the suburbs came into view.

As he lay spread-eagled and half clothed on the hard motel bed, exhausted from the day's drive, his mind turned to Ka-Litan and his many mysteries. What kind of spacecraft was buried under the deep end of the pool? How could Litan have stayed alive for so long? Hundreds of years? Was it possible that there really was such a thing as stasis? Science fiction writers had invented stasis as the only way to get to distant star systems in one lifetime. If Litan could stay asleep or control his metabolism, how was it that he could wake or revive whenever someone came near? How did any of that really work? How long was a lifetime for a Dzuran warrior? How did they communicate?

He could almost convince himself of some sort of mass delusion, something in the air, anything except space aliens if it weren't for the metal artifact. What was it Litan had said as he was leaving? "Talk you soon?" No, he'd never heard Litan say or express "soon." "Send you?" It had the sense of "Talk to you later" or "I'll send you."

"Send talk you!" That was it. How could Brad only talk to him when he was within a few hundred yards of the pool but have vivid dreams from a thousand miles away?

Brad lay in the quiet of his cheap west Texas motel room, trying to recall the last conversation he'd had with Litan. The sounds of late-night interstate traffic rushing by had been his soundtrack after finding that the TV only got one channel and it was fuzzy. Bright parking lot lights flavored with neon filtered through the edges of the room's curtains. He longed for the familiar comforts of his dorm room at Arizona State. As sleep began to edge in, he wondered about Connie's dorm room in Chapel Hill. She'd be out of her graduate program next spring. He was undecided about what to do after graduation; he decided that undecided was good enough for now. Inevitably, his thoughts alternated between Connie's living with him in his room and shopping for apartments. Maybe he should apply for grad school at Chapel Hill? For her last semester? But not that night; that night, his thoughts drifted into darkness.

Deep Space 5

Litan was locked into his hyper-accelerated curve through and ultimately flanking around and behind the Erran battle lines. Checking his rear screens, and then, as his angular momentum changed, through the port side of his canopy, he could see the growing formation of Erran cruisers and battlewagons. How could it be? More of the ugly ships were dropping in as he watched. Ugly to his eyes, as none of the deep-space Erran vessels were atmospheric ships, and equipment, decks, weapons systems and com towers seemed to sprout at random. A squadron of more Erran fin fighters had been dispatched to intercept him, but apparently, they had not accurately gauged his velocity and were soon outpaced. His strategy was working. By maintaining the velocity attained in the attack on the Erran cruiser and using his starboard field-effect modulators for course correction, he was making a long, wide sweep around to the rear of the Erran battle lines and burning the incredible velocity he'd gained in his chem drive dive.

If his strategy worked, he would either be in position to make a sneak attack on a vulnerable pulse engine component on one of these big battlewagons or he could get back to his own lines. Maybe he could get back to the carrier, or maybe even a small ammo ship that would provide a little nourishment and rearm his rail gun munitions. Ka-Litan assessed the changing battle lines, and by yawing to port and kicking in his forward thrusters at the right time, he eventually slowed and began to approach the rear of one of the huge dreadnoughts. Three had popped through and were getting oriented to the battle line.

Looking between the hulking behemoths at his own lines, he saw that the claw formation had failed to deal with the new arrivals, and the remnants were consolidating into a shield sphere for mutual protection. Moving in close-order array, they presented a simpler target, but their multiple shields could be phased and combined to provide an incredible energy-absorbing barrier that would be barely affected by the combined barrages of the Erran fleet. At the edges of the shield sphere, a carrier and two flanking destroyers were trying to coordinate blending their shields in with the larger formation. Nine green flashes grew out of the three nearest Erran dreadnoughts, and the Coalition carrier's starboard destroyer escort simply evaporated in a flash of yellow.

222

Seeing the blast in the distance as well as the blinking red signal on his dash array, Litan was glad that, from this great distance, he could not see the unsuited bodies of his confederates boiling into space. The Dzuran carrier escort had somehow failed to coordinate with the phase of the Coalition shield sphere. A tangle of green rays converged on the control deck of the carrier and began to move down the hull. Litan had never seen the Errans coordinate fire like this before. This was horrible. Soon, the luckless carrier began to split open like a seed pod. But instead of seeds spilling out, his comrades, ships, containers, everything was blown from duty stations or berths or from hallways and bunkers by the terrific forces of depressurizing hull gasses.

Masses of equipment, structural beams, bulkheads, and ships of all description spilled into space. A magazine exploded and then another; finally, in a horrifying instant, a starboard fuel pod blew, and the giant ship disintegrated. Some of its pieces flashed on the nearby shield sphere; some spiraled away as space junk for a future metal scavenger. As the flight deck spilled open, Litan saw fuel rams, armorers, shuttles, and small, unmanned messenger pods spill out. Most would be captured by the nearby gas giant and become exotic heavy metal planetary fuel for its hydrogen plasma core. He zoomed back the scale and changed his visual pad array to schematic so he wouldn't have to watch the details.

Litan's fighter was now closing in on the rear of a dreadnought, and he began to assess the plumbing and control lines, looking for weaknesses. He knew he could penetrate the big ship's force field within the cone of the giant pulsed thrusters. He could then maneuver within the shield like an insect in a tent. He was unsure of the best place to make his limited attack do the most damage. Drifting around the rear thrust plane of the dreadnought, he saw a large view screen. It was huge, and it was protected to forward by a rail gun emplacement.

"Jai, off all yaw and roll controls."

Off yaw and roll. Lights on his control panel went from amber to blue as some of his field loops and gyros powered down. Soon, he looked like tumbling space junk. Any observers would see his out-of-control little boat and think it was no longer functional. His plan depended on looking like inert metal with a dead pilot. With each roll, he nudged a little farther forward along the massive hull. He was approaching a point at which he would have to make his final decision. He still had a lot of positive vector, and he'd have to decide soon. He could see through the large viewing screen port that dozens of Errans of all ranks were viewing the battle in person rather than from one of the many nearby display stations. He understood that nothing quite beat seeing things play out in real life rather than on a display.

"Jai, bring carbon fuel thrusters on line and be ready to burn. As I give the one, two, three count, restore yaw and roll control; do not engage collision avoidance as I hit the chem thrusters."

In attack conditions, pilot and computer communicated in psi mode for clarity. *Ka, you wish to get closer? Much danger in wreckage*

Do not question, Jai. My target is the interior of that screen. Litan had known of AI control units that had frustrated attack sequences by overriding their Ka's control commands and instituting collision avoidance protocols. Ka-Litan closed his eyes and thought his last thoughts of the Maker of Lights and the universe and its wonders. He touched the small, triangular Maker totem on the sill of the instrument panel and took deep breaths to cleanse his thoughts. If he got close enough in his random drift as space junk, he hoped to use the skeeter itself as a mass ram and damage or possibly crush the huge viewport that was beginning to fill his screen. He was counting the timing of the skeeter's rolls and was about to begin his power-up sequence when a blue flash broke his final Maker thoughts. A squadron of Coalition skeeters was burning a hole in the dreadnought's shields. Green energy rays, diverted from the main battle, began to cut through the formation. Nine groupings of skeeters in triad formations had made up the attack, but they were being taken out one pod at a time. They had succeeded in thinning the shield enough locally to blow one shield generator and were focusing their rail guns in a lethal cone of fire.

The combined impacts focused on a cross member supporting four transparent panels. The structure failed spectacularly. In a burst of debris, outgassing nitrox blew into nearby space. The skeeters were now too close to avoid contact with the ship itself. A lone surviving turret gunner, forward of the screen, took out one of the skeeter triads, but the rest rushed into the maelstrom. Explosions began to shudder within the big ship. Suicide skeeter pilots were loose in the guts of the battleship. In minutes, fire and pieces of structural metal and dead and dying Errans were spewing into the vacuum through a widening breach.

Jai, ignore last orders. Impose all yaw, roll, and avoidance routines. He stopped rolling immediately. Litan yawed to get oriented away from the impending disaster area when a massive fireball of exploding chem tanks burst the hull. He could see nothing but white and yellow incandescent gasses for a long time. He could feel his tiny ship being hit by debris, and as the gasses outside his cockpit cooled, he could see the dreadnought going the way of the Coalition carrier. A huge chunk of fuselage with attached pieces of decking from at least three levels and structural spars hurtled toward his tiny ship. Litan made a reflexive movement toward the controls, but it was too late.

The collision was stunning. A blast of white and then blue filled his eyes until his tunnel vision turned to black. Ka-Litan, lieutenant group commander and last survivor of his skeeter attack squadron, was tumbling away from the explosion. This time, he was out of control, being buffeted by ejected debris. The Ka was unconscious, and Jai's control systems were useless until the red-hot metal junk tumbling around his hull cooled. The little skeeter appeared to any observer in his own fleet like inert junk, indistinguishable from the several derelict skeeter hulls mixed in the debris. Litan hung loose in his straps, not quite lifeless, but unconscious. This had been the intended impression he'd hoped to create with his earlier maneuverings; now it was real. Jai and his unconscious pilot tumbled randomly amid the dispersing cloud of Erran ship components.

Chapter 13

*No sooner does man discover intelligence than he tries to involve it
in his own stupidity.*
Jacques Yves Cousteau

December 31, 5:00 a.m.
El Paso, Texas

Brad awoke with an uneasy stomach. He felt for bruises, sure that he had
just lived through a violent explosion. He went to the window and blinking
against the harsh parking lot lights, pulled back a corner of the shade slowly
to see if there was a white Taurus in the parking lot. That there wasn't didn't
mean much, because Jenks would have had to swap out vehicles. After a
quick shower, he decided his upset stomach was due to hunger, so he went
to a drive-through for a pre-dawn breakfast and headed out on the last leg of
his trip, El Paso to Tempe.

The dream, Ka-Litan's solo attack on the Erran dreadnought, came
back to Brad as he drove through the mountains of southwestern New
Mexico. By the time he reached the outskirts of Phoenix, he had decided that
Litan had sent him another dream experience that tied in with the other
"chapters" he had received a few years ago. Ka-Litan had done this over
several hundreds of miles! Or had he given him this dream back at the pool
but Brad had to be relaxed enough to play it back? Good questions! It had
taken some time to calm down from his encounter with Jenks. The more he
thought about it, the more the latter idea appealed to him because it made
more sense than Litan's being able to telepath to him over that much
distance. He had never heard from Litan during the seven years he had been
out West, and he had only received another installment after he had gone
back to the pond.

On the last leg, a little less than two hours from Tucson to Tempe, he
considered graver thoughts. Jenks had promised to leave him alone. At
gunpoint, the operative admitted to him that they were in search of the metal
rod, that it was important to national security. He told Brad that the team

226

who killed his father and the two FSU scholars were relieved of duty and that their superior had essentially retired to avoid a court-martial for allowing the termination of US citizens. Brad had been scanning his rearview mirror since El Paso. It was an easy thing to do on a desert highway with minimal turns or changes in grade. Climbing a rise, he could see every car behind him for miles.

He pulled off the interstate into a tired-looking, dusty town and found a mechanic's garage. Trading in the truck, all of the tools his dad had left in the truck box, and half of his cash reserve, he left a few hours later with a 1979 model F-150. The tan-and-brown paint job was a change from the blue and white he'd come to love but knew was a liability. In a world full of pickups, every third vehicle in Arizona seemed to be a truck, and an F-150 was as anonymous as you could get. His dad's Koenig work box was just too easy to follow. He pulled back onto the interstate, smiling and wondering if anyone was backtracking, trying to find the F-250. He'd made the mechanic promise to keep it in a garage for two days. When the mechanic learned that Brad was ducking Feds, he'd promised to tell anyone who asked that he'd traded it for a light-green Corvair.

Thinking about who might be following, he began to rerun the gunpoint conversation with Jenks. Jenks was terribly sorry; it had been a horrible misjudgment. All they wanted was to locate the metal rod. Brad told him that he had thrown the metal into the Gulf of Mexico the night they'd killed his dad and that he didn't know where. It was somewhere south of St. Marks and east of Shell Point if they cared to go look for it. Could he trust Jenks not to follow or had he gone straight to a phone? Well, at least Jenks hadn't gone straight to the sheriff's office a few miles down the road from his ambush. He'd have been taken by now. When he told Connie of the encounter with Jenks, she was horrified that he had done it but also proud of him.

Connie. What to do about Connie? Could she come to Tempe? Should he go to North Carolina after this semester? Should he just wait and see? He found a familiar Tempe radio station and turned it up so loud he could no longer think. Finally, a large, green rectangular sign rose out of the mid-day glare. *Tempe 17*, damn! Winter semester at school would start up in a week.

January 1, 1985
Wakulla

Lucy Hitchens stared at the TV. It wasn't on. She had misplaced the remote again. She had been told by parents, coworkers, Whit, and almost anyone she let into her inner circle that she could be a little more than scatterbrained when anxious. The TV gave no hint as to where its box of magic buttons might be; it just stared blankly back at her in the dimming evening twilight. The visit with Connie and Brad had been a wonderfully busy time, and the ability to fill six days in a row with long kitchen talks and plans for the future had made it possible to get through the high Christmas holidays and a week off from work.

Now, she was back in the not-quite-fulfilled state of gainfully employed loneliness. She sometimes joked that she was gratefully employed because the hard times in the desert were only a few layers below her surface and too easily recalled. Closing her eyes to the familiar shapes in the darkening room, she took herself back as she often did to the last cigarette of the days before Whit came home from the shop. He had quit smoking almost as soon as he was discharged from the army because he refused to pay more than the post exchange price of twenty-four cents a pack. Sitting there now, she almost wished for one of the damned things, and if you could buy only one at a time, she'd be tempted to go up to the corner and get one.

Sitting like she often had, listening for Brad's noises in the yard or Whit's truck tires turning into the drive, she could almost take herself back. They were good, easy times. Cricket noises were nearly frozen out for the winter, and they wouldn't be a significant background noise for another three months. A lone woodpecker was having a late meal on a pine somewhere out back. Hearing it brought moisture to the inner lining of her eyes. The mind's eye picture she drew of a solitary bird pecking away for a meal on what was going to be a cold night made her shiver a little too. When the bird finally got his prize or gave up, it was truly quiet in the house. Sitting still, focusing on breathing, Lucy was startled when the only mechanical noise in the house, a quiet circulation fan in the refrigerator, suddenly stopped. Snow silent. She reminisced on how quiet it had gotten in the desert when snow buffered everything with soft round edges and the wind stilled.

One of the most unusual experiences of modern life, she realized, was true quiet. She drew in a deep breath, stretched, and stood up. Peace and quiet in the country wasn't what it was cracked up to be. Sometimes, she thought, it just plain gets lonesome. She knew a lot of old widows and widowers: Mrs. Perkins down the highway, Dolly's Aunt Bethany, and old man Sunny. They'd all been alone for years now. Feeling as if the dark stillness was going to fuel another episode of depression, she flicked on a table lamp and rooted among the sofa cushions for the TV remote. Finally, a satisfying clunk of plastic on pine plank told her she'd loosened it. She knelt to fish it from under the sofa.

With light in the house and the familial banality of broadcast color companions, she set about making dinner. Tomorrow, she thought, I am going to have to go for a walk. She had considered taking the walk since she'd moved back into the house. She knew that to finally convince herself that neither she nor her son was delusional; she would have to do it. Ka-Litan was real to Brad and, apparently, to Connie, who had made repeated trips out to Dreamland, as they now called the place. His presence was real enough to motivate them to plan to recover the piece of junk metal that had gotten Whit killed. He or it was real enough to draw Brad and Connie together. Lucy smiled. They looked good together; maybe it would work out for them. She did some quick math and decided that if it did, she would not be a doddering old woman when she became a grandmother. Heck of a thought for a New Year's Day.

Living in Vegas and then in Indian Springs, Lucy had pretty much given up on the continuity of family. She had met a number of older couples and many more singles of all ages who would give an embarrassed cough and change the subject if kids or kin came up in conversation. Why was the place so attractive to loners and losers?

She had gone out there because of the Area 51 hubbub. She thought that if there were any place on the planet where she might wait patiently to meet others who had been "visited" or who had "come into the presence" of or survived a "close encounter," that would be it.

Too eager at first to share her story, she soon learned to be especially subtle about broaching the subject of alien encounters. Some of the crazies she met were just that—crazy, unfortunate wanderers turned loose on the world by shrinking state mental-health budgets. Others were fellow seekers, and a few had credible stories—or at least their stories didn't vary from telling to telling. No one she'd met in Indian Springs could claim a presence or personality like Litan in a particular spot that never changed, that was always there, and that was always welcoming, soothing, and curious to learn.

Twelve years in the desert had seemed like enough. One day on the way to the casino, she knew she was ready to leave. It wasn't that the work had become intolerable. She enjoyed knowing she had the chutzpah to make it in a harsh social climate full of belligerent, lying cheats and broke and brokenhearted losers. In the mix, she had made friends—work friends. She'd taken a few lovers to salve the loneliness, but on more than one occasion, she found that others were looking to her for solutions she couldn't provide. Brad had moved to Tempe almost three years ago, but she knew there was only one place where she could get her questions answered. So she came home to confront Ka-Litan. That had been a year ago, and she still had not gone to meet her devil in the woods.

The next morning lit cold and thin. A high frost in the sky circled the sun and seemed to keep its meager rays from warming the air. When Lucy finally emerged after nine, there were still patches of rime on the trunk of her car, and frost ran in peppermint stripes down the panels of her sheet-metal roof. Grass crunched underfoot, and her breath billowed before her. It was a refreshing cold that she met with the gusto of a downhill skier. She trod off on a well-remembered course that was now pretty much overgrown and might have been truly invisible if not for Brad's and Connie's trips out to the pond over the holiday. She would have known the way even if the brush had been waist high, for it was the trees that stood as place markers in her memory, not a path through the ground cover. She had never marked her trail to the Cathedral of the Palms with paint daubs because she didn't want passing hikers in the refuge to find her way in.

Now, scanning from tree to tree, Lucy picked her way into the familiar forest and stepped into her past. Here and there, she noticed a gap and looking about, discovered a prone reminder of an old waypoint. She paused for a gulp of coffee from her thermos and was pleased to be making no sound when a forty-odd flock of Canada geese passed honking overhead. Did they always honk? What did they have to say all the way from Canada?

Nearing the desired spot, she thought something did not look quite right. Lucy saw the ragged root ball of the big cypress protruding from the brush. That must be where Brad found his artifact. She became aware of the light, an unusual amount of light, and then saw the titi thicket. It was gnarled and tangled, but she could tell where the kids had passed through and taken the same route. She loosened her bag, unfurled one of Whit's purloined US Army blankets on the ground, and sat. Looking down, the reflected sky's electric blue provided backlighting in the surface of the pool, creating a high contrast with the dark filigree of nearly barren branches. She knew reflections such as these had been the inspiration of many of M. C. Escher's works, and she loved to gaze at the three-dimensional thicket rendered flat by the dusty water surface.

hello, friend Lu-cee … Lu-cee not come long time … Litan like talk Lu-cee

She sighed, he was still here, and leaned back against the pine, not knowing that it was Brad and Connie's favorite spot also. She rubbed behind her ears with the heels of her palms and lacing her fingers, melted back into the support of the tree. "Hello, Litan. It has been a long time. I have been away for a long time."

not so long … Litan feel Lu-cee not near … same feel Lu-cee not far
Whoa! she thought. He could feel her presence from the house?
yes … Litan feel Lu-cee home … Lu-cee not come talk

She remembered now. She couldn't plan what to say next; he heard it all anyway. "No," she answered. "Lucy not come to talk Litan for long time."

She tried to think of what to talk about next, the short list of things she had crossed out on the way to Litan's Pool, as she thought of it, or Dreamland, as the kids called it. "Litan, I am sorry. I should have come a long time ago, when I returned to my home."

Litan talk Ka-nee when Ka-nee come … talk B-rad when B-rad come … talk Lu-cee when Lu-cee come

"Litan, did you ever talk to Lucy when Lucy was a long time away? Very far away?"

Litan try … hard talk long away … must rest after long time, The voice kept going far longer than his usual triad responses. *Litan talk Lu-cee long away … same Litan talk B-rad long away … difficult*

She tried to think back to the one time she had been visited by the "voice" in Indian Springs. She had been resting after a hard shift and had started to daydream about home. That had morphed into a dream about her jogging trails in the woods, and possibly because she had just seen a tour bus full of space cadets come through the UFO gift shop, she had thought of Litan.

They had "talked" about her home. The discussion had moved to an explanation of Litan's home, and her mind was flooded with images for which she was unprepared. She fought the mental connection and woke with such a start that she had surprised her friend Marina, who had covered for her on the casino floor when she took a break.

yes, Lu-cee ... Litan remember Lu-cee in ne-ve-deh ... Lu-cee say go away

"That's Nevada," she said, correcting the pronunciation with the long soft middle vowel the locals used. "And again, I am sorry. I thought I was going crazy. Talking to you like I do is not something most of my people understand." She waited for the response. It took longer than she expected.

Ka-Litan and Lu-cee friends ... Litan share pictures of Litan home ... same Litan see Lucy home

"I don't know why, friend Litan. The pictures of your world, Dzura, scared me."

Litan home name Dzura ... Ka-nee say Dzura very pretty ... Litan show only Lu-cee, B-rad, and Ka-nee home Dzura

Lucy shifted on her cold bottom to double up the blanket against the cold damp earth. The higher sun angles were finally bringing some warmth to the early January morning but not to the ground beneath her. When she settled back into the relative comfort of the cypress tree, the vision before her changed. The thin, cold blue of the sky darkened to violet with streaks of pink and purple clouds. Shapes seemed to blow by her in space, and the surroundings she knew so well were replaced with a surreal landscape in which green seemed to be absent, at least in nature.

Clumps of what might be vegetation shone in iridescent reds and lavenders with white and yellow highlights. Clusters of yellow and yellow-green structures were arranged geometrically around a central triangular plaza with three triangular structures to a side of the plaza. Individuals, almost canine in form, but erect, seemed to stroll about the plaza area and meet in groups of three or larger. Looking closer, the groups of bystanders seemed to be self-segregated into those with white colorations and some with almost a cinnamon color. Her first thought was that they seemed to have almost the appearance of an earthly fox, but with a shorter snout.

Her camera view seemed to change, rising or gaining altitude above the surface as the nine-house structure was revealed to be part of an array of countless more homes laid out in nines across rolling terrain. The viewpoint started moving. She realized she was a passenger in a small craft flying over the planet's surface. The craft approached a dark spot on the horizon that increased in size as she approached. The dot resolved itself into a circle, which the craft flew through or, rather, into. The circle was a port in some sort of a transmission system. Soon, the scene changed again as the craft slowly approached a docking station inside a dark structure. Lucy's craft or viewpoint rose in the structure and docked in an open bay that seemed to be one of hundreds.

Her viewpoint changed to a corridor with a view pane back into the launch/docking bay. The view was of an incredible display of logistics organization: fueling ports, drive-through ammunition bays, landing craft, and docking for fighter squadrons. Although signage was unreadable, somehow, she understood the utility of the equipment being displayed. Below, or what seemed like below, an opening revealed the violet-and-white edge of a planet with a deep, reddish-gray background. A sudden burst of vertigo overtook her when she realized she was peering down into open space above an unknown planet's atmosphere. She startled awake.

Lucy opened her eyes to palms, pines, and Spanish moss, and a multitude of grays and greens illuminated by bright winter sunshine. She closed her lids to keep the thought of what she had just seen clear. She understood the layout of the larger ship's loading and docking facility. She realized that she hadn't just had a vision but had been given a shared memory of the layout and purpose of every fitting and pipe in the larger ship. "Litan, was that your home world? Your home ship?"

my home ... my ship ... my world

"Why, Litan, they are simply beautiful!"

home gone ... ship gone ... world gone

Lucy heard and felt this with a visceral sense of sadness and loss, and her heart went out to the lost soul under the pool. Off in the underbrush, a scampering creature broke the spell. She shivered in the January chill and realized she was cold to the bone.

March 3, 1985
Tempe, Arizona, 6:30 a.m.

"Hey, Brad, I hope I didn't wake you up."

On the other end of the line, a suppressed yawn was obvious and then a sleepy, "Huh?" rose above the hiss of dead air.

"Brad, it's me, Connie." Then she realized she had done it again. "Oh, my gosh! Sorry, I forgot about the time-zone thing. Should I call back? Do you wanna call me when you wake up?"

233

Brad stumbled out of bed and into consciousness. "No, I'm fine," he lied."It's just that mid-terms were last night and there was sort of a party to kick off spring break." He suppressed a yawn that wanted to take over his face. "What's up, Con? How's school going?"

"Great. Listen, remember you'd wanted me to get diver certified before summer vacation? Well, I will be by next Friday."

"That's great, Con. Umm, how many classes in the program?" he asked, looking through the bathroom door at the vacant-eyed, hungover recluse in the mirror. A few brain cells began to click. "Is this a basic class or what?"

"Three weeks classroom, two in a pool, and we'll get two sessions outdoors in real water. It's real basic, Brad. One step up from snorkeling, really. No exotic airs, no double tank. Simple calculations of dive time versus depth, how to use the basic equipment, and how to get out of trouble. Let's see, buddy diving and drown-proof survival too." Connie's voice was enthusiastic. But it was 8:30 a.m. in North Carolina and 6:30 a.m. in Arizona. He listened, yawning and blinking until she finished with, "they said we'd be good for basic shallow reef diving in the Keys."

Four hours earlier, Brad had been celebrating a major midterm exam series with a few friends in his dorm. The few hours of sleep had not been enough to counter the cumulative effects of two pizzas, several beers, and a brief transition to tequila. Two o'clock hadn't seemed like too late to stay up since he didn't have a class until 11:30 on Friday. But Brad hadn't counted on a 6:30 wake-up call. He shook out the fuzz and tried to think. "Does your dive school have any specials on equipment?"

"Yeah, I picked up a shorty wet suit, a buoyancy compensator, and a snorkel, a mask, and fins, but no tanks. That stuff is way beyond my budget. I'm fine with snorkeling for a while."

"You know, Connie," he said, smiling at his own inner joke, "if it wasn't such a bad pun, I'd say you sound almost bubbly."

"Ouch!" her reaction was instantaneous. "It's said and done. Anyway, isn't that great news? Next time I come out to Tempe, you can take me down to Lake Roosevelt or one of those cold desert rivers you've been telling me about."

Brad was fully awake now, wishing it weren't rude to talk on the phone while you brushed your teeth. "Actually, since you bring up traveling, I have a better idea." Last night's sins had taken up occupation in his mouth, and he really wanted to freshen up. Then he had a thought. "You haven't bought any tickets or anything to surprise me, have you?"

"No, Brad, that's your trick. What's your better idea?"

Brad asked a simple question that later would very nearly end his life. "Can we borrow the sea skiff from your dad?"

April 1, 1985
Gulf of Mexico, South of Apalachicola

The happy coincidence of their simultaneous spring breaks provided an opportunity for Brad and Connie to spend time together and with their families back in Florida. It also sealed Brad's resolve to locate the *Lou Anne's* final resting place and make plans to retrieve the artifact. A check for the airfare from Mom helped make it possible.

The trawler *Lou Anne* had been a graceful vessel for a working girl. At forty-three feet, she had not been the largest ship in the Apalachicola shrimper fleet, nor had she been anywhere near the smallest. She'd had a pronounced rake to her bow that gave her a sleek, fast look. If her working gear had been removed and she had been refitted as a pleasure craft—a rich man's toy or a navy man's retirement plan—she would have brought joy every time she came into sight. Her twin diesels could get her out of sight remarkably fast. Rising out of the roof of the forward cabin, the captain's bridge had been a graceful, glass-paneled semicircle that cut through wind-driven spray.

Her wide prow had been graced by an anchor sprit that gave her an elegance rarely seen in a working boat. Chase had applied a scrollwork in blue with gold appliqué immediately behind the sprit in homage to the filigrees that graced the wooden ships of the early navy.

She now lay submerged in twenty-five feet of water, pulled onto her starboard side by the weight of her steel outriggers as she sank. Except for the wide expanse of her port-side hull, which was scrubbed by wave action, most of her other surfaces were alive with anemones, sea grass, barnacles, and sponges. With a sixteen-foot beam, the port side of the dead ship lay within easy snorkeling depth from the surface. Like most captains, Chase had given the hull a thorough painting of marine-growth inhibitors up to the sheer line just below the heavy planking of the gunnels. Everything else topside simply got exterior-grade gloss paint, which provided little resistance to marine life.

All the captains who regularly dragged nets across the bottom knew the general area where she lay. Where she was exactly was anyone's guess. Unfortunately for Brad and Connie, Nav Chart 11401 was a large-scale map and the small shape he'd scribed on its surface covered a lot of area.

From the surface, it all looked exactly alike: dark-green waters glistening in the sun. To the north, the thin, bluish line of Little St. George Island spread across the horizon. The sound of the thin, white line of surf was well out of earshot. To the east, a row of cumulus clouds was building like popcorn on steroids, their rolling tops in a slow boil as they pushed into the bright-blue canopy. To the south and west, skies were unbroken even by high ice clouds. The dark-blue line of the southern horizon jumped and twitched, indicating a fair swell of five to seven feet in the deeper waters south of the shoals. At anchor, the twenty-foot sea skiff pulled at its chain as three-foot swells rolled under it.

The bearings 30 and 320 were two numbers Bradley had been carrying in his head for seven years. He had been unwilling to write them down anywhere in case someone should find them and figure out their significance or, worse, find them and force him to tell how to use them. He didn't relish the idea of what forcing might mean. The government had too many exotic chemicals for that purpose. Torture wasn't even necessary.

The azimuth from the foundering *Lou Anne* to the red, flashing channel marker south of Sikes Cut was 30 degrees, and 320 degrees was the azimuth to the lighthouse. He was pretty sure about the sighting on the channel marker to within two or three degrees of error, considering how stressful the situation had been. He was less sure of the 320 azimuth to the lighthouse. First of all, it was unlit, and the pale-white stripe of its brick tower wasn't as easy to read in the roll of the sinking boat. So he'd allowed five degrees of error on that sighting. He hadn't been sure, but he had thought maybe a little north of 320 degrees was more like it. He scribed the four outer lines of uncertainty beside the remembered bearings; he had understood that the irregular box created by the uncertainty lines from both of those fixed points spread out over scores of acres of sea bottom.

In the years since the loss of the *Lou Anne*, none of the fleet had reported snagging a net on it, so its actual location was still an unknown. Brad hoped to get a good fix on the wreck, so he and Connie could plan a dive later in the summer. Guthrie was due for knee surgery in June, and Brad was going to crew in his place for the summer. The plan for spring break was simple: set up the search grid for the lost shrimper and leave one of the buoys on site to mark the wreck so other bottom draggers wouldn't rip their rigs apart on it.

Brad and Connie had spent the morning boxing the search square with his homemade buoys. The box was a few degrees off to each side of the directions he'd sighted from the Lou Anne's pilothouse the night of her sinking, creating an irregular square search area. He knew he'd probably never be able to see crab-trap buoys in the size of ocean he was going to search, so he'd been inventive. No one in the contractor's supply in Eastpoint would ever have guessed that the four lengths of six-inch sewer pipe, two hundred feet of heavy nylon rope, and eight bags of cement were going to turn into the corner buoys that boxed the location of a lost shrimper.

Connie was handing him the end of a length of heavy chain and said, "Sure doesn't feel like an April Fool's Day!"

Brad cocked an eyebrow at her. "Are you trying to be sarcastic?"

He saw that she was beginning to get too red. "Or are you referencing your imminent sunburn?"

She looked down at the pink beginning to spread between her orange freckles across the tops of her shoulders. "Damn, I must be sweating the sunscreen off." She grabbed his shirt from the seat of the sea skiff and put it on. "No, I mean usually some idiot tries to pull a prank or something. Oyster Radio might give out some goofy news or something."

He watched her covering up her slender frame with his soiled shirt. "Well, I guess that proves the law of unintended consequences," he said.

"What does?"

"Here I am, looking out for your well-being, worrying about your sunburn, and I lose the best view in a hundred miles!" He shook his head in mock disgust.

In response, she threw a dock bumper at him.

"Just look at it this way, Swamp Boy: any chance of getting close to Freckle Face depends on her not broiling like a lobster." Sunny Rogers, true to form, had branded Connie 'Freckle Face'. She had hated that moniker and similar taunts as a kid in school when her freckled, sunburned nose was the cause of much teasing, but somehow, from Sunny, it was sweet.

Brad looked up at the sound of a noise in the distance; a small plane was making a turn on a course that had gone from the approximate location of the Apalachicola airport toward Sikes Cut and was now moving southwesterly toward them. He shielded his eyes against the bright sky and peered at the high-wing small plane that was approaching at several hundred feet above the Gulf.

Connie followed his gaze and spotted the light plane. "Do you think it's just sightseers?"

"I hope so, but I don't think so. They usually just cruise the beaches looking for bikinis." As he watched, the light Cessna flew over and then banked east. He was about to ignore it and get on with setting the last buoy when he noticed that it had turned again as it crossed the southeast corner marker they had just set. He said, "This doesn't look good." He tossed his pocket flip-top notebook over to Connie and grabbed his field glasses. "Take down these numbers." He then called out the ID numbers of the small plane and re-cased the glasses. Stewing to a slowly building anger, he continued to attach the anchor chain to the large, stainless-steel eyebolt protruding from the bottom of the concrete plug in the plastic pipe.

Connie saw Brad's face and demeanor harden, transformed from that of the smiling, relaxed man he had been all morning.

"It's them, isn't it? The Feds?"

Brad hissed without moving his mouth, "It's got to be those bastards again. I don't figure on us being newsworthy to anyone else." He put the marker buoy's homemade anchor on the side of the boat and let it fall over the edge with a backsplash that would have been rewarding and cool a few minutes ago but now was annoying. "Connie, I was hoping to come back in June and do some serious pattern dragging and diving for the *Lou Anne*, but I think we need to step up the schedule. We need to get back out here tomorrow. We also need to see who's flying that plane." As he said this, the plane finished the approximate shape of the defining trapezoid marking his search area and flew off west, as if it were simply flying around. Turning to pull the starter handle on the outboard, Brad allowed himself a curse with each pull of the rope.

April 2, 1985
Gulf of Mexico

Sitting on the polished wooden gunnels of the sea skiff, PQ, Brad adjusted the fit of his mask, shrugged again against the shoulder straps of his air tank, and fell backward over the edge. He and Connie were investigating another snag that was probably not a hit but needed to be eliminated. Brad had constructed a simple rig that when underway would send two spreader planes suspended on a double length of PVC pipe to each side of the boat that pulled against a floating row of net floats. Below that hung a simple snag line of quarter-inch wire rope suspended by ski rope. If the spreaders were doing their job underwater, he was clearing an eighty-foot swath on each tow. He didn't want to think about how many it might need; it could take a long time. They tried to pull at about five knots so that the wire skimmed about twenty to twenty-five feet below the surface. Occasionally, the drooping center would grab a rock pile and indicate snag when there wasn't anything below but an agitated grouper.

He quickly found the cable snagged in a rock pile with one of its knotted ends caught between two growth-encrusted lumps of stone. As he worked to free it, a silver-plated barracuda patrolled at about a ten-foot radius from him. He couldn't tell if the barracuda was sizing him up or just waiting for a meal to be scared out of hiding in the rocks. He knew that he was a lot bigger than the fifteen-pound barracuda, but brevity was best in these situations, and he didn't linger. Returning to the surface, he tossed his mask, snorkel, and fins into the boat and hauled himself up the rope ladder. His hair was atypically short for his generation, and the bristles glistened in the sunlight. He was muscled and taut. Hopi influences had brought him self-discipline and strength of will. That strength didn't always hold up when great planning bore no results. He was disappointed already, and the plane had spooked him into accelerating the search for the *Lou Anne*.

"Okay," he said, "there must be a better way to do this. We've covered almost three passes across the southeastern face of our search box. That's less than 10 percent of our search area. It feels like this could be a several-week process, and I have to get back to Tempe by Sunday noon at the latest."

Connie handed him a cold bottle of water from the cooler. "Yeah, and I have to get back to Chapel Hill. But we've only hit three snags, maybe we won't hit as many in the rest of the box." She was wearing drawstring cotton pants and one of her brother's old dress shirts with the shirt tails tied at her waist. He thought she looked great, but then he was smitten and he knew it. With her scarlet hair pulled back into a ponytail that she had passed through the hole in her baseball cap, she was a fine mixture of tomboy and bathing beauty. He made sure that just enough water splashed on her to ensure that her light clothing clung in the right places.

"Con, I guess we can only do what we can do and come back in the summer to finish it if we don't get lucky in the next few days." Brad pulled off the shoulder harness and laid the tanks against the fish well bulkhead. He took a long pull on the water bottle and squinted at the horizon. It was the same view as four hours ago, just a little warmer. Looking back at the tank apparatus, he said, "Next time, I'm going to see if I can do it free diving. It's taking too long gearing up each time we hit something." He looked thoughtful and added, "I think if I can rig a float so the middle of the snag line doesn't hit bottom, it'll go a lot faster." He leaned over to give her a kiss on the forehead, but she leaned up to meet him with her mouth. The kiss lingered and threatened to grow into a real distraction before she broke it off.

"Make hay in the sunshine, boy. There's plenty of time for recreatin' later." She playfully pushed him to arm's length and held him there. "Promise me we'll play later?"

In response, he only wagged a finger at her, before pulling the Mercury outboard to life. "Anchor up!" He hadn't needed to say it. She was already leaning over the bow pulling on the anchor rope. He was just about to pull on the starter rope when he thought he heard something behind him. He looked back and sat down on the rear seat. The plane was back! He didn't even have to look at the wing numbers. It was the same green-and-white Cessna that had given them a quick recon pass yesterday, noted the four buoys, and flown off. This was no coincidence. He tried to look casual and reached into the cooler for a sandwich. He handed one to Connie and leaned back in the captain's chair. "Any chance they won't figure out what the spreaders and floats are for?"

"No," Connie replied, "I can't see how they'd miss 'em, and I don't see how we could take them in without them noticing."

"If they mean us harm, not much we could do. We can go about thirty knots wide open, and they can go about one-forty." He continued after chewing a bite of turkey sandwich, "Doesn't seem like a very fair horse race, does it?"

She countered. "It doesn't seem that way, but you have cunning and luck on your side." She gave him a light fist tap to his shoulder. "You've outsmarted them several times already, if I remember right.

"So why do I feel like the turkey at a turkey shoot?"

They watched the plane as it circled the four bobbing floats and then began a crop duster's pattern back and forth across the boxed study area, only at a much higher altitude. It was obvious the pilot knew his stuff, as he could maintain a slight aileron roll while keeping the plane from turning by applying opposite rudder. They were searching!

"Holy crap!" Brad stood up angrily. "Of course!" He pulled thin lips together and beamed hatred at the small plane. "From a few hundred feet up, they can probably see the *Lou Anne's* hull. We watched it go down on its side. The side of that boat is a forty-foot-long white billboard reflecting light down there. I once found a capsized sailboat over in Apalachee Bay by seeing the big, white triangular sail through the murky water." He let out a sigh of exasperation. "This isn't even murky water."

"Are those his friends?" Connie was pointing northeast at a small craft that was approaching their search area from the direction of the cut. Brad sat down, teeth clamped, arms rigid, and fists clenched white-knuckle tight. He was almost trembling he was so angry. He had kept his secret for a long time, and now people with serious resources were going to steal it from him. They'd have to know where to look, but what the heck? "We just staked out the search area for them, and the Feds don't have to get back to school in a few days. Can't friggin' believe it." Brad slumped into his seat alternately looking at the Cessna and the small boat heading toward them. He guessed that within five to ten minutes the boat would be in the search box—his search box. "Adversity is a mother!" he said. Looking up at the plane again, he struggled for an idea.

Connie, with a slight choke in her voice, said, "Brad, what now? Everything we've been doing here is going to be for nothing if they get the artifact." She tried to talk through an increasing heaviness in her lungs. "If you lose the artifact, there's no proof of the alien craft."

"We could dig up the spaceship," he offered. "We could introduce Ka-Litan and the little green people to the good folks of America."

"Yeah, sure, you could dig up a spaceship in the middle of the wildlife refuge and no one would notice." He picked a piece of seaweed off his diving watch and flicked it over the edge. "That, my dear, will have to be plan C, D, or E."

They sat for a minute as the two other searchers began to coordinate their movements. Connie took the field glasses and focused in on the boat that was bouncing toward them. Brad settled into his seat and watched the graceful turns of the plane as it made the practiced 180's of a crop duster at the end of each pass. He finally said, "Well, you got any better ideas?"

"Yes," she said looking through the glasses, "I do." She handed him the field glasses. "Why don't we stick around to see how this works out."

Brad was sitting up looking through the glasses at what was now recognizable as a center-console Boston Whaler. It came to and powered

241

down as it got to the first corner buoy. Connie said, "Brad, there's only one guy on the boat."

"Yeah, and there's only one guy in the airplane," he said. Brad was thinking quickly, but Connie was ahead of him.

"If the guy in the boat is going to dive, he'll have to go down and leave his boat. He'll be needing a ride home!" She laughed.

He laughed, as he realized how simple the next step would be. "Let's just move up the pattern a little and see if the spotter plane finds *Lou Anne*." He stepped back to the outboard and pulled it to life while she hoisted the anchor line. They had just gotten the sea skiff turned when they saw what they were hoping for. The Cessna had made a ninety-degree turn and dipped. It made another turn to pass over the same spot again from the south. "Look, he's verifying the sighting." Brad pulled back on the throttle, letting the sea skiff drift to a stop. He began to dismantle the tow apparatus and stow it. The Cessna made another turn, and a small package was thrown out. Immediately, the small Boston Whaler sped into action and closed on the splash site.

~ ~ ~

Martin Jenks approached the inflatable float and tossed an anchor over the Whaler's side. He looked overboard and knew that his plane spotter had been correct. Waiting for his next approach pass, he stood and waved the spotter plane off with an okay sign. Beneath him, he could see the band of lighter water marking the white side of a hull. He could see the two kids a quarter mile off and smiled to himself. Finally, he thought, I'm ahead of you, kiddo. He strapped on his tank and gear and prepared to splash. He loved the transition into scuba. One moment, you're on the surface, being rocked and tossed about, especially in smaller boats, by swells and chop not always moving in the same direction.

Tank, flippers, buoyancy compensators, weights, and equipment belts all made a diver feel especially clumsy. The next moment, peace. He back-rolled over the side. After turning around and getting oriented, he had stability, weightlessness, and grace, and the soft, rhythmic mechanical exhale of his scuba blocked out most other noises except the light slap of water on the small hull above him.

He looked down. Less than twenty feet below was the planking of a flat-sided boat. Undulating streamers of filtered green sunlight danced across the white hull. This has to be the *Lou Anne*, he thought. He turned parallel to the hull and gave a light kick of his powerful flippers. As the curve of the hull brought him into slightly deeper water, he could see there was more algal growth on the prow obscuring the lettering. He brushed away a thin layer of loose green slime and some slightly more tenacious algae and was rewarded with the clear outline of "*anne.*" With a few more wipes, he had the whole name exposed. He popped to the surface, found the circling plane's pilot, and waved at him. When he got a return wave, he gave a thumbs-up and dove again. If he had waited but a second more, he would have noticed the pilot signaling something else.

Turning his attention to the search, he swam along the port-side rail, looking over the edge at the pilothouse a few feet deeper but noticeably more encrusted by marine growth. The *Lou Anne* had become an artificial reef. One of man's greatest gifts to a nearly featureless benthic plane is his shipwrecks. The slightly modulated terrain typical of a near-shore, sand-and-shell bottom is not inviting to the many species that require solid anchors and provides little cover beyond sea grasses for small fish hoping to become bigger fish. The hull and its superstructure provided stability, vertical surfaces, and the protection of its many crevices. It was only minimally disturbed by anything but the largest surface waves, and new life in many forms had adopted the now-dead *Lou Anne*. And it made her more dangerous.

Waving sea grasses obscured dangling wires and cables. Cabins that had been lit by sun through glassed openings were now darkened as the plates were obscured by algal slime. Shapes darted in and out of openings that had not been intended as escape routes for seafood. As Jenks approached, larger carnivores readily gave up their places to the new bubble-blowing visitor, but only grudgingly.

Jenks reached for his tool belt, found the sealed beam light, and shone it into the hold. After dealing with the two kids, he would come back with his pilot and diving partner tomorrow. First, he would get a look around and see if he would need more advanced tools. He had, after all, found the *Lou Anne* where he had thought the artifact might have been hidden, but it was a large boat to be gone over in a dangerous environment.

His wreck-diving classes had taught him never to dive a wreck alone and never on a single tank unless it was a recreational, photo-only dive of the exterior. He would have to come back. Seeing the broad, open entry to the captain's cabin, he swam toward it, intrigued by the small amount of light filtering in through the incompletely clouded windows. The interior was a surreal impressionist construction of a man-made space, except that it was covered in anemone, barnacles, and sea grasses, and it was turned on its side. When he approached, a small school of something silver and black darted out. He held on to the door frame and peered inside.

If he mentally turned the whole world ninety degrees, he could make sense of the space. The wheel was forward and down to the right, its shaft protruding from an instrument panel covered in growth. To the left, or up, was a locker box, or seat and an interior companionway leading down into the hold. Good, he thought, there are two ways into the hull. He hadn't checked yet, but he hoped that there was clear access from the bow back to the stern decks below. Still, a diver could never be too careful about getting out of sight of a diving buddy, and each dive on a new wreck would have to be planned ahead based on what had been learned from the previous visit.

Jenks looked at his dive watch and saw that he still had over twenty minutes left. He looked up at the outline of the fiberglass boat waiting on its line and looked back into the cabin. On the bulkhead above or to port was a rack holding equipment lockers. Below, on the starboard bulkhead, he could see a tangle of circled cables or ropes. They had probably been hanging on hooks when the boat was upright. Shining the light around, he realized he could improve overall visibility on a future dive if he broke out the windows. It would allow disturbed sediment to disperse faster and increase current flow through the entire hull. He'd do that from the outside before he left today. He filed away the thought and planned the tools he would need for tomorrow's dive with a diving partner. And, yes, I'll have to deal with the kids.

A glance at the watch told him he had eighteen minutes left. He slowly drifted into the cabin, careful to tuck his legs under him to minimize disturbing silt, which could cloud the cabin in seconds. Pulling himself along a railing, he made it a few feet forward to the locker box. He could see that it had a simple hasp, now certainly rusted beyond use. Reaching for his knife, he slid it under the lid, which hung vertical from its rusted hinges. He began to pry, and as he worked the blade into the stubborn crack, his motion caused his large rubber flippers to stir sediment into a growing cloud behind him. Had he seen the cloud of silt billowing behind him, he might have gotten the message and left.

He did not realize that his own sense of adequate time on the tanks, the nearness of the doorway to open ocean, and his overconfidence in his own survival skills were about to be trumped by the sea and its utter disregard for human plans. He also did not hear the small boat overhead.

~ ~ ~

Brad approached slowly. He knew from his dives in Lake Roosevelt that a high-speed boat can be heard for miles underwater because of the high-frequency engine noise and the high-frequency generation and collapse of cavitation bubbles forming behind the prop. A slowly moving boat just above an idle does not cavitate; it gently pushes water behind it. His outboard made all of its noise above water and little underwater. He had asked Connie to take a time check when the diver splashed and to keep a mental note of when thirty minutes was up. He was approaching with about fifteen minutes left on his estimate of the diver's safe downtime. At a hundred yards away, where he could now see the rhythmic boil of the diver's bubbles rising from the wreck, he rolled back the throttle to low idle still in gear.

He guided his wooden boat closer to the smaller fiberglass craft. "Connie, let's borrow this gentleman's boat, shall we?" She was ready to jump across. He sidled up to it, and Connie jumped onto the Whaler's foredeck. They quickly lashed the two together, let the anchor line drop from the diver's boat, and moved away from the bubble stream. He looked at his watch. Twelve minutes left.

~ ~ ~

Martin Jenks was in serious trouble and knew it. He had gotten into trouble one small step at a time. He had made most of the mistakes that an inexperienced wreck diver could make. He was alone, and he didn't have twice the air he actually needed for the length of his dive. Well, he would have had if he hadn't come into the cabin. He had managed to drop his knife and, turning, had seen the billowing cloud of silt. Startled, he had jumped slightly. When his regulator had snagged on an unseen dangling line, he had incorrectly, but instinctively, pulled on it. As he did, his legs uncoiled, further silting the small cabin until his entire field of view was uniform dark-brown silt.

The fine edge of panic had come on him then, creeping like a dark monster into his thoughts. He now could not see the small hands on his dive watch, the rear door to the cabin, any sign of the dropped sealed beam light, or any hope. The pounding in his head was his own racing pulse. He slowed his breath, trying to squelch the building horror. Twenty-five feet from air! He could easily free dive if he could get the tank off. Slow down, breath slowly, dammit! He reached back to his wreck-diving class. The few short steps to tragedy were unpreparedness, lack of planning, lack of caution, and at any time, panic. Panic ate up time, muddling the mind and its ability to think out options clearly—and it ate up air. Panic's rapid, short breathing could halve the time left in a tank. He listened to his breath. Still too fast. He took a long, deep breath and very slowly let it go. Reaching out into the dark murk, he thought he saw a rectangle of light. Was it the doorway to the rear deck?

He reached for the light, full of hope. No, it was a glass window at the front of the cabin. He felt the small dash under the window and tried to visualize which direction was directly behind that. He reached over his head for bubbles to determine which way was up. He did not want to take off the tank until he was sure of the opening. That would really be stupid. If he dropped the tank and still hadn't located the exit, well, he'd drown.

Bracing on the instrument panel behind him, he pushed off toward the rear of the cabin, hoping to clear the sediment cloud and find the doorway or at least the rear bulkhead. As he pushed off, the line snagged on his regulator and went taut, jerking him generally up toward the port bulkhead. His outstretched hand jammed against a metal locker handle, and as he reacted, his elbow slammed into a metal door. Suddenly, his world collapsed around him. The metal cabinet had been suspended from a rotting wooden wall for years, its several galvanized mounting screws rusting in their watery afterlife until only the barest metal still had enough grip on the wood above it. The hard shock of Martin Jenks's elbow on the cabinet was the final jolt, and it fell from the wall and pushed him hard eight feet across the cabin, pinning him at the waist and facedown against the starboard bulkhead.

He felt a sharp jab in his side as a rusted rope hook pressed into his gut. His own sharp cry startled him into awareness. He had gone from careful, cautious, thoughtfully planning a next dive to curious, incautious, and stupid. He had no idea how much time was left on his watch, but he knew for the last two or maybe four minutes, he had been breathing at more than twice the normal rested rate. He was in trouble—damn serious trouble.

~ ~ ~

Connie and Brad had been watching the bubbles boiling on the surface. They had been discussing what the diver would think when he looked up and saw two hull shapes above him and no anchor line. "Brad, I show that he only has five or ten minutes left." She looked a little worried. "Do you think he's all right?"

"He's probably Navy Seal or Green Beret and has hours and hours of this kind of training. Surely, they wouldn't send in an untrained diver."

She countered, "How many divers can there be in the Air Force? Isn't that the branch that runs Area 51? Isn't that who's after you?"

Brad looked at the bubbles. There was now a sharp increase in their density and duration. He could no longer distinguish individual breaths. "What the hell is going on down there?" He started the motor and moved closer to the bubble stream, noticing that they were pulling dirty water up with them. "Connie, I'm going to go down. He's in trouble. His bubbles are pulling up silt! Toss our anchor over there," he said, pointing upwind. "Try to keep the PQ over the bubble stream."

Brad donned his gear as quickly as he could. Hatred had dissolved completely. There was a man in trouble down there, and he had almost no air left. He grabbed a spare tank, splashed, and followed the bubble stream down. He found them coming from a small vent hole in the port cabin bulkhead. He whirled, kicked, and brought himself quickly to the aft entry into the captain's cabin. He quickly had a vision of his last moments on the afterdeck and oriented himself so that he could think of where real vertical was. Safety and life were up, and up was where the former port bulkhead had been.

He rolled around the edge of the old cabin roof overhang and saw a billowing cloud of silt spreading outward from the opening. Christ! he thought. What have you done in there? He pulled his knife and began tapping on his tank—three sharp taps, tink, tink, tink, pause, three more tinks, pause, three more tinks. He listened, but all he heard at first was the rasping bubbles of two regulators, one a little faster than his own. He moved closer to the opening and then heard it: thunk, thunk, thunk.

Whoever was in there had probably thought through his own death by now, had not expected anyone to be able to get to him, and then had finally heard the rapping and registered that help was at hand. Brad rapped his tank again: tink, tink, tink. It was answered by an immediate thunk, thunk, thunk from inside the cloud. The diver was alive, and he knew someone was near! How do you approach a man on the verge of panic? Brad moved slowly into the doorway, spreading his legs at the door frame so that they gave him a plane of reference. He thought of Connie above; he thought of his mother at home; and he thought of a man on the verge of drowning a few feet away.

Reaching into the murky brown water, he felt around the shapes piled on the starboard bulkhead. He was surprised when a hand grabbed his, gripped it, and then slowly released it. He was amazed at how joyful he was. The hand actually shook his in a "How do you do?" motion. Brad laughed into his regulator, spurting a burst of bubbles. He pulled back out of the companionway and looked around him.

A shrimper is a boat full of long lines, cables, and chains of all description and lengths. None were small enough or short enough or even handy to be immediately useful. He could see the dark framework of growth-encrusted outriggers disappearing into the blue-green sea. He remembered that the coils of line hung from the starboard cabin wall. That was where he was? What could have gone wrong?

~ ~ ~

Martin Jenks had come slowly to the realization that his legs were loose, but flapping them only stirred up more silt. The flippers were great for open-water power swimming, for which he had trained, but were dangerous in tight quarters. He had calmed his breathing rate down and was trying to test the weight of the metal cabinet that had fallen on him. It was too much for him on the strength of his arms and elbows alone. He was attempting to rotate under it when he heard the tapping. Any diver would know the sound of metal on dive tank. There was no sound like it.

The tink, tink, tink sounded like angels' voices to him, though he knew it had to be the kid! He could not find his knife in the dark green-brown murk. His sealed beam must be lighting some muddy corner of the cabin, but he couldn't prove it right then. Finally, he answered by tapping on the metal cabinet itself. Doing so loosened more silt, but that was almost meaningless now. Reaching toward what seemed like the stern of the ship, he had found the hand. Oh joy and celebration! A human hand had found his! He would take his bride to every possible church service when he got home—maybe even join his baritone to the choir. Thank you, Jesus! Another human's hand!

~ ~ ~

Connie had watched Brad's bubble stream move in pulses away from her spot over the other diver's stream. For a half minute, his bubble stream had stopped entirely, and she had almost jumped overboard until she noticed that the stream under her had increased. She looked around and saw no other watercraft, not even a shrimper. It was a weekday, so no sport fishermen were out. No help for miles! Her calculated time for the missing diver had passed zero. Could they be buddy breathing? Did Brad get the spare tank to the downed diver? Could the diver be wrestling Brad for his own precious air hose? She heard a subtle change in sound. She looked down again and saw no bubbles at all. "Oh merciful heavens!" She was on her feet and stripping down to her bathing suit. She had one flipper on when she saw bubbles rising from ten feet away. Then two heads popped above the surface. One was Brad's bristle, the other a tight-kinked dark nap. She cried out, "Over here!" The two heads turned as one and began to move toward the sea skiff.

Brad lifted himself over the gunnel first, throwing his mask and two flippers over the side before climbing in. Connie's arms encircled him, and she threatened not to let go, but he pulled away, making two practiced moves that dropped the tank and bent over the side. Brad got Connie to help him with the other diver. She first saw the closely cropped top of a black man's head followed by a row of white teeth in what started as a grimace of pain and then turned into a wide smile. As the mask came off, Brad shouted, "You!" Impatiently, he pulled Jenks's exhausted frame into the boat. "You son of a bitch. You, of all people."

Jenks flopped onto his back and looked up at the clear blue sky he had thought he might never see again. "Yes, Mr. Hitchens, it's me again." He looked into Connie's startled face. "Miss Chappell? Martin Jenks, glad to meet you." He took several deep breaths of free, unregulated air, feeling like he might never be talked into a dive mission again. Facing Brad again, he said, "I think that makes two times you had the chance to leave me a dead man and didn't."

~ ~ ~

After a few minutes of shifting positions, shedding diving gear, and harsh muttering at Jenks, Brad and Connie ended up sitting on the two seats behind the skiff's windshield and Jenks sat straddling the small ice cooler amidships. Jenks looked Hitchens in the eye and said, "Kid, I should be dead. Right now, I should be thirty feet down, stuck in that boat, eyes bulged out, not seeing the brown cloud of mud I disturbed when I finally croaked." He shook his head in disbelief. "But you saved my black ass for another day. I don't know what to say."

"First of all, who's a kid? Last time I saw you, you were staring up the barrel of my shotgun. Hell, man!" Brad's stare bored into him. "You should be asking, 'Why am I in sunny Apalachicola instead of wherever people are plotting the overthrow of America?'" He stood up. "You should be asking, 'Why am I screwing with two American citizens who are lawfully minding their own business?' You should be asking, 'What's in it for me?'" He sat down. His own shouting in the quiet, sunny afternoon on the water surprised him. "Why are you still bothering me? Jinks, is it?"

"Jenks, Martin Jenks; officially that's Staff Sergeant Jenks." He raised his hands wide, palms forward, tilting his head slightly to one side. "I am in the service of the United States government on an assignment that has no regard for your life or welfare, whose only interest is in suppressing information that would be injurious to the safety and welfare of the American people."

"Do you practice that stuff in the mirror?" Connie said. "You are so full of crap!"

"No, but maybe I should; perhaps I wasn't clear."

Brad said, "You were clear, especially the 'no regard for your life' part."

"So my problem," Jenks rejoined, "is what the hell do I do about you two?"

"We two?" Connie started to rise. "Do you know how unpopular your African-American self will be 'round here if something happens to me? I'm third-generation in this town, and I'd say it's safe to assume a new age posse would be tracking you down before you could find your spit-shined shoes and re-enter the air farce!"

Anger levels rose again when the joy of salvation had been dampened by reality as hunter and prey squared off. Jenks knew that in a few seconds, he could dispatch the two, leave them for chum, and plan the next day's trip, but it had become complicated. He knew in his Christian soul that he could not harm Mr. Bradley Hitchens or Miss Connie Chappell. He was alive now, contemplating the future precisely because they had saved his life. He tried again.

"Hitchens, one of the gladdest moments in my life was finding your hand underwater. I could not deny that to you or to myself." He paused, searching for the right words. "If you had blasted my face to hamburger last year, there would be a lot more bad guys still running around in South America torturing, maiming, raping, and coercing young girls into smuggling cocaine into the country in their guts. I have done some good things for the world and this country since then." Brad started to respond, but Jenks raised a palm at him for quiet. "I have a degree of latitude here; my boss does not care what happens to you, as long as I come back with the artifact."

"Artifact? Is this still about that?" Brad stood and waved his hand at the blue horizon surrounding him on all sides. "Whatever that piece of metal was, it's nowhere near here! I told you back in the woods, it's somewhere on the flats south of St. Marks." He could feel Connie's stare burning him from the adjacent seat, but he couldn't look over lest he betray the lie. "That first night after your partners killed my dad, when I left, I took a canoe down the Wakulla River and paddled it back to the beach south of my house. I had a lot of time to think that night. Whatever it was, whatever fantasy my fourteen-year-old self had about what it might be, it was killing people. Hell, your people killed my dog, too!

"You wonder why you disgust me? Your people, your agency, whoever the hell you are, have forgotten that we, Connie and me, Dad, and those geologists at Florida State are the very American people that you were sworn to serve and protect." He paused for a breath, to control the venom he felt.

He looked down at the pile of wet dive equipment on the deck. "Jenks, Sergeant Jenks, did you kill my father?" He saw his dive knife handle buried under the pile and wondered if the answer was going to make him have to dive for it. He knew that Jenks was older, stronger, and well-trained, but he didn't know how he'd react to the wrong answer.

"Connie—Bradley—listen. I know who did. It was not supposed to happen. Like I told you in the woods, your dad drew a shotgun out from behind a couch cushion so quick one of the rendition team freaked and pulled his handgun. He hadn't meant to fire; he was a trained dark ops agent, lots of licensed wet work behind him, and he always went into a hot room with the safety off. When we left, we thought he might survive, but I guess there was too much internal bleeding."

"We!" yelled Connie, outraged now. "We!" All five foot three inch, one hundred and ten pounds soaking wet of her was in a fury. She started to jump on Jenks and both men rose; Jenks to hold her off and Brad to pull her back. "You were there, you sorry shit!" She pulled into Brad's shoulder but didn't take her eyes off him. "You were there. You killed those men in Tallahassee too, didn't you?"

Jenks had backed to the small stern deck. "That's all history; I had directives, orders. The two in Tallahassee were, well not intentional. Your dad…" He paused, looking into the bilge. "Hitchens, believe me. Like I told you before, your dad was supposed to be pulled for questioning. He was a lead; only a lead. The two men in Tallahassee, well, they possessed critical, actionable scientific knowledge that had to be suppressed. That was the directive—suppression. Like I said before, they were scheduled for removal. In my world, removal means rendition to Nevada for questioning and psych treatments. In Captain Richards's world, removal means elimination. He and Lassiter were trained, highly skilled black ops cleaners. They misunderstood the order for removal. That was a mistake made by pulling in temporary talent. Your dad was a mistake that was never supposed to happen, and no government can ever apologize enough. I know this one will never even try. For them, at all levels from sheriff to the joint chiefs, there will never be an apology because the official record of a B-and-E gone bad will never be changed."

"So, Jenks," Brad said with disdain, "what's your game plan? I could point to a chart and show you where I paddled. I don't know how you'd find it. It's in one of the largest grassy beds in the world, spawning ground to every kind of fish and crustacean in this ocean." He spread his hand behind him. "I don't think the Army Corps of Engineers is going to let you drag and filter five hundred acres of those grassy beds to find a piece of metal because a fourteen-year-old thought it mighta come from a spaceship. I don't know who knows who in DC, but have you ever tried to get a permit from the Corps of Engineers?" He remembered his dad's ranting about the goddamned Army Corps this and the goddamned Army Corps that when he was trying to work with developers on a project at the coast.

Brad could feel Connie's chest jerking beside him. He looked down expecting to find tears and was shocked to find her suppressing laughter. He couldn't help but smile at her irrepressible sense of humor. He looked back up at Jenks. "What's your plan? Are we still fish bait?" A corner of his mouth pulled down as he tried very hard not to catch Connie's sudden attack of mirth. Apparently, the Army Corps of Engineers' reputation was worse than he'd thought.

Jenks, sensing some relaxation, tried again. "Guys, listen … I mean, Bradley, Connie, I said first that I owe you. I owe you big time. You can go back to doing what college kids do; I'll go back to catching bad guys. But I need two things from you to wrap this up."

"Yeah, what?" Brad put on his deepest sincere voice. "If dragging your sorry Air Force ass out of the ocean doesn't quite satisfy your need for closure here, what can we do for you?"

"It's simple, really. One, I need to say that under subsequent interrogation, you broke and admitted to the general area of the drop in Apalachee Bay and showed it to me on a chart. Two, well, what the hell were you looking for out here?"

"You beat us to it. You found it!" Connie said. "You found the *Lou Anne*. That was my father's first boat. He loved it; he rebuilt it, and he named it for my mother. She looked down at the lighter-colored band of green glowing from the depths beside them. "You found my dad's boat; we figured it might take us the rest of this week and maybe we'd have to come back this summer, but sure as toads croak, you found it in fifteen minutes. Maybe we ought to thank you for that." Brad pinched her on the tight skin over her kidneys, but she shrugged, adding, "And for not killin' us."

"What's so important about finding a boat that's been lost for over seven years?" Jenks wasn't sure yet.

Brad took over the lie. He was afraid Connie might take it into unrecoverable territory. "Two reasons. One, it being out here unmarked, has kept boats from coming anywhere near here for seven years. There's good beds down there, and knowing where the boat is and where it isn't lets all those fisherman in Apalachicola feel safer fishing this bottom. We were going to put one of those pipe buoys over it and tell the shore patrol folks to come out and mark it permanent."

Jenks nodded and said, "And two?"

"My mom left a pair of stud earrings on board, in a compartment below the bridge, rubies circled in diamond chips." Connie said. "She had worn them on the boat. Dad gave them to her after I was born. Cause of our red hair. She didn't want one of them getting snagged on something and gettin' lost, so she took 'em off whenever she was aboard, and they got left on the boat." She eyed Jenks to see if it was going over; he was looking off at the horizon. She followed the gaze and saw nothing.

"I don't know if you read the papers, but she went down at night and we didn't have long to get off her. Mom wasn't even on board that night. No one even remembered them for a few weeks." She stopped before she got too far from something verifiable.

Jenks looked over into his own boat at a pile of clothes and said, "Kids—Brad, Connie, you may not believe this, but I do burn badly. You might not think it," he said, rubbing his left coffee brown forearm. "I need to get clothes on. Why don't we call this a day to remember and move on?" He spread his palms again. "Deal?" He extended his right hand to shake.

"You're done with us?" Brad asked. He took the extended hand.

"Through with chasing us around?" Connie added.

"Done," Jenks said. "I'll write it up tonight, send them a note, and maybe get you cleared. It doesn't mean that your case will ever be closed.

The government's got a long memory. But I think I'll be done with this case."

Connie began untying the lashings, releasing the Whaler from its hold on the PQ. Both boats were quickly put in order, with Jenks's equipment transferred over and loose articles tied down or stowed. From the console of the Boston Whaler, Jenks called over, "One more thing."

Suspicious, Brad called back, "What?"

"I may owe you, but try real hard not to need a favor."

Moments later, both boats were powered up and heading back to different docks in Apalachicola. Standing behind the captain's chair, Connie held on to the back of Brad's seat, her ponytail streaming behind her in the wind. She ran a hand through the bristly stubble of his hair and then bent over and kissed his ear. She remained there and whispered, "It felt like I almost lost you today. I don't want to lose you, you beautiful boy!"

He pressed a hand against her scarlet mop of hair, holding her head against his as they sped northeast toward the Number 1 channel marker. A smile spread slowly across his face. "Let's go to Dreamland!"

Chapter 14

I have come to believe that a great teacher is a great artist and that there are as few as there are any other great artists. Teaching might even be the greatest of the arts since the medium is the human mind and spirit.

John Steinbeck

April 7, 1985
Wakulla Beach

Connie Chappell rapped on the front door with three tentative taps. The screen door knocked loosely in its frame, magnifying her taps into louder bangs than she'd intended. Nothing happened for a while, and she was about to knock again, on the frame this time, when the door opened. Lucy's face lit up immediately when she saw Connie through the screen. Lucy opened it reached to give her a hug. "Connie, honey, come on in and set yourself down. Can I get you some iced tea?" Then she offered the *pièce de résistance*: "Would you like some cake? It's double chocolate."

Ten minutes later, they were sitting at the kitchen table. Connie had eaten all of the cake but pushed around a large wad of chocolate frosting with her fork, deciding whether to eat it. "Lucy, can I ask you something?"

"Sure, hon," Lucy said. "What's up?"

Lucy had fallen back in love with coastal Florida. At first, the stark beauty of the treeless Nevada landscapes had reinforced the hollow hurt in her chest when she thought of everything she had left behind. Her husband, her son, and her home had seemed irretrievable. She had found herself wrapped in fear, self-doubt, and, as she had come to learn, paranoia. Moving back to Florida, to her old home, provided some solace. Having her son listing the same house as a home address was a comfort. But the shadow of Whit's absence, even when she factored in his intolerant reaction to her fears, was still devastating. She looked at Connie's troubled face, as the young woman gathered her thoughts. "Are you okay, sweetie?"

"Yes, ma'am, I'm fine. It's just that ..."

"Girl, you don't look fine. What's wrong? Is everything all right with your family? Are you and Brad still together?" She stopped, thinking she may have overstepped. She reached over and offered her hands to Connie.

"Yes, we're all right," she replied, taking Lucy's right hand. With her own right hand, she still worried the lump of frosting. "Brad told me that he didn't tell you about the last dive we took Tuesday. It's been bothering me." She nibbled at a twist of frosting on her fork. She looked up at Brad's mother. "Can I tell you about it? I need to talk to someone about what happened."

"Sure, hon." For the next twenty minutes, they walked in the yard, and Connie confided almost everything that they had been doing: their search for the *Lou Anne*, the plane's flyovers, the diver down rescue, the short discussion they'd had in the sea skiff before they split up, and the near retrieval of the artifact.

"Wait a minute," Lucy interrupted her. "You weren't trying to find your mother's earrings?"

"No, I'm afraid we were trying to recover the artifact, and it's still down there in the *Lou Anne*."

Lucy slapped her thigh. "The two of you!" She shook her head in mock disgust. "And that boy!" She pointed her index finger up to make a point. "Remember this, Connie!" She then wagged the finger at her. "When you have kids, they will lie to you. They will lie behind your back; they will lie before they sneak out; they will lie when they sneak in later, much too late; and they will lie in front of your face lookin' pitiful like it was all someone else's fault. He told me he threw it out into the Gulf of Mexico the night Whit was murdered!"

"Mrs. Hitchens—Lucy?" Connie pleaded. "He told you that to protect you!"

Lucy Hitchens looked at her, puzzled, and then a hint of good humor took over. "So those guys crawling over the flats looking with metal detectors?"

Connie caught the shift and gave her a lopsided grin. "That little waste of the federal budget is courtesy of your son, who can lie to your face and look pitiful doing it."

Lucy started to walk over to the porch but stopped and turned back to Connie. "Sunny told me about those guys and scratched his head in his real peculiar way. You'd have to know him, but he got a funny look, like he was the model for the Gomer Pyle character, and scratched his stubble. You should have heard him describe the 'Tom fool waste of money.'"

"Lucy?" Connie pointed at the house and tapped her ear.

"Right, I know, I'm probably bugged."

"I need to go for a walk in the woods," Connie said, placing her hand on Lucy's shoulder in invitation. "Are you interested in coming with me?"

"No, Miss Connie. You go right on ahead. I've got some things to do before the workweek starts tomorrow, and, actually, I just don't want to go out there again real soon. I went down there for a chat New Year's day and don't need to go back for a while." Lucy put on a "no nonsense, absolutely not" attitude that had served her well in the Vegas game rooms. She had had plenty of reasons to say no. She turned to go into the house where she knew Connie would not press the idea. "And Connie, if you want to drop by after and get something for your dinner, come along to the kitchen door when you get back, y'hear?"

"Yes, ma'am, I'll be back in a few hours, okay?" As she walked to the blue Honda, she could hear muttering coming from the kitchen.

~ ~ ~

Connie entered the glen hesitantly, reverently, as if she were entering a church, aware that something or someone was resting there and being respectful of its space. She squeezed through the thin branching trunks of titi and settled on the bank of the little pool.

Leaning over the edge, she cupped a handful of the tannin-stained water and took a sip. It was cool and refreshing even with its musty taste and odor. She directed her thoughts to the deeper end of the pool opposite the titi thicket and expressed the thought, "Hello, Ka-Litan."

hello Ka-nee ... is long time ... many suns?

The thoughts were forming right behind her ears, closer to the occipital lobe sight centers than the auditory cortex. The familiar sense of being talked to from behind was far more welcome now than on her first visit. "Yes, Litan. You are getting better at making questions. That is good."

thank, Ka-nee ... Litan try inflect ... last phoneme make question

Connie thought his vocabulary was improving, but he had a long way to go on syntax. They ran through some of their now standard greetings and settled down to his English lessons. She had been coming there more or less regularly when she was home from Chapel Hill. She had found that she could hold mental images of real things and project the word at the same time. Using simple language techniques she might have used with a pre-K student, she had helped Litan build up a basic vocabulary list of simple objects and then, with substantially more difficulty, verbs. He seemed to have no inclination to use articles, and she was unsure if he understood gender.

After only about forty-five minutes or an hour, she would get a headache and have to quit the lesson. This afternoon, she sat, mentally exhausted, looking out at the shaded woodlands around her. The voice returned.

trees ... water ... ground

"Not now. Litan, I am tired."

Litan see same tree Ka-nee see

Startled at this revelation, Connie blinked; she consciously looked at the water and framed the thought "water."

"Now?" she said aloud.

water

She looked at the large pine at the edge of the pool and held the gaze.

tree

"Yes, that is correct." This was as cool as it was disturbing! She looked up at the blue circle of sky through the trees and held the view.

space

"No, not space—sky." She said aloud, "Sky!" Then she thought of the difference. "Litan, the space close to the planet where there is nitrogen and oxygen or other gasses is called atmosphere or sky."

sky same cielo?

"Yes, but cielo is Spanish, you know, from your old friend Guillermo." Litan had told Connie of the several friends he had spoken with over the centuries. They varied from English, Spanish, and French to Indians from unknown tribes. "In my language, English, the visible atmosphere is called the sky."

Earth ... sky ... light blue ... Litan home Dzura ... sky dark blue ... sometimes reddish blue ... atoms not same

Interesting, she thought. He understands that sky color would depend on atmospheric chemistry or maybe density.

"Litan, we need to have a chemistry lesson. Chemistry is the study of the basic elements and how they react. Do you understand chemistry?" She wondered if this was going to be productive. She had taken a year of chemistry in her pursuit of a degree in education and had started a second year in inorganic chemistry on prodding from Brad. But the second year was

258

too difficult. The only way she could think to express herself intelligently to Litan about her atmosphere was to get to the basics of chemistry and physics.

Litan understand kem-stry ... atom basic ... atom same gi ... more than one gi we call 'fera.'

She thought about that for a bit. "Same atoms, just atoms. Maybe solid, liquid, or gas, all one kind of atom. If different kinds of atoms, connected, we call it a substance."

different ... gi together ... 'fera.'

Connie thought, If he can see what is in my field of vision, I could probably bring books with pictures and work on his vocabulary and an understanding of a lot more than I can talk about. She looked at her watch and then the sky.

She thought, "Litan, how many, umm, what number different gi on Dzuran? How many different gi or elements?"

Litan pilot ... not trained kmist ... only know basics ... 212 gi

"Whoa!" She thought. "That doesn't sound right." She stood, dusting off her jeans, and said, "Litan, I'll be back in a few days."

Chapter 15

Mother, mother ocean, I have heard your call
Wanted to sail upon your waters since I was three feet tall
You've seen it all, you've seen it all.
Jimmy Buffet

May 1985
Tempe, Arizona

Graduation seemed pointless when you were staying on in preparation for grad school. Spring semester at Arizona State had been challenging enough. Taking on the multiple roles of graduate student, teaching assistant, and weekend dive-shop employee was probably not too different from what many bootstrap students endured. Brad Hitchens lived, studied, and worked in Arizona, but his major thoughts were about a waterlogged boat a few miles off the Florida coast. Connie had left Chapel Hill for Florida, and he didn't have the money for the phone calls he'd like to have made every night. His side job, weekend sales and tank filler at Mountain Divers, kept his mind focused on his goal of wreck diving and allowed him to practice in cave dives in Lake Pleasant. There were no interesting wrecks to dive in Lake Pleasant, so he practiced in confined areas. He had made numerous dives under the floating docks at the several marinas near the Lake Pleasant dam.

By the time he was packing to head home to Florida, he had learned to wear strap-heel flippers that could easily be removed in tight places where flippers were a detriment. He'd learned to always go in with a guide rope to get out of trouble, and he'd learned that he should never, ever go into tight places without a buddy diver nearby. He'd learned to plan each dive carefully, to map out what could be done in thirty-minute segments, and to break down goals into doable tasks. Taking what he'd learned in the *Lou Anne* into his dive classes, he realized that the rules of survival made perfect sense. But the nagging question from the spring dives persisted: would he have been better off if Jenks had died on the boat?

June 10, 1985
Apalachicola, Dive 1

Long-frequency, two-foot swells, created in a storm off the Mexican coast, rolled gently under the *PQ*'s lapstrake planking. A gentle three-knot breeze kicked up a very light chop from the east. An eleven o'clock sun was approaching zenith, ensuring maximum visibility for at least three hours. Sitting on the edge of the captain's chair, Brad simply wanted to get the artifact back in hand and see what he had. He needed to find out what was so important to the Feds that his father and at least two others had been killed to keep it quiet. Connie had arranged to borrow, for at least a week, her dad's sea skiff, the *Pain Quotidien*.

The name derived from Chase Chappell's French Acadian roots in Louisiana and from his underlying, but lapsed, Roman Catholic rearing. Not many boats hailing from Apalachicola boasted French names. Most, like the *Lou Anne*, were named for wives, girlfriends, or daughters and boasted block lettering in house paint rather than the *Pain Quotidien's* gold leaf on the varnished wooden stern. Instead of trying to pronounce it, many of the locals simply called Chase's restored '55 sea skiff, the PQ, and thought it too dandy to do any serious work.

Brad hoped to prove them wrong. Behind the two seats in the cockpit lay a pile of tanks, diving gear, nylon lines, and other equipment meant to make his search as safe as possible. Connie asked, "You really got a plan for all of this stuff?" He looked at her in her oversized, floppy sun hat, which shaded her tanned, freckled shoulders.

"Yes, dear, I really have a plan." He waved a hand over the pile. "If Jenks had had a plan, I wouldn't have had to drag his waterlogged butt out of trouble. This pile is this big because of the failure of that plan. I'd really like to get this done in one day so the powers that be don't notice that we happen to be diving on this wreck." He looked back over at her and winked. "The only thing we don't need down there is suits."

"Wet suits? I don't see any wet suits."

"Bathing suits. We don't need bathing suits!" He grinned at her with his best boyish grin. "Haven't you said you always wanted to dive naked?"

Connie threw a towel at him that almost went overboard. Not removing her bathing suit, she began to pull on her buoyancy compensator and belt. "Bradley Hitchens, I need to tell you that I don't want to have to go in after you today. So you be careful!"

"Yes, I will be," he said playfully. He was centering his weight belt, and as he secured the lower tie of his knife sheath to his thigh, he added, "Con, I've been planning this dive for over two months now, and unless something really strange happens, I think we'll be back up in less than twenty minutes. Maybe we'll even have some time to go after some fresh dinner."

"You're sounding awfully cocky for someone who got pretty freaked out last time."

"Yeah, well last time, I was rescuing a first-class party crasher, too!" He stood and helped put Connie's forty-pound tank on. At near rest at fifteen feet, she should be a good safety observer for almost thirty minutes and have spare air in case he got into trouble. His own forty-pound tank would allow him to do some light lifting or a little heavy work for about twenty minutes and have extra air. As hard as the scuba apparatus made maneuvering above sea level, it also made it so nice to be down in the calm, blue-green quiet below sea level. With a little attention to the buoyancy compensators, they could approach weightlessness.

Grace was another matter entirely. As humans invading a hostile world, they were slow, encumbered by the mass on their backs, limited by the loss of peripheral vision, and denied the near silence of the realm by the constant pulsing hiss and boil of their regulators. Connie and Brad sat on opposite gunnels of the boat and did a final visual check of each other's gear while they pulled, tightened, and adjusted their straps and snaps. Eventually, everything was as good as it could be, and after a shared thumbs-up, they splashed backward.

The *Lou Anne*'s hull was beneath them. They had anchored by tying up to a cabin house window frame. Brad was not wearing flippers but had on rubber reef-walker shoes. He had decided to sacrifice maneuverability outside the boat in favor of minimal silt disturbance inside. He pulled himself down the tie rope as Connie swam down beside him.

Yellow green shafts of sunlight flashed through the darker blue-green waters. The two divers approached the hull, stopped for an ear-popping pressure equalization at twelve feet, and then reached the railing. They pulled along it aft toward the afterdeck. Brad stopped to tie off a medium-weight yellow nylon line to a deck cleat and then moved down to the aft hatch.

When operating on the surface, the four-by-five raised hatchway allowed fish, shrimp, or other harvested seafood to be tossed into two different freezer boxes. The boxes, buoyed by Styrofoam, had broken free of their rusted mounts and floated up or to port, and the resulting opening to starboard allowed ready access to the interior. Prying the starboard hatch cover open, the two divers lowered themselves and looked into the darkened hold. The shaft of his sealed Q-beam revealed swirls of sea slime clinging to wooden surfaces, anemones, stars, and slugs combing many of the interior surfaces in their never-ending hunt for the next meal. The various soft attachments on nearly every surface waved in rhythm with the swells passing overhead. Motes, stirred by subtle currents, floated in the few shafts of light. Otherwise, clarity in the hold was remarkably good.

Brad knew that this was a temporary condition and that if he caused any turbulence, he would cloud one corner and the next until visibility would be gone and he would need the nylon lifeline trailing from his belt to get out. His great advantage over Jenks was that he knew where he had hidden the artifact. Connie was looking intently through her mask at him as he gave one more thumbs-up and pulled himself in under the lower edge of the cooler. His tank bumped it lightly, causing a rain of brown scum to fall, dropping visibility in the rear hold by about half. Cursing his stupidity, he pulled himself along handholds to the bulkhead that had been the anchor for the chiller machinery.

The chiller's original sheet-metal housing had turned to rust in the hold in a very few years, and Mike had built a protective wooden casement around it. It wasn't as pretty as the woodwork on the *Pain Quotidien*, but it had been stout. Now, slime and calcified boring worm traces covered the once-oiled woodwork. He turned his body sideways, making it easy to orient himself to what had been down. He pulled himself "down" to the backside of the wooden case and knew where he had to reach to get at the artifact. He thrust his hand into the darkness, and there was no gap.

Was he confused? Had he misremembered where it was stashed? Disoriented himself? Pausing to slow his heart rate and calm himself, he thought back. He remembered many years ago when he had shown the piece to Connie. He looked around and then turned his attention to what had been the back of the chiller case, which was now flush with the inner planking of the hull. Every surface in the hull was covered in slime, anemones, sea fans, or some other wiggling, swaying life form that made identification of original objects and shapes challenging. Reaffirming his bearings, he saw that the case was now flush with the hull. The metal artifact was somewhere behind or below the wooden case that housed the chiller and that he estimated to be a few hundred pounds. The heavy case had remained intact, but it had broken loose from its deck screws. The simple retrieval dive had just become complex.

It would have been far simpler had the housing been constructed of marine plywood. That would be a spongy mess by now. But Mike was a craftsman, and he had used cypress planking with tenon joints reinforced with stainless-steel screws. He had justified the extra effort by saying he didn't want the damn thing tumbling about below decks in a storm. The cypress was in near-perfect condition where the worms had not been active and the casing was jammed on some part of the chill compressor inside it. The casing wasn't going to budge without some sort of leverage. Something began to block the shafts of sunlight falling through a porthole window.

Turning, he was amazed to see a cloud of brown water blossoming between him and the hatch. He fought an urge to bolt as the soft brown cloud roiled in front of him. Something closer to panic than fear began to bang in his chest. Bits of material floated at the edge of the cloud, mocking his planning. He was aware that his heart rate was high; the dreumbeat in his temples almost drowned out the regulator noise. Brad rolled and looked up. Yes, up was up! The silver cloud of air lining a corner of the cabin trunk, which from his vantage looked like a puddle of mercury, was snaking out of a vent. Breathe slowly, breathe slowly, breathe slowly, he ordered himself. The mantra traced across his consciousness and took hold. He repeated and listened until his breathing rate returned to a little above normal.

He turned again and tied the line around the top of the chiller box; securing it with a hitch, he now had a tight line between it and the hatch. Shining his high intensity Q-beam along the line, he pulled himself along it. He bumped into a few things that seemed out of place, and when his regulator bumped the Styrofoam-lined floating ice boxes, he knew he was close. Soon, his hands found the edge of the hatch, and he pulled himself through. Connie was waiting outside the hatch and helped guide him out through the opening.

He pointed up, and using her flippers, she took them both up to the rope ladder hanging from the side of the skiff. As they broke the surface, they both threw their masks into the boat and gulped fresh, clean air.

"Well?" Connie asked. "Did you find it? Was it easy to get to the chiller? Where is it?"

"I don't have it. It was easy to get to the chiller, but it's still down there." He watched her face melt in disappointment and said, "Come on, let's get out of these things."

Taking their places on opposite gunnels, she asked, "Brad, talk to me; how did it go?" He went over the dive in detail—the easy approach, the shifted chiller casing, the array of junk lining the new "bottom" of the boat, and the covering of marine life that coated almost everything, as well as his inability to get at the artifact. After a short pause, he admitted his near panic when he saw the way out blocked by the cloud of sediment.

"Is there anything else we can do today?" she asked.

"Yes, we need to go back down and break out the forward bridge windows to let currents clear out sediment faster. If we can do that and get the forward hatch open, it might clear itself naturally so we can get in tomorrow."

"But what about tomorrow? How are you going to get at the artifact?"

Brad realized that he had just invented his next dive plan on the spot and answered, "Well, I go down tomorrow with a crowbar, and you attach a float bag to the lifeline. We loosen the casing, the line pulls it out of the way, and, *voilà!* We have it."

June 11, 1985
Dive 2 – Gulf of Mexico

The following afternoon, Brad and Connie splashed again to find the increased ventilation through the hull had, in fact, cleared it of sediment. It was safe to dive. Added to their complement of dive gear was an iron crowbar, a military surplus duffle bag, and a hundred feet of half-inch, heavy nylon cord. "Hey, Con?" Brad said as they sat on their pre-dive pile of equipment. "I've been thinking about yesterday. I think we need to establish two ways out. If I'm in trouble and start tapping the trouble signal, I don't want you to glide into another brown cloud not knowing what trouble I'm in."

"Is this a plan revision?" she asked. "Another midstream invention?" She looked concerned. For eight weeks, Brad had been planning and working out what he needed to bring, thinking about what could go wrong.

Brad said, "Connie, listen to this and see if this is not reasonable." She was struck by the no-nonsense look on his face. All traces of the boyish grin and the twinkle in his eyes had vanished, and she was looking at a grown man. He was an adult in a hard world. She thought about all the crap he had gone through to get to this point, and it made sense. The early loss of his mother, the murder of his father by Jenks and Company, having to flee his only home, and later the showdown with Jenks using a drawn weapon, all while protecting a secret that could change how mankind looked at its place in the universe had made Brad grow up. She realized she had not been listening, and his words had broken in on her distracted mind. "… then if we get silted out, I can pull on the opposite lifeline to find a way out."

"I'm sorry, Brad, I zoned out and missed a lot of that. I don't want to screw up down there; can you start over? A second lifeline sounds like a good idea."

With a hard look, he started over from the beginning, outlining his plan to provide a lifeline for a second exit. The second lifeline traced through the pilothouse into the hull would approach the chiller unit from the opposite side, so he would have two exits.

On the next dive, they went down with Connie pulling Brad, who was again finless. Since she had no wreck-diving experience, she would not go in unless she got an SOS from Brad. This was to be repeated banging on his tank with the blade of his dive knife—a noise she had heard underwater and would never forget. The first stop was a look into the hold through the afterdeck hatch. Their plan had worked; opening up the hull in as many places as they could had allowed natural currents to blow silt clear of the lower hold. They next tied the duffle bag with heavy line through its grommets to the original lifeline that had been left wrapped around the chiller case. Connie had a small marine fire extinguisher tied to her equipment belt. She could insert it into the bag, and when she pulled on the trigger, the CO_2 burst would fill the duffle. Once inflated, if the gas wasn't enough to fill the bag, she could augment it with her own bubble stream. The line would still be tied off to the deck cleat and would only pull the chiller case a few feet so as not to plug the after hatch opening.

They faced off mask to mask; a grin slowly spread across Connie's face, and in turn, spread to Brad's. Instead of a thumbs-up, she blew a bubbly kiss, which he returned. At the entrance to the pilothouse, he tied off his second line and pulled hand over hand into the boat, keeping the new escape line taut as he worked his way down into the dark teal gloom inside the the hull. His sealed beam told him that there was still more silt down there than he would have thought from their glance through the rear hatch, but he could still make out all of the basic shapes clearly enough. As he swam down to the chiller box, he could see his second rope leading out of the stern. He found a perch for the Q-beam that would light up his work area and got ready to pry with the crowbar.

Crowbars worked on the simple principal of the lever. In most cases, there was a hard surface around to get purchase on with either the recurved end or the bent end. But Brad found that most of the plywood surfaces were too soft to allow him any purchase. Each attempt had stirred up a little cloud of brown silt mixed with floating wood slivers. These would vanish astern after a few moments if he was patient and let the slow current wafting through the hull take them away. Waiting took up precious minutes. Looking at his watch, he saw he had only twenty minutes before the red zone. His red zone could be set on his countdown watch to beep when he was at a point where he would have to stop the day's work and head for the surface—no matter what.

~ ~ ~

Connie was looking at her watch from her station near the rear deck. A shadow passed over her, which she welcomed, because a few dolphins had circled the PQ earlier and then come down to investigate her bubbles. Dolphins were always welcome on a dive because they had an aversion to sharks of all kinds and would chase away or kill most varieties if they had a calf in the pod. She looked up her bubble stream toward the PQ for a sign of movement. She had not expected to see the bright flash of silver reflecting off the upper flanks of a barracuda.

The fish was examining her from a point above and exactly in front of the sun. From the barracuda's point of view, Connie was well lit. The yellow-green, undulating shafts of sunlight provided good lighting on something that moved and might be food. It did not look like most of the food it had ever encountered, but it seemed to be attached to something.

From Connie's point of view six feet below, the dark shape was menacing enough even with its mouth closed. She knew they rarely attacked humans unless there was a smell of blood in the water. They weren't seen hunting in packs often and liked to snap up small fish from schools. They could be caught by accident by fishermen who were dragging for school fish because of this.

Her thoughts went to an early snorkeling dive with her father in St. Joe Bay when she was six. They had been scalloping in its shallow waters. Connie had been wearing one of her mother's hand-me-down US Divers masks that had a stainless-steel band securing the glass faceplate. The silvery shine glinting off that band had attracted a barracuda that was almost as long as she was. She had frozen in place, slowly floating to the surface to breathe. Chase had noticed her stationary and come up. He too had frozen when he saw the fish. The toothy mouth was opening and closing, drawing water through its gills as it maintained its position five feet away. A sudden strike by this fish would not be fatal, but it would certainly maim. Chase had acted first. In the shallow water, he made a sudden lunge at the barracuda while opening his arms and screaming through his snorkel. The fish vanished and was not seen again.

Drawing on the memory, she released her grip on the lifeline, slowly drew her hands in front of her, and with a kick of her fins and a bubble-encased scream, spread her arms wide to increase her visual size. It worked. The fish left. Then she heard brad tapping out shave and a haircut, the signal to inflate the bag.

~ ~ ~

Brad had found purchase on a ship's framing timber, but he hadn't been able to move the cabinet. The weight of the chiller was pinning it and, consequently, the artifact, to the inside of the *Lou Anne*'s hull. He had stirred up more silt than he was happy with and decided it was time to give the air balloon tactic a try. He started tapping to the rhythm of "Shave and a Haircut, Two Bits." The first lifeline almost immediately went taut. The sudden release of CO2 into the duffle bag gave it incredible buoyancy, and the lifeline was straining against the chiller housing. His second lifeline was also tied to the wooden cabinet. He wrapped a length of cord around his right wrist and placing two feet against the former deck, strained to loosen it.

This was where all the planning broke down. With the buoyancy of the air-filled duffle pulling on it, the chiller box suddenly released, sliding three feet toward the stern hatch. At this sudden movement, a cloud of silt exploded from the casing as it and Brad shifted aft. The sudden shock of movement and the disorienting tug that had inverted him was surprise enough, but he soon realized that the second lifeline was entangled around his left ankle. He was trying to visualize the wrappings that he could not see when the first lifeline jumped again.

~ ~ ~

Outside, Connie had been pleased with the results of their "on the cheap" buoyancy bag. The burst of gas from the fire extinguisher had filled the duffle immediately, and a few seconds later, the rig had jerked to the limit of the lifeline's grip on the deck cleat. She thought they must be almost through with the dive and was almost going to miss the adventure. This was the kind of stuff you could tell grandkids about! Hey, there might even be a book in this someday, she thought. Then, unexpectedly, rust and decay finally took its toll on the deck cleat. The buoyant duffle, ballooning to hold about thirty-five quarts of buoyant air, provided seventy pounds of urgent pull against the aging bolts securing it to worm-softened wood. The cleat broke away from the rail still wrapped in the lifeline and dragged everything attached to it another six feet toward the surface.

~ ~ ~

Inside, Brad was trying to figure out what was wrong with his dive plan. He was enveloped in a blinding cloud of brown silt. He was hamstrung from right wrist to left ankle by the second lifeline that was now pulling hard to dislocate either a shoulder or leg joint. He could tell where "down" was by a dim glow coming from the Q-beam. A brief struggle against the line proved fruitless. He could move the line by pulling against the buoyancy of the duffle, but he could not get enough angle or rotation to free either wrist or ankle.

Brad could bend just enough at the waist by exercising the most extreme abdominal crunch he had ever attempted to get to the hilt of his dive knife. But with his free left hand, he couldn't reach the clasp on his right thigh that meant his deliverance. He tried three more times before giving up. He pulled his dive watch close to his face and in the dim brown light that filled his world could make out the needle just a few degrees from the red zone. He cursed uselessly for a few seconds and then began the mantra again.

"Breathe slow, breathe slow, breathe slow, breathe slow." Slowly organized thought took hold again. The dive watch! Reaching around, he began to tap the watch's stainless steel bezel steadily on the tank. The tink, tink, tink was much quieter than he would have made with the dive knife, but he had few options. He was suspended in a brown cloud and strung out and along part of the lifeline that was supposed to have been his salvation. He had not kept it taut and one of the coils had wrapped an ankle. That was his first mistake. Great! At least I can die knowing what I did wrong. His world was dark brown and becoming painful as the strain on his joints increased. It was a world without form or void. Suspended as he was along the length of line, he couldn't seem to touch anything solid. Tink, tink, tink. *Please, Connie, hear this!* Tink, tink, tink, tink. *Please let this be loud enough.*

Another sound joined the rhythmic tapping of his watch housing on his tank. His dive watch timer joined in with short bursts of high frequency: beep, beep, beep! The three beeps followed by a long pause repeated as he tapped. Five minutes of air left!

The miracle came slowly to his consciousness. The pressure on his right elbow was decreasing. He pulled at the waist and found he could pull against the line; it was giving! He flexed his left knee and with much less effort than he would have suspected, got the hasp of his knife sheath open and freed the knife. It was no longer necessary. He had enough movement now to release the curl of rope around his wrist and only had to reach down—or was it up?—to get at the tangle of rope at his feet. He reached for the glowing sealed beam, grasped it, and then reached for the rope at his ankle. He pulled along it and into clear water in the forward cabin under the pilothouse. He looked at his watch, realizing that it had been beeping for some time. The needle was halfway through the red zone.

Bradley had been exerting and scared, no telling how much air had been lost to struggling against the lifeline. He grabbed at handholds and bulkheads and burst into the welcome window-lit brightness of the pilothouse. Pulling with both arms on the companionway, he jetted toward and through the doorway to the aft deck and found Connie, staring at him through wide eyes.

As they ascended, being careful to not outrun their own bubbles, he could the taste the change in his air supply from the easy breathing of a freely flowing rush of fresh air to the sensation of sucking vacuum out of a lifeless metallic substance. This time, as they reached the boat and each hung from one arm from the gunnels, he tossed his mask over the edge, spit out the regulator's breather, and pulled Connie to him. When she had cleared her face gear, he kissed her hard. They hung that way for a minute or two before he noticed that he was hanging from his right arm and his right shoulder really hurt.

He had difficulty pulling himself over the rail and allowed Connie to go first and pull him up—a reversal of their usual pattern. They shed their tanks, and Brad collapsed into the captain's chair. Connie didn't have to ask if he had it. They had been down too long, and he had been intent on getting up as soon as possible. Her eyes asked a thousand questions, but she waited for him to speak.

Brad stared, realizing that she had done something to save his life. From some past literature, the phrase 'hoisted on his own petard' worked through his many rushing thoughts. But he knew that the analogy was wrong. His own lifeline had nearly strung him out to die. He wondered if there were any old wreck divers, or did they all eventually make one last mistake? He thought of the many plans he had made over the last months of spring—how they had all changed yesterday when he saw clearly the conditions inside the boat. "It's a good thing we are out of air!"

Connie didn't laugh at the gallows humor. "Okay, dive master! How is it a good thing? Were you thinking of going back down today?"

"When I was leaving, after the rope went slack, I reached down to get the Q-beam, and I saw it. I saw the rod." He allowed himself a smile and a sigh of relief. He was alive; the rod was attainable. "We need the hull to clear for a day for visibility. And then we can snatch it."

"Is that all?"

"No, I—"

She cut him off. "How about a 'Thanks, honey, for saving my bacon!'"

~ ~ ~

That evening, sitting around the Chappell dinner table, they found that the only way they could relate the dive to Chase and Lou Anne was to infuse humor. Connie was telling her side as the outside observer. "So there I am watching this six-foot barracuda head off toward the front of the boat. I'm wondering if it has gone back into the hull, if we'd rousted it from its safe haven. Then I hear the signal tap to gas the duffle bag, and I blow the fire extinguisher into the bag. So, it goes perfectly, fills up like planned, and pulls hard on the line, and as it fills, I can tell it's really pulling on the chiller. Then, wham!

It breaks loose. It can only get so far because we tied it off to a deck cleat, but the cleat breaks, and the line is being pulled like crazy by the duffle bag. So when I'm expecting for the chiller end of the line to be loose, it's tight as hell. I could have played music on it, it was strung so tight."

Knowing that they were both safe, Chase and Lou Anne wore expectant, thin-lipped smiles on their faces as if they were waiting for a tightrope dancer to fall. Lou Anne asked, "Did you know right away that he was in trouble?"

"Almost right away!" Connie looked at Brad who had gone sheepish in embarrassment. "You know when you get a really good-sized cobia or snapper on a hook and it starts to panic near the surface on a tight line?" Heads bobbed around the table. "That's what the line started doing. I didn't know what was going on except that a big brown cloud of silt blew out of the rear hatch and this line was jerking hard."

She paused for effect. "I was beginning to think Bradley was having it out with the barracuda inside the boat when between breaths, I heard a really faint tap. I swam down to the edge of the hatch and heard it louder: 'Tink, tink, tink' in the SOS pattern just like we'd planned, only weaker.

"Now, I'm scared. My watch says I have about five to ten minutes left. I haven't been doing any work or wrestled any barracudas, but I'm thinking I don't want to go in there with no visibility and find a dead Brad being eaten. My next thought was if it isn't the barracuda, then maybe he's stuck in the line somehow." She sighed, closing her eyes, recalling the moment of horrible realization of what was happening. Opening her eyes after a brief moment, she continued, "So, I slashed the line to the duffle. It zoomed to the surface, and a few minutes later, Brad comes blasting out of the cabin like it was about to cave in on him." She paused again, leaving out a lot, and simply said, "And here we are."

Brad cut in. "Yup, not quite like I'd planned it, but I guess I need to add another rule to wreck diving, maybe at the top of the list: 'the unexpected always happens.'"

Chase asked, "You said earlier that you know you saw the metal rod?" He was reluctant to call it an artifact despite his daughter's explanation of what it was and what it might mean. His military background made it hard for him to believe that the US military or some wing of it had been the agents of Brad's father's death. And his own belief system made it hard for him to accept the UFO business that both kids seemed convinced was real. "Why don't I go out with you tomorrow to retrieve it? If the water in the hull has cleared, and we both think it's safe, we'll all three go down and make sure this is the last dive."

Connie and Brad looked at each other. First, he shrugged, and she followed suit. "Sure, okay. I'd appreciate your advice if it's stuck in anything else." Brad was quietly grateful that he wouldn't have to put Connie at risk again, if anything else went awry. "Have you ever been in a wreck before?"

"No, but I used to dive the caves up in Jackson County and the sinks over in south Leon. So, I'm pretty good in tight places."

Lou Anne said, "Hon, are you sure? It has been a long time since you used your tanks."

"Yeah, I'm sure. And besides, we can put a serious sea anchor line on that buoy, so we know where the wreck is, and no one will drag their nets on it." He waited for Lou Anne to nod in agreement before adding, "Besides, I'd like to look at her one last time before her timbers cave in. Just to see how she's holding up."

Chapter 16

When something is missing in your life, it usually turns out to be someone.

Robert Brault

June 20, 1985
Wakulla

The teal green rod, the artifact, lay in the middle of the kitchen table, an innocuous piece of very important junk. Lucy Hitchens was happy to have a last dinner with her son, his girlfriend, and sister

Susan at home before listening to the outcome of the much-discussed plans. She was not as happy to find out that Brad had come close to drowning, more than once, trying to retrieve the artifact. Connie and Brad had learned from dinner earlier at the Chappells' house that trying to make light of it made it go a little easier. It did not appear that the strategy was working on Brad's mother, though.

Lucy said, "So after you risked your life saving this federal guy last spring, you work hard to kill yourself in the same way, in the same place, twice?"

"Mom," Brad cut in once more, saying, "one, I didn't know he was who he was until he was up and gasping for air. If Connie hadn't been there, I don't know. But she was there. Two, we obviously didn't go out there to try to repeat his experience. We had planned carefully, but things didn't go as planned, and three, throwing up his hands in a shrug, 'it ain't nothin' but a thing!'" He quoted one of his dad's sayings from "the Nam." He knew it covered all cases from very bad things that almost killed you to simple disagreements within the squad. It was the all-inclusive dismissive expression.

"See what I mean?" asked Lucy, looking at her sister and then to the heavens—actually, the tongue in groove pine paneled kitchen ceiling. Then in mock prayer, she said, "Lord, if you love me, you will make sure he has children of his own to torment him." She glanced back over at Susan and

274

asked, "This is what I get? Nothing but worry and aggravation." Susan said, "Luce, he's a good kid, a little crazy and impetuous, a little big on himself sometimes, but a good kid."

Connie laughed and looked at Brad. "Now there's a ringing endorsement for you, Brad." She counted off on her fingers, "Crazy and impetuous, big on himself—" She looked at Brad's mother and aunt, who were sharing in the roast. She began ticking off more traits on her fingertips. "—good at dive planning, likes to test the limits of his tank air, bad at knots underwater, and to be fair—I could add, not bad looking in a bathing suit!"

"Hey, hey!" Brad broke in. "No fair ganging up on me. Three against one isn't fair."

Grinning, his Aunt Susan said, "She did say, 'not bad looking in a bathing suit.'"

"All right, all right," Brad said. "I get it. No amount of luck can make up for better planning."

"Brad, honey," Susan said, "You said you had planned to get samples of the artifact to some labs for analysis when you got the piece back. Do you have any id—"

Brad put his hand up palm out, in the universal stop motion, and Susan stopped in mid-sentence. He looked over at Lucy who frowned and then, understanding, said, "Don't worry, I think. We had a couple of Sheriff's deputies come out a while ago and sweep the place for bugs again. They found two with dead batteries and one with so weak a signal it was worthless. Maybe you are no longer on their list?" She tried her best reassuring smile.

"Well, okay then," Brad said. "I've got some connections back in the department at ASU. I plan to try my hand at it myself. That's why I've been working on my engineering and chemistry degrees. I want to understand what I'm looking at. I also don't want to chop it up too much. It was almost twenty inches long when I found it, and we gave almost an inch of it up to FSU seven years ago. I hate to cut too much more of it up for analysis, but I want multiple labs to independently analyze the metal." He took Connie's hand. "We need corroboration."

"Brad, sweetie," Lucy asked, "is this hunk of metal worth all the trouble and aggravation you've been through? It's basically a piece of cosmic lost-and-found. Somebody's spare parts!"

Brad was silent for a moment. "Mom, it's way more than a bit of space junk. If it were a piece of refined aluminum, or something else, even exotic earth metal, it would just be a location anomaly. I'd be trying to figure out how it got in the bottom of that tree. You know, if it weren't for Litan and all of that, I'd be willing to think that maybe the tornado that had knocked the tree over had blown some piece of someone's boat into the root ball. But it's not."

Now he started ticking off on his fingers: "One, we have a piece of metal that is extremely unusual in its physical properties, stronger than titanium, tinted throughout, probably not from this planet. That alone, if substantiated, is worth a week's worth of headlines.

"Two, the US government, specifically the Air Force Office of Special Investigations, is especially interested in covering up its existence, which I think is utter BS. We have a right to know more about our place in the universe; and, very importantly;

"Three, there's Ka-Litan, marooned alien pilot. I wouldn't dare try to get him out of the ground until there was at least a conversation going on in the major media about the probability, not the possibility, of there being nonhuman intelligent life capable of space flight."

The three women watched him, expecting more. He paused and then said, "And I really need to figure out who to trust in getting more samples of the artifact out to others."

Susan let out a barely audible "hum" sound, reached down for her purse, and after a short rummage through its bottommost contents came up with a folded piece of paper. She opened it and slid it across the table to Bradley. "This is a contact you will find interesting, Dr. Walters in Detroit." As he reached for it and picked it up, she added, "This is the guy that Dr. Hill was contacting just before he died … or was killed."

"Whaaat?" Brad looked at the much-crumpled paper. It looked like it had been riding in the bottom of the purse for all seven years. "How did you—"

"I did a little research of my own when the three deaths hit the papers," she said and shrugged. "We don't get accidental death dealt to us in Tallahassee like that. It wasn't even a hard connection to make." Brad got up to refill his Coke glass.

"Thanks, wow! This is a really big break." He looked in turn to the three others around the table.

In the pause, Susan and Lucy looked at each other, not quite mirror images, but certainly recognizable as a sister act. They both looked at Brad and then back to each other. Susan nodded her head, and Lucy smiled in agreement. Susan glanced at Connie subtly and got another affirmative from Lucy.

Lucy sighed, paused, and then said, "Bradley, there's something else we need to talk to you about. There's something you don't know; some ... umm, family history that you need to understand." She looked at her sister who was looking back at her with questioning eyes. "Go ahead, Sue, I don't care. It certainly doesn't matter now. And we both owe it to him." She looked at Connie. "And we owe it to both of them to put everything out there."

Connie looked puzzled. Brad leaned on the opened refrigerator door, mouth agape, eyes darting from sister to sister, from mother to aunt.

Aunt Sue stood and took Brad's hand. "Hon, your mother and father had a great marriage while it lasted; I am glad that they fell in love and got married." She gave his hand a squeeze. "Before they were an item, your dad and I were ... " She could feel Brad's muscles in his hands tensing; his forearms grew rigid. "I knew him before your mother did, and we were an item, a major item."

Brad's mouth sagged open in disbelief; his glance again flicked from sister to sister. Connie just stared, awaiting a bomb. Susan looked from Brad over to her sister. Lucy said, "Brad, we should have told you a long time ago. You deserved to know about this long before now."

"What?" He was thoroughly confused. "What, for crying out loud?" he asked, his voice thickening with emotion.

Susan pulled him close. The room was quiet enough now to hear water dripping slowly from a downspout outside as she said softly into his ear, "Brad, honey, your father and I ..." she said and paused, feeling him tense, arms wide. She smoothed his stubbled cheek with the back of her hand and held him harder. "Your dad and I knew each other long before he fell for Lucy. We knew each other from freshman year, and well, Brad ..." He began to squirm, but she held him close. "I'm your mother, sweetie." She was crying into his neck, trying to keep talking. "I could not handle it back then; I left. I came back through before I left town and dropped you off. That was my last stop before Denver and Boulder, before LA, before Frisco, and, finally, Vancouver, before a lot of lost time on the road. You were three before I came back to town and to Whit and Lucy. I hadn't called, written, or checked in on them or you in any meaningful way." She was sobbing softly. "Not cool, I know, not cool." She brushed tears from her cheek with the back of her hand. "Those were the sixties; dropping out was just that, dropping out, and it was wrong. I was wrong." She blinked at the moisture in her eyes, shifter her glance to her sister. "I guess Lucy isn't the only one of the DeLaney sisters that's good at pulling a disappearing act."

Brad was rigid; his were the only dry eyes in the house. Susan pulled away slightly, holding Brad's face in her two palms. "Every bit of it is my fault, sweetie. It wasn't about your father; it wasn't about you. It was me. I was a glorious little hippie chick who got pregnant. Whit was wonderful; he was so happy that you were coming. When he found out you were a boy, he was bouncing off the walls, excited. I ... I was scared witless." She pulled him in again and hugged him close.

Brad wiped at his eyes and shuddered, trying to gather his thoughts from the shock. He looked over at Lucy. "Mom?" He suddenly squinted. "Aunt Lucy? So you're my aunt?"

Susan, caressing his hair, said, "Lucy is your mom; I gave birth to you. So, yes, I am your mother, little 'm.' Lucy is Mom, capital 'M,' the one who raised you, fed you, changed your dirty diapers, read you bedtime books, held you when you were scared, and most important, loved you. She loves you now and always. Lucy is your Mom." She stood looking at him and broke into shuddering sobs. Slowly gaining control, she said, "I birthed you and freaked, left you a few weeks old, and came back three years later to find Whit and Lucy married and happy, and you running barefoot in the yard, a perfect little blond-haired child of God—"

Lucy interrupted. "Susan, please. It's okay. Bradley, sweetie, I got what I couldn't do on my own. That's why you don't have a brother or sister. But you grew up happy and loved. And as I got to know Whit better as he was trying to figure out what to do as a single dad, I did truly fall in love with him." She got up to go to her sister and son. The three of them hugged, the two women wrapped in their son's arms, comforting him and each other. Connie sat stunned, with tears running freely, sobbing softly as the flood of pent-up emotion flowed from the two sisters. She listened as the three whispered, "I love you" to each other. Brad looked over Lucy's head at Connie and with a nod motioned for her to come to them. He opened an arm and took her into the circle. As she took a place at his right, he said very clearly and un-self-consciously into her ear, "And you, Connie, I love you."

~ ~ ~

As breakfast was cooking the next morning, Brad pulled out the piece of paper. "Susan, Mom?"

She said, "I think it's best for us all to stay on first names, okay? It's too confusing now, right?"

"Right, okay." Looking at the paper, he set it down next to the hard-won artifact. It looked as if it had never seen seawater. That was pretty amazing in itself. Very few metals or alloys other than high alloy gold could spend that much time immersed in the ocean and look that good. "Susan, how did you get this name and number?"

Susan sat down with a cup of steaming tea, circling a spoon around, mashing the bag against the cup's inside to speed the leaching process. "I dated your father through over a year of his undergrad at FSU. I knew some of the girls in the department office. Some of them have worked there since they started working." She took a slurping sip from the cup. "Debbie Mullins is still there now. She was at the department when we were students, and she was there when your dad was killed. After the police left, after I had come down here and seen the mess, I began to think about the two supposedly random deaths at the department and Whit. As I was clearing up the mess and straightening up, mail kept coming."

She gave a breathless chuckle and took another sip after blowing chamomile-scented mist across the table. "One day, the phone bill came in, and being curious, I ran through the numbers and called to see if anything made sense. That bill had this house phone and your dad's business phone on the same statement, and I found that your dad had called FSU several times, a few days before ..." She stopped. "Before he was killed, he called Dr. Hill three times. Twice the week before Dr. Hill died and again on the day of his accident, Whit called the geology lab." She took a slurping sip of the still-hot brew and set the cup down. "There was also this call to Detroit. I called this number and found Jason Walters."

Brad thought back nine years to when he and his dad had driven to the shop to cut off a piece of the rod in the bearing press and then on to Tallahassee to drop off the sample. He remembered the long halls of tile— not the kind of Clorox-clean tile you'd find in a hospital, but dusty, institutional tiles lining the lower walls of the department's hallways—and the glass cases full of important rock and fossil samples collected by past field exercises all over the world. He remembered the sprightly, energetic man introduced as Dr. Hill and the true affection he'd shown for his father. "Son of a bitch!" he muttered softly.

"What's the matter?" Susan asked, coming into the kitchen.

"I should have killed Jenks when I had the chance, either time that I had the chance." His knuckles were white on his balled fists. "That lying bastard even admitted having something to do with those deaths, at least to being there, an accomplice, and he's loose somewhere. He's messing with people's lives, and some of them are honest, tax-paying citizens of our fair country."

"Brad, honey." Susan's voice was soothing comfort itself.

"Yeah?"

"Let it go; you've got your artifact back. You have a plan; it's a good plan. Go as public as you can from multiple sources and let the conclusions fall where they may. Let the public know. That's been your point all along, right?"

"Yes, ma'am." He got up to pour a cup of coffee, as the machine's gurgles announced it was nearly finished. "But I'm going to need more than this guy, Jason Walters."

"If he's still in the business and even if he's retired, he would know others from the industry who would also work at major labs. It's a shot—a damned good shot." She looked at him proudly. *How could I ever have been so selfish, so stupid? Look at him. He's as strong-willed and bright as his dad. Given a problem, he won't quit until there's a solution or at least a next step.* Then she said, "It's a next step, honey."

He picked up his coffee cup and held it out to her. "A toast to next steps," they clicked cups, "Mom!"

~ ~ ~

Brad approached the titi thicket with a mixture of apprehension and anticipation. Bright rays of white light jostled for space in the thick carpet of summer ferns at his feet. Greenbrier tugged at his ankles as he left the new refuge trail and made the last few hundred feet to the thicket. As he approached, he considered that Connie and Ka-Litan had been making phenomenal progress in vocabulary and awareness of human—or at least American—culture. She had said that he had an almost vernacular understanding of her speech but that he still didn't know what to do with articles. He knew he had to ask himself and Ka-Litan some questions before he left for Detroit. As he approached, in a dark recess below ground, an indicator light brightened.

Before he had even reached the edge of the thicket, a sort of welcoming question mark formed in his mind. *yes?*

He pushed the thought into the space around him, *It's me.*

280

Their chatter continued as he crawled through the maze of branches, found his spot, and leaned against the trunk of the cypress at the edge of the pool. "Litan, from the parts of your life that you have shared or sent to me, your people, your race seems to have the ability to move from star to star with ease. Do Dzurans move within this galaxy only, or are you able to go to other galaxies?"

Dzuran starships travel star system to other star ... travel in other dimension ... human travel is only in four dimension.

Brad considered this for a minute. "Yes, other dimensions. Is it possible to move out of this star system without using other dimensions?"

yes possible ... four-dimension travel possible ... take long time

Brad knew that he had never felt anything like emotion from these mental conversations, but he could have sworn that he felt something like humor in the last response.

"Did Connie tell you that humans have traveled to our moon, umm, our satellite?"

yes, Ka-nee tell story ... humans travel to moon satellite by drift ... chem thruster then slow drift

"Right." Brad thought of the Apollo flights to the moon, slow drift. He couldn't remember how many thousands of miles per hour the lunar missions reached. He moved on, asking, "What fuel do you use for propulsion? Do you know about our names for elements?"

Ka-nee talk with Li-tan human kemstry ... understand more hydrogen helium ... earth kemstry much basic

"Yeah, I suppose you would think it is." As they talked, Brad came to understand that Litan's Dzuran science was to human science as modern postgraduate human sciences were to alchemy and superstition. He remembered the simplistic shell explanation of energy levels he had been fed through high school and the much deeper electromagnetic theoretical explanations he had been taught in third-year physics at Arizona State. Although he had been force-fed the theories, he still had problems processing the "look" of string theory. No one had yet animated what it might look like if you could see the structures.

He could barely grasp the simplistic terms that Ka-Litan tried to use to explain why there were no real gaps in the Coalition planets' periodic table as there were in the chemistry of modern human understanding. After Brad had reached something approaching mental gridlock, Litan explained briefly and simply that human science was limited to the understanding of physics and the chemistry provided by the humans' star and its planets. He explained that many star-planet systems had only rudimentary elements based on the composition of the primary star's elements before it went nova. Some planet systems had more elements, many more elements than the human star system. Sol, it seemed, lacked some of the ingredients for a full cosmic cookbook.

Brad was stunned by the realization. How simple! It would be like trying to explain to a color-blind person what red was like or trying as a human to visualize the ultraviolet world of insect vision or explaining to a person born deaf that hearing was a refinement of the coarse vibrations felt by our bodies. Why wouldn't a star system that evolved from much older, heavier primary stars generate a gas field rich in higher level, heavier elements that sol system scientists simply wouldn't think of because they didn't exist in our experience? Gaps in the periodic table!

Most of the elements that we had artificially created had nanosecond half-lives. But what if complementary elements were created in the same maelstrom with others that would satisfy the needs of those atom's energy levels? What if, instead of collapsing or shedding electrons, those unstable elements found compatible companions that rendered them stable? What would you call these compounds? Would they actually be hybrid elements that could not exist without their shared electron cloud? Brad slowly emerged from the communication state or reverie that had totally occupied his senses and discovered that his back hurt from pressing against the pine's lumpy bark. His shoulders were hunched, and he was shivering.

He opened his eyes to twilight. He had been talking with Ka-Litan all afternoon, and the darkening woods were cooling. His sweat-dampened T-shirt was now cold and clammy. He quickly surveyed his arms and legs, finding something less than a hundred mosquito welts. A throbbing on the outer rim of his left ear led him to a yellow fly bite that began to really hurt. *How could I have slept through that?*

He felt mentally tired, as if he had been in a long lecture series and taken thirty pages of furiously written notes, yet he had been passively listening for most of a few hours. No, that was not entirely true; it had been more than listening. He felt as though he had been in an immersion learning session, only without the darkened, water-filled tank. Images began to flood back into his mind—three-dimensional models of molecules of compounds that he could not name, that existed slightly above or to the side of the ranks of known chemicals in the periodic table. Yet, as compounds, they should not belong there. If they could exist in those positions in the known periodic table, they would be so unstable as to decay immediately to lower states.

Apparently, Litan had not shared these insights with Connie. As he oriented himself on the outside of the titi thicket and headed for home, he reasoned that she had not been so illuminated because she had not taken any chemistry or physics beyond the most basic general science course required of Chapel Hill undergrads. Her basic sciences curriculum had offered only slight elaborations of the simplistic models explained in the grade schools; the onion model of atomic structure.

Litan sensed her understanding and had not shared with her. That evening, as he lay in his bedroom looking up at the sole plastic model twirling in slow circles on its string, he tried to replay much of the afternoon's exchange of knowledge. As sleep came over him, he felt a familiar tug on his dream state and surrendered. Brad could not remember the last time he had let Litan take him into a dream state, but he was happy to oblige. As usual, his viewpoint began in a familiar place, the cockpit of a P-51 Mustang.

The panel array was familiar; he had memorized the instruments when the Confederate Air Force had visited the Tallahassee airport years ago. The central altimeter was spinning clockwise as he gained altitude; his azimuth indicator lower left was stuck on due north. The rate of climb was steep, and his throttle was full back. The clear blue sky outside the canopy was darkening. He checked the airspeed indicator as it approached and then pegged the five-hundred-mile-per-hour max. Stars began to appear, and as he looked out into the purpling sky, the structural ribs of his canopy disappeared.

Deep Space 6

A hard thump to Jai's hull brought Ka-litan back to consciousness. Looking down now, Litan saw a very different array of indicator lights in unfamiliar hues. Indicators that were normally amber were now mostly blue, some of them flashing for attention. These indictors lined a display console that put his ship's 3-D image at the center of a 3-D grid space, surrounded by vaporous spheres, indicating distances on a logarithm scale. One sensor's alarm was flashing blue and providing annoying audible pings. A quick glance showed it to be a collision avoidance alarm. Images on the inner sphere rotated and yawed wildly. The black outside the cockpit was absolute now, and blurred images of stars flew by in rapidly changing directions. The field of view slammed violently to the side as a large piece of space junk caromed off the side of his starboard force field. The collision avoidance alarm went quiet.

Ka-Litan, squadron commander without a command, became aware that Jai was insisting on attention, aware that he was now awake. Slowly, he lifted an arm out of its crash cradle to tap an autopilot control. The arm hurt. Instead, he told Jai to autocorrect. Short bursts from chem jets fired in succession, correcting for roll and then pitch and finally and hardest, yaw. The last was sluggish. He sighed. Now not only was he nearly out of chem thruster, he was running short in the chem attitude stabilizer jets too. If he lost much more in the way of propulsion options, he would be little better than a tumbling rock. The stars stabilized, and to his amazement, he saw his ship was nowhere close to any of the battlewagons from the Erran fleet nor any Coalition ships. How long had he been out? A tap of lateral jets rotated Jai's main jets to port, and a correction to starboard stabilized him. He was drifting away from the battle scene amid a debris cloud from the dreadnought. Tanks of fluids and gasses were spinning haphazardly in the mélange as their contents spurted into vacuum. The random thought passed his consciousness, If I could only get some of that propellant!

Framing materials, body parts, and a hundred kinds of loose jetsam littered his near space. Off his port bow, at a great distance, he watched the Dzuran Coalition's battle lines reforming in two X-claws. He could tell from his battle array that its outer ships were blacked out and com-silent, hoping to evade the detection of the enraged Erran commanders who had just lost a flagship.

His shields were still on, which might be a mistake because they would surely show on even the most primitive Erran weapons display; without them though; he might easily be smashed by the tumbling wreckage around him. Litan reduced them thrusters to half power to decrease their signature and slowly began to apply a lateral vector to slide his ship out of the expanding debris field so that he could accelerate safely. The terribly slow acceleration of outer-system ion pulse drive was his only tool for redirecting his velocity from what had been a death dive. Ka-Litan had meant to meet the Maker of Lights and found himself alive!

After what he felt was too long, he was clear of the junk and about to hit his main plasma thrusters when a stab of green energy cut across Jai's bow. He instantly spun on his axis and jabbed for full chem power. It wasn't much, but another slice of green energy passed by, missing his cockpit, but too close. Another beam of deadly laser darted past on the port side as his ion pulse engines kicked in and he began slowly picking up intentional velocity on a vector that would get him closer to safety—and farther from the battle lines. He didn't have enough maneuvering fuels left to be useful. As he checked his arrays, the direness of his position began to set in. He was on the wrong side of the battle line—far behind it. Chances were good that his pursuers were rear-guard scouts that spotted him in the debris field and probably blamed him for the destruction of the dreadnought. He would have to take a very long, sweeping turn around the main Erran lines or cut through them. With the two or more trailing fighters, he would not be able to do the latter and he would have to get perilously close to the gravity well of a nearby planet to get back to his lines for refueling, rearming, and minor repairs. Checking his panel, he saw that his shields were in horribly poor shape and his tanks were all but empty—green across the panel, except for one.

One of the halide coolant tanks had been blasted away. His primary near-space com unit had been damaged by a laser strike, but his deep-space com was still amber, as was his life support. Close-combat maneuvering fuel was a problem. There was enough charge in the main battery array for a short-star jump. Last hope, he thought, if it comes to that, and those batteries had no rail gun ammunition left anyway. He had accumulated pulse ion velocity now, and the Erran fighters were trying to flank him. They were slower, but only slightly, and he couldn't get around the corner of their formation without coming into range of their deadly laser bursts. He opted for a quick burst of his nearly depleted chem roll thrusters, which saved him from one burst of green light but propelled him into another. The blast was horrific, and the shock and rebound inside the shield reverberated through the hull. The ka unit Litan lay limp in his harness. Stunned, blinded, and for the time being, unpiloted, Jai maintained the last course Ka-Litan had issued—a course that took him and his pilot much too close to the nearby planet's gravity well.

Jai continued to accelerate until the rear chem jets sputtered their last bit of combustible hydrogen into space. Although he was now incapable of forward thrust other than the slow-to-build pulsed ion drive, the little ship still hurtled into the gravity well, lost and forgotten by the behemoths still engaged in mortal combat above. Jai was a Class IV fighter, one of the best in the Coalition's fleet. He possessed most of the recent tech upgrades, and his psi core had been extensively reworked by his ka himself. His automatic controls had been trained by Litan to anticipate and correct.

He waited for Litan to revive; the life support indicators showed no permanent problem. The ship and its inert pilot continued along a parabolic descent toward oblivion. Jai noted the moment when the planet's gravity threshold was crossed. Litan and Jai were now locked into an unpowered dive toward the planet with only pulsed ion thrusters. These would never be able to negate their asteroid-like plummet. There was too much mass in the planet and no time to decelerate.

Litan woke to audible alarms and a nearly full array of flashing green indicator lights. "Creation's Light!" he swore. This was no way to make planetfall. Litan saw the circle in his forward screen resolving into a sphere as he plunged toward it. It was a few hours away, but the plunge would follow the inexorable laws of physics. Soon, he would watch the blue nitrogen gas bag fill his screen, and he would pass into its soft outer atmosphere. Gradually, he and Jai would pass into a darkened inner atmosphere and drop for however long until they impacted either a condensed liquid nitrogen sea or a rocky core. No matter, Jai would have imploded by then. His only hope now would be scooping some volatiles in the outer clouds to use as chem fuels. He began to scan for chemical concentrations in the outer cloud layers.

A glance at his rear screens showed that all but one of the fin fighters were gone. They had ample maneuvering fuels and could avoid planetfall! A cloaked fighter was tailing him out of range, but closing in. The Errans hadn't realized that when they were cloaked, they still had a detectable signature in the ultra-high frequencies. He was being chased, and he had only yaw and roll maneuvering chem jets left. He shut down the pulsed ion drive; no use in depleting his reserves! There was only one option left: jump! He palmed up the jump screen and hit recall. He was no longer at the last destination point; he was over a full quarter quadrant away and considerably closer to the nearest planetary mass. It was getting uncomfortably closer each tick. But he was close enough. He should be able to jump to the system from which he had just escaped. Perhaps … no, wait! Something flickered at the corner of his rear screen display.

Chapter 17

Destiny is a good thing to accept when it's going your way. When it isn't, don't call it destiny; call it injustice, treachery, or simple bad luck.

Joseph Heller

June 22, 1985
Det 2, 336th Training Squadron, Fort Meade, Maryland, 1615 Hours

Gloria Shefly looked at the message in the yellow pop-up box on her screen. The urgent message flashed green in imitation of the green hit lights on its predecessor, the old five-hundred-line call boards she and a room full of analysts had occupied until the late seventies. The military always seemed to lag behind the private sector everywhere but here. Spyville was funded! Spyville was her private moniker for the basement of the training school at the Air Force's training detachment at Fort Meade. The fort's primary mission was teaching everything from Morse code to basic trainees at sig int school and forensics 101 to future MPs to advanced cryptanalysis to anyone who would not normally go to the company farm at Langley. Shefly had gone civilian after her tour was up but had been convinced by the recently promoted Colonel Henderson to stay on as a G-11 employee. With the G-11 pay grade and the high-stress security augmentation of leave and comped hazard pay, it was worth staying on in Spyville.

When she clicked the pop-up box, its annoying beep in her speakers stopped and a screen opened that provided a rough phonetic voice-to-text transcription that had started as soon as enough key word operators had appeared in the conversation string. She read the string of text and put on the headphone set to listen in. Her eyebrows furrowed as she followed the conversation.

Brian "Bud" Henderson liked to dress in civvies and downplay rank. When he had to, he could boast a medal board on his chest with ribbons from hot-spot conflicts all over the world from his command of field listening posts. When he didn't want to, he wore jeans and loose sweaters—thin ones in the summer—thick ones in the winter. If he didn't spend mental energy on wardrobe, his acute mind bored into complex communications webs and found the next outbreak of news of spaceships, space aliens or their sightings. The "witnesses" seemed to disappear shortly after he told the special ops field types where they were physically located. They usually returned a few days later, less sure of their story than they had been when they first called nine-one-one or the local press or their cousin. He looked up as Gloria approached.

"Bud, we seem to have an old friend surfacing again," she said, handing him a transcript. He scanned it, calling up memories from several years back. "Isn't this the same kid we orphaned a few years ago? Kitchens or something?" She handed him the file before he could ask for it. He pulled back several layers of paper to get to the initial entries. In truth, he forgot very little. Eidetic memory could be a curse for some, but he had honed his over a long career. As a result, if he had actually read an entry to himself, he could usually retrieve it years later as if it were fresh. "Hitchens, yeah, I remember. Bradley Hitchens is on the screen again? The kid from the cracker shack!" Shefly had the uncomfortable feeling that he could remember every word of that prior conversation. He had made her feel inadequate in so many ways.

Henderson sat back in his chair and rubbed his eyes as if trying to conjure a memory. He looked up at Gloria. "Yeah, notify the B-Team and keep me posted." He flipped the file open and scanned down a few of the more recent pages. "One more thing, this agent, Jenks. I think he's burned on this case and shouldn't be recalled despite protocols. This last report looks like he may be compromised and will no longer be able to act *sans conscientia*. He's a good agent, but not on this one anymore." He turned to his desk computer and keyed in a simple query and waited. "Looks like he's out in Dreamland anyway for advanced ops training." He mused more to himself than anyone. "Good role for him." Aware that Shefly was still standing in front of him, he looked up at her over the rims of his glasses.

Gloria was tempted to ask a question, but despite her own one-twenty-six IQ and her increasing involvement in caseload, Colonel Bud, as she thought of him, was often impatient with her ideas. She caught the 'anything else?' question unexpressed and excused herself. As she left his office, she found she was still wondering if the unwarranted radio transmitter placed on the Chappells' speedboat should be retrieved. Could citizens mount a civil right to privacy case if they found it? Or were they simply untraceable and expendable? Ten steps from the door, she heard, "Shefly!" from behind her.

Well, she thought, at least he didn't wait for me to get seated. She stopped at the threshold to his office with an arm braced against the doorjamb. "Yes, sir?"

"Make sure this time it is understood that all effort is to be made not to harm this kid!"

"Yes, sir. Is that all?" She knew it was; the Hitchens file was already closed on the top of the "Refile" pile, and he was scanning another folder. She saw his distracted nod and that he was already immersed in the next issue. She slowly backed away, smiling to herself. He's got a soft spot for this one, she thought. But he can be formidable if he wants to be. Before she was out of earshot, she heard him shout into the folder, "Have a good weekend, Gloria!"

This last brought back the all-too-brief six months that they had spent together on weekends. Those days were gone. "Get over it, Gloria," she said to herself as she had a hundred times before. "Get over him. The man is a machine. He has no feelings. You can do better," she said over and over as she headed down the stairs to the unmarked door in the hallway of the military com-ops training facility.

June 23, 1985
Detroit, Michigan

Brad Hitchens climbed the granite steps of the dark, redbrick, three-story home in the Lakes District west of town. A balding head, which had been keeping watch through the cut-glass-paneled door, bobbed out of view to the rattle of door locks. The dark oak door opened and Jason Walters invited him in. The sitting room, dominated by decor from the thirties through fifties, was a little stuffy but surprisingly comfortable. Colored bands of light flooded into the room from the leaded beveled glass bay window. Walters waved a welcoming hand, indicating a richly brocaded lion's-foot sofa.

"Please, Bradley, please have a seat. I hope you traveled well?"

"Yes, yessir. And it's Brad to most who call me anything." He was a little nervous but mumbled, "I had a bumpy flight up from Atlanta, and, umm, I have a present for you." Before sitting, he took a ring box out of his inside jacket pocket and handed it over to Walters.

290

Walters took the red-papered box with its thin gold thread embellishment and opened it slowly, expectantly. He peeled back the tissue Brad had used to keep it from rattling around and examined the small bit of metal in the box. He immediately noted its greenish sheen with minute flecks of black. Handling the small bit of metal, he examined both the two sheared ends and its original sidewall. "You said this was in seawater for a few years?"

"Yes, the Gulf of Mexico since seventy-seven."

Walters lifted his eyebrows in absorbed study. "Did you polish the artifact or wash or scrub it at all since you brought it up?" he asked, rolling it over in his fingers.

Brad set six other ring boxes on the edge of a marble inlaid mahogany side table and thought of the effort involved in bringing it up and then the trip to a small car repair shop that agreed to shear off several pieces in a hydraulic press. "No, I wiped some slime off of it before it set up drying. No real scrubbing; marine slime can be pretty hard to clean once it hardens."

"Yes, I suppose it is." Now his brows, wild and salted with gray, furrowed. "You probably didn't know Dr. Hill. He first called me about this 'project' as excited as a boy at Christmas." He made quotation marks with his index fingers and looked up at Brad. "I can see why."

"I did meet Dr. Hill, but I was in high school back then." He looked a little embarrassed. "I went with Dad when we gave the first sample to him."

"Yes, hmm ..." Walters turned the piece over and over in his fingers, alternating his survey of the mirror-smooth original skin and the sheared, strained ends. "I suppose that was the last possible time you could have met him. It's too bad he died; he was extremely excited about what he thought he had, or rather, what you'd found."

"Dr. Walters?" Brad asked. "Are you aware of the circumstances concerning Dr. Hill's death? I mean, did you know about the other deaths that occurred at the same time?"

"Why no." Walters looked up surprised but distracted. He said he had been disappointed by the death of his old colleague and the end of the mysterious inquiry but had not thought further of it for years.

Brad explained, "When Dad asked for him at his office a few days later, they simply told him that he had passed, and we thought that was that." Brad told him of the nearly simultaneous deaths of Hill and his assistant, and then with some difficulty checking his emotions, he told Walters about his father's murder. As they talked, the light coming in the window became flecked with the shadows of the trees across the street. He told Walters of the search and wrecking of his home, the reasons for his fear of the authorities, and his journeys to Apalachicola and Las Vegas.

Walters told Brad about his long friendship with Dr. Hill and how they kept in touch since their graduate studies by exchanging family vacation host duties for over twenty years. Walters became interested in Brad's studies in chemistry and physics and asked about the program at Arizona. They discussed his possible career paths and options, but the conversation kept coming around to the artifact.

Walters said, "We have very different perspectives of the last several years. For me, it's just been eight or nine years. I have the same job now that I had then. I'm just older, but for you?"

Brad replied, "I was just starting high school then. I've changed states twice, been to college, and now I'm about to go on to grad school. Seems like an entirely different universe to me than it was when all this started." He did not add any of the possible insights into Dzuran metallurgy that he had "learned" from his telepathic discussions with Litan. He wasn't sure if he could express his limited understanding of these impressions to a seasoned materials science professional.

Walters cocked his head sideways to look at Brad. "Perspective can be everything, especially in inquiry, and that's a good thing." He leaned back, putting his fingertips together, palms apart. "Bradley, you've developed a very good plan for getting the samples out to different labs. Is there any more of this?

"About a foot of it. Thanks for letting me know that the samples could be quite small. So, I still have a little more than two-thirds of the original piece. That is in a safe place, well out of the way. The first piece that was cut off showed the distressed end at its original point of attachment disappeared in the fire at FSU, unless the Feds found and recovered it." Brad was thoughtful for a moment, noting that the sun was no longer coming through the beveled-glass door, and asked, "Who have you thought about for labs? Who do you trust to take a blind assay and not go flying to the press as soon as they figure out what they've got?"

"Well, I've made some calls, carefully at first," Walters responded, "but then I couched it as a competition of sorts and said that best estimates of manufacturing method would be compared in a conference call next week. Some were reluctant, but then professional jealousies took over when I told each of the others research labs on the list. I also added that the conference call was to be chaired by an NBC news anchor. We got Lawrence Livermore Labs first. Their Dr. Chang was actually very interested up front. Cal Tech came on, too, right away. Harvard didn't call back." He looked up at the ceiling, trying to recall the sequence of events. "Cornell came in after they checked up on me with Chang's lab, and MIT jumped at the chance when they heard who else was in it. They have a new guy in materials science. A Frenchman has just taken over their department, very big deal for them. He's from the school of engineering in Cherbourg." He paused, trying to pronounce the *École d'Ingénieurs de Cherbourg*, as it had rolled off the tongue of Professor René Étienne de Larcy. "And we got Princeton when they heard that Harvard had declined."

"Wow!" Brad found himself sitting up as the list played out. "I'm impressed, Dr. Walters. So we have six, right?" He ticked off on his fingers: General Motors, Lawrence Livermore, Cornell, MIT … mmm, Cal Tech, and Harvard. Is that right?"

"Princeton, not Harvard, but that's the list, Bradley. Good memory." He got up and crossed the room to a small antique rolltop desk. "We actually might get Cherbourg, too!" He pulled out a pair of jewelers glasses with several swivel-mounted magnifying lenses and sat at the desk, turning on a bright desk light. After looking at the piece for a minute or two, he asked Brad, "Have you looked at this piece?"

"What are you seeing?" Brad asked, peering over his shoulder. "It's kind of hard to see because of the crude shear cut, but do you see this fine circle of darker metal here?"

Brad tried to look closer, but without magnification, he had to say he couldn't. Walters continued, "And the color, it is definitely a characteristic of the base metal, not any coating or admixture." Walters rotated one of the ends under the bright light. "Just inside this ring of dark bits, there's an indent that almost looks to me like there are two pieces of metal here, one inside the other."

Brad said, "I've taken a look at one of the slices under a scope back at AU and that was one of my conclusions, too."

"Really!" Walters rotated his head left to look at Brad. "What other observations did you make?"

Brad cleared his throat and said, "Well, there is also a greater magnetic field generated when the material is chilled, but it seemed out of line with the amount of current, almost like you could do more work than you put in. If this bit is an appendage or extension of some kind from a spacecraft, well, that would put this thing's natural working environment at right about zero degrees kelvin." He paused, thinking, and then continued, "Umm, the magnetic field strength just doesn't seem to match what we'd expect from any iron alloy or wound copper or any other traditional coiled conductors. We'd need to develop a different set of resistance and field strength criteria for this stuff."

"Stuff!" Walters gave a short, gasping laugh. "If it truly is new, we could call it Stuffium! Have you thought of a name for a new element? How about, maybe, Hitchensium?"

"Really? Do you think it really is a different element? Not an alloy of existing metals?"

Walters rubbed the end of his mustache and allowed, "There is room for that hypothesis—if the provenance you described is correct. There is the chance that it is something we do know about but is just extremely rare or we'd have to make it in a collider and figure out how to stabilize it." He noted the increasing darkness outside and sat up. "Why don't we get up and see about some dinner? I'm sure there's something in the fridge that would serve." He stood and led the way to the kitchen. "Brad?" he said. "There's something I need to ask you about Arizona State."

"Arizona State?" Brad asked, perplexed.

"The list of schools we were talking about earlier? Those schools have the best physics and materials science labs in the country. If I asked ten of my colleagues to name the top ten or fifteen physics schools in the country, those schools would all show up. But Arizona State?" Walters's peaked eyebrows told him it would never show up on the top twenty. He backpedaled quickly. "Not that it's a bad school, to be sure, it's a great state college. But have you thought of where you might do better?"

"It's what I can afford," Brad said somewhat defensively. "I got Arizona residency as a freshman and with my assistantships and work-study scholarships, I can make ends meet."

"Look, Brad, you have an almost perfect scholastic record as an undergrad, but for a master's degree or better, to become a leading professional in the field, you should aim higher." Brad started to object, but Walters raised a hand and continued, "And with your 3.95 GPA I think I can get some departments to make offers based on scholarship, not your willingness to babysit undergrads. Are you interested?"

Brad sat on a bar stool at the end of the kitchen counter, a little stunned. "Any in particular?"

Walters smiled. "Well, almost any of them, but I have already had some conversations with colleagues—one who has just taken over Cornell's Physical Sciences Department. He's set up an interview. Another interested party is the fellow from Cherbourg, France, who is a visiting scholar now at MIT. How's your French?"

"I ... I ..." Brad stammered. "I don't know what to say. I wasn't thinking past getting back on campus next week."

June 26, 1985
Det 2, 336th Training Squadron, Fort Meade, Maryland, 0940 Hours

Gloria Shefly and Anna-Marie Durrant were looking through intel briefs from the listening posts when Anna-Marie's eyebrows lifted. "We get some weird stuff through here sometimes. I swear, Gloria, there are more nuts and fruits out there than in a bowl of granola."

Gloria put her stack of reading briefs down and looked across the partners desk at her friend and coworker of four years. Anna-Marie was a skeptic, not just hard to convince, but she truly believed that the Lord only blessed one planet with life and created only one species in his image and that all the ballyhoo about space aliens was either information planted by the Russians to distract the American people or just plain whackos feeding on each other's hysteria. She hadn't seen or heard anything in four years at the base that shook her set of beliefs. She liked her partner, but felt Gloria was almost dreamy enough to believe some of the storylines they came across.

Anna-Marie shook her head in disbelief as her eyes scanned the copy on one of the new facsimile message tracers they had recently begun monitoring. Gloria put out her hand for her turn to read. They had developed their own system of backing each other when something came up in the dailies that might warrant field action. With a grin and arched eyebrows that said, "Here's another good one," Anna-Marie handed over the briefing sheet. Below the intercepted fax's phone address line the message read:

```
To:   Dr. Jason Walters, Dir. Analytical Services, General
Motors Corporation
30003 Van Dyke Ave 2-7, Warren, MI 48093

From: William Chang, Spec. Projects ofc.
Lawrence Livermore National Laboratory
```

Dept of Energy, National Nuclear Security Administration
7000 East Avenue—Livermore, CA 94550

Re: Materials Test on Metallic Sample Submitted
6/24/85

Dr. Walters:

Sample size insufficient for advanced electro-magnetic analysis. In preliminary testing, irradiation of the subject demonstrated a high degree of stability of the substrate material. Chromatography results are not conclusive, however carbon is a subcomponent noted in the sample but not related to substrate matrix.

Matrix materials are rare earths with chromium admixture. Noted enhanced magnetic properties when chilled below minus 80d C. Apparent major component is technetium isotope 99^+ not previously produced in quantities.

X-ray laser attempts to separate components resulted in extreme damage to laboratory test equipment and operator injuries.

Review of bombardment analysis demonstrated heavy particle tracers indicative of heavy metallic (99Tc) components in admixture with stabilizing common chromium in unknown structure.

Staff agreement on post investigation evaluation conclusions:

1) Further testing is not indicated in a non-secured installation.

2) High gauss magnetic test equipment should be considered expendable as current methodologies may result in loss of test bed.

3) Recommend cessation of any high energy testing at other test locations.

4) Recommend collaborative approach to materials testing.

5) Recommend top-secret clearance for team members. Minor sample supplied represents 700% more than known non-medical technetium produced to date as documented in the radiological research literature

6) Based on analysis of crystalline matrix structure and component materials, donor material is not likely of terrestrial origin.

Will submit results to moderator as scheduled.

Regards, Bill

Gloria said just loud enough to ensure that Anna-Marie heard, "Six, Donor material not likely of terrestrial origin!" She stared at the words, puckering her lips in an airless whistle.

Anna-Marie looked back with a disgusted smirk. "Some people just have to explain what they don't understand by laying it on space aliens. Seems to me like a need to have an explanation when reality doesn't fit what they think they should know."

"For real?" Gloria was truly curious. She knew her partner was decidedly unimaginative, but this was Lawrence Livermore, not a backyard video of a pie plate. Her tone had been neutral enough to hide both her excitement about the note's contents and her disdain for Anna-Marie's parochial outlook.

"Yeah, for real," Anna-Marie said. "So, imagine you are an Indian tripping through the western plains, never seen a white man, and you look down and see a thing on the ground that you can't understand. You go back to your chief and tell him the gods have left you a silver talisman with a golden eye but you need to do a smoke tent or something to figure it out. Meanwhile, somewhere farther down the trail, a buffalo hunter is looking all through his kit for the lid to his coffeepot." She paused and let the superior smirk firmly settle on her mouth. "The two men in our example are from different cultures and places. For guy number one, a mystery of the universe has been dropped in his lap. For guy number two, a trivial piece of his kit is lost, not found."

"But, Anna-Marie, you just made the counterpoint to your own point of view. A man in his own genuine world of experience is introduced to a far advanced culture. Even though it's a trivial component of that culture, it has no significance or reference in the finder's experience. He knows his people didn't make it and couldn't make it." She shook her head in disbelief at her friend's narrow world view. "To him, he found an alien artifact, from an alien land."

"Yes," Anna-Marie said, her black eyes flashing, "but that alien land was on the other side of this planet." She punctuated the last two words by smacking the table with the heel of her palm.

"Still," Gloria said, "this letter more than triggers our protocols. This is Lawrence Livermore here. I'm taking it to Col. H."

Anne-Marie adopted a denigrating smirk. "Okay, but not on me. It's prob'ly just a of coupla profs trying to put one over on a colleague!"

Occasionally, the wheels of government do turn quickly. The letter made it to Colonel Henderson just before 1030 hours. By 1500 hours the following day, a pickup team was contracted to be on the ground in Boston for the intercept.

June 26, 1985
Over Boston, 2:30 p.m.

The Boeing 727 throttled down slightly and began to lose altitude. A brief mechanical whine outside Brad's window woke him, and he lowered his head to the window port to watch air brakes descend partially from the wing's trailing edge. The plane had made ground speed on the heels of a low-pressure ridge over the mid-Atlantic states but had not reduced speed accordingly. Since the gates and ramps at the usually overcrowded Logan Airport had no spare room, the penalty for making good time was a long, slow oval thirty miles by ten miles over the South Boston megalopolis.

Brad had been thinking of the connections he had made in the last few days. Whoa! Susan and Lucy, the good sisters—aunt and mother, mother and aunt—together and each in her own way, they had provided for him. He thought back to the cleanup of the house and the restoration of his room when all this started. That had been Susan, the secret mother. Their disclosure had helped him to better understand Lucy's disappearance when he was ten. She had known that Susan would fill in if needed. Now again, Aunt Sue, or Mom, had come through with Jason Walters's phone number. Walters, what a character. And he might even get him a connection to a full academic scholarship!

With Walters's help, his plan was partially implemented. The samples were in the mail. Within a few weeks, the world would know. Leading scientists would have to come to a conclusion about the samples, and the government would not be able to stop the news.

Soon, he thought, he might get funding and government buy-in to excavate the wreck he knew had to be buried in a shallow grave a half mile from his backyard. Rethinking that, he wondered if he could trust the government with the life of his interstellar friend, Ka-Litan.

He had only to make a stop at Boston for an admissions interview with MIT. Then, if that didn't develop, it was back to school at AZ State. The thought of going back to the plain and mundane life at school while six top science labs around the country worked to crack the mystery of his artifact was almost overwhelming. Grad school had recently lost its luster.

Later, leaving baggage claim at Logan, he spotted a sign with his name on it held by a limo driver. The dark-skinned man was nattily dressed and in a perfectly tailored three-piece suit complete with watch chain. But his knotted Rastafarian dreadlocks hinted of some origin in the Caribbean. His shoes were buffed to a high gloss shine. Brad had not expected to be greeted, but it sure beat finding a cheap shuttle into town and then some number of bus transfers to MIT. The airplane tickets had been on Walters's credit card, but the rest of his travel had been on his own dime. He thought to remind himself to thank Walters for this attention to detail.

The diminutive Rasta driver's obsequious attentions were disarming. He kept up a rattling pidgin that had Brad preoccupied and distracted as they moved toward the curb and a limo with blacked-out windows: from the first, "How dey you, Mistah? You Mista Hithchen? Go you Bostown, sah? I takee Bostown, fee paid, you no pay nating!" to his "Go you M-I-Tee? Say, you pretty smart fella." They had reached the curb where the driver clicked open the trunk of a black Lincoln Mark III Town Car.

"Yes, MIT!" Brad was relieved to hear a familiar phrase in the prattle. The driver had taken Brad's backpack with an authoritative air and with a slam of the trunk, hopped around Brad and whisked open the back door. "Sit you, sah? Please, sah!"

Brad climbed into the dark interior of the town car and was immediately surprised to see another passenger on the other side of the backseat. His startled expression brought a thin smile to the stranger. Immaculately dressed in a dark-blue pinstriped suit and holding an expensive maroon leather briefcase on his knees, the middle-aged man eyed Brad's casual traveling clothes and seemed on the verge of a comment. The door shut behind Brad as he tried to think of something beyond, "Are you going to MIT also?" The man only smiled to himself and faced forward, as if checking for the driver. An hour-old haircut formed a silver halo around a tanned face that didn't look old enough to have earned the color change. Brad saw what he was supposed to see: the definition of poise, style, and breeding.

The driver got in and pulled into traffic. As the limo gained speed, door locks engaged and a glass privacy screen rose behind the driver. The gentleman beside him answered finally, a hint of a French accent coloring the response with a thick layer of gentility. "Yes, Mr. Hitchens, I am also going to MIT." He smiled again, but it seemed to come from somewhere far off.

Brad casually raised an arm to rest on the window ledge, allowing a finger to extend near the door lock pull. To cover the movement, he made a clumsy show of turning to face his fellow passenger. "Are you with Dr. de Larcy?"

After a pause, *"Qui,"* then, "yes, I am with Dr. René Étienne de Larcy." The Parisian accent intimated continental grace, and he played it. "I am in fact he, Dr. de Larcy, with the *École d'Ingénieurs de Cherbourg*. I am at your service." The gentleman offered a hand and then faced forward, hands on his briefcase, looking into traffic ahead. A traffic-metering cross arm lifted, letting their car onto an acceleration ramp, and the car's powerful engine quickly matched traffic and merged. The Frenchman looked over at Brad. "Relax, Mr. Hitchens, it's not very far." He turned again, facing the front.

Brad was confused. He didn't know what to expect of his reception at MIT, but Dr. de Larcy was cold, seriously cold. He was considering ways to avoid giving de Larcy a sample of the artifact. He thought about calling Walters and asking for a different laboratory when the man turned the briefcase around in his lap so the clasps faced him. Brad looked out at the fast-moving traffic and saw they were entering a descending ramp to a tunnel.

De Larcy smiled again looking forward and muttered, "Not long now. You've come at a good time of day. Some days, the traffic backs up all the way to Rhode Island!" He laughed as if this were a funny joke. Tire noise gave way to a dull roar as the double line of fast-moving cars entered the yellow-lit tunnel. A car to the right rear honked at its neighbor, and Brad looked back toward the noise. A whirr forward accompanied the partial opening of the glass barrier behind the driver. He heard a click in the car and turned to face the small black circle of a .38-caliber automatic pistol's stubby snout. As the man's arm relaxed on the briefcase, its locks clicked shut again.

The "Frenchman" then intoned in a perfect East Texas drawl, "Son, like I said before, relax yourself; we won't be long." Brad didn't like what was happening. This scene had gone from Bubba Goes to the Big City to the French Connection or 007 within minutes.

Brad Hitchens felt cold sweat beading on his forehead. He knew his chances of getting away from this man were slim—worse than slim. He was not equipped to fight this fight. "So, de Larcy, who are you really? And did I detect Oklahoma or was that East Texas?"

The Suit with the gun smiled widely. "Not bad, son, not bad. Just relax, someone likes you. You'll be fine." He looked forward at the driver and tapped on the glass. The heavy, dark glass rolled down. The Suit said, "Hassan, DISCO! Button up!"

From the front seat, the cabbie in a clear New Yorker's accent responded, "Yes, sir, got you covered." The glass rolled back up.

The Suit, whoever he was, looked back to Brad. "Now, son, I know it's going to be hard, but I need you to just relax and enjoy the ride. Oh, and please put on your seat belt. We wouldn't want anything untoward to happen now, would we?"

Brad took in the dire implication of the two personality shifts and felt around for the straps. "Do you have a name? Or do you prefer a number? Are you Double O something?" He looked closer at the man in the dark-blue pinstripe. He was muscular; he looked strong and fit. Even sitting, he exuded strength.

"Hey now, I'm on your side. I work for the US of A, mostly on contract. That 007 stuff is fiction. They'd be MI-5 or 6, anyway, British intel. I just need to make a delivery of one American white boy to my bosses, and my day is over and their day begins. I'm guessing that the folks at DISCO might have some questions, but I'm sure they'll be polite." He chuckled at that. "Oh, name's Michael; you can call me Mike!" Smiling as if genuinely amused, he added, "It's Dallas, McKinney actually, a little north of Dallas, but I moved to the Big D just out of high school."

Disco? Brad ran through images of Saturday Night Fever and the falsetto soprano sound of the Bee Gees. "Disco?"

"Ah, yes, D-I-S-C-O. That's Defense Industrial Security Clearance Office, or DISCO for short." He smiled thinly. "Not everyone in government lacks a sense of humor. We mostly handle industrial clearances for personnel applying for contract work in sensitive military applications and locations.

301

We do the occasional pickup. An old friend of mine asked me to do a favor for him, and here we are."

"Where are we exactly? I mean, what is my situation exactly?"

"You, Mr. Hitchens, are going to be the guest of the United States Government for a short time. I am sure you will have some interesting conversations with the boys."

"Where are you taking me?"

"That, son, is classified; couldn't tell you if I knew." He looked over and winked. "If I told you, I'd have to kill you." He chuckled softly. "Just kidding, son." Brad watched, frozen in his seat as the Suit calmly reopened the briefcase, put the gun down, and pulled out a small plastic baggy. It appeared to be filled with lumpy mashed potatoes—no, a damp white cloth. As soon as the zipper lock on the baggie opened, Brad smelled a familiar sickly sweet odor—antiseptic, no, anesthetic. Eyes wide in horrific anticipation, he backed into the corner of the seat and tried to fend off what was coming. But the big Texan was all over him, and the bag full of saturated cotton was covering his mouth and nose. Brad tried not to breathe in.

In that frozen moment, he was aware of the underarm stink of the agent who was drugging him, a spot of whiskers below his right ear that had been missed shaving. He was aware of the driver's eyes in the rearview mirror, calmly watching them. He was aware of the traffic moving alongside on the other side of heavily tinted glass, oblivious to his peril, his fears. Something was roaring in his ears; the windows were now down in the front of the car, ventilating it for the delivery team. He could not hold his breath any longer and let the air out of his lungs. The agent, Mike, had expertly gotten inside his defenses and had his arms pinned open with his elbows.

With his left hand, Mike held the baggie firmly over Brad's face as his right forced Brad's face into it. Brad tried to think of himself as a diver, holding on to the one last breath until he broke surface. Cars continued to pass. He couldn't hold it any longer. One excited inhale later and the scene around him narrowed to a darkening tunnel. A cold shock wrapped around his world. His chest weakened; his arms turned to rubber. He was aware of sweat rolling down his temple. His eyelids, wide with fear only seconds ago, began to droop. On the next breath, his world went black.

June 26, 1985
Det. 206 B, Nellis AFB, Nevada, 2030 Hours

Martin Jenks sat in his temporary office, feet extended and resting on a lower desk drawer, as he reviewed the thick Hitchens file. Smoke curled in lazy S-curves from a cigarette lying in the military-issue, six-inch-square glass ashtray with a one-inch ash hanging over the bowl. He was not a happy person. "Damn!" he said aloud. How did this get to be so screwed up? he thought. He wasn't supposed to be on this case anymore. He'd been compromised, big time. But here he was, and here they were coming. Guess it wouldn't matter if they went through the psych scrub before being put back in the world. But still!

Jenks had loved being a cop. Donning the uniform of a military police officer the first time had made his chest actually swell with pride. Each new stripe and service pin had done the same. It was the same uniform as most other airmen at first, but the MP insignia made the man. He no longer wore it, of course. He dragged his faux leather briefcase from behind him and pulled out the flip wallet that now housed the uniquely numbered badge. He rubbed his number with his thumb, thought about his old mentor, and wondered if he could ever justify some of the things he and the team had done in the service of the Dreamland's B-Team assignments. He longed for his usual assignments in the Air Force Office of Special Investigations.

AFOSI usually had him tracking down fugitives; his specialties were natives of Central and South America. He'd just completed a little work for the Drug Czar in Ecuador. Recently, he had been less enthusiastic with the service. The increasing number of assignments for the Dreamland's B-Team had made him question his own oath of silence and, more recently, whether he had it in him to reenlist. At sixteen years in, and with an excellent record, both he and his superiors assumed he was a lifer.

He had not known his father and never had the benefit of a stable male figure during most of his youth. He found what he had been missing on a racquetball court at the downtown Billings YMCA. Out of curiosity, he had checked out a racket and tube of balls and was working up a sweat trying to keep up with the seemingly erratic bounce of the little blue balls when a forty-something-year-old, looking like a businessman out of uniform in nylon shorts and a T-shirt, stepped through the low opening at the back corner of the racquetball court and changed his life. Over the next few months, the older man had taken him from the basic skill set to playing one-on-one and to serving as a good back court partner.

His racquetball mentor, Lieutenant Detective Toby Drake turned a page for Martin. The first and only black detective in Billing's metro force, Drake knew how close Martin fit the profile of an undirected, one-parent kid with no role model. He recognized that young Martin was on track for a ten-to-twenty-year sentence for grand theft. Martin needed a channel for his energies and a sport that required tough mental discipline. He was not big enough for football and not tall enough for basketball and thought these stereotypical routes out of the poverty cycle were closed to him. Drake directed him back to school and the military.

Drake had related his own struggles in Houston's Fourth Ward projects and how he had used the military as a step out. During the calm between Korea and Vietnam, Drake had enlisted. Most of the available military occupations seemed to have no well-paying civilian counterparts. His enlistment sergeant had tried to steer him to cook school or mechanics. He had no interest in a lifetime in a kitchen or a garage. He didn't have the science for the electronic jobs, drafting didn't interest him, and mortars, M-16s, and machine guns didn't sound like an occupation with a long life expectancy. He'd signed up for the MPs. He reasoned that every city in the country needed cops and that he could work anywhere he wanted. But he swore he'd never go back to Houston and the human horrors of night life in the Wards.

Drake shared his passion for life and sport with young Martin and showed him a way up and out of a statistically bad start. At seventeen, GED in hand, Martin Jenks joined the Air Force and trained as an MP. At twenty-one, he used the GI bill to pursue a degree in criminology with a specialty in forensics. At twenty-six, he discovered a color barrier in most cities large enough to need forensics specialists. Reenlisting had provided him with a satisfying job and the skills he picked up, as well as his careful attention to the task at hand, resulted in promotions. As a thirty-year-old and divorced after a bad life choice, he had been tapped for special assignments that varied significantly from military police work.

He and a small group of black-shirt operators worked in Nicaragua prior to the official invasion, making sure that key personnel were not available when needed. These "cleanup" tasks were supported by US Marine Special Forces and other men whose branch he never did know. All that mattered was that they were successful, and the four-week assignment had been exciting. He was then tapped for service in the Air Force Office of Special investigations, where his forensics training resulted in challenging assignments behind the Iron Curtain posing as an embassy staffer.

By the early 1970s, he had been given the occasional assignment to the Dreamland B-Team. These assignments he often found unsavory. He was not happy about rendition, removing civilians from their private lives for questioning. He knew that they would be reinserted with altered or implanted memories, but then somewhere, it changed. Under Captain Richards, they had been more aggressive, doing things to Americans that he could not be proud of.

Jenks tossed the Hitchens file on the desk, stubbed the largely unsmoked cigarette out, and left. Passing through the small kitchen and dining hall, he looked through the door at the far end of the room that accessed the dormitory. The girl was due to arrive in the morning. The Hitchens boy had been in custody for two days. He'd been given nothing but basic sustenance, mess hall meals and water with a sedative over the night shift. Jenks had been flown in to meet with them one last time before the scrubbing was to begin. With nothing better to do, he thought about grabbing a few beers at the NCO club. Later, he would try to sleep. He knew sleep would not come tonight, but he'd try.

Chapter 18

Hay una mujer desaparacida
Holly Near

June 28, 1985
Area 51, Nevada

Connie woke slowly. Her arms ached, her head hurt, and she had not liked the dream she'd just had. She was exhausted and, feeling consciousness coming on, resisted waking. She rolled over and became aware of a terrific argument going on somewhere. It's just the dream and all its psychic turmoil, she thought. Just shut your mind off again. At least it's still dark out; I can sleep some more. Despite her best efforts to shut off and shut down, her mind began to come out of deep rest. She had the familiar confusion she often had on a Sunday morning when she had to convince herself that it really was Sunday and okay to sleep a little longer. Letting sleep back in was hard in those moments as the possibilities of a wide-open Sunday were weighed against the threats of being late for Monday's routine. Finally, she couldn't do it any longer, and she stretched an arm out to find her clock.

Her reaching fingers failed to find her nightstand. The confusion returned; consciousness flooded in, and if she had not been drugged, she would have snapped awake. Instead, the confusion reigned. The argument was still going on within earshot. It was not part of the dream. *No, I'm still in a dream; that had to be it. What the hell?* Her knuckles went to her lids, and she tried to grind herself awake by pulling on her eyelids with her curled knuckles. No good, it was still dark even with her eyes wide open. *Is that Brad's voice? How could that be?*

With great effort, Connie managed to swing her right leg over the edge of the bed and then the left. After two failed attempts, she got her right elbow under her weight and pushed herself to a sitting position on the edge of her bed. This is not my bed! She ran her hands over the corner of the mattress.

This was definitely not her bed. Exploring further, she found a hard steel frame with a spring mesh support under a thin cotton mattress.

Not my bed. Where the hell am I? It's still dark. What's with that? Focusing on the sounds of an argument outside, she thought. *Is that Bradley.* She had to almost verbalize her thoughts to maintain focus.

"I've been drugged, dammit to hell!" she finally said aloud. The molasses in her forebrain fought every attempt to make a decision or come to a conclusion. Part of that consciousness wanted to lie down and wake up properly in her own bed, to end the nightmare.

She had been living alone in an apartment in a modest complex on Tallahassee's east side that made a point of discouraging college students and attracting young couples and working singles. She had been proud to show off the two-story apartment to Lou Anne and Chase when she had gotten settled and finally thrown away the last cardboard box. Her first six weeks as a working college graduate were frugal, with many of the weekends spent on treks back to Apalachicola to help out with the business. Her mother had finally convinced her to start cutting some of her old ties, and she had started to take more of an interest in decorating her own first place. In the club room, where the tenants mixed after hours and on weekends, she had heard the conversations about break-ins and had heeded the warnings.

Security at the complex was a joke, she and her fellow tenants had all agreed. Every unit was furnished with high-strength steel doors in unitized steel frames at their entrances and rear courtyards. Each steel door was fitted with heavy unkeyed deadbolts and a drop chain security lock. Unfortunately, each unit with a patio deck was furnished with glass sliding patio doors. Over the previous year, five units with her rear patio plan had been burglarized without any bodily harm or mayhem. Mostly, residents had lost their cassette and new CD players, TVs, microwave ovens, cordless phones, and other easy-to-carry-and-pawn items. One lost over a hundred LPs, some of which were classic collectibles. As they commiserated in the residents' lounge, they could only hope that anyone arrested for the crimes would not blab in the cell block about the ease of getting into these apartments.

Connie had installed both a top key that prevented the doors from being lifted off their tracks and a length of broomstick to prevent the door from sliding.

Later, as the drug's effects subsided, it would come to her that the intruder had been lurking in the downstairs entry, waiting for her to return from work. As she passed through the door, the drug-soaked rag slipped in front of her face, muffling her initial cries until she stilled. She would never remember the outrage and fear in that first contact or the burning in her eyes from the aromatic ethers. For her DISCO captors, she was, for the next two days, little more than a logistics problem: how did one get an inert human being from Florida to Nevada?

The muddied efforts to make sense of her darkened surroundings were emboldened when she finally realized she could stand. She took in everything she could from the senses she could muster: light, none; scent, overused air-conditioning; humidity, low; taste, awful. How long had it been since she'd had a drink of water? Touch? She raised heavy arms forward.

She stood, wobbling. Feeling like a newly blinded person with leaden limbs, she stepped cautiously away from the edge of her bed. She met a wall in two steps. *Okay, where's that sound coming from?* The head of the bed had been to her right as she sat on it, and two steps made for a very small walkway. She turned left, assuming that the arguing would be coming through a door rather than through the walls.

Connie took a few steps with arms outstretched before her and her right elbow tracking along the smooth wall surface. Again, she ran into a wall. She took two steps back and sidestepped to the left where she felt the metal of the bed frame. She bent and moved along the back of the bed to the opposite wall. The bed was against that wall. Turning right, she advanced again, arms outstretched but with her left elbow against the wall. In two steps, she bumped her shins into something hard. She reached down to touch cold metal. She ran her hands across its contours, appreciating for the first time the difficulties the blind have in interpreting the shapes around them.

Suddenly, the shape made sense: it was a toilet. Somewhere in a movie, she had seen pictures of built-in stainless steel toilets in prison cells, and this couldn't be anything else. *What the hell! I'm in jail?* She tried to assemble the small floor plan in her head. Sure enough, just beyond the toilet was a sink and a small shelf on the end wall next to it. She could feel her pulse rate increasing. This was bad. She turned slowly and walked, she thought, toward the opposite wall but kicked the bed frame instead. "Ouch!"

Feeling the bed frame for guidance, she maneuvered around its sharp corners and sat on the thin mattress. She swore to herself and wasn't sure if she was loud enough to be audible or not. Shaking her head to clear it hurt. She still heard voices somewhere, muffled by concrete—an argument.

The slowness of her thinking was slipping away, but answers still didn't come. *Crap, I don't even know how long I've been here!* She knew she was thirsty and soon realized she was hungry. *Where the hell is the door?* Although the voices seemed to be coming from her left, the only corner she had not tried was to her right. Standing carefully, she again advanced to the wall and turned right. She found the door almost immediately, but there was no handle from the inside. Hinged to swing into the room, it could be pushed open from the outside, but it had no pulls from the inside. From her side, it could only be pushed closed.

But the voices were still coming from behind her, from the other side of the cell's back wall. She turned, oriented herself to the sounds, and moved to the wall. The argument seemed to have settled to a conversation, but it still seemed that one male voice was resistant to the more even tones of the other male voice. *Maybe that isn't Brad; it sounds muffled. What the hell? Why am I standing here in the dark?*

She shouted, "Hey!" And then louder. "Hey!" She began to beat on the wall. "Hey! Bradley! I'm in here! Get me out of here!" The voices had stopped so she tried again, keeping the pounding going. "Hey! Help! Bradley?" The voices picked up anew; she heard the intensity level increase and then a bang of metal furniture smashing around. Connie had her ear turned to the wall and so was startled when a heavy weight smashed into the wall from the other side. More loud voices. More struggle. Then she shrieked in surprise as a painfully bright light flashed on.

When she could remove her hands from her eyes, she saw a small, single prison-style cot with a coarse, gray woolen blanket. It was color-coordinated with the dull gray wall and the dark gray bed frame. Now that her captors knew she was awake, when would the door open? She stood in place and waited. The sounds of struggle withered to low conversation. She could almost sense the movement of bodies going from the room on the other side of the back wall, down a corridor, and to her door. Keys rattled; her breathing stopped. A voice on the other side called out, "Step away from the door! This door opens in!"

"I'm okay," she mumbled and then louder, "I'm clear!"

The door swung open and a familiar face appeared, smiling. "Hello again, Miss Chappell. May I call you Connie?" He stepped into the small space followed by a heavily muscled attendant garbed in dark gray scrubs and a no-nonsense expression. Martin Jenks extended a hand, which was not taken.

"You!" She almost spit it out. "I'll give you this much," she said. "You gotta lot of damn nerve. Jenks, isn't it?" She could have hit him. "Is that Brad you were beating up in the other room?" She got no response other than a pounding in her temples that was clearly audible. She palmed her ears to shield them.

Jenks said, "You will find if you don't get excited, the sedative will not hurt as much as it wears off. It has to do with your blood pressure."

"Where am I, Jenks?" She could feel her blood pressure spiking with her anger. "What possible crime could I have committed that warrants kidnapping?" The pain started to mount again in her temples. "Where the hell am I?"

"Please, Miss Chappell, it will only hurt more. Please have a seat." He turned to the attendant in scrubs. "Please fetch a cup of water for Miss Chappell." The orderly/guard left them standing, and suddenly aware of her weak knees, Connie wanted to sit. She collapsed onto the mattress and felt her energy drain away.

"I want a lawyer. I am not going to talk to you about anything but the menu until I get a lawyer and know the charges, whatever they might be." The pain was subsiding a little; she hoped that it was weakening. "Where is Brad? Why have I been kidnapped or arrested or whatever you'd prefer to call it?"

"First of all, it is not technically kidnapping and you have not been arrested." She turned her head up to give him an icy stare. He continued, "Technically, it would be called rendition. You have not been charged with any crimes."

She found she couldn't hold the stare because it hurt and raised her stress levels and blood pressure, and the resulting headache was worse. She rubbed her temples, trying to force blood to circulate to her forebrain.

"I'm sorry this is so difficult for you," Jenks said. "We had hoped that you would have slept longer, allowing the side effects to wear off a little before you woke."

Connie tried to keep her emotions in check. "Do you have Bradley? Was that him in the other room?"

"Let's talk about Mr. Hitchens, Brad, a little later, Connie. Take some deep breaths, and try to clear your head first."

Connie looked up at the encouraging face of Martin Jenks with pure malevolence. She curled into a fetal ball on the mattress, rolled over to face the wall, and said with conversation-ending finality, "I want a lawyer."

310

~ ~ ~

Bradley Hitchens was trying to learn to live with boredom. The battleship-gray walls were well-painted and free of graffiti. He had quickly learned that there was almost no room above the two-by-four-gridded suspended ceiling. There was no possibility of crawling over a wall since the walls were constructed through to a concrete ceiling. He had performed all of the rituals of the newly incarcerated. He had memorized the dimensions in paces so that he could pace, turn, and pace with his eyes closed and when the lights were out. He had developed a workout routine that left his biceps sore and his abdominals aching. He learned that he could not work out all day; exercise would have to be paced.

The once-a-day interviews with Jenks were going nowhere. Two opposing forces with no apparent resolution. But Jenks had promised a surprise for tomorrow. Footsteps approached down the hall but passed his door on another errand. He had learned which guard was approaching by the cadence of their steps. This was a real advantage, since even though the lighting and meal regime was designed to confuse his sense of time, guards still worked on eight-hour shifts. He estimated he had time for a nap.

Deep Space 7

Litan stared at his display, mesmerized by the growing blue sphere filling his forward view screen. The planet seemed to be boiling, but he knew this was unlikely on a frozen gas planet. Unless there were some more active gasses at depth, they were very boring places to visit. What about the trailing Erran fighter? He boosted gain on his rear display and got the signature of an Erran fighter using cloaking. It was tailing him, but would soon be unable to match velocity without dedicating his ship to a plunge into the gas planet.

But then, he too, would be unable to do anything but plunge into a planet with no useable fuels. The fighter was on cleanup detail, and he was the trash. He was out of options. If he continued falling into the gravity well, he and Jai were finished. He had one last tool in his kit. He could jump. He was by then more than a quarter quadrant away from his drop point and very much closer to a large gravity node, but he could probably pull it off. He palmed up the jump screen and asked for the recall menu. Dzura, his home world, was no longer an option. It had been rendered uninhabitable in the civil war that had consumed his planetary system. But its coordinates were on the menu for every ship ever built out of tradition. Most of the federated worlds of the Elioi were on the list, including the mining belt he had just jumped from. Dzura, his home planet and its orbital twin Erra were now smoking wrecks with fires of destruction still smoldering under cloud decks that might persist for decades.. He had seen the vids, home was a ruin, but at least it had fuel in its oceans.

He called Dzura's coordinates up and began preparing Jai's bio life support appendages for his jump. Pulling the life mask over his face, he tightened the body restraints on his ship suit and began the long, slow breathing technique, clearing his mind for the jump. His concentration would be as important as Jai's numerical instructions to achieve the jump. Through narrowed eyes, he pushed the jump countdown button. Jai's audible countdown began at twenty-seven and dropped. He began to lose consciousness, to let his thought stream take him to the targeted system.

Something shook the ship. He allowed one eye to open to the stimulus. A green flash burst just outside the canopy. No! Not now! Jai's shields were about to drop to zero in advance of the jump. Space around the little fighter began to elongate; threads of time and consciousness began to ravel around him. Another green blast, this one unnoticed, rocked the ship. It was too far away at maximum range to do any real damage, but it did distort the growing energy field building ahead of the fighter. Jai had committed the ship to its jump routine, and his attention was absolute. Ka-Litan, nearly unconscious now, held the mineral belt around his planet firmly in mind. Long years of practice had taught him to obliterate all outside thoughts while prepping a system drop.

The pursuing Erran pilot gave a final burst of thrust from his kickers and pulled slightly closer to his target. A jump bubble was forming around the fighter's bow, and the Erran pilot knew there was only one more shot possible. He just wanted to finish off this escapee. Another long, green spear of deadly energy reached out for the escaping Coalition fighter, but to the amazement of the Erran pilot, as the energy flare died down, there was nothing but the blue ball of a nitrogen giant in front of him.

Jai began sounding alarms as soon as the drop sequence was complete. Ka-Litan came out of jump state much more slowly. Damn the Lights! Jumps in these small ships were always tough. He much preferred the comfort of a full stasis drop on a carrier. Go to bed and wake up—no headaches, no twitching muscles. He heard the alarms after he noticed the flashing strobes. The headache was that bad. The blue giant was gone. Instead of a mineral belt semi-cloaked in red-oxide dust strung around the wreckage of his home world, his forward screen was black with an unfamiliar star field. He loosened an arm restraint, palmed up the star field computer, and managed to reach across to the match array toggle. Jai quickly drew up the solution, and a large yellow star popped into the array's center. Yellow? There was no sign of the asteroid ring. Concerned with the sensor array, he called up the rear screen display, which immediately filled with the blue and white swirling bands of an atmosphere that was far too close.

Lights of Creation! He couldn't jump again anytime soon. It was not physically possible with Jai's energy levels depleted from this last jump. Scanning his displays, he saw that they were in a rapidly deteriorating orbit around the blue-white ball. No, it was actually a shallow dive into the atmosphere of a planet that was not supposed to be there. Ah, yes, the Erran had been blasting as he jumped. No wonder. But no time now to worry about the Erran fighter who had blown his planned drop. Maybe a planet in the neighborhood was better than the cold black of deep space.

He rapidly called up more displays and scanned all pertinent sensors. He was relieved when he realized this planet had oxygen and some upper-level hydrogen for the taking, and it appeared to have about a 1.2 Dz-gravity quotient. Immediately, he reached to extend scoop sails, but Jai had just done it. Maybe he could get some nav gas collected before he smashed into the surface of … of … wherever this was.

He punched some quick options into Jai's orbital calculator and found there was a possibility that he might be able to bounce off the atmosphere and free himself from exile on a lonely, primitive planet. Jai's calc screen popped up to report the planet's brief entries in the Coalition logs. Yes, it had been visited occasionally; most records though were from old survey contacts. Another few taps into the near-space database and he was horrified to find that the planet was inhabited by primitive sentients. He swore again and briefly thought about not committing a sacrilege to the Light. Contact with sentient species was to be made with special teams, not crash-landing warriors. Concentrating again, Litan made his best visual correction for the angle of incidence for an atmospheric bounce and then, looking at a break in the cloud deck ahead, saw that if he miscalculated, he would make a hard rock landing, meaning death. He hoped the deployed fuel scoops and accumulators could draw enough hydrogen out of the thin leading edge of this planet's atmosphere. His surface scanner revealed that he was coming down over a long peninsula. He needed at lease water for a landing site, preferably salt water.

He made a fine-adjustment lateral course correction that would bring them down over water. Checking for the component readout on the atmospherics, he read with resignation that nitrogen was high, oxygen was good, but hydrogen and methane were too thin to draw sufficient fuels to control his rate of entry. At least, he thought, as he scanned the database for the planet's atmospheric and liquid assets, if we splash on this planet's oceans, we can refuel the chem rockets and the field generator. We can get back out of here. He was alert, scanning all displays, when he realized that something was not right. He was going to

314

impact too hard. Soon, his shields would heat sufficiently to blind his sensors, and he couldn't extract enough chem fuel yet to soften the blow.

The superheated nitrogen-oxygen atmosphere impacted his nearly depleted shields. The Jai unit's fuel scoops automatically retracted. A flashing display indicated that a jump space nav antenna was still deployed and refusing to retract. *Not much good that will do if we don't survive this crash.* Litan watched the growing planet through the canopy rather than the panel display as his options dwindled to one.

It became inevitable. Neither he nor the Jai could find a solution. They were not going to bounce off the atmosphere. They were going to hit the surface of an ocean going much too fast and much too close to exposed land. Litan spent the last of his newly acquired fuel in the forward chem thrusters and pushed all the ship's remaining power to the weakened shield. When the ship's field impacted the water surface, Jai skipped out of control. Litan nearly lost consciousness on the first bounce, but as the ship rolled from the bottom friction, it skipped the second time onto its back. The shallow trajectory translated into a series of skipping bounces; a slow, out-of-control roll became a high-speed, end-over-end spin; Litan passed out. The last impact caused the ship to crash through some light land vegetation, and Jai came to rest at the end of a long furrow plowed by the shield. Slowly, water seeped out of the saturated soil, filling the furrow as Litan and Jai disappeared under a brown layer of groundwater. A thin line of steam emerged from a stream of bubbles and drifted into the thick green vegetation covering the alien world.

Chapter 19

The only way of discovering the limits of the possible is to venture a little way past them into the impossible.

Arthur Clarke's Second Law

July 3, 1985
Building B, Area 51, Creech AFB, Nevada

The images faded; the last transmission had finished the story that Litan had been sending for months. He had told the story eloquently in first person in video form, as if it had been painstakingly assembled from first-person memory and the ship's records. How else could it have included Jai's alone time when his pilot was unconscious? Running out of things to preoccupy his racing thoughts, Brad tried to push images or thoughts to Ka-Litan. He received no response. He was especially angry at Jenks and found it difficult to keep from wasting mental energy on going over their briefings. For two—or was it three?—maybe four days, they had gone over the same ground.

Where did the artifact come from? Why do you think someone would have put it under the tree? Are you sure about your father's conclusions when he looked at the root ball? Where is the picture you said you took? Are you sure the camera you used was the one that was smashed in your bedroom? Why did you tell me you threw the metal rod out on the salt flats? Where were the samples sent? Where was the remainder?

And on and on, argumentum ad nauseam. Sometimes Brad took over the conversation, demanding to know under what constitutional authority he was being detained. Why could he not see a lawyer? Where was he being detained? Why couldn't he get one phone call? Whatever happened to Miranda rights?

After less than two hours into each session, silence had been Brad's responses to questioning, and the interviews stopped. In the most recent interview, on hearing her shouts from a nearby cell, Jenks announced that Connie was coming out of sedation just down the hall. Brad exploded. What had been a particularly contentious verbal contest quickly became physical.

Jenks had underestimated Brad's attachment to Connie and had been unprepared when the younger man rose to his feet in spite of being cuffed to his chair and charged through the upturned table at him. Three additional guards and a hypodermic with sedative were required to get him back to his cell.

His head hurt, and his tongue felt like leather. Brad was trying to think back over the last two, maybe three, days to determine whether it was daylight or dark outside when he heard the door to the hall open and footsteps. They paused immediately, and he figured the guard must be looking in on Connie. He knew that she was across the hall at the other end of a hallway that was about fifty- to sixty-feet long. He had to walk down that hall to get to the interrogation room, and he planned to call out to her the next time he was taken for questioning, if only to let her know he was there too. He found that they could not communicate by yelling because of the sound deadening construction of the walls. At present, he was intent on listening to the footfalls in the hallway. He did not recognize these footsteps, which seemed to hesitate.

Pausing halfway to his door, the steps were soft now, almost furtive. A deadbolt slid in the lock, and Brad watched as the door opened inward a crack. Jenks' voice asked in a whisper, "Bradley, do you want to see Connie? You can take lunch with her, if you'd like."

With no internal handles, Brad knew he could not pull the door open. He simply replied, "Yes, I would." Then he added, "Thanks."

~ ~ ~

As the door opened Brad jumped up from his seat in the small dining room in which he had taken his meals alone. He saw surprise register on her face and then joy. "Brad!" He took her into his arms and cradled her tightly, feeling her rib cage shudder with emotion.

"Shhh," he whispered, stroking her head gently. "Shhh, it's okay. We're together."

"Oh God, Brad, I was so exhausted with worry, and now, I'm so happy you're okay!" She looked up at him. "They wouldn't tell me anything, just asked a bunch of questions."

"Same here, Con, we're good." He lied; he didn't feel that he had the right to say it, but it felt good. "We're together; we can at least talk. Jenks said we could have dinner together."

They sat and let the stories flow. Brad was understandably restrained about what he shared. He knew not to say anything about Walters and the samples. He understood that their conversation was probably a listening opportunity for Jenks and crew. He subtly tapped at his ear to get her attention and then waved his finger around pointing at the ceiling to warn her of bugs. So he talked about his college recruiting trip to MIT and how it went wrong. Connie shared her story of being taken, attacked, and drugged in the stairwell outside her apartment, and of waking up in her blacked-out cell. They held hands across the table from each other and soaked in each other's faces. As they talked, Brad pulled back a little, and his eyes drifted.

"What's wrong, hon?" Connie asked.

"Nothing, keep talking," he whispered. "Tell me anything about home and family—just keep talking." Connie did as he asked, somewhat out of sync, but tuning in rapidly. "Son of a bitch! Con, casually look over my shoulders and tell me if you see any surveillance cameras."

"No, I don't see anything that looks like a camera," she said, her expression puzzled. "So? What does that mean?"

"I don't see any behind you either."

"I'm not following you; where does that get us?"

"Maybe nowhere," he answered, "but behind you, on the last table in the room, there's a roll of duct tape. I'm going for a piece of it. Let's go for a little walk together around the room." Hand in hand, they walked around the perimeter of the room a few times. In case there might be a camera in a vent, Brad guided Connie so that she could be turned and pressed with her back against the far table. Wrapping her in a hug, he kissed her, long and with genuine feeling, as he pressed into her. She melted into his embrace, answering his kisses and caresses. She also felt his arm reach beyond her, pick up the roll, and with both arms behind her, remove several inches of the sticky cloth tape. That didn't stop her from enjoying the kiss. She needed it; she was beginning to admit to herself, she needed him. He folded the small bit of duct tape and tucked it into a pocket.

The door opposite the cell block entry door opened, and the usual cook or cook's helper entered, pushing a cart with meal trays. Brad kept up his passionate embrace, and eventually, a guard came over and broke them up. Through dinner, Brad kept up a steady banter about school, how he was late for his second summer session, and how ungrateful Jenks was for having his sorry life saved. He talked about anything but the artifact and his plans with Jason Walters to get it analyzed by the best labs in the world. As they ate, he folded the scrap of tape into a wad that he hoped would meet his purposes.

~ ~ ~

318

The interrogation room met all of Brad's expectations, which were based on crime shows he had watched on television. A heavy table and three folding metal chairs were the only furniture. A mirror, which they understood to be a one-way observation glass, was mounted on one wall. Jenks sat with his back to the mirror. He and Connie faced it. There were no light switches on the wall to control the wire-screen-covered ceiling lights. The bland, light-gray wall paint matched that of every other room—the few he'd seen anyway.

The conversations had not been going well, but after day two, they had become repetitive. Brad said, with some resignation, "So we are not allowed to A) talk to a lawyer, B) make a phone call, C) get out of this building, D) see daylight." He looked at Connie. "What else?"

"E) expect a future?" Connie answered laconically. Out of boredom with the third interview attempt, she found herself tuning out and counting the holes in the ceiling panels. This was a habit she had picked up while waiting for anesthesia to work before the arrival of her dentist. It kept her mind occupied when she didn't want to think about the present. This interview was different because now they were together, but the questions were the same.

Jenks shared that he had been brought back on their case in spite of his long priors with Hitchens because he happened to be in the area on assignment. Something about a place called Factory Butte. So, how did that affect them? Maybe he was just being conversational. Neither Brad nor Connie could tell how much Jenks knew of their personal communication, written and spoken, that they had thought secret.

Jenks had not expected to see them again and in truth, kind of respected their spunk. For civilians, they seemed dedicated to a plan and were not sharing what it was. He had not appreciated the four days he and a squad of airmen had spent combing the sawgrass flats with sophisticated metal detection equipment based on Brad's offhand comment that he had tossed the artifact into the grassy flats west of the St. Marks estuary.

Martin Jenks looked at the two young adults across from him and thought of Brad's ambush in the pine woods and then his subsequent rescue while diving. Twice, he had been incautious, and these "kids" had gotten the best of him.

Finally, Jenks broke what was becoming a long silence. "Brad, Connie, we've been through a lot. Most of the we in 'we,' admittedly, was me watching you, surveilling you, and reporting on you."

319

Connie looked over at him. "Oh, I feel so much better knowing we've been so well protected." She looked back at the wall and started to hum.

"Point is, I kind of like you two. I don't have to remind you that I might be fish food if not for you."

Brad bristled and said stiffly, "That makes me want to ask you something. If that had been me caught down in the *Lou Anne*, stuck and running out of air, would you have rescued me? Would you have simply let me have a diving accident? That would have reduced your caseload considerably."

Jenks's momentary pause prompted Connie to interject, "Figures!" She shook her head in disgust, looked back up at the ceiling, and continued humming.

"If I'd had time to think about the problem, probably not. Look, Hitchens, I know you have reasons to believe we came to your house with malevolent intent. Truth is, we just needed to ask questions to …" He paused. "… to assess the level of threat, to find out how much your father knew about the metal sample. But we've discussed that." He got back to the point. "On your question, if I'd found you stuck underwater, it would certainly have been easier to let you be. But then, you knew where you were looking on the boat; I didn't. It took a few more months for you to get back to it, and you got it." He smiled smugly. "And now I have it, at least a few parts." He stood and backed up to lean on the mirrored wall. "You will probably be happy to know that we have the three samples you sent out for assessment."

Brad and Connie shared a look that Brad broke off immediately. "You son of a bitch! You got all three of them?" He looked to Connie again. "Shit, Con, they got it all? What the hell?" He wondered if it could be true. Maybe he shouldn't make too big a deal of it. There was no telling what kind of shrinks might be behind the glass or would watch on video later.

Connie picked up the thread. "Well, Brad, there goes a year of planning." Then she looked over at Jenks. "I must assume that the metal samples were important. When do we get our finder's fee?"

Brad added carefully, "So, what did you do to these researchers? What you did to Dr. Hill?"

"Actually, Brad, it was pretty simple. Lawrence Livermore actually called us. They thought Dr. Walters's story was a little over the fence. They do get a lot of their funding from us. And you know, we have the one from Dr. Walters, and oh yes, of course, we have the one going to MIT. Dr. de

Larcy was very cooperative. He seems to enjoy the continued use of his work visa."

Brad responded with what he hoped would appear to be an air of defeat. "You don't have to gloat. Christ, you have the samples and us." He put his head into his palms. "It seems like you got dealt the straight flush, and I busted."

Trying not smile a victory grin, Jenks added. "Walters gave it up and gave us the other two."

The two captives exchanged knowing glances. Connie posed a question that had been bothering her for a while. "You showed up last March, literally out of the blue. What did we say or do, specifically, that put you on to us again? Why after several years of no tails, no strange cars parked a block or two down the road, all of a sudden, you show up ready to dive the Titanic?"

Jenks let out a short burst of air that was supposed to sound like a laugh but didn't convince them or him. "Simple misunderstanding." He rubbed his chin thinking. "We sent out a simple recon team to replace bugs, check on some things. The crew called out here to ask about something you'd said on your dad's runabout, the PQ. Connie, you'd said you were going to Dreamland. We wondered about that. Why in the hell would you be going to Dreamland? We couldn't figure out why you'd want to come here. There are a lot of spacer cranks that want to take a clandestine tour of Area 51, or Dreamland, as some of the pilots call it. We couldn't figure out from your file if you knew what IS at Dreamland. The short of it is, the supposed crack team of field agents that replaced me lost you. Couldn't follow a college kid out of a paper bag.

"They hustled out to Nevada and waited for you to show up. They spent almost four weeks patrolling Indian Springs and Vegas—nothing. Then we pick up phone calls between Tempe and Tallahassee, but now it's a Hitchens listing in Arizona, not Williams. It got our attention; it got the attention of my bosses and their boss, and we went from monitoring to tracking again."

When he finished, Brad and Connie both asked, "Dreamland?"

"So when you said you were going to Dreamland, where is that? To you?" After a few moments with no response, Jenks asked directly, "Where is Dreamland to you?"

Connie laughed. "It's a place in the woods where I go to meditate. That's it." She shrugged, trying to look convincing. "Bushes, woods, a hole in the trees where the sun comes in. That's Dreamland. Brad's mother showed it to me a few years back."

Brad interrupted, lest Connie try too hard to string the lie. "It's where Connie and I first ... umm..." He let the silence fill in the blank. Relieved that a few secrets still remained, he asked, "Where is Dreamland to you? You said the tail crew hustled out to Nevada?"

Jenks drew himself up and spread his arms wide. "Welcome to Dreamland, boys and girls. You are here!" He looked down at Brad. "Son, you were a few miles from here seven years ago, when you tracked down your mother. If there had been a road, you could've walked it in a day, if you didn't roast in the desert."

"So, it's true?" Brad was incredulous. "Area 51 and all the crazies? It's true?"

"What's true?" Jenks deadpanned. "What's true exactly? Does the Air Force develop and test advanced airframes? Yes, we do. Did we crash a few that looked like saucers? Yes, we did. Do we collect and do computer analysis on UFO sightings, looking for parallels and patterns? You got me. We do all that here and at Ft. Meade in Maryland. Do we go way out of our way to discredit civilian sightings of UFOs? Yes. Do we have carte blanche authority to listen in on you and Citizen X and his grandmother? Obviously. Sometimes, it suits us to let the locals think we have aliens in the neighborhood. Keeps the headlines rolling over the same old controversies."

Connie looked blank. "I thought the whole idea of Blue Book was to discredit or disprove all of the alien sighting reports."

"Well, it's complicated," Jenks replied, thinking that it didn't matter if he told them because short-term memories would be wiped anyway. He said, "The Russians have been dealing with their own UFOs for years. Ever since what has been called a meteor hit Kamchatka, they've been trying to either officially prove or debunk UFO stuff. Depends on who's in power. We still don't know if they were honest about it being an iron nickel meteorite or, well, who knows? With all that uncertainty going on over there, it makes it convenient for our public to report the random fast-moving lights." He smiled, saying, "Kids, we have some god-awful fast airplanes here, and I don't think we want the Russians to know that. Better they think we have alien problems of our own."

"What about Roswell?" Brad asked. "Didn't they go out and scrape a crashed alien craft off the desert and bring all the bits here?"

"Well, they did go to Roswell and scrape something off the desert floor, and, yes, they did bring it here."

"And?"

"And now," Jenks continued, "they know what happens when you take a test balloon to the edge of the atmosphere and it drops like a rock. Lots of little pieces of airframe in a deep hole, and the pilot dies. That was a well-kept secret." He grinned. "Better to let the Ruskies think we have a hushed-up alien than a balloon capable of passing undetected above their airspace on the jet stream.

"We are all pretty much innocent guys out here, doing research, playing with the public's perceptions, but pretty much keeping our go-faster and go-farther airplanes secret until we have a tactical mission for them."

"And you also have carte blanche to kidnap and murder?" Brad retorted.

"We don't murder anymore, and like I've told you, that was a mistake."

"Anymore," Brad said sarcastically. "I like that policy shift."

Connie added, "What about kidnapping?" She opened her hands and raised a russet eyebrow in question. "What exactly are your plans for us?"

Clearing his throat quietly, Jenks answered, "That's a detail we still have to go over." He looked at his watch again. He had been checking it, sometimes casually, as if he were trying to keep from being noticed. Brad had noted the attention to the watch because he had no idea what time or day it was and because there was so little else to notice in the featureless room. Jenks continued, "Well, I need to make a visit to see someone. I do hope I can trust that you two won't go anywhere?" He stood up, nodded at the mirror and then turned toward the door. There was a soft buzz and a click, and Martin Jenks walked out, leaving the two alone.

Brad noticed the visual communication with the mirrored panel and said, "He may have gone, but I have no doubt we are not alone." Connie closed her eyes to block the overly intense lighting and tried to relax.

Brad continued, "I see now why there is no light switch in this room." Connie looked at him, her eyebrows raised in question. He answered, "If we could turn out these lights, we might be able to see who's on the other side, and maybe even see if we could find out if the way out of here is through that mirror."

"You nuts? Do you actually think you could put a chair through that mirror?" Her tone was flat, clearly despondent.

"I don't know. Maybe if we could see out, we'd be able to see through a half-opened door or something." He walked over to the window and cupped his hands around his eyes. Just then, he realized he was looking through mini-blinds into a room with a few people in it. He saw a wrist quickly reach for the pull rod, and the blinds closed. "Damn."

Connie began to hum, a pulsing, not quite monotone, like she was trying to remember a melody. He thought, Even humming, she has a pretty voice. The melody developed with a very distinct pattern and a peculiar arrhythmia. It repeated; she had found it, and the hum became clearer, almost voiced.

"That's pretty," Brad said. "What is that?"

"I was just trying to remember the words; they're mostly Spanish." She hummed a few more lines. "Do you know who Holly Near is?"

"Holly Near? No, don't think I do. She a singer?"

"Yeah, she's pretty big on women's rights. It's one of her songs." She began to sing it softly, trying to deliver it as plaintively as the recording. *"Hay una mujer desaparacida, Hay una mujer desaparacida, en Chile, en Chile, en Chile."* She repeated it, even though she knew the song went on from there, something about the junta; that was it: the junta knows where she is. She said, "It means 'there is a missing woman, a woman is missing in Chile.' The song was a popular protest song against the Pinochet regime for silencing dissident women whose husbands had been openly murdered. Of course, most of the missing women were murdered, too, and by their own government."

"Connie, Sweetie." Brad bent over, elbows on the table in front of her. "Look, hon, until they put that needle full of forget-me juice in my arm, I am going to keep on thinking of how to get us out of here. That's us, you and me. You asked why I wanted to know what's on the other side of that glass. It's because I already know there's nothing above that suspended ceiling but concrete and some wiring. I have kept my eyes wide open whenever we or I have been guided anywhere. For the last three days, maybe four, since we woke up here, that is all I have been working on. The only thing I haven't seen anywhere is a window."

"So," she continued, "what makes you think that our government, the government that killed your father, that has obviously invested heaps of dollars on suppressing or discrediting any knowledge of alien visitors, wouldn't keep us disappeared. We are the disappeared ones; we are *los desaparacidos!"*

July 4, 1985
Independence Day

Entering his cell, Brad paused and faced the guard. "Thanks, man. And when he gets back, tell Jenks I appreciate it, the dinner together." He paused as his left hand pushed the wad of duct tape into the door lock's striker plate opening. "If it'd be okay, would you ask if we can continue to at least eat together?"

"Sure, no sweat. See what can be done, right?" Specialist 4 David Moody had been a stockade guard for four years on his first enlistment tour. The reenlistment spiel had been sweetened by the offer for a low-stress gig on the outskirts of Las Vegas. They hadn't told him how far out the outskirts were. But Moody knew how to keep up the mood of his inmates, how to maintain distance when needed, and when to come on like a bad dream. These kids, the only guests at present, seemed like innocents. It's too bad about them, he thought. The talk sessions had not gone well, and after the holiday break, they'd be under the needle. A session or two with the psych team and the appropriate cocktail and anything that seemed like memory of certain events would be remembered as bad dreams, hallucinations at best.

"See you tomorrow," Brad said, trying on model prisoner behavior. With one hand still on the door frame, he tried to pat the duct tape smooth.

"Not me—off tomorrow. Shift change in ten minutes, and I'm outta here. Probably won't see Jenks for a few days." The guard gave him a wry smile and gently pushed Brad in through the door. Moody pulled the handle, and both men heard the soft click of the latch bolt. The guard had no reason to suspect it had not seated its full depth into the door housing. Okay, he thought. Let's give it thirty minutes for shift change and another hour for them to do rounds and get bored. For what seemed an eternity, Brad was left to wonder if he could dislodge the bolt that must be hanging on by a millimeter or so. After the sound of steps passed and the night shift's leather boots squeaked through the hallway's outer door, Brad stood holding his breath at the blank darkness of his cell door.

He gently pressed against the door and released it. It did not rebound. The automatic closer, pulling from the outside, frustrated any attempt at a fingernail's grip on the door edge. He stooped to look at the clearance between door and jamb; a faint glow indicated about an eighth of an inch. Just before the lights went prematurely out, he turned to check out the steel cot frame. Now, in complete darkness, he knelt and quietly removed the

325

bedding, placing it under the spring mattress support. Checking for something that would resurrect his plan, he ran his hands over the elements of the bed frame. He noted slots in the end braces that had tabs from the long side frames. Feeling as if he were making a wildcat's racket, he pounded the frame's connectors loose with the butt of his palm. Slowly, very slowly, he had to remove more than twenty spring attachments from one side bar of the frame. Each spring's release seemed to rattle the walls as the chain-link mattress support clattered on the mattress.

As he worked, he went over the last conversation. What was it the guard had said? He was off tomorrow? That guard, Moody, had bragged to one of his cohorts that he was an eight-to-five weekday guard, almost always off on weekends. Brad was trying to figure why this seemed wrong. He sat for a moment, trying to recalculate the days he had been there. Except for a bit of inept foolishness with lights and meal timing, he was pretty sure that he had been incarcerated for only a few days, less than a week. He wondered if tomorrow was actually July 4? That would account for the guard's off day. Then he realized the gap in his day count. He had no way to account for how long he had been in transit and unconscious. It could be any day of the week and anyplace in the country.

Why would Jenks have told the truth about Dreamland? Damn! These people had left him in a black hole. Brad laughed quietly to himself in the darkness. *I am literally in a black hole!* He stooped carefully by the side of the bed frame, feeling the end of the frame metal; an edge protruded from the angle iron. He wasn't sure until it slid just barely into the slot between door and frame that his plan might work. He pried the frame sideways a little, and it snapped out with a metallic pop. "Dang it!" He realized he needed to be able to pull on the door as he pried the frame away from it. He had to bank on the fact that the bolt wasn't spring loaded. If it were, no matter how much he deflected the frame, the bolt would follow it. Well, nothing for it but to keep trying, he thought. Wasn't it a prisoner's duty to try to escape?

Slipping the angle iron frame back into the door just above the lock, he pried sideways while pulling gently outward. Nothing at all happened except he made too much noise. He felt sure that the metallic clanging must be reverberating around the building. He imagined a skeleton crew in a break room, bitching about pulling holiday duty. On the fourth attempt, he adjusted the angle of attack slightly and found a way to get between the wall and the angle iron. With a quick prayer, he twisted the angle iron a little for maximum friction on the door, pried slowly against the frame, and was rewarded with a soft click, as the deadbolt slipped out of its hasp. He felt a light breeze on his arm as he reached for the thin edge of the door. Dim overhead light from the hall flowed into the room as the door swung open.

Minimal though it was, the hallway light now flooding into the room made him blink a time or two. He set the piece of bed frame down with a seemingly overly loud clank. Looking down the hall, he detected no motion. There were no visible cameras, either. Maybe, he thought, this place doesn't like to make tapes. Less evidence to have to hide from Congress. Six doors to a side, one at each end—the hall was perfect for a comedy routine, though he found nothing humorous at this point. Only two doors interested him now: the one to Connie's cell and the last door at the end.

He trotted as lightly on his feet as he could to Connie's door. He whispered through the door. "Connie?" He paused a second. "Psst! Con, it's me!" Brad looked down at the lock; there was a simple deadbolt with a keyed lock. He tried the door at the end of the hall; it opened to palm pressure. Low-bid prison! he thought. Just inside that door was a small, tan metal box on the wall. He recognized the type. His dad had had one in his office to hold the keys to all the various equipment and cabinets in his office. He slid the catch and opened it. He prayed that if the room were monitored, that the guards were sufficiently bored to not be paying attention to their screens. There were numbered keys, matching the twelve numbers on the cells in the hallway. He looked into the hallway, saw that Connie's room was number twelve, and pulled the key. It fit the tumbler, and he was relieved to feel the pressure release on the door. He pushed it open slowly. "Connie, wake up."

"I'm awake," came out of the darkness, followed by a flying ball of energy. She flew into him and hung on.

"Ouch!" he exclaimed, pulling her into the hall and shutting the door. "Come on."

"How did you get out?" She pulled back. "You didn't attack the guard?"

"No, I'll tell you about it when there's time to stop and think." He led her along the hallway to the end door. "Right now, we have to get out of here." He had also locked his door, figuring there was no sense raising any early alarms. Returning to the room he'd just visited, he returned the keys to their hooks and shut the door. As he closed the door to the cell block behind him, he noticed a swipe-card security lock. No going back, he thought. A half glass door revealed the interrogation room to the left; to the right were a few offices with desks and lockers. All were lit and empty. A radio farther down the corridor indicated some human presence.

Cautiously, quietly, they worked their way through connecting office doorways, until one opened onto another hall. At the end of the hallway, they caught the glorious sight of an internally lit red exit sign next to a government-issue battery-powered emergency light array.

The exit door opened to stairs that led up to a small landing and another door. A simple push-bar release would open that door. There was no sign warning of an alarm, so he pushed cautiously. "Con," Brad said, "I don't know if this goes to a roof, a parking garage, or Grand Central Station." As she looked at him, he saw the same intensity in her gaze he'd seen on the sinking trawler. "Connie, remember when your dad's boat sank?"

A puzzled look passed briefly across her eyes, as she answered, "Yeah, sure, why?"

"You were pretty damn calm that night. I have no illusions that whatever is out that door will be easy. But some of these guys walk around in uniform, some in civvies. If we just act like we are supposed to be here, we'll attract a lot less notice than if we run bent over like we are about to be shot."

"Sure, that makes good sense. Okay. So, do we have a plan?" she asked, one dimple forming in her left cheek.

"Sweetie, I plan to marry you and make grandchildren for your mother," he answered, "but first, we have to get out of here. We just need to play it like we belong. Nothing real furtive."

She popped onto tiptoes and kissed him. "That, sir, is the worst proposal a girl ever got, but I'll take it." She kissed him again, took a deep breath, and said, "So, let's do this thing."

He pulled her face to his and gave her a lingering kiss. "If an alarm sounds, be prepared to run like hell." Brad pushed slowly on the handle until the door began to move. They heard nothing but a mechanical noise somewhere above and nothing through the door, which opened into a cone of yellow light coming from above the door. It painted a bright circle immediately around their doorway in its garish glow. In front of the door was a small concrete pad and then dirt. A row of painted rocks on either side of a walkway led to open space—a lot of open space. Brad stepped out with Connie right behind him. They let the door close and wondered at the cool night air and complete lack of activity. "Night shift!" Brad quietly exulted. "Connie, we lucked up. We got the night shift."

Brad pulled at Connie's elbow, and they slid quietly along the side of the building out of the cone of sulfuric light. He sniffed the cool outside air to relish its freshness. A second sniff confirmed that he was back in the desert. The musky scent of dew on dust recalled to his mind the many nights he had spent alone in the desert. At Arizona State, he'd liked to go up into high country. Unfurling a blanket on a bare spot of desert gravel, he'd watch the slow rotation of stars pass overhead. On a good night, just after full darkness, satellites would silently fly by, reminding him that humans could and did hurl great lumps of technology into almost permanent orbits. He could stare at Jupiter for hours at a time. By midnight, dew would be settling on him and his blanket and the layers of dust lightly covering almost everything around him. He'd always remember the smell.

"Connie, we need to make a move. It's sometime after midnight, and we only have a few hours of darkness left." He scanned the compound around him—apparently military from the numbered or lettered buildings. Their entrances were bathed in halos of yellow light, but he guessed they were air-force gray. The security lighting was unevenly distributed. In fact, he noted that it was almost dark in some places. The base appeared sparse, though Brad wondered if this was the less-busy end of a larger installation. To his left, down the valley, he noted the revolving green-and-red light of an airfield's control tower. A row of light-blue landing lights spread out to the edge of nowhere, indicating a runway. To his right, buildings thinned out to darkness. Ahead, a central roadway with infrequent overhead lighting lay between him and a row of metal buildings.

Connie said, "Brad, you are a miracle man, but we need another miracle. We need to get out of here!"

"Yeah, no foolin'." He pulled her out of the darkness of the shadow cast by their former jail and into a more anonymous darkness near a utility post. She looked behind at the building. There was no identity on it save a large block letter "B" at the building's corner.

"Check that out," she said, pointing at the large, iconic capital B. "Didn't Jenks say his unit was nicknamed the 'B-Team'?"

He simply huffed in acknowledgement. Scanning across the street, he said, "There, that looks like it might be a repair garage. Lots of trucks outside, four large roll-up bay doors for maintenance, and hey, there's no fence around the back of the building." Connie pulled him across the street.

Smiling, he followed. "We seem to have a plan," he said. "And if we can pull any more karma out of the universe, this may be the Fourth of July!"

"And that's a good thing?"

"Heck yeah!" he said breaking into a trot. "That means half the troops are out on the town rolling craps."

"Craps?" They reached the darker side of the building and stopped to see if anything moved besides the dust raised by their sprint.

"Yes, craps; dice. I know where we are. It fits perfectly."

She turned and looked up into his face. "Really? You know where we are? Where?"

A glint of light reflecting off teeth sparkled in the dark as he smiled back at her. He pointed to a signature red-and-white water tower a little farther down the valley to the left of the airfield and then pointed out the runway lights. He gestured to the right at a huge patch of white earth bathed in the light of a quarter moon, explaining it was a salt evaporation pan. He cupped her face in his hands and kissed the bridge of her nose softly. "My dear, at this moment, we are standing next to the vehicle maintenance building in an almost secret section of a hush-hush Air Force base that almost everyone knows about." He spread his arms out toward the yellow lit buildings arrayed below them. "It's in a large area sometimes known as Area 51, but pilots nicknamed it Dreamland." He panned his hand across the brightly lit center of the base farther down the valley adjacent to Broom Lake's white, salty expanse. "That, my dear, is Dreamland, home of one of the Air Force's ultra-secret advance flight vehicle development facilities. The other is in California at Edwards. But this place is also thought to be the location of dead aliens, space junk of all kinds, including ..." He looked back at her for effect. "... including the remains of the Roswell alien spaceship."

"Dreamland?" she whispered to herself. Yellow ovals of light scattered across the valley floor, highlighting the few dozen structures in view. "This is *the* Dreamland?"

July 4, 1985
East Gate, Area 51, Nevada, 0315 hours

Exactly fourteen point seven dry desert miles east of the small base's main crossroads, Senior Airman Hal "Perky" Perkins was cussing angry. He was angry that his girlfriend had actually written "Dear John" at the top of the letter that he had just finished reading for the umpteenth time. The writing was such a tortured attempt at pentameter verse that he figured it had to have been written with the help of one of her girlfriends, or worse, a new boyfriend. And he was angry that he had drawn night duty at East Gate. The only thing to watch at night was starlight.

By 9:00 a.m. the slopes down mountain would begin to shimmer with heat. On cloudless days, it was nothing but a sunburned hell in glaring white heat. Night shift was, if anything, worse. East Gate seemed barren and hostile by day. At night, things moved in the dark. East Gate! Just his little guard shack and a whole lot of scrub and rock. Hell, the fence only went a few hundred feet either side of the road. He rarely saw anything and only heard sounds of desert life. Between the extremes of heat and cold and boredom, he might catch a coyote sneaking up the road. When the atmosphere bounced just right, he listened to KXPT in monotonous eight-hour stints. When he couldn't get that, he suffered through country and western that was more LA than Nashville.

Tonight, he stared north at the ops area. He flicked off the overhead lights above the guard shack and scanned the night sky. Sometimes, he'd see the lights of the new fighter bomber being run through its paces in night operations. Usually, after settling in and reading through the previous shift's activity record, he'd stroll yards out into the desert and sit on a low, rounded rock. The shift then settled into a monotony shared by tower guards, night watchmen, and soldiers on perimeter guard duty the world over. He allowed himself only one cigarette per half hour. With PX pricing, he knew he was getting addicted to nicotine at a level he would not be able to afford on the outside.

He crossed off the days on his calendar as each one passed. He was down to 147 days and a wake-up. Occasionally and, unfortunately only occasionally, the monotony would be broken when spacer groupies drove up the road to see if they could get pictures of the installation.

Sometimes they took pictures of the "Do Not Pass, Restricted Area" signs, and even less occasionally, they would park out of sight of the guard shack and scale the small hill called Black Top to get a look into the valley. They were always intercepted by the motion detectors that let loose an ear-blistering klaxon and a call to the dog-team handlers. Immediately east of the guard shack, Black Top rose almost two hundred feet above the surrounding, gently rolling terrain, and the cameras there could be controlled from his desk. Glancing at the monitors, he saw no movement anywhere in the camera's night vision along the eastern approaches to the gatehouse.

He jumped as his radio hissed and clicked. It was Sergeant Gomes calling in for a communication check. "Got you loud and clear, Sarge."

"You gonna stay awake for me tonight, Perkins?"

"Yes, Sergeant. I'm wide awake, thank you." He muttered other responses under his breath.

"Say again?"

"Nothing, Sarge. I was just coughing."

"Well, keep it together. Half the base is off tonight. I can't spare anybody to relieve you if you think you're sick."

"No, that's okay. Just some dust."

"And turn down the radio, Airman. Stay alert and turn your overheads back on. Base out."

"East Gate out." Perkins leaned over his desk and turned up the radio. It was one of the good nights, and he loved the E Street Band. A glint of light to the northeast caught his eye. A white light with halos of brilliant blue streaked across the horizon hugging the hills. The aircraft took a sudden vertical and climbed. As it gained altitude, it arched back toward him, and he could no longer see its baffled exhaust as it winked out. No wonder the spacers thought these things were UFOs. He looked at his watch. Only 3:30 a.m. The sky was beautiful; he decided not to turn the overheads back on just yet. He went back into the shack to get his binoculars to sky gaze.

The radio started to buzz. When he realized the sound wasn't the radio, he barely had time for a "What the hell?" The buzz turned into the high-pitch grind of gears and a highly revved diesel engine. With a burning pit of acid growing in his gut, he looked for the source of the sound and saw none. As he stared back toward the base, a lights-out deuce and a half troop-truck came out of the darkness, moving much too fast for the turn, much less for him to stop it.

He tripped backward getting out of his shack too quickly and lost a few seconds getting back on his feet. Damn. Not on my shift! he thought. Another coupla drunk airmen, stealing a truck to go to town. How cliché can you get? He grabbed his weapon and scrambled to get out in front of the gate. He began waving his arm to slow the truck. There was a grinding of gears as it slowed, and the transmission ground as the driver missed a gear or two. With sickening certainty, he knew that he could not stop the speeding truck with his 172-pound, burr-headed self. The truck's brakes squealed but didn't seem to slow the gray monster. He leaped aside and rolled to the

332

ground as the truck jerked, hopping on its brake pads to a stop just inches from the stop bar.

In the rolling dust cloud and the excitement of the moment, he wasn't sure what happened next. He would report later that he was blinded by dust and grit in the air and something knocked him on the head. It was better to say that he had been blindsided in the dust than to say that a gorgeous redhead had materialized out of the dust cloud in an orange mechanic's jumpsuit and had karate kicked him in the side of the head. The truck was gone, snapping off the two-by-six striped drop bar and busting the chain-link gate off its hinges.

As the truck revved up, leaving behind the broken entrance gate, an empty guardhouse, and twelve unwatched video monitors, Brad swore softly at having to find out the hard way that hydraulic brakes were the reason the truck was in the motor pool for maintenance. Connie looked at his face, which was illuminated by the few dashboard lights. "I thought you were gonna run over that guard, Brad. What if he hadn't jumped out of the way?"

"He'd be very sore right now. I was worried that when he rolled to the right, I'd run over his legs or something." He chuckled, saying, "I'll never forget the look on his face when he saw you. He never saw that kick coming!"

"What are we going to do with him?" In answer, he used gears to slow for a small turn and then continued to slow to a stop, pulling hard on the emergency brake handle. "Let's turn him loose while he's within easy hiking distance back to the gate. It'll take him a while to figure out what to do next."

Perkins felt himself being slapped awake. Coming to, he saw red. At least, the only things that were lit were red. As he tried to focus, he saw a man in an orange jumpsuit and wool cap pulled down to cover his eyes was shaking him. "Okay, good, you're awake," Brad said. "You should be able to get that knot off your ankles in a few minutes. Your guard shack is only about a mile and half up the road." Perkins felt himself being dropped back onto the rocky shoulder of the road, and heard footsteps running away, a squeak as the truck adjusted to the weight of the driver getting in, and, finally, the slam of the door. The red glow of the truck's brake lights dimmed. The engine roared as it revved to catch first gear and was gone. He listened to it run through some gears and then heard it diminish with distance as he struggled in the darkness with the cord wrapped around his feet.

Getting to his feet, he could barely hear the truck. Or could he? It might just be ringing in his ears from the kick. Dusting himself off, he set out on a trot back up the road. He tried to work on an excuse that would minimize the pile of trouble he would be in when he had to report in. In less than ten minutes, he was back at the guard shack. Taking in the broken gate, the snapped off-drop bar, and the deep gravel ruts in the road, he fought to suppress an urge to get sick. This was serious trouble; the phrase dereliction of duty came to mind.

Once inside the guard shack, he reached for the radio set's hand mike and was stunned to see it gone. It was simply not there; a small black hole labeled "mic" was the radio's only answer to his search. Instinctively, he looked at the slot that held the low-res video recordings from the security cameras covering the gate. The slot was empty. "Jesus!"

Then he went for his government-issued car keys and found the key rack empty. "Damn!" Looking out into the desert, he could no longer see the roving white glow of the truck's headlights heading east. "Dang it!" he shouted at the desert night. He thought about the fifteen miles back to headquarters. It was now just past 4 a.m. It would take more than two hours. He shouted to the overhead stars. "I am screwed!"

~ ~ ~

At 10:30 hours the next morning, the truck was found at a Kentucky Fried Chicken in Rachel, Nevada. Brad and Connie's escape to the east misdirected the search. Specialist Perkins, dreading a court-martial, found the truck and convinced half of the search detail to redirect search efforts to the north up Highway 375 toward Route 6. The other half of the search team, led by Jenks himself, took the more likely search south toward Las Vegas.

Three days later, Brad and Connie emerged from an aging, sunbaked camper trailer parked behind the only service station in Rachel and breakfasted with a grizzled former prospector and the current proprietor of the service station. The name "Lucky" was somewhat of a misnomer for Lucky Magee, who had divorced or been divorced five times and had no use for the nearby Air Force and their lying ways. He knew there were secret things going on over the mountain, and he didn't like any part of it. Some of what he saw in the night sky made him sure the "gov'mint" was lying to the world about captured alien spaceships. He told some great stories, some of which might have been true.

By July 11, with Air Force security throwing a feeble net across the southwestern states and the Florida Panhandle, Brad and Connie met a wiry truck driver with a salted burr head of hair. The cab-over candy-apple-red Freightliner was headed for La Jolla with a reefer load of South Texas citrus. That met their need to stay out of Florida for a while, and Dink loved the opportunity to retell road stories.

Chapter 20

And ye shall know the truth, and the truth shall set you free.
New Testament, John 8:32

August 16, 1985
Tallahassee, FL

Summer rain was still dripping from the eaves outside Susan Delaney's Tallahassee residence. A low fog had begun to form in the oppressively humid evening air, and the deluge had silenced even the usual cricket chorus. Down the street at almost even intervals, cones of light filled with clouds of circling insects. The small gathering became used to a rapid tat-tat-tatting on a garbage can lid as drops from a second-floor gutter banged away in monotonous metronomic regularity. Connie Chappell, her hair still wet from their sprint down the street, was grinning lopsidedly, chin in hands. Brad, leaning back on one of the four dinette chairs, crossed his feet on another and got comfortable, hands behind his head. Susan Delaney, pleased to have them both back, was looking at the teapot, expecting it to whistle at any moment.

"So you stole an Air Force truck?" she asked, astonished.

Brad responded, "It seemed like a good idea at the time. As it turned out, we drove it much farther than we could have traveled on foot. We'd have become vulture food if we had tried to escape on foot long before we ever got off the base proper."

Connie cut in, "You should have seen the eyeballs popping out of the guard's head as he realized that he was about to be run over. Looking back, it seems funny, but we could have killed the poor guy if he hadn't jumped."

Susan asked Brad, "You were going to run this guy down?"

"No, no, nothing like that. We had stolen the truck from the motor pool maintenance shop. There were a few curves getting off the main base and out of there. Most everything was uphill toward the east gate. I didn't know that brakes were the problem with the truck until we stopped, er, tried to stop at the guard shack. I'm just glad I found the hand brake in time." The teapot interrupted, cycling up from a low, breathy whistle to a shriek. Susan, set in her ways, always waited for the full boil before dousing the decanter's worth of tea bags with scalding hot water. She felt it made better iced tea in the long run.

He continued, "It's good that we found out when we did, 'cause a few hundred yards down the hill, there was a pretty good hard right turn that I might have missed if I hadn't known the foot brakes were dead."

"Sounds like good luck all around," Susan said.

"We had tremendous luck, but I'm not sure we weren't 'allowed' at least to make an attempt to escape," Connie said. "I wouldn't think we were actually let go, but let's say, Jenks might have felt guilty for abducting us."

Brad broke in, "You think that SOB understands guilt?"

"Well, maybe not guilt, but he sure should understand payback," Connie replied. "Who knows? Maybe even karma. We did save the jerk from drowning and he won't ever forget that day!"

"I don't know, Con. I don't think I can accept that one roll of duct tape left in the dining room constitutes an offered option to get out of there. We had to do a lot on our own based on the availability of that tape." He sounded convinced but wasn't sure of his own conclusion, even as he said it. He wondered, *Could Jenks really have put the roll of tape there? It was surely helpful that it was there on the evening of July 3. Jenks would have known that half or more of the research base's personnel would be on liberty on July 4.*

"Either way," Susan said, "it was very handy at the time, and no telling what drugs they would've used on you if you were still in there." All three exchanged glances. Susan continued, "I think it's safe to assume that you'd still be in there."

Brad said, "I read a lot about abductions. There's a case to be made that some of the people who think they've been taken by aliens were in the 'business' of alien spotting. They caused a bit of a ruckus locally and generally spooked the local population wherever they were. So the black hat guys, this Dreamland B-Team detachment, made a practice of snatching these folks up and then doing hypno on them. They'd go back raving about big-eyed, white-skinned aliens and being poked and prodded, all by suggestion. Hell, the medics could easily make a needle insertion here or there, a cut or two, whatever fit the profile. Meanwhile, the unit comes in, confiscates anything that looks like physical evidence, and then turns the guy loose so certifiably sure of what he thinks he's been through that everyone in town thinks he's loony, including the spouse, kids, shrink, or whoever."

"Brad, honey, stop a second," Susan said, waiting for his rant to slow down. "You're making a case for everybody else being deceived. What is it you've been talking to in the woods? Are you certain of the time line that has you talking to it, or him, or her before anybody had you in custody? Are there any gaps that you couldn't account for? Were there any times you woke with a headache after a longer-than-usual sleep? Are you absolutely sure there's something in the woods?"

Brad said, "We're just saying that the official policy is that there is nothing to alien visitors or abductions. We don't know how much they know about what's really happening."

Connie interrupted. "I know there's something there, Aunt Sue. Brad, you first took me down there to explain why you were so committed to finding out what your piece of metal is. That thing, person, alien, or whatever it is, introduced itself to me. I know that. You know that, Brad."

He met Connie's intense gaze. "I know! I know, but still, I don't trust those guys for anything. If what you say about Jenks is true, I'm sure he thinks he's leveled the field and anything is fair game from here on."

"What about from here on?" Susan asked. "Where do you go from here?"

Brad looked at his mother. He was still getting used to the idea that Susan Delaney, who had been "Aunt Sue" forever, was his mother. "I need to contact Dr. Walters. Jenks said all three samples were recovered and that Walters and the laboratory's directors have assured secrecy and compliance with the agency's directive to smother any evidence gained in tests they've already performed." He stood up, realizing that the government was only going to be more determined from here on, and exclaimed, "Holy crap!"

"What's wrong, Bra—?" Connie asked, interrupted by Susan's, "What's the matter, Bradley?" They turned to each other in amazed wonder.

"Man! This sucks!"

Again a synced chorus of, "What?"

"They have three samples and data!" he shouted, waving his hand in frustration. "They can't help but find out what that thing really is! Even if they gave it to a metals tech for only a few hours, it would not take long to find out that it isn't manufactured on this planet." Their faces showed intense interest, but no understanding.

They are going to have to make sure they get the rest of it. They will have to make sure they can discredit me and you." He pointed at Connie. "We both know of the Air Force's little secret summer camp, and we weren't released under the usual drugged-out circumstances."

"So you need to go into hiding or into second gear," Susan said. "I guess you won't need the Wakulla Beach house, after all."

"Exactly!" Brad said. "Sure, we could go into hiding, but I could never get a job that required fingerprints, or even a résumé. I could never serve in the military. I kinda wanted to keep the option of going into the armored infantry. That could never happen. Heck, I don't even have ID. They took that from both of us. I'm not sure we could get those renewed without getting busted."

"I don't think we could stay hidden for more than a few more weeks, unless we find some tiny town in Idaho, and I don't like cold that much!"

Susan asked, "Do you know anyone who can help?"

"Well, yeah." Brad looked at Connie who was still sitting at the dinette.

"What was the name of that guy…you remember, Marina introduced us to the guy with the beret?" Brad rubbed at a two-day stubble in thought. "He had round-framed glasses and a little mustache. What was his name? Angle, Dangle, or something like that?"

"DeAngelo?" Connie offered. "Stan or Sam DeAngelo?" "That's it, Connie, perfect. Sammy DeAngelo!"

Susan looked expectant, waiting for an explanation. Brad asked, "Mom, do you remember we told you that we met up with Marina, the woman who connected me with Lucy? While we were waiting for a ride east with Dink, Marina introduced me, er, us. He introduced us to Sammy at the Indian Springs Casino."

Susan blinked. Brad had not called her "Mom" spontaneously before. A quick, knowing glance passed between them. She said, "I remember hearing about Lucy's friend Marina. Wasn't she a hostess at the casino?"

"More of a concierge in that she knew everything about the casino, the hotel, what was going on at night at which venues in Vegas, and everything about anybody in the little town of Indian Springs. This guy DeAngelo was a past president of the Extra-Terrestrials Committee, or ETC, only they spelled it in lowercase like et cetera."

"Too cute, huh?" Connie quipped. "Not many in their group. I think he said there were no more than fifty of them all over the world."

339

Susan asked, "So how can etc help out?"

"His etc network, no matter how small, has connections at NASA, JPL, Hale, and on the Hill in DC, and also a small number of possible screwballs."

"Hale?" Susan asked. "What's Hale?"

"Hale is the observatory at Mount Palomar. It's the biggest set of optical eyeballs in the Southwest. It's about a daylong trip from there up to Indian Springs or Area 51."

Susan looked at Brad, her head cocked to the side. "How much do you know about all of this ET stuff?"

"I read a lot. It was sort of my extracurricular life back at AU," he answered, shrugging. "I guess I'm as informed as I can be, given the state of official government intervention. And their intervention is pervasive, persistent, and effective. Just a word from them and very professional people shut up. Careers have ended because of them. Lives have been taken—Dad's, for one; Dr. Hill; and others in Spokane and in Nevada. An Air Force pilot who was 'last seen' chasing a UFO across Lake Superior into Canadian airspace, was actually debriefed by the pros at Dreamland and then disappeared. If he's not dead, then he could be deranged and homeless on the streets of Los Angeles. There are literally hundreds of sightings and more involved incidents across the globe, and all the world governments interfere, obscure, and deny. I wouldn't be surprised if there is a secret committee at the UN."

Connie asked, "Brad, what do you want to do next? It seems Susan is right, and you're right. They're going to be very motivated to get you and, for that matter, me too."

"I think we need to find a way to New York. If he hasn't spilled that part of the plan, Jason Walters was supposed to have lined up access to producers at NBC news. I think with Sammy DeAngelo's help, we might be able to get to New York."

"Brad, honey," Susan said, "what makes you think your story is more compelling than any other?"

"I have an ace in the hole!" he said smiling. He opened his arms expansively. "I have evidence. If I can get reports on the remainder of the artifact to the studio, I can get word out. Also, I have to get word to Walters, because when Jenks was trying to get us to talk to him, he mentioned that he

340

had three of the samples and had shut down inquiry at all three research labs."

"I'm sorry, Brad. Don't you have to start over?" She got up to get ice from the freezer for the tea. "Do you have enough to get to some other labs?"

"I didn't make my point, yet. I clearly remember that Jenks said 'three.' He had all three of the samples from the labs. So there's the three he intercepted from labs and probably the one from FSU. There are still three labs out there working at Walters's competition, trying to figure out what they've been given. It's been almost two weeks, and they should be close to getting their results ready for the mini-conference that they don't know is canceled yet!"

"If enough noise starts to come from widely spaced respectable sources at the same time, there will be press." He emphasized, "Lots of press. As long as no one starts a war, we should be above the fold in major papers all over the place."

Connie said softly, "Brad? We have another card to play besides your ace."

Surprised, he turned to her. "What?"

"A good friend of ours. You introduced me to him."

Furrowing his brow, he offered, "Sunny? Dink?"

"No silly, Litan. Ka-Litan. We need to get help from Ka-Litan. How could his reality be obscured? He is not a wreck that can be hidden. Well, I mean he is hidden. But, if we can get him free, we can ask for his help in telling his story. It will set world governments on their butts. They are not paramount. They might even begin to cooperate."

He sat back in his chair. Watching Susan stirring the dark, hot tea into the pitcher full of ice cubes, he said, "Well, I guess I know where we need to go tomorrow. Mom? Do you wanna come?"

"Well, yes. I think I'd like to." She thought for a moment. "I have to get a report out to the governor's office by tomorrow afternoon, but the day after, I can do it. If you two want to get into the house, I can call down to Sunny and get it opened up for you." Two blank stares met hers. "Oh! I guess you guys didn't get the news yet. Brad, just after you went to Detroit, Lucy got a call from her old boss. They're opening a new casino in Vegas and wanted her to come out and train some of the floor help."

Brad asked, "Don't they have a surplus of part-time and former dealers to choose from? She had to go all the way out there to train?"

"I don't know, honey; all I know is that it was, or is, good money for a short time, and she left. But I'll call down and get Sunny to light the pilot and open the house up. It's only been a few weeks, but the air gets so funky in there in the summertime when the house is closed."

She looked at Connie. "Con? You've been talking to this thing in the woods; what do you think it is?"

After a pause Connie said, "I really don't know. Whatever it is, it's intelligent. Last year, I'm talking to him about our culture in general. You know, basic stuff about humanity. Then I start to bring books, and it turns out he can learn to read our language by 'being' in me while I'm reading. As he explained it, he could see the pages I was reading by understanding what I was thinking as I read it. Next season, he is asking for more detailed science books, and I'm reading chemistry texts to him and physics." Her face turned up at the twirling blades of the ceiling fan above the table, but she was looking into the memory. "The chemistry was easy to read because that was my old text; the physics wasn't easy to read 'cause I didn't actually take it myself. But you know? It was one of the few times he seemed to have a sense of humor." She came back to the present and presented one of her lopsided, single-dimple grins. "He seemed almost to be laughing as I read about atomic structure. It seemed like he was trying not to offend me, but it gave me the impression we were missing something."

"I'd expect as much," Brad cut in. "I'm surprised he didn't laugh at the chemistry text too. Hey, did he respond to the periodic table? I mean, did he ask if there was more?"

"Yeah, he did, only...let me think. It was more like he thought I'd skipped a page, like he expected there to be more on the next page. I felt a little embarrassed because I wasn't the ace student in chemistry in the first place, but I felt like he knew a lot more about it than I did."

Brad nodded, and Connie continued, "There are times when I get a glimpse of what he's thinking. I got the very strong feeling that Ka-Litan thinks human understanding of chemistry or physical chemistry has a long way to go.

August 17, 1985
Wakulla

Sunny picked up the phone and growled a hello into the receiver. His initial scowl softened into a smile; he'd been expecting it to be another call from a telephone solicitor. "Sure, Miss Sue, I'll go over and turn everything on. Right, 'cept the lights. Yes, ma'am, next twenty, thirty minutes at worst." He picked casually at a dry liver spot on the back of his hand. "What'd she want to go back to Las Vegas for? Uh-huh, uh-huh." He listened attentively for a while with an occasional "do tell" and "don't say," as he took in what was apparently an interesting story.

Jasper got up, went outside, and relieved himself of most of the last two light beers, and came back in. Sunny was just hanging up the phone. Jasper, one of Sunny's longtime fishing partners and a regular at the men's breakfast club, was known locally as "Jazz" even though his musical tastes ran to sixties country and western. He was another victim of Sunny's naming system. "Jazz, don't set just yet. Miss Sue asked me to go over to Miss Lucy's and turn on the water 'n' AC, 'n' air it a bit. She says to 'spect company in an hour'r two." Without much more conversation, the old friends hitched up into Sunny's old pickup and headed out of the drive.

"Miss Sue hire you to take after the place?"

"No, sir, she does not."

Jasper pulled at an earlobe thinking. "You got history with her the county don't know about?"

"Yeah, but it ain't the interesting kind ends up in the paper for weeks on end." There was a silence for a while. Sunny's lower lip was moving like he was considering what to say. Jazz sat looking over every now and then as if to urge on the reply. When it came, he was dumbstruck.

"Jazz? You believe in flying saucers and space aliens?"

Jasper waited in the momentary silence for Sunny to continue.

"You know, not like in the movies maybe, but do you allow that of all them stars that maybe some of 'em might have smart critters on 'em that can visit now and again?"

One and two did not make three. Jasper considered his response to the question and asked, "You sayin' that Miss Sue is a space alien?"

"Naw!" Sunny reached out and flicked Jasper across the knees. "Don't be an idjut! I'm askin' the question: Do you think it's possible that maybe bein's from another planet might have been to earth?"

"Well, heck! Almost anything is possible, Sunny." They rode in silence for a little while. "So you're saying you do? You do believe in flying saucers 'n' such?"

"Ain't sayin' any such a thing." He thought a moment and continued, "Guess some people I've knowed a long time do, and they come on pretty convincing." He let go of the wheel with both hands in a palms-up gesture of simple acceptance. "I saw this bit of metal that was found down in the woods that we, er, some folks think fell outta space or got knocked off'n a spaceship or something like that, and, well, Jazz, it sure did not look like anything I'd ever seen before. And I've worked on about every kind of metal that comes through a shop. I've welded on brass, bronze, steel, 'luminum, mag, stainless, and all sorts of exotic alloys, and I gotta admit I's stumped when I saw it." He explained about the coloring and the ring of tiny black dots that seemed to be extruded or formed into the length of the rod and the peculiar details of how it was found.

Jasper listened, saying nothing for a while. Finally, he grinned and punched Sunny on his knee with the back of his knuckles. "Man, that was a good one. You had me for a while there, Sunny. I had taken the hook, and you was reelin' me in. But I only had two of yore beers. I ain't that far along!" He laughed a deep, rich guffaw and slapped his own thigh. "Man, I gotta remember that one. I bet I can pull in half the guys up at the barber shop if I can work it into a conversation somewhere."

Sunny looked sideways at his friend as he drove, wondering if he should push it. He considered it for a while and then laughed aloud and said, "Ha, Jazz, you jumped all over that bait shore as a gator'd go after a pup on a rope." He laughed again, and Jasper joined in. Sunny realized that not everyone was as liberal a thinker as he was.

After a moment, Jasper asked, "So, what was the history with you and Miss Sue?"

"Now that's a whole n'other story." As he pulled off the coastal highway and down the short run to the Hitchens house, he began the story. "Long time ago, say '66 or '67, Miss Susan and her sister Lucy were just a couple of pretty, young hippie chicks. Real pretty, too, neither was into makeup or nothin', and you never saw such goods in pigtails and coveralls. They had not too much to care about in the world. Sort of in school and sort of not; their major up at the university was how not to get knocked up while trying yore best to fake it. Well, that worked out for a while." He paused to gather back-story. "You remember old Charlie Hitchens got this here place from his daddy?" He pointed at the little white house as they drove up.

"Charlie from up at the gunpowder plant?"

"That's the one, he was a supervisor or something in the loading docks. Anyways, Charlie was real pissed off when one of the young girls took a shine to Whit 'cause Whit was studious. Did real well up there at the

344

college. He was afraid that Miss Susan and Whit was getting too close for comfort. Charlie knew the two Delaney girls was trouble when he first laid eyes on 'em. No bras on, no makeup, but real pretty anyhow like I said and way, waaay too friendly. Somethin' about Whit. He was smart and a good-lookin' kid, a lot of fun afore he went to the war and got serious. Miss Susan and Whit used to come on down to the beach and talk to me and whoever was around. They'd pass their pipe or joints around with whoever was interested and generally just be good, fine folks. I got to like 'em both quite a bit, and you know me and Charlie was fishin' a lot then." He paused, putting the memories together. "They didn't pass anything around when his daddy was down to the beach.

"Susan was his sweetheart first, and after a while, it got fuzzy. Well, afore it got fuzzy, Susan and Whit did the mambo, er, without protection." He looked over at Jazz as he was leaning down to hit the pilot button on the water heater. "She was with child, out of wedlock, as the preacherman says."

"Well, there was a lot a' that goin' around back then." Jasper shrugged. "That so unusual? Fact, it's been going on way longer than that. It's just people can't behave when it comes to sex, and you know—" He started to ramble, but Sunny took back the lead.

"Like I's sayin', after Miss Sue got herself in the family way, she got weird. Closer it got, weirder she got. It caused a lot of trouble later with her sister Lucy who'd always liked Whit, and I think she wasn't too put out to take over when Miss Sue lit out."

"I thought Lucy was the one that run off?"

"Miss Sue, she was the one that run off when Swamp Boy was just a tiny baby. It was Lucy that run off when he was older. Wasn't more'n two weeks after it dropped, Sue comes over to sit with me and the missus. Real broke up. We talked and set and talked and set and tried to get her to understand that every mother goes through this hard time. 'Post-partin' depression,' Maybelle said. We thought we had her put straight, but two days later, I'm comin' out the door and damn near stepped on the basket. If the baby hadn't'a peeped about then, I might'a done it too."

Jasper let out a low, sympathetic whistle. Sunny continued, "Well, I guess you coulda said we should'a seen it comin', but it's true; lots of young mothers go through that scared-to-death phase and grow right out of it, post-partin' and all. Not Miss Sue. Guess she got more scared and couldn't fall in love with the baby. Well, we drive right on over to Charlie's place with the baby and find everyone there but Sue.

"Charlie and Agnes are there with Whit and Lucy, and they're all tore up. They have a note from Sue say'n she's gone, and they all thought with the baby too and maybe that was Sue's first thought." Sunny paused at the front door, flicked the panel of light switches up and down to ensure the lights were on. 'But she couldn't do it, that is to say, she couldn't run off with the baby and she left it with us on her way outta town."

Jasper let out a low and slow, "Jeeesus H. Christ!"

"Yeah, well, what really took my heart away was that little Lucy, who'd been all tore up about the pregnancy from the start, grabbed up that baby and that was that."

"But I thought that Whit and Lucy were, wait, I'm confused"

"Yeah, you're right. Whit and Lucy were. And it didn't take more'n a coupla months or so after Miss Sue lit out." Sunny dusted his hands on his pants and locked the front door. Walking back to the truck, he said, "Coupla years later, Sue come back. Let me tell you, there was a lot of crying and gnashing of teeth. Lucy let her sister Sue back into the family circle. Just by agreement and all, Miss Sue moved up to Tallahassee and went back to school. Miss Lucy stayed on being mother to the child and married Whit up at the courthouse quiet like.

"Now, Miss Sue, she's still up to Tallahassee, got a real job and done real well. She married once but not for long; I think she never stopped loving Whit and finally got attached to the little boy." Getting in and slamming the truck door, he looked over at Jasper. "Jazz, you remember Bradley, right? Swamp Boy? He'd come down to the beach pretty regular?"

"Yeah, Bradley is Whit's kid—the baby, right?"

"He's the one. Great kid, too. So anyway, Lucy, the new mom, is struggling, but her sister Sue helps out a lot. They raised the boy together, it seemed. Then Whit, outta college at last, decides he needs to join the war and goes off to Vietnam. Sue actually moved down to the homestead after Charlie had his stroke, and for two years, the two sisters, no longer hippies but young women with jobs, raised the boy. When Whit came back from the war, I think it broke Miss Sue's heart to move back to Tallahassee."

"Jeez, Sunny, does this story stay depressing?"

"Not for much longer." He glanced over at his friend. "But it does stay differ'nt! Back a while, maybe ten years ago, Miss Lucy started goin' strange. She complained of hearing things, said there were aliens out in the swamps; it got real uncomfortable around here as people started lookin' at her strange and talkin'. You know how folks are! She finally drug up and

346

left town. She disappeared and stayed gone. She was real conflicted, but she was gone!" He emphasized the finality of the last word.

"So that's the ones you're talkin' about believes in space aliens? What about Whit and the boy?"

"Well, they toughed it out; Brad was about ten at the time, and he took it hard. Whit and Sue did what they could to keep some kind of family up for him. But they didn't marry or anything. Fact is, you couldn't'a told that there'd ever been any close history 'tween Whit and Sue, but I kinda think after a while, they got close, just between you and me, that is." He shrugged. "It ain't gospel, just a feelin'."

"So, it's all good?"

"Naw, it ain't all good. Whit got hisself shot!" Getting out of the truck back at his house, he shot a hard glance over at Jasper. "That was what? Eight or so years ago? But you knew that." He pulled off the road and up to the side of his house. Getting out, he stopped and leaned on his fender. Jasper leaned on the opposite fender facing him.

"Jazz, I helped the boy get out of town. He was being pursued, least he thought, by the burglars who shot his daddy. Got him a ride outta town on a friend's rig."

"So the boy, he's comin' back? That why we went over to open the house?" Jasper nodded, thinking he'd absorbed most of a complex story.

"Well, yes, in short. But he's the one found the thing from outer space."

Jasper cussed and spat out the window. "Jeezus, Sunny, leave it alone. I ain't gonna bite on that one again."

August 18, 1985
St. Marks National Wildlife Refuge

The three hikers were sweating from the heat and humidity of a midsummer's morning in the pine flatwoods. Brad had warned Susan to wear long sleeves and pants or lots of bug spray for the hike. Connie knew better, so the three of them were relatively well protected from the cloud of gnats and larger insects. Connie showed Sue how to slip through the thin branches of the titi without snagging clothing or slipping into the water-soaked depression it depended on.

Susan's first reaction was like everyone else's. She looked over her shoulder for something coming at her from behind. She became conscious of her confusion and glanced around to see both Connie and Brad smiling at her. Brad told her to sit and get comfortable. They all settled around the small, dark pool. Its tannic waters teemed with small life from diatoms and spirogyra to their larger predators, mosquito larvae and surface scavengers like water spiders. The voice came to them all, speaking in psi, thought forms they knew the 'presence' had perfected a few years earlier. He had been trying to talk to visitors for much longer—much, much longer. Almost all of the other visitors to the place had run away, terrified.

~ ~ ~

At first, there had been no reaction. The buried intelligence paid particular attention to the psi brainwaves of the beings he learned later called themselves, in various languages, "the people", "humanos", or "humans." He realized that he could actually project his thoughts into them. With the lower life forms, he could only get sensations of hunger, caution, fear, and, sometimes, curiosity. But with humans, it was different. He had learned to recognize their thought patterns and welcomed them into his lonely isolation. He knew he had been embedded in soft bedrock for a long time, four hundred seventy-six of his home world's cycles or more. He had been prevented from communicating with his battle fleet for all this time. He had no idea if he was the last of his kind in the galaxy or if the Dzuran Coalition had beaten off the Erran attack and he had long ago been written off as missing in action.

But sensate beings were above again, and his sensors had activated, warming up usually cold circuits and synapses. He sensed two old friends and a stranger; he felt trust bonds between them. One of these was "Ka-nee"—his teacher of the planet's written language, or as he had learned, one of the planet's prominent languages. She had made many visits in the past. She had been brought by the one named "B-rad." He was here today, too, and had become a trusted, but less frequent, visitor. He had determined the teacher was not a pilot commander, but he had not learned why Ka-nee had been given the honorific of an pilot's title 'Ka' without the training.

The new visitor, he was told, was "Ss-san." And he did not know why she had been given the Administrator's title of Ss. The presence of this caste was surprising to the underground listener and he had to remind himself that the language might have some similar sounds, probably from a similar soft body morphological similarity with Dzuran vocal structures. It was just possible, though, that the random beings that had chanced upon his ship knew an administrator from the Ss caste.

The discussion with those on the surface was much different from the many he had had with B-rad and Ka-nee. Perhaps it was the administrator Ss-san's presence. He almost enjoyed the interview; they had brought up some interesting questions for him to process: What happened to his thoughts when no one sentient was around to trigger his monitors? Why did his processes go quiet when they left? And what might they do to help him get himself out? What did he need? Would he need to be extracted physically? Were there lifting points? There was much to think about; how long would the sentient interval last before he went dormant again?

The one called B-rad had mentally asked about the end of his story. B-rad had enjoyed the full-immersion episodes he had been able to upload and cast via carrier wave. He had not been able to project these to Ka-nee. He had promised to pull up camera and event files from the logs to put together the last jump and fall to Earth for the others. When could he send it? He set to work while the ones above were still there. Maybe he would be able to package it in time to embed the sequence.

The one called Ss-san was agitated, as most of his visitors had been when he first made contact with them. She had been wary, though she did not exhibit chemical fear. Her scanning abilities were not clear. She seemed to be very much the same as Lu-cee, who had come before B-rad. The Ss-san was probably not an administrator, after all. As usual, the visitors spent a short span of time and left. Gradually, the psi energy fields they projected faded to nothing, and his own buried antennae could not pick up their communications. As time passed with no inputs, his feedback loops faded and began to shut down. Lights in the cockpit dimmed to black, and time ceased for a while.

Not far from the dark pool in the titi thicket, the three humans stopped near the fallen remains of a massive cypress. Brad showed Susan the dirt-encrusted root mat in which he had found the teal-blue artifact a little over seven years earlier. It had changed his life forever. A little farther down the path, he rolled over a crumbling section of pine log and scraped a little to dig up the remaining fifteen inches of the artifact from its hiding place.

An indeterminate time later, a month, a moment, or a week later, a light blinked on again. Jai's time clocks had been damaged at some point in the Erran battle. They had been repaired, but they were no longer synchronous with fleet time, if the fleet still existed. Lying almost inert, logic circuits in the ship had been processing communications for content in low-power mode and one of the questions from B-rad began to loop again. "What did he need to get free?" B-rad was forbidden to bring digging equipment into this area. Could he bring something? For Litan's part, he had communicated clearly that in order to get free of the limestone bedrock prison, he needed coolant for the field generator.

There were little or no chem fuels left, but these were readily available in the nearby ocean in which he had almost successfully landed. The rare materials he needed to synthesize coolant were in the ocean too, in small quantities. Stupid bad luck and Litan's injuries had led to the miss and this imprisonment in alien bedrock impregnated with non-saline water. How could he communicate to either B-rad or Ka-nee what he needed? An indicator light glowed a soft blue at low power as this question was considered. An indeterminate time later, it too went dark.

August 21, 1985
Cherbourg, France

Anton Dupres read the data off the gas chromatograph with disappointment. He had taken the shaved samples with care himself. He had fired the sample in a negative-pressure electric crucible to blow off any contaminants. The tiny sample had been ground with considerable difficulty to fine powder. He had supervised the preparation of the sample for the incinerating microtube gas chromatograph. The test results rather pissed him off. He read carbon and silicon, chromium, and another large spike where there should not have been a spike—the same results that his lab tech had gotten. Furious at the young chemist's result, Anton had undertaken to do the retest himself. Silicon and carbon, SiC would get carborundum and, yes, there was the chromium signature. His problem was the massive spike where it shouldn't be. He looked back at the calibration sheets for the chromatograph.

"Michel?" He shouted across the lab at the earlier chastened tech. "Michel, come here!" The young man was afraid of being reprimanded, afraid that his vain, inconsiderate, and boorish boss was going to dress him down again for blowing the sample prep on the chromatograph. He'd known that the material was precious and that a blown test would jeopardize the ability to do further testing. The lab had already exhausted most of its standard protocols for alloy analysis and drawn a significant blank.

350

"Sir?" he asked softly in the obsequious manner that Dupres seemed to prefer from his lab rats. Dupres handed the printout over to him abruptly. Michel took it and, turning it upright, saw the nearly identical profile to the sample he had run that morning. "Is this my sample?"

"No," Dupres answered as if the word were a curse. "That." He gestured with a nod at the paper. "That is two minutes old. How sure can we be that the powder you ground from the parent sample is not contaminated?"

"As sure as I can be, sir." He paused, gathering his thoughts, and said, "I agree, there should not be a spike there. It's spiking at a mole weight that should be giving us both radioactive poisoning, but we only get the barest twitch from the counters."

"I agree," Dupres said, softly, sounding almost defeated. "How much more sample do we have?"

"A few cc's at most."

"Let's try something fun, eh? Are you up for some fun?"

Michel's eyes narrowed momentarily, not sure where his lab super was going. Dupres had not been known for his own creative testing, and Michel was unsure of what was coming. "Sure, yes, by all means. What did you have in mind?"

Dupres handed his assistant a thick manual of standardized testing procedures and said, "Look up the isolation and test procedures for technetium."

"Monsieur?"

"Technetium."

"But it's radioactive," Michel said, and after a pause, "and the only technetium we've seen is a plutonium decay product from nuclear reactors." He paused looking at the small sample, "and it's not as radioactive as it should be."

"Yes, but ^{99}Tc has such a long half-life that it is virtually stable," Dupres said. He allowed a smile to creep across his usually impassive face.

Michel, still obviously perplexed, asked, "But that's theoretical. Who could make enough of the metal to … to chop it up like scrap metal?"

Dupres's eyebrows lifted in uncharacteristic good humor. "That, my friend, is the big question." He picked up the business end of a Geiger counter probe, flicked the switch to on, and heard the unmistakable clicking, the sample was giving off very low level radiation. The were looking at a small sample of powdered ^{99}Technetium isoptope.

Chapter 21

Everyone has a plan till they get punched in the mouth.
Mike Tyson

August 22, 1985
Manhattan, NYC, 1:30 p.m.

Sammy DeAngelo handed some dollar bills to the tollbooth attendant in the queue to enter Manhattan via the Holland Tunnel. "You know, Brad, that there is no toll to leave? You'd think it was a theme park attraction or something. You have to pay to get in, but you're free to leave." They surfaced into the busy grid of streets and made their way across Thirty-Ninth and took a left on Sixth Avenue. Sammy pulled over as traffic paused for a light and reached over to give Brad a reassuring pat on the shoulder. "Go get 'em, son. This is really going to be big!"

Anyone's first visit to New York City could, in itself, be exciting, even intimidating, for the uninitiated. Brad looked at the crowd outside the car. Who were these hundreds of people passing by? Which of them might be watching his movements? Had any cars followed them into the city? He looked over at Sammy. "Thanks, man, I guess it's time for the show!" He started to step out of the seat to the sidewalk, but stopped and turned back to Sammy. "Thanks man, I'm not sure I'd have gotten here without you. You're a life saver."

He got out, walked half a block and, feeling conspicuous, went to the nearest doorway. Looking back, he saw that Sammy's car was gone. He stepped inside the doorway, realized that he was in a restaurant, and quickly stepped outside again. He could hear his pulse in his temples. He closed his eyes; the noise surrounding him was disorienting—honking cabs, a siren several blocks away, another one more distant competing for attention. A thousand vehicles pulsing down the avenues of New York City. Brad thought, *seven million people make a lot of noise.* He took a few deep breaths, stepped out onto the sidewalk, and made the very public trek from the semi-shadowed protection of the side door of the Pig and Whistle pub to the parking garage entrance to Rockefeller Plaza with extreme caution.

Brad was tired of looking over his shoulder for a tail. He was tired of feeling like a criminal subject to arrest, imprisonment, or worse, and he was exhausted. He was exhausted from the long journey up I-95. Sammy DeAngelo had been great. As an expat New Yorker, he'd left Vegas, driven cross-country in only two days, and, after a recharge sleep and a quart of coffee, had been game for delivery up the East Coast. Sammy had history in the ET debate; he had helped set up the SETI array and the first attempts to use spare calculating space in networked private computers to do calculations required to sort through the mountain of radio data coming into the receivers. As a friend of such disparate types as Carl Sagan, Stephen Hawking, and Bob Lazar, DeAngelo had the confidences of many on the pure science and sci-fi aspects of alien contact. He'd told Brad how excited Stephen Hawking had become when he'd shared with him the essentials of Brad's find.

The drive up from Florida had been ruined by Brad's paranoid certainty that every car that was content to follow Sammy's two-tone Dodge Dart was actually a Dreamland operative. The beauty of the eastern piedmont in the full flush of summer did not escape his notice, however. He'd just wished he could enjoy the view more. A night spent in the parking lot of the Great Falls of the Potomac Park seemed safe enough, off the beaten path enough. Then again, maybe it was too remote, too easy to disappear from. Brad was tormented, asking himself, "Who am I kidding?" The question prevented him from getting a well-earned sleep. If they were being followed, could they really lose a tail or outwit a trained team of field agents? He knew he had been lucky getting the jump on Jenks in his home woods, but here? Or anywhere he did not know all the back roads? The next day's drive, begun well after sunrise, had been relatively easy through Maryland but was slowed by suburban New Jersey traffic that seemed to increase in density at every interchange as they approached "The City."

Despite DeAngelo's assurances, Brad was now alone—a stranger in a strange land. Walking across the street between stopped cars, he tried his best not to look up at the glass towers over his head, not to look like just another tourist in the big city, but he could not resist. Four seconds later, he bumped into a rushing pedestrian, excused himself amid a brief torrent of nasal inflected insults, and continued into the bowels of the Rockefeller Plaza's parking garage. He followed signs to the Lobby and stopped just inside the door. The three story tall entrance was impressive. Grand. He was the picture of a jaw-dropped tourist, standing still, eyes up, and gawking. He quickly recovered and found the information desk and got the needed directions to the NBC news center.

Now, closing in on his final destination, he wondered if his was a fool's errand. Would he just be turning over the remains of the artifact to an agent posing as a news producer? Brokaw's contact person had assured him that the "item of interest" would be secure, that he would be protected until showtime. It appeared that his fears had been groundless. A pretty receptionist led him down very ordinary hallways through littered and busy offices to a cluttered, glass-walled cubicle with an outside view. This must be someone important, he thought, and glancing at the walls, saw numerous black-and-white photos of world leaders, entertainers, and an autographed photograph of Edward R. Murrow in his familiar black suspenders. He finally found, amid the cluttered detritus on the desk, a small three-by-five gilt frame photo of Tom Brokaw with family. The frame fell on its face as Brad tried to put it back in its original location. He muttered a quiet, "Oh crap!" under his breath and heard a familiar voice behind him.

"Please, not in here."

Brad turned around to see the familiar face and smile and was a little surprised; the famous newsman was taller than he had expected. Brokaw walked around to his desk chair, tapped his chin thoughtfully, and asked, "So, you are the young man my producers tell me has proof of an alien visitor?" He sat and motioned for Brad to sit.

"Yes, sir, Mr. Brokaw. I wouldn't waste your time if I didn't." Brad reached for his backpack and pulled out the artifact. Handing it across the table, he said, "I found this about nine years ago in the backwoods near my house, and it's been trouble ever since."

"I have a few minutes," Brokaw said, looking at his watch. "Can you give me the ten-minute version?"

Brokaw listened intently while Brad told of his walk in the woods, the upturned cypress, and the discovery of the artifact. He nodded with understanding as Brad described his father's assessment of the historical significance of where the metal rod had been lodged. Brokaw's brows furrowed with concern as Brad related his father's murder and his two run-ins with Agent Jenks, who was believed to be in a special detachment of the Air Force, and his removal, questioning, and incarceration at the Area 51 B-Team facility. For brevity, he had omitted the episode in the Gulf of Mexico and only indicated that there was more to the story of how the artifact had been kept safe for most of the intervening years. He elaborated with names and research facilities and how many of these had been shut down.

Brokaw took notes as Brad related the kinds of research that had been done to date, including at FSU in the 1970s and the "accidental" deaths of both researchers within a day of each other. Brokaw interrupted. "Wait a second, you are saying that you don't believe that these deaths were accidental?"

"No, sir, I do not. Dr. Hill was killed one morning on a quiet rural road with minimal traffic that he drove every day to work. His assistant was killed the following afternoon in a fire at his lab, in which all three fire alarms on that floor were discovered to have dead batteries. He apparently died of smoke inhalation, but the coroner's report was summary at best. My father was killed in a staged B-and-E the next night. That's three deaths all connected to this one strange piece of metal in two days."

"Why do you think you were't killed also?"

"I thought about this, and I don't think it was out of a sudden attack of scruples. I think they wanted to let me lead them to the original piece of metal. It could have disappeared into a junk pile and been dumped into a landfill forever or it could resurface to haunt them. I don't think they wanted to take that chance. Agent Jenks, or Sergeant Jenks, whatever, said that Dad's death was accidental, too much testosterone at the wrong time." Brad shrugged and said, "I suppose they have plausible deniability of any connection to the three deaths, and they would deny ever having taken Connie and me and transported us to Nevada. I think they call it 'rendition,' not kidnapping, when the government does it to a citizen. The US has an official policy of denouncing it in the third world." He trailed off, temporarily out of steam.

Brokaw sat silently, hands folded in front of him. A glance up at the large digital clock opposite told him they'd been talking for most of twenty minutes. The kid had a story. He twirled in his chair to look out at the Manhattan skyline. His view from the his building was a canyon of glass, brick, and concrete. The street was filled with yellow cabs jostling for position and an army of bug-sized New Yorkers and more gaily dressed tourists bustling about down in the plaza. Finally, he said, "Mr. Hitchens? This will change a lot of things and, of course, you know that we will have to get confirmation from the remaining labs." He looked at his notes. "I have a friend at Princeton and our researchers can contact, General Motors, Cal Tech, and Cornell."

He twirled the truncated metal rod in his hands. It was down to less than 15 inches in length. "You said, parts of it had been shipped off for testing; so you keep losing bits of it. How long was it originally?"

"About twenty-one inches."

"And what did the end look like before it was cut off?"

"I was no metals expert then; I was fourteen. But I've had advanced physical sciences classes since then and I would say now what I thought originally—that it looked to have been broken off by violent force."

Brokaw gave a silent whistle through pursed lips. "Any guesses what kind of violent force?"

Brad had given a lot of thought on the drive up about whether he should tell Brokaw about Ka-Litan and had decided to keep that part of the story secret for the time being. He would retain that ace for further play. "I really can't say, possibly a crash landing or some collision event in or above the earth's atmosphere."

"Why in our atmosphere?"

"Well … just speculating, here. The material is very durable in itself and chemically resistant to almost everything we can think of to test it with. But if it fell from even low orbit through the atmosphere, even with no initial horizontal velocity, it would have scorched organics out of the air as air friction heated it on entry." Brad hated what he was doing now, basically spinning a tale that would be very different from his own true knowledge, if and when the ship became public knowledge. "Perhaps these visitors came into our air space not realizing we had filled orbital space with hundreds of communications and military satellites, and they accidentally blundered into one."

Brokaw gave a sideways nod and said, "If the piece has been buried for hundreds of years, there wouldn't have been anything in orbit."

Brad, embarrassed at being caught out on his extemporizing, said, "Right, maybe it wasn't something we had in orbit. I was just guessing there. I'd really hate to say more until we get the results back from the labs."

"There's more? Mr. Hitchens, do you know more than you're telling me?"

Brad fidgeted. "Yes, sir, but for the time being, let's see what the lab reports say and then we can discuss next steps."

Brokaw held the piece horizontally in front of him supported by the tips of his forefingers. Looking at it, he said thoughtfully, "If this thing is what you say it might be, it will be one of the biggest discoveries or revelations since the discovery of the New World." He was thinking about how to break a story like this. Sagan was a friend who could be called in to help with assembling a diagnostic team. But the church? The church would have a heck of a time adjusting to a reality in which we were not the sole intellect in creation. He saw that Brad was looking through the window at the glass tower across the street. A little over a hundred and fifty feet away, office workers could be seen typing, sifting through papers, and peering into computer monitors.

"Bradley? Can I call you Bradley?"

"Yes, sir."

Brokaw turned to face Hitchens. "Bradley, I often look out at these other buildings and see a hundred short stories going on. Usually, I just see people doing their mundane work-a-day jobs. Sometimes, I see things that should have required a little more discretion. But mostly, it reminds me of the fact that while we are all individuals, each of us is a part of a much larger machine. Our culture, if you will, is a vast interconnected organism that has slowly evolved from tribal societies that could make only minor changes in the appearance of their world to the billions of individuals who have since made great changes to this planet."

"If you think about how we might have changed the appearance of the planet from a visitor's perspective, unless they come here quite often, one might speculate that we are far different from the species that would have been encountered five hundred or a thousand years ago. And you are right, we are now a space-faring species. How long would that skill be tolerated in silence, if there are star-traveling beings out there?"

"I guess it would depend on if there are gate keepers."

"Sure, sure. If there were a far advanced civilization out there monitoring emerging cultures—"

"Mr. Brokaw?" Brad cut in on the newscaster's thoughts. "My goal from the beginning has been to fight the government's attempts to keep this a secret. I don't think they have the right to not only deny and confuse actual or potential sightings but to rewrite history. I don't know if there is an alien craft at Area 51. I certainly didn't see a building marked 'Alien Wreckage Stored Here.' I was too busy escaping. But although the Air Force says it shut down Operation Blue Book, they really just took the operation underground, politically and physically. I think Blue Book's existence eventually gave credibility to the story that they were actively hiding something. Eliminating it simply indicates that there is no problem: nothing to this alien issue to even spend funding on." He paused and then continued, "I would like for you to do whatever you can to get this story out."

Brokaw nodded, still in deep thought.

Brad continued, "I know a lot of people will object at many levels to the idea that we may not be the preeminent species in the universe, the sole creation of God Almighty, made in his image. But don't you think we deserve to know for sure?"

"Yes, Bradley, I do." After a brief pause, Brokaw added, "As a boy in South Dakota, the summer sky opened up to all the heavens. Here in the city, all we see is an orange glow; even on clear winter nights, only a planet or major star burns through the back scatter of city lights." He smiled. "One of the things I do on the first clear night when I am back out in plains country, or at some high mountain retreat, is to simply look up. I love to trace the Milky Way and search for the nebula in Orion's sheath or vainly try to fix the Seventh Sister. And, like most of us, I have always wondered if we could possibly have neighbors."

"So, you'll do the story?"

"I don't know if there is a story—I mean, let me check on your sources, the laboratories, and we'll do an independent analysis of our own. I'd like to get a better fix on how to present your story. Do you mind if we don't cut this up any more? The whole thing could be subjected to nondestructive analysis. If it is a real article, I'd hate to see more of it cut up. And, we don't do any story without research."

"Can I follow the research? I don't want to just hand it over to NBC News." Brad cleared his throat and added, "Not that I don't trust you, Mr. Brokaw. NBC is a big corporation with obligations, stockholders, and I can't even guess at its connections with the government. I have every reason to be extremely skeptical about the long, and not too scrupulous, arm of the federal government."

"I can certainly appreciate your perspective, Bradley. Why don't I find a place for you to stay for a few days? We make arrangements on some occasions for our guests who need to lie low for a little while. I will try to see that you can accompany this to a university lab here in the city so we can cut down on exposure to, let's just say, other elements."

"Thank you, that would be great," he said and added, "I think there is a particular sense of urgency, at least as it pertains to my personal security."

"I see. Have a seat out in reception, any empty chair, for a few minutes. I'll make some calls."

Brokaw's call was taken by a receptionist, and he left a message. He was about to flip through his card file for Stephen Hawking's card when something, not usual for the streets of New York, caught his eye. Parked across the street was a large, black bread-truck-sized van with the white letters "SWAT" and the vehicle number "203" stenciled on its roof. Black-garbed figures were exiting and moving toward the front of Rockefeller Plaza below him. He turned and looked at the sandy-haired young man sitting on the other side of the glass wall. He thought, this young man is the cause for the SWAT alert.

He punched a programmed number on his desk phone. "Buzz? Tom here. I need your help. We seem to have an issue developing downstairs."

"I'll say, NYPD SWAT just ran through here."

"Did you find out what's going on?"

"No, they had a short word with security and ran to the elevator banks. Wait, four of them just went for the stairwells. Do we have a camera crew moving?"

"That's probably happening; I'll be sure we have somebody on them, but I need you up here right away. My office—no, wait. Meet me in the men's room, admin side, as soon as you can get there without attracting notice. Everyone's going to be shut down in about two minutes. I have a story to protect from the SWAT."

Exiting his office in a hurry, he ducked into a side office and picked up a gray windbreaker with NBC and the peacock logo prominently displayed on the back. For good measure, he snatched a baseball cap from the back of the desk chair. He came back for Hitchens. He tossed the jacket and hat to him, and they took off at a brisk walk. Looking back, he reached over and snatched off the clip-on visitor's badge. "Quick, put those on. You've just been hired by NBC News."

"What?" Brad was confused. "Hired?" He was trying to keep up in the maze of back office hallways as the newsman led the way through the labyrinthine halls. They hustled across the newsroom reception lobby and into another hall door just as the elevator dinged and the stairwell door burst open, spilling out black-clad figures.

They paused in a stairwell to catch their breath and listen for footsteps. "Mr. Brokaw, what's going on?"

"Your story about government interference just gained credibility. If you are not the subject of their search, then we can calm down. If you are, then we figure out in a hurry what to do."

"Whose search? What are you talking about?"

"My offices just got invaded by NYPD's SWAT. Chances are great that they were turned on by the local FBI office because I saw at least two of their jackets down on the curb." He pulled Brad through a restroom door and faced him. "Brad, an old field producer friend of mine is going to come in here in a minute. I'm simply going to tell him to take care of you, that you need to be kept from arrest for at least the next twenty-four hours, and we'll see where we are this time tomorrow. I'm going to have to go back and either answer some questions or plead the First Amendment."

"Not the Fifth?"

"No, son. The First Amendment will allow me to not reveal a source or lead on a story, and, right now, you are my source for what could be a game-changing story."

"You think so?"

The newsman stopped and put his hand on Brad's shoulder. "Son, if what you told me is true, it is a historical place marker. There will be human philosophy before this, and there will be human philosophy after this. It's about as big a game changer as the change from BC to AD—it's big!" He told him to stay put until Buzz got there and then left.

Brad stood in the gleaming green marble and stainless bathroom, eyeing the folded linen hand towels, the small bottles of cologne, and the polished counter and concluded that he was in the network's inner sanctum. He thought of Brokaw's last comment and finally got the significance of the change from BC to AD and puckered for a silent whistle. He knew he had an important story, but that time shift reference took his breath away.

A man appeared with a stack of banker's boxes and a rolling cart. Sean Michael Flynn to his mother alone, he was Buzz to everyone else. His bodybuilder physique, topped by a flat-top haircut unchanged since he left the Marine Corps ten years earlier made him, if anything, a more imposing figure than he had been in his thirties. Thickly muscled forearms extended from the short sleeves of a white cotton dress shirt. His khaki trousers and wingtips looked misplaced on his frame. After brief introductions, he directed Brad to look like he was assisting in moving files down to storage in the basement. The ruse lasted as far as the lobby where the elevator had been interrupted by security. "What the ...?" Buzz argued with the agent at the ground-floor lobby. "We're supposed to get these down to storage and get right back up to Studio A."

"Just take a break then, sir." The agent was eyeing them but realized that there were hundreds of employees in the building. He turned to a flip chart. "I'm sure we can reopen the building in a few minutes."

Taking the initiative, Brad said, "Come on, Buzz, let's grab a cup of coffee; this stuff'll wait." They covered the distance to the front doors in seconds, looking like any two frustrated employees in a New York hurry. Behind them, the agent was just catching on to the Southern accent he'd heard. He flipped back to the one-sheet the team had been handed. He rushed to the door and saw the pair of NBC jackets heading across the street.

The distance from the glass-walled offices of 30 Rockefeller Plaza down West 50th street to the stone-lined rose windows of St. Patrick's Cathedral was less than a few hundred yards and took less than two minutes, but the change of place stepped two hundred years into the past.

Buzz led him down a side aisle to a rack of candles, took one for each of them, and gave one to Brad. With strict instructions to mimic his actions as he approached the prayer bench, Buzz knelt before the altar and bent his head in supplication. Brad knelt a little less gracefully, but soon found himself on his knees, head bowed, next to the muscled man at his side. Brad listened to the whispering giant next to him on the bench for instruction as to what to do next, when he realized that Buzz was actually praying.

A few minutes later, Buzz told him that a sanctuary was actually just that. There was no specific statute on the books in New York, but there was a long tradition of protection in a sanctuary that even the mobsters honored. Besides, it was a quiet place to wait while the NBC offices across the street were searched. He told of recent use of churches as sanctuary from deportation. Those cases had been prosecuted, but after significant delay and embarrassment to immigration officials.

Buzz sized up his companion. Brad was looking up in awe at the architectural detail, the interlacing fingers of the roof framing, and at the suffused glow coming through the windows. In the few hours a day that sunlight actually found the building's south wall, the sanctuary was an incredible sight. At other times in daylight, it was merely beautiful. That afternoon, buildings to the south were just beginning to let serious light into the sanctuary.

"Say, umm, Bradley, is it?"

"Yes, but Brad is okay."

"Do you have a place to stay in the city? Is there someplace you'd like to be next?"

"Mr. Brokaw mentioned that he had a place where some of his guests stayed … umm, people who had to lie low."

Buzz held his palms together but was looking beyond them at the floor. "Yeah, the apartment is about forty blocks south of here, just north of the Village. It's pretty comfortable, actually. We just need to get there without you being found out."

"Mr. Brokaw said you were a producer?"

"That's right. I've been with the company for about six years. I mostly work in the war zones. That's because of my background, Marine Corps."

"Dad was armored infantry, Vietnam."

Buzz nodded. "Good man. Nam was a hard place to be." He looked at Bradley. "You know, they didn't spend very much time in that armor, don't you?"

"He didn't talk about it much. He didn't really get to use the armor too often, although he named me for General Bradley."

Buzz chuckled quietly. "Bradley, er, Brad, I sure hope you have something important going on; this could be illegal as all hell." A slight increase in traffic sounds indicated the slow, quiet opening of the small doors at the back of the church. The big ex-Marine slipped Brad's NBC jacket off, dropped it to the floor, and hissed, "Get up and go slowly to the front left corner of the altar. Stop at the stairs to the choir loft; I'll be there a few seconds behind you."

Without looking back, Brad moved to the head of the church and took a left at the altar. Footsteps behind him quickened. He tried hard to seem interested in the programs in a small rack of wooden trays on the wall. Buzz's hand gripped him hard and pulled him along with him. A side door swallowed them up, and as it closed behind them, he heard the steps behind them accelerate to a run. He tried to keep track of the turns, but the narrow hallways, stairways, wooden doors, arched stone hallways, tiled spaces, wood-paneled spaces, painted hallways, and more stairs were too confusing. As the last doors closed, he heard no following footsteps. They emerged into what looked like a white-tiled hallway. A small turn to the left revealed a concourse of the subway's "F" line.

Brad followed his guide through the turnstiles and waited at the edge of the platform. Buzz took a fast look around the platform and then turned Brad so that he faced the tunnel's southern end. He positioned his large bulk between the lone camera that had a view and his charge. Bradley, nervously waiting for something to happen, eyed the famous third rail and feeling the rush of air preceding the southbound train, stepped back, bumping into Buzz. "Whoa, stay put, I don't need you on candid camera just now."

"Oh, sorry. This is my first time in a subway."

Buzz grinned to himself and said softly, "That a fact?" Then louder, he said, "I don't think those guys'll find a way out of that maze of hallways anytime soon. Some of those digs were cut in bedrock in the eighteen hundreds, some were dug later to connect to the subway."

"How'd you know how to get out of the cathedral?"

"Back in a prior life, I was an altar boy at St. Pat's." He whistled in silently. "That was a long time ago." He thought back to his early teens, tending the racks of votive candles, preparing the offering, sneaking a few wafers of host when he was hungry, and later, when he was a little bolder, sneaking a few sips of sacramental wine. "Yeah, that was a long time ago." The southbound train stopped in front of them, and Buzz guided Brad to a middle car. "In a few minutes, God willing, you'll be tucked away safe and sound—a needle in a haystack. Not many cities in the world better to disappear into than Manhattan."

He was wrong; partially concealed behind a tiled column at the other end of the platform, a homeless man whispered into a handheld radio set concealed in a Cracker Jack box.

~ ~ ~

Brad found the small apartment, if anything, a little too ordinary. A third-floor walk-up, it resembled a stage set of too many urban dramas set in the city. He thought an NBC property should be a little more posh. Its light-green walls were almost gray from age. A miscellaneous collection of popular art in cheap frames adorned the walls; the furniture was not new by any means, but not shabby either. Bookshelves lining one wall housed enough reading material in enough genres to salve boredom and even allow some minor research in a number of current affairs topics. At a desk he found a computer and one of the largest dictionaries he'd ever seen outside of a library. The tiny kitchen was stocked with non-perishables, and as he examined the contents of the cabinets, he realized that someone could be put in here for a short or long stay and become almost invisible. The building's street front housed a green grocer, a deli/pizza parlor combo, and a dry cleaner. Across the street, in either of two directions, were enough other vendors to supply most anyone's needs for an extended stay. Buzz left him with instructions to stay put, told him that the phone was expense accounted and scrambled if he absolutely had to use it but he otherwise shouldn't, and that he'd be back with fresh milk, bread, and Chinese takeout.

Brad settled on the couch and pulled out his small notepad. He looked again at the three labs that he had left to depend on. If something went wrong with the NBC gamble, there was hope that one of these labs might still be working on the research, and the strongest possibility was France. The US government was less likely to have fingers in France. Princeton was still a possibility, as was Cal Tech. But what was that college in France, the school for engineers? He pulled the pencil out of the metal spiral binder and scratched out "Jason Walters" and "Dr. Chang." What was that school in France? "École," he said and snapped his fingers. "École d'Ingénieurs, in Bayeux or Bordeaux, one of those." He looked around the room for what to do next. The phone was good for long distance, but what about overseas long distance? He settled into the desk and dialed zero. Maybe he wouldn't need plan B.

August 22, 1985
Manhattan, 3:45 p.m.

The small troop of plainclothes agents passed unnoticed through the crowded sidewalks of lower Manhattan. With sport jackets over Kevlar vests and shoulder holsters, they simply appeared to be a little beefier than the average New Yorker. They had unloaded into a side alley two blocks north of their target address and separated to avoid attention. They converged on the apartment block that held the NBC safe house and entered its foyer at random one- and two-minute intervals. With rear exits and stairwells secured, Colonel Henderson nodded to his team members, and the three trusted operatives moved silently up the stairwell. Dark shapes in a darkened stairwell, they moved like wraiths on a limb. Silent as ghosts, they gathered around the door. Jenks nodded an affirmation to Colonel Henderson, who looked at his companions and allowed a wry grin. He rapped five times on the door. Footsteps approached the door and paused. "Buzz, that you?" from inside.

An exchange of curious glances passed between the dark huddle of agents outside the NBC safe house door. One of the agents cupped his hand over his mouth to muffle consonants and said, "Yeah, Brad. Open the door, would you? My hands are full." Brad was making too much noise unlocking the several hasps on the door to hear Buzz shouting from two flights down not to open the door. He opened the door with the security chain still attached, but that small opening was enough. While fleeing an agent in chase, Buzz shouted out from the foyer, "Brad! Remember Plan B!"

Not waiting to find out what plan B might be, Henderson, Jenks, and friends forced the door. Brad found himself on the floor being handcuffed before he could shout much of a protest. As the events of the last few seconds sorted out, he absorbed the message for Plan B. He would just have to wait it out and see if it developed. Meanwhile, he had to concentrate hard to get the overwhelming funk of fifteen-year-old carpet out of his nose. "Jenks, so glad to see you again."

"Don't worry about it, kid. My friends like to wrap their packages in a bow. The handcuffs are only to get you off the street."

"I was perfectly safe where I was; I didn't need your help here."

"So, this is Mr. Smart guy, back with us?" Colonel Henderson appraised the bound kid on the floor; the central figure in a year's long case.

One of the Suits came back into the room. "Sir, that other guy is gone. Vanished!"

"You get an ID?" Henderson asked.

"No, Sir. Just a voice from the crowd."

"Not so surprising. New York is a big place and they probably have cut-aways."

Henderson helped Brad to his feet and made a show of dusting him off. "Mr. Hitchens, or is it Mr. Williams? Or are you someone else this month?" Brad only stared back at him. "Any chance you're going to share what Plan B is?" After a few seconds of silence and no visible change on Brad's face, he guided his prisoner out of the apartment to a waiting limo. Limos and yellow cabs were the rides of anonymity in New York. Almost no one bothered to notice the black stretch town car heading uptown, except Buzz, who was now wearing a pin-striped Yankees baseball cap and a muscle tee with a messenger bag over his shoulder. He put a ten-speed bike over the curb and took off in pursuit.

New York's mid-afternoon avenues resemble a slowly moving parking lot full of yellow cabs with a sprinkling of delivery vans, limos, and, very occasionally, a sedan. Buzz on bicycle had to hang back a block to keep from being noticed. He had the legs for serious distance on two wheels and a mastery of the required two-wheeled acrobatics of dodging and weaving between the pulsing surge of checker cabs. Ahead in the black limousine, Brad was pinched between two muscled agents in the back rear-facing seat; two others sat facing him on either side of Agent Jenks and the new figure of authority, Henderson.

Henderson said, "Listen, Bradley, hey! Listen up!"

Brad hadn't been particularly inattentive; he was upset at the arrogant disregard for what he thought he knew of law enforcement. There had been no identification, no offer of a warrant, no Miranda, only a heavy kick on the door once he had the deadbolts turned. If there had been a peephole lens, he'd never have opened the door. He thought to himself, If I ever see Buzz again, I'll have to mention that deficiency.

But Henderson was persistent. "Hitchens! Earth to Hitchens, are you with us?"

"What? Yeah. I'm sorry. Were you talking to me?"

Henderson and Jenks sat across from Brad and the two unnamed suits in the rear facing seat. Henderson, meeting the young Brad Hitchens for the first time wasn't impressed with the surly object of attention. "Matter of fact, I am. Do you want to see your girlfriend again?"

"See her? What have you done with Connie?" He had just gone from really ticked off to furious with a large helping of concern. "What have you done with her?" He tried to surge forward, but two elbows, one from each agent on either side, pinned him back to his seat.

"Easy, boy," the blue serge to his right said. "Have some respect."

"Dad always told me respect had to be earned. From all I've seen so far, all you should expect is a subpoena."

The gray suit on his left said, "Son, don't know which pile of dog mess you stepped in, but you really don't want to piss off the colonel here."

Brad looked at Jenks, his longtime antagonist, and the new man they'd called the Colonel. "So, you're the man behind the curtain. How long have you been in on this little chase?

Henderson smiled and answered, "Do you mean your drive up from Florida? Or your diving adventures last spring? Or your illustrious career at Arizona State?"

Brad pushed against the restraining elbows of the two plainclothes agents on either side. "And where's Connie? Where have you taken her?"

Henderson, looked aside to the raised eyebrows on Jenks's questioning face, then back across to Hitchens. "I imagine she's deciding whether to keep hanging around with trouble makers like you."

Jenks motioned palms up to the two agents restraining Hitchens. They lightened up the pressure on his ribs a little. A flash of white shirt passed across the rear window of the limo, catching his attention. He couldn't be sure, but as the car moved forward again, he thought he saw Buzz on a bike changing from one lane to another and pulling casually aside the rear bumper of the car. They made eye contact.

Buzz nodded, pulled ahead of the car, and then, making a light that the Lincoln didn't, pulled over and searched in his messenger bag. Looking back casually down Third Avenue, he made a show of entering a shop and coming back out in less time than it took for the cross light to cycle. As the limo continued north up Lexington, Buzz pulled casually out behind the car and followed at a distance. He could see Hitchens in the rear-facing seat yelling at someone in the backseat. Ballsy kid, I'll give him that, he thought.

The car and bike took right turns onto East Fifty-Eighth, and in a few blocks, as the limo pulled into a dead end blocked by the East River Drive wall, Buzz veered off and made a false exit north. He ditched the bike and looked around the corner to see five suited men guiding Hitchens into a nondescript midrise tower overlooking the East River. They had placed a black sack hood over his head and had him in a side-by-side armlock. Buzz returned to the bike and made for Rockefeller Plaza.

Brad could see only vague shapes through the weave of the sack. It had been pulled over his head while they were still on Lexington, and he could tell only by a lurch to the right that they had turned toward the East River. The first thought that flashed through his mind was of crime movies and floating bodies being fished from the East River. The second thought was of Connie. *Would she be there too? Had one of the tracker teams captured her? What about Plan B?*

The stale air in whatever building he was in proved that its utilities were normally off. It was cooler in there than outside, but not by much. His beefy guides dragged him sideways through a doorway, led him to a bench, and sat him down. He heard a metal door close, and abruptly, the sack was removed. He had shut his eyes against bright light and then, opening them, slowly found to his surprise that he was in a dimly lit room. The walls were painted some color between beige and gray-brown, which was broken only by pale rectangles of long-ago-removed posters or bulletins. The furniture consisted of a few metal chairs and an ancient metal desk. The room had no windows, and the sole light came through a low-watt bulb in a wire-meshed ceiling pot. Through a door, he could see open floor space and painted-over industrial windows styled from the early 1900s. His two suited guards got their orders from Jenks and hovered in the outer room, discouraging any thought of leaving. They conferred, checked their watches, and left him behind a closed door.

He was alone again with his thoughts. He compared his current surroundings to the dark hole he'd woken to at Dreamland. At least there was some light from the low-wattage bulb. As soon as he thought of it, a central air system began pushing even staler air through the aging building's duct work. Shadows of a former row of file cabinets lined one wall, so maybe this the office from an old manufacturing building, on the waiting list to be turned into river-view loft apartments. He'd been taken up in an elevator; he didn't know how many floors. A window, if he found one, would not be an escape option. He could hear voices through the vent tubing. He guessed these were his escorts, and since Jenks had been with them in the limo, maybe he was out there too. Wasn't one of the older guys called "Colonel"?

Brad's thoughts returned to Connie. How was she doing? Had she also been picked up? Was she on another floor in another room? Was the mention of her earlier just another ruse? He pictured her dimpled, off-center smile, which brought a reflexive smile to his own face. He missed her. He missed the calm comfort of relaxing with her, her insights, and her intelligent problem-solving. Outside his door or through the vent, he heard raised voices.

He stood on the chair to get closer to the vent. The voices were muffled by the blowing air, but he could clearly make out Jenks's softer tones amid the New York accents. There was also the tinny track of a television in the background. Jenks's volume increased several decibels as he shouted, "Not on your life. You will stay here as ordered. I don't care how locked up he seems to you. This kid escaped from an Air Force detention facility in the middle of three hundred miles of desert, took his girlfriend with him, and disappeared!"

There was a blend of objections, and Jenks again outshouted them. "Yes, all three of you. Every button we could touch on the grid produced nothing. Dammit! We were checking and rechecking all over his old university haunts, all known Arizona and Nevada addresses, his old diving buddies. Nada. Zip. Two live, full-sized human beings disappeared from one of the most inhospitable deserts in the world. We halfway thought they were coyote food. All of you will stay here and watch that door!"

Brad heard footsteps and a door slam. Through the vents, he could hear mechanical sounds, which he took to be an elevator.

Standing on the chair to listen, Brad smiled at the memory, at the relief of getting out of Area 51 or Dreamland, Groom Lake, whatever, and his sweet, brief layover with Connie in an aging camper. He sat on the folding chair and put his feet on a box. The cross-country trip with the help of his mother's friend Marina had been exhilarating, if not full of the necessary paranoia. She had helped him get back in touch with Sunny and eventually get a ride west and back east in Dink's sleeper cab. The low-profile transit had not required cash or credit card and the "off-the-grid" travel had allowed Connie and him to beat the surveillance net thrown over Nevada, Southern California, and New Mexico. Six thousand trucks a week passed east out of the Nevada badlands and not every nook and cranny could be searched without stopping interstate commerce.

August 22, 1985
NBC News Central, Manhattan, 4:50 p.m.

Tom Brokaw was angry. The frustration he felt showed in the tremble of his hand as he set the phone back in its cradle. He might have just as easily thrown it across the room. Buzz had called from the lobby to report that his primary source had been nabbed by large men seeming to belong to the Feds. That in itself lent credibility to the kid's story of harassment and a cover-up. His phone lit up from his secretary's inside line.

"Yes, Debra, what's up?"

"Mr. Brokaw, there's a Dr. Kevin Sturgis from Cal Tech, and I've taken a message. I also just took one from a research lab in France on the same topic. Something might be breaking loose that we should be in on."

Debra's news savvy had been bred by a career in broadcasting. She was far more to Mr. Brokaw and his staff than a secretary; she was more like an in-house referral service whose excellent memory could retrieve contacts and make connections that left most speechless.

Brokaw took the call.

370

"Yes, Mr. Sturgis, this is Tom Brokaw. What can I do for you?" The PhD from Cal Tech proceeded to brief Brokaw on a fascinating competition that had been proposed by one of his peers on the industrial side to determine by any nondestructive means the composition of a metal sample. They were to provide a best guess at means of manufacture of a small piece of bluish-green metal that had been shipped to his lab. As he listened, Brokaw waved at a passing producer in the hallway and invited him in to listen on speaker.

The tinny speaker intoned, "So you see, we were at first convinced that we had been shipped a fragment of something that our industrial side brothers were stumped on and wanted some free advice about. We had actually sidelined it, but one of the new researchers got curious. We let him run with it." There was a pause on the phone while Sturgis caught his breath. "We are not convinced that we could come up with this material based on our knowledge of contemporary metallurgy. Having reached this conclusion and with the time limit on the competition expiring, we were asked to call this number."

"I see, umm, Mr. Sturgis. Is that Dr. Sturgis? I'm sorry." Brokaw paused, looking at the notes in his yellow steno pad he had taken a few hours earlier from the Hitchens kid. "Did this sample, this bit of blue-green metal come from a Dr. Jason Walters in Detroit?" There was a silence on the phone and some muted, indistinguishable conversation. "Dr. Sturgis, I ask this because we were pursuing a very interesting story about this exact piece of metal, and our source was abducted minutes ago by agents appearing to be from our government."

A cough on the other end of the line indicated it was still open. "Dr. Sturgis? Is everything all right there?"

"Yes, ahem, Mr. Brokaw, I'm sorry, we just had some confusion here. Some of my fellows here weren't aware that this phone number led to NBC News. That has some of us concerned."

"I can appreciate that, Dr. Sturgis; I can assure you that nothing will go on the air that is not verifiable. I can appreciate your professional concern and your interests." Debra stood at his doorway, waving. "I'm sorry, doctor, one moment."

Brokaw looked up, questioning his assistant. She hissed, "That French lab is back on the phone; they've been talking with another lab." She looked at a sticky note in her hand. "Princeton."

Brokaw said, raising his eyebrows, "Princeton called earlier, just before all that ruckus downstairs, and before SWAT and the FBI came up here!"

He removed his palm from the receiver. "Dr. Sturgis, we are beginning to get a lot of activity on this story or issue. Umm, do you know how to get over to our Los Angeles affiliate, NBC4? It's on—"

"Yes," Sturgis broke in, "I've been there."

"This is a fast breaking story, how soon could you be at that studio? If you wouldn't mind going.?"

"I can be there in thirty, no, make it forty-five minutes."

"That would be great, Sir. I'd really like to talk to you further. We can do it where we will be assured of a positive link, and if you would allow me to, I'd like to take a statement on video. This is developing into quite a phenomenal story." He paused, listening. "Yes, tell them I've requested a live interview. Yes, thank you."

From the doorway, Debra said, "Princeton is back on line three. The French lab, her pronunciation was perfect, is on five. Same lead topic!"

~ ~ ~

Connie stood at the edge of Rockefeller Plaza, leaning against one of the many flagpoles lining the plaza's edge. She moved hesitantly over to the base of the Statue of Atlas, working up courage. She blended in with a clutch of pedestrians working their way along the pavement and stopped at the magnificent entrance. It was intimidating. The lobby seemed designed to separate tourist from employee. You could not enter those doors for the first time and not look up in awe at the gilded and marbled display. But, this was not her first entrance into this building. She checked a directory kiosk and thumbed the entries and then found her way to the elevator bank.

With no call from Brad updating her on Plan A, it seemed that Plan B was going to have to kick in. When the elevator delivered her to the right floor, she stepped into NBC reception and asked for Mr. Brokaw's assistant. She had a message for him relating to Bradley Hitchens.

August 22, 1985
Manhattan's lower east side, 1830 Hours

Brad was tired of standing on a chair listening through the vent for a sign of what was happening or what might be about to happen. He found if he sat still, he could just about make out what was on the television. Lately,

372

mid-afternoon soap operas were running and not much was going on to keep his attention. Brief flares of volume change usually meant commercial breaks. A news alert at three thirty informed him of a tropical storm east of Florida, which immediately had his attention, but he could not hear well enough to understand its intensity or direction. More was promised later. Frustrated, he began to pace. From the low, mumbling voices outside, he could tell only that he was still being monitored. Just for grins, he walked quietly toward the wooden door. Looking at the handle, he saw it was an older type handle secured with a screw onto a square shaft.

Knowing how to remove the handle would do him no good. The question was whether the door was locked. He wondered from which angles he was being watched. Softly, he gripped the handle. It turned, and he could feel the bolt sliding out of the striker plate. As he pulled ever so slowly, the door moved and then stopped. A simple galvanized door hook was latched over a ten-cent eyebolt in the door frame. From his vantage, he could not tell what stopped the door. Footsteps approached. He stepped back.

He heard a click and a rattle, and the door opened. "Youse getting curious?"

"Umm, yeah. Prisoner's duty and all that."

"Well, technically, you're not a prisoner, so technically, you don't got no rights. Get back and wait till we say diffrent."

"Listen, I overheard on the TV that there's a hurricane near Florida. I have folks down there. Could you listen to see where it's headed?"

"Yeah, sure!" It sounded like, "Yee-ahh, shooahh," but Brad understood clearly enough that it wasn't going to be one of his captors' priorities. He was also left with an impression that these guys might be hired locals and not from Jenks' usual cadre.

~ ~ ~

The news desk studio was hastily cleared for action. Rolled out of its bay, it was being pulled to its stage marks and lit as Brokaw entered, trailed by a sound tech. The technician tucked an audio wire under and around the news anchor's coat lapel and asked him for a sound check. Brokaw looked over at his guest across the interview table. She looked great. She had a face made for television—not the news, but prime time. Connie had been given a once over by makeup to give her face shape under the harsh camera lights, but she was really lovely, he thought. As on-set makeup made last adjustments to both their faces, he said, "You going to be okay?"

"Yes, yes, sir."

373

"Ever been on camera before?"

"No, but I'll be okay. I did some Toastmasters in school."

Brokaw smiled at her reassuringly and said, "I'm sure you'll be fine." He shuffled his stack of papers, spreading them slightly so they'd be easier to open. "Just remember, there is no one in this room but you and me, and we will have a simple conversation. We aren't live, so if you have to back up and get your facts straight, there's plenty of time to edit for the newsbreak."

"I think I'll be fine." Connie rolled back and forth on her hips getting as comfortable as she could.

"I'm sure you will be." Then looking into the lights toward the engineering station, he said, "Ben, do you have the photos and video cued?"

A "yessir" floated out of the darkness beyond the array of lights. From another quarter came, "Quiet! Keep it down. Quiet on the set!" A previously unnoticeable murmur in the shadows diminished until it truly was quiet. The disembodied director called out again, "On one, then five, four, three, two …"

"Good evening. Tonight, we have a special guest with quite an unusual story, one that I, at first, had a hard time believing; one that more or less bowled us over earlier today; and one that we feel has major implications for our government and our military, which appears to have abused our private rights. All of this is only a thin covering over a much larger story, one that has been in the shadows of illegitimacy for a very long time and has been so denigrated by official channels as to sound absurd at first hearing."

Brokaw looked again at his notes as if concentrating on what to say next. He had actually mapped how to unwrap the story layer by layer. He had planned for a later intro on the evening news and a one-hour special at nine that would blow the doors off the US Air Force.

"This is a story of a very unusual piece of metal that was found in a very unusual place and time. The young man who found this piece of metal lost his father under suspect circumstances, has been pursued by agents of our government, has had to live in hiding for almost a decade, has had to take on an assumed name, and, at this time, is probably again in the custody of this government with no known formal charges filed."

Brad's photograph appeared in a box on the screen. "This afternoon, this young man, Bradley Hitchens, came to our New York studio to share a story, which at first, had us perplexed. The story he brought to us suggested that there might be others in our universe with technology and the ability to move between star systems. Quite simply, there really are extraterrestrials. This idea has been repressed by the now infamous Air Force Blue Book Project from the early 1950s through 1969," he said as an image of the cover to a Blue Book report appeared on-screen. "According to the US Air Force, this project of purposeful denial of any and all claims of extraterrestrial contact is supposed to have been closed." He paused for effect. "It is apparently living on in some other form. Mr. Hitchens brought to us a piece of physical evidence—a small piece of metal that has been evaluated by some of the top minds in the field of materials analysis."

He paused for breath. "This is a what remains of that original bit of metal." A video of the remaining metal resting on red felt and rotating on a small turntable appeared. "I will state for the record that this small sample of metal is not at this studio in New York, and we will hold that its location is protected by First Amendment principles. We took this precaution based on the appearance in our studios earlier today of several paramilitary operatives dressed as a SWAT team demanding the delivery of Bradley Hitchens on national security grounds without a bench warrant. Our NBC security briefly slowed that inquiry, allowing for the secure removal of Mr. Hitchens off-site. He was subsequently tracked by federal and NYPD forces and taken into custody." He pierced the camera with his stare, "We have asked for comment from NYPD and have yet to get a response.

"It is a very uninspiring piece of scrap metal at first glance, but it has a pedigree." The camera returned to a head shot of Brokaw with an inset of the turntable. "Samples cut from this remnant have been sent to some of the most prestigious laboratories on this planet with no presumptions made as to its origin. They were simply asked to hazard a guess as to the method of manufacture and the identity of the base material. They were instructed to spend up to ninety-six hours in the analysis and to call these offices by three o'clock today. Two of them called in; we called a third for their verification. A fourth and possibly more were shut down by personnel of an American military agency that is unidentified at this time. But," he paused for emphasis, "the results we do have are simply amazing."

He pulled the pages closer to show that he was reading: "From Cornell University, Dr. Lee Park, I quote: 'The material provided for analysis is still of unknown manufacture. We have determined that there are systematic inclusions of carbon structures that we are familiar with in cutting-edge theory, but to our knowledge have not been fabricated successfully. Put simply, they resemble what we understand as Buckminsterfullerene constructs. We have only recently known spheroids, popularly called Buckyballs, to have been fabricated. It has been theorized that these structures could be constructed as fibers, but no lab has published any successful attempts at creating fibers or filaments as we have seen embedded in this material. We repeat, for emphasis, these are the first known examples of these fibers to researchers at our laboratories. In structure, the filaments appear to be woven at a molecular—no, atomic—level into fibers of extreme strength and fairly unusual electrical characteristics.

"These carbon inclusions are phenomenal on their own. The primary metal matrix at first presented as a crystalline form of a metal that has heretofore usually been created as a result of nuclear reaction in supercolliders or as a decay product from nuclear fission in reactors. The material, technetium, is normally extremely unstable, has a six-hour half-life, and emits low-energy radiation. The isotope found, ^{99}Tc, is much more stable, has unusual magnetic behavior at very cold temperatures, and does not occur on this planet in any significant quantities. Technetium, if you will, is a relatively midrange metal. Think of something twice the weight of titanium and half the weight of lead. This material's light weight is due to a matrix or crystalline form of the metal with inclusions of chromium, a much lighter metal. The resulting metal matrix is about the weight of titanium but is considerably stronger. We have never encountered this construction before and have not found mention of anything similar in the literature."

Brokaw looked down at the notes he had compiled from his earlier conversations with the three labs. "The known occurrence of technetium on Earth is as a decay element produced in nuclear fission in power plants, and very small quantities of it have been isolated from spent fuel rods. It is thought to exist in very old red giant stars, but not in any significant amount in our much younger sun. As it obviously exists somewhere in sufficient quantity to have been subjected to an unknown manufacturing technique, we can only conclude, without substantive additional material to examine, that this sample is of extraterrestrial origin."

Brokaw, pausing to let the effect settle in, continued, "From our studios in Los Angeles, we are joined by Dr. Kevin Sturgis from the California Institute of Technology. Dr. Sturgis …"

The interview lasted only two and a half minutes, with the questioning establishing confirmation of the Princeton report. Dr. Sturgis revealed that there was an impurity in the technetium matrix, probably chromium, that imparts stability from chemical attack and provides for the lighter specific gravity due to the lattice structure of the compound. Dr. Sturgis finished the report, which he had been asked to keep brief and not overly technical, by saying, "The resulting compound, which we have not named, has a hardness above steel, is lighter than aluminum in its matrix form, and has an unusual, light green-blue color under natural light but fluoresces yellow to white under ultraviolet."

"Thank you, Dr. Sturgis." The box inset from the interview disappeared, and Tom Brokaw's head and shoulders again filled the screen. "We have similar reports from two other laboratories: Princeton University and the School of Engineering in Cherbourg, France. The latter was originally compromised by US State Department intervention but continued its program anyway and reported in with similar results. These four research laboratories, I need to emphasize, are all in the top schools for materials science, as are the several laboratories whose invitations to this research were aborted or interrupted by authorities.

"Do we know for sure now that at some point in the past an alien visitor to this planet lost a spare part?" He let the pause linger and then said, "No, we don't. The origin of this piece of metal—" The artifact on the turntable again took the main screen. "—is still an enigma. All three labs that have responded per their original directions have requested additional time to perform more studies. We would hope that agents of the US Air Force are not at this time proceeding to those laboratories to secure and hide away these amazing little bits of metal. Much more study, with juried peer review, should be conducted to better understand not only the basic atomic physics, but the sophisticated metallurgy involved."

A full head shot of Brokaw looking straight into the camera appeared. "Obviously, even the idea that there may be physical proof of alien technologies left behind on this planet, perhaps even by accident, leaves us with larger questions. Who? How often? How many? And When? There is, perhaps this time, conclusive proof: a physical artifact that had to have come from somewhere else, because the ability to manufacture it doesn't exist here in our time. Nor does their appear to be enough of the technetium isotope on our planet to fill a thimble much less to create this artifact."

Mr. Brokaw appeared again in a full studio shot at his desk, looking somber. As the news special developed, he introduced the credentials of the science team leaders at each of the three schools and laid a solid foundation for each school's credibility. He laid the papers he had been reading on the desk and continued, "This is not a shaky, fuzzy video of what might be an aluminum plate on a string. It appears that this is no hoax. This time, I hope that science has time to weigh in before the opportunity is hidden away in a desert wasteland."

He paused and glanced to his left to warn the producer he was about to introduce Connie. "We have in the studio now a close friend of Bradley Hitchens, the young man who visited our studios this morning shortly before his abduction by federal agents." The camera pulled back to include Connie facing Mr. Brokaw from the end of the news desk. "Miss Chappell has been a foster sister to Bradley Hitchens since the murder of his father over nine years ago by agents of the US Air Force."

"Miss Chappell, can you share with us what happened this morning?" Connie began an account of their entry into Rockefeller Plaza, waiting for Brad's interview to end, and her escort to rejoin Brad at a supposed safe house by one of the network's security specialists. She described the short trip with NBC security to get Chinese takeout, and her spotting of a known agent of the Air Force's special detachment and of a small crew as it entered an NBC safe house. She related Buzz's reentry into the building as she waited outside and her fears when she saw Buzz's rapid departure and the subsequent removal of Brad from the building under the control of Jenks and four other men. She finished with a description of the limo heading uptown and the pursuit by Buzz on a "borrowed" messenger bicycle.

"Miss Chappell, thank you." Brokaw faced the camera again. "I hope you agree with me that this abuse of civil liberty by an out-of-control wing of the US military is unwarranted. This is not the freedom our young men have fought for from Saratoga to Saigon." He paused, collecting his thoughts and organizing the papers into a simple stack, and continued, "Prior to going on the air today, we've received no comment from media services of the Air Force, and we were told that they did not know from which agency we might be able to obtain a response. We sincerely hope that this appeal will result in Mr. Hitchens's release from custody." Brad's face again appeared in a side box. "We hope we will find someone from the Air Force to point us to anyone who has an idea of what happened today, who ordered it, and under what constitutional authority. We have a news crew outside of the abandoned, warehouse where we believe Mr. Hitchens has been taken and are awaiting developments."

"That is a small part of an ongoing story that we will continue to investigate. Less important, but certainly an integral part of the larger question, is who or what left this artifact on this planet?" A full-screen shot of the artifact on its turntable appeared. A text box popped up, advising the viewer to tune in at 9:00 p.m. Eastern for more coverage.

~ ~ ~

Several blocks north and east of Rockefeller Plaza, on the fifth floor of a boarded-up and, apparently, vacant six-story brick pile, two guards halted the deal of yet another game of cribbage and looked at each other. Had they just seen their captive's face on television? What the hell? They debated for a few minutes whether the face on the screen was the same as that of the kid in the room. The third guard sauntered in from the hall yawning. He croaked, "You boys seein' things?"

Blue Suit said, "No, boss, I really think it was him. The kid in the other room. NBC just had him on the news!" The aging, thirteen-inch portable RCA they had been watching didn't have a VCR slot. Even if the story came back on, they couldn't record it for Jenks. Almost as soon as they said his name, the elevator door hissed open and Jenks walked into the room.

Blue Suit stood and said, "Agent Jenks, I wish you had been here a second ago."

"Why is that, Capriotti? Need help with your cribbage scoring?"

"No, sir, we were just …" Brown Suit was scooping up the cards and hastily putting them into a suit pocket. "We were just filling up some time on the shift, and there was a newsbreak. One of the news guys said there was evidence of aliens from outer space and our kid, least we think it was our kid, was part of the story."

Jenks had been heading for a small refrigerator to get a canned drink and stopped in midstep. Turning on his heel, he asked, "What did you say?" His expression was neutral, but his eyes held a dark intensity.

Brown Suit added, "Yeah, we was just arguing if the guy on the TV was our guy."

"They had a picture?"

"Yes, sir," offered Blue Suit. "Tom, uh, what's-his-name, came on with a special news announcement." The two hired guards tried to fill in the story, but their versions were not a perfect fit. Jenks got up and walked to a wall of painted-over windows whose cracks and flakes added to the dismal aura in the room. He picked up a standard-issue brown metal trash can and hurled it toward the elevator. The two guards exchanged glances.

He turned on them. "This Tom, was it Brokaw? Tom Brokaw?"

"Yes, sir," they chimed in unison. The Blue suit puffed up importantly, even   though   he   had   nothing   to   say   on   the   subject.

"Dammit!" Jenks began to mutter and curse. He walked over to the wall phone and jabbed at the dial. "Colonel Henderson?" Jenks was stressed and tapped his toe as he waited. "Sir, Jenks here. Have you seen the news?"

~ ~ ~

Brad was listening at the grate again. He had not been sure at first, but he thought he'd heard Jenks's voice overriding the three Staten Islanders. A sharp metallic click at the door gave only momentary warning before Martin Jenks entered the room. "Hello Mr. Hitchens. We are famous—you are famous, that is. Maybe even for more than fifteen minutes." He motioned to one of the chairs. "Please, Bradley, would you have a seat?" To Brad's surprise, Jenks took one of the cheap folding metal chairs and straddled it with its back to Brad, sat, and waited quietly. "Please, we need to talk."

Brad pulled up one of the other folding chairs and sat facing him. "Okay, what's up?" He was hoping that by now, Plan B was well underway and the secret was out—irretrievably out of the box, no putting it back. You could not reskin a cat. He smiled and said, "Have you seen the news?"

"Actually, no. I haven't. Apparently, because I've been running around Lower Manhattan trying to pick up the track of your girlfriend. I am one of the only two or three people in this country who has not seen the news by now. We might as well go out and take a look in a minute." He raised his palm indicating that Brad should remain seated. "First, though" Jenks paused, leaned over with elbows on knees and his fists clasped so tightly that his knuckles bleached to a light tan. "Bradley?" he said, looking up. "You win."

Brad smiled, not without some sense of victory. "I win?" He waited while Jenks gathered his thoughts.

Martin Jenks looked almost pained. His forehead wrinkled in consternation, and his stare, fixed on nothing in particular across the room, underlined his concentration. He began slowly, "For years now, I have been occasionally assigned to a unit that at first, I had to believe, was almost a frivolous adventure. Some of the senior cadre in the unit were sincerely convinced of the moral imperative behind the unit's mission."

Brad wanted to interrupt and ask, "What unit?" but he waited silently.

"At times, I almost believed them," Jenks continued, looking at Brad. "I will tell you honestly, I came to believe you or your father and the good professor were part of some elaborate hoax. But I took a picture of the screen in that geology lab. I was told that that my picture or the image on the screen had to have been faked because the structures it depicted could not exist."

380

"Please understand that over the last six or seven years, some of the missions I've been on have conclusively proven to me to be nothing but BS on a large scale or simple lunacy. We certainly had cases of elaborate fakery. I had no reason to believe that you were part of something bigger. And only by finding your artifact would I have proved or disproved your story." He shook his head remembering.

"God knows, I felt foolish as hell running back and forth across the salt flats with five guys and metal detection wands. At times I wanted to believe you and hoped we were going to find conclusive proof of extraterrestrials. We, I, felt absolutely stupid, and I was livid when I realized that you had actually kept the thing and then lost it in the boat. A few of the guys would've enjoyed running you through the treatment just for grins."

"Treatment? What treatment?" Brad asked, though he was pretty sure of the answer.

"Nothing to worry about now. It's over." Jenks looked genuinely contrite.

Brad, alarmed, asked, "Jenks? What treatment?"

With resignation coloring his response, he said, "It's what you avoided by getting yourselves out of Area 51. We'd have used an amnesic drug, what amounts to a chemical eraser to your memory." He spread his hands open, as if exposing all secrets. "Under hypnosis and psychotropic treatment, we'd insert doubt into your own accounts of what you believe or what you think might have happened."

Brad engaged; he was curious, but still doubting the sanity of Jenks's 'mission.' "That implies that you find people who actually have had valid experiences with aliens or have actually witnessed phenomena not explainable by current science."

"Actually, some of the people we reprogrammed were probably seriously mentally ill to start with." He paused and tried to shift out of defensive mode. "I was introduced to that level of the unit's operations four years ago." He smiled to himself and said, "I was truly amazed, I got to tell you. I can't tell you any of the things I've been witness to—maybe that will be declassified at some time, but for now, I can't discuss it. I'll just say my world view was rocked." He sat up in his chair, leaned back, and simply repeated, "You win, man. We were focusing on you and missed the big one. We thought we had your research quest locked down, and we blew that one, too!"

Brad pursed his lips in a silent whistle and said, "So what now? How'd we do?" He didn't know what kind of impact Connie might have had, and although he knew he might expect one of the labs to have reported by now, he just wasn't sure.

"You kids hit it out of the park. I just called my boss, and he said to be as nice to you as I would be to my mother. Essentially, in a few minutes, you will be a free man. The networks are going nuts. My role is about over here. In fact, I don't know if the unit will survive after Congress has a turn grilling the bosses." He appeared to be seriously thinking out the implications of public scrutiny of a program that had been super-secret for decades. "Glad I'm not Colonel Henderson."

Brad looked at Jenks closely. He seemed older than he had remembered him; there was more salt in the pepper, especially around his close-cropped temples. He looked tired, too. Sagging shoulders and bags under the eyes hinted at lost sleep or release of anxiety, or both, and the rich brown tones his skin had shown on their 'boating adventures,' had the look that his down-home acquaintances would have called "ashy." Jenks looked up from the floor, which he had been studying, and Brad met his gaze. "So what now? Any reason I can't walk away?" he asked and stood.

Jenks stood also, signaling the end of the conversation. "This is a big, big city. Can I give you a lift?"

Brad looked at him incredulously. "A lift? Are you serious? A lift?" He shook his head in disdain. "I think I'd rather walk back to Florida, than—"

"Wait," Jenks interrupted. "At the very least I am to deliver you to some safe haven. This is not a good neighborhood when the sun goes down." He glanced at his watch. "That's very soon. Listen, your girl is over at NBC." Brad looked at him suspiciously. "Brad, we've got some history, not all of it good, but certainly some high-quality memory material. Let me at least deliver you to NBC's doorstep. That, apparently, is where Connie is. From there, you are a free man." He extended a hand, a genuine peace offering.

Brad squared off, staring at the hand of his longtime adversary, those "quality memories" running through instant replay. As Jenks's mouth stretched into an infectious grin, Brad found himself shaking his head in wonder. "Man, you really have no shame, do you?" He took the proffered hand and found a firm, no-nonsense grip.

"Not much," Jenks said. "Come on." He extended his left palm toward the open doorway, as if to guide Brad out of the room. "Come on, let's get the hell out of this dump."

From a darkening corner across the street, Buzz and his newly arrived news crew watched as Jenks and Hitchens left the building by a door on the side loading dock followed by three guys who looked more like "made men" than government security forces. There were no signs of distress, trauma, or danger to the boy. At the curb, he watched as Hitchens walked freely to the passenger door of the black Lincoln. As it sped west, Buzz briefly announced to a small two-way radio that the "package" was moving out apparently under no duress. Pocketing the small hand radio, he nodded to the camera crew to break camp and follow. He was surprised when the Lincoln pulled up at the curb in front of Rockefeller Plaza. He got out of the car and met Brad on the sidewalk outside the still opened door of the limo. "Sorry I lost you downtown, Brad. Let's go upstairs. There's a whole lotta people want to talk to you." With only the barest glance at Martin Jenks, he put a hand on Brad's shoulder and guided him into the building.

Chapter 22

I consider it an extremely dangerous doctrine, because the more
likely we are to assume that the solution comes from the outside, the less
likely we are to solve our problems ourselves.

Carl Sagan

October, 1985
Wakulla Beach

Life began to settle down after almost six weeks of dealing with the painful presence of news reporters, media investigators, private investigators, and, he was sure, some of Jenks's cohorts from the Air Force Office of Special Investigations. The publicity ordeal had been far worse than he had ever imagined.

Somehow, a lifetime of watching the way the media treated controversial figures failed to convey their ruthless persistence and intrusion into every facet of their lives. After the initial shine of fame wore off, Brad lost many of his friends at Arizona State, not to mention his job as a resident advisor at one of the undergraduate dorms. The initial disruptions in class led him to leave school and come home only three weeks into the fall semester.

As he drove around his own home turf, he no longer wondered if he was being followed. He pretty much accepted it. His anxieties had transitioned into his wondering if the SOBs would actually follow him into his driveway. He worried that if one of the news hounds did follow him home looking for an exclusive interview or photo opportunity, it would embolden others to drive into the yard. The sheriff had been called on more than one occasion to evict the press on trespassing charges. The clustered vehicles at the entrance to Wakulla Beach Road had almost caused two accidents, and the sheriff was no longer patient with the antenna trucks and semi-sized RVs. Brad and the Sheriff were relieved when the satellite trailers finally departed Wakulla County. As September faded into October, he no longer expected to see his face and some other minute factoid of his life on the nightly news.

One adventurous news crew had gone diving over the wreck of the *Lou Anne*. Brad and Connie had watched that particular episode billed as a "special news feature." The coastal towns of Apalachicola, Carrabelle, and St. Marks had been happy to host the visiting news and camera crews from the multiple networks that simply had to have their own angle or take on his life in their fair locale. Although there had been great temptation to take book and movie advance money, his old friend Sunny had been instrumental in advising him, saying, "Those idjutes don't have any idea of what life is like down here. No sooner'n you'd tell them your best stories and deepest secrets, than one a' their writers'd decide to spice it up with stuff that wasn't quite true." He'd allowed that "Not saying that you ain't had some pretty amazing adventures; it's just that I never seen any a' them git it quite right."

Brad and Connie decided to heed this advice and that of the senior Chappells to keep their own counsel and talk to almost no one outside of their personal circle. He had given three more interviews to NBC and even invited Tom Brokaw home to show him the house, so he could tastefully recreate his entry into the living room and then the master bedroom and explain how he had found his father dying.

By agreement, their walk in the woods to show the world their own Dreamland had to be faked. To deflect the press that shadowed Brokaw's team, Connie and Brad took the news crew to a different portion of the Florida Trail and posed near a different downed tree with a fake segment of the artifact, sized and colored to mimic the piece of metal before it was cut up. He explained how he had found the artifact in the root mass and that in the last nine years, most of the dirt had been washed away by the fifty inches of rain that the area got every year. Most of the news crew members were so taken with the pristine beauty of the woods in the St. Marks National Wildlife Refuge that they didn't look so closely at the surroundings to see that it didn't quite match Brad's earlier on-air descriptions. Based on the ratings, the public ate up the story. Word was out that HBO would soon be contacting them for rights to a miniseries that would pay off all college debt for both Bradley and Connie and provide living expenses for them while he finished grad school.

The nine-year odyssey from discovery to disclosure had been a massive blow to the Air Force's prestige. The special branch of the Air Force Office of Special Investigation, known loosely as the B-Team, was disbanded. Congress demanded that the holding pens in the basement of Building B at Groom Lake be bulldozed or turned into records storage. Two different congressional subcommittees, one Senate and one House, sent members on tours to ensure that the facility was closed. President Reagan gave Connie and Brad a personal tour of the White House. The curse of fame, though, followed them home. Brad often wished for the usual "fifteen minutes" of fame, because that would have meant that he was no longer a person of interest. And he would no longer have to see his face on the front of the National Enquirer with some made-up story and faked pictures of aliens.

Connie also found the persistent pressure of paparazzi and especially the locals almost unbearable. A simple trip to buy groceries could turn into a high-pressure event as first one person and then another would whisper in line next to her. One would eventually either politely and with good intentions or in simple rudeness ask, "Aren't you the girl from the spaceship?" Some of the ridiculous comments and questions convinced her that many of her fellow citizens got more news from the Enquirer than from the serious news outlets. It was disturbing when perfect strangers would approach and ask, "Dearie, did those aliens try to have sex with you?"

Over the next several weeks, both Brad and Connie realized the strength and wisdom of Sunny's advice about not talking to the "idjuts." Brad had also taken the advice of his aunt and mother to accept an offer for book rights with Random House to publish his official version. The family was still negotiating over which ghostwriter would be brought on, but the twenty-thousand-dollar advance had provided him with a good sense for the immediate future. It also gave him the patience to wait to see which scholarship offer he might accept; MIT or Cal Tech. Both were a long way from his roots in the Florida Panhandle.

Connie and Brad found refuge in fishing offshore in the *PQ*. After having the craft swept for surveillance bugs, the little boat provided the ultimate in privacy. They could talk, plan, and share the simple pleasures of an uncomplicated life punctuated only occasionally by a jerk in a small plane circling overhead to see if they would bring up more artifacts. Eventually, news of Palestinian terrorists hijacking an Italian cruise ship overshadowed their old news in the major press. The checkout-line tabloids continued to make up stories for months.

~ ~ ~

The larger issue of who or what had left the now-famous piece of metal behind as well as when and under what circumstances still fueled debate on smaller stages, far below the front pages or the lead stories of the day. After all, nothing could really be said that wasn't complete speculation. The laboratory reports agreed along a central line of discussion. They believed it was an isotope of technetium, ^{98}Tc, which in any large quantity would not be as dangerous as the more available ^{99}Tc, known to be a beta radiation source. Sunday panels of learned scientists discussed the formation of ^{99}Tc from the decay of ^{235}U in reactors. Those who cared to listen were told that the much rarer ^{98}Tc had a spectral signature found in much older stars than the sun and that it was possible for a planetary system formed from the explosion of an older star to have much richer deposits of the metal than were found on Earth. Some proposed that specific missions to Venus and Mercury might find beds of the metal because of their nearer sun orbits. Some commentators suggested that there might be Tc-rich asteroids orbiting inside the Mars orbit for the taking. Others noted that no one had determined the utility of the object and wondered why anyone would venture on such hostile missions to replicate a piece of scrap metal.

The more puzzling discoveries coming from the empanelled TV scientists concerned the pentagonal lattice form of the carbon filaments embedded in the larger matrix of technetium-chromium metal. How were they formed? What was their purpose? How were they manufactured within the much denser metal? The structural comparison to the darling of Earth physics, Buckminsterfullerene balls, was startling, and many planned experiments to develop the processes that could be used to create the same filaments. If the extreme hardness of the little carbon matrix spheres could be imparted to a cylinder, it would impart great strength while providing excellent electrical conductivity.

Much more misunderstood, but no less hotly debated in laboratories around the world, was the mysterious ring just inside the outer skin. Deformation of the samples, created when they were sheared off the original, obscured the fact that it was electrically isolated from the interior. So questions were more pragmatic: Was it a protective layer? Was it a sheath within which the inner part could move? Much discussion revolved around its manufacture. Some argued that the material was extruded. A few posited that the exotic material was grown in a crystalline process or deposited layer by layer in a process not yet envisioned and certainly not economical by mass production standards. And underlying the discussion was the tacit understanding by most commentators that no one had any clue as to the artifact's purpose. It was known that the material had unusual electromagnetic properties at very cold temperatures, and, it was pointed out, it was very, very cold in space. Was this a factor or simply a property of the metal? And the debate continued, if not on major networks, at least in academia.

November 18, 1985
Wakulla Beach

With close media attention following their movements, neither Brad nor Connie felt they could go back to their Dreamland, the pool in the woods and Litan. With mixed feelings of selfishness and protective concern for him, Connie and Brad had almost certain knowledge that if he were dug up by the government, he'd be dissected and debated. If there was a live entity still in that ship, he'd be treated like a lab rat, not a learned interstellar ambassador.

Before the New York trip, Litan's diction and understanding of vocabulary had blossomed enormously. With Connie reading to him from all sorts of materials, from science and math books to sections of the World Book Encyclopedia taken from Brad's reconstructed bedroom, they had brought their interred telepathic friend an awareness of human culture beyond simple physical knowledge.

Occasionally, now that they were back in the "neighborhood," he reached out to them. The conversations seemed to be shorter, perhaps because of the longer distances. Connie had just crossed over the bridge marking the Franklin-Wakulla County line when she felt the familiar presence in her head and pulled over to the shoulder. An Indian summer spell had choked the highway with cars full of beach umbrellas and coolers and pickup trucks pulling boats for what might be the last warm week of the season. It was no place to lose full awareness of where she was. She closed her eyes and let the feeling fully develop. The few dreams she had "received" from Ka-Litan had been awesome. Soon, the channel developed. A line of cars and trucks following a slow-moving RV with out-of-state plates passed by in staccato blasts that rocked her little car. The buffeting continued as her mind slipped into the dark. This was not a dream transmission; he was there and "talking."

Ka-nee is close ... Litan feel Ka-nee ... Ka-nee talk with Litan?

388

"Hello, Ka-Litan, yes, I am close. Do you remember I described our personal surface transports? I am driving nearby."

Litan think of chemistry lesson ... need ask question.

"Okay, I don't have my books with me, but go ahead." She thought, man he's getting better with syntax.

not need book ... can query memory ... Litan need chloride ion ... chloride salts basic to field effect engine coolant

"Sodium, I think I can buy some. No, wait, there's sodium all over the place. It is very common on this planet." She carefully expressed the thought in order for him to understand. "Sodium chloride salt is in solution in our ocean. Your position is not very far from our ocean."

ocean?

Surface water; not far from you; very big ocean. She laughed to herself; his diction was improving, and she was beginning to think in three-part stanzas.

how to bring ocean to Litan? ... Litan not go to ocean ... big ocean ... need sodium salt of chlorine

Connie considered this; salt was usually poisonous to life. As essential as it was in minute quantities, in any concentration, it was deadly. *Litan, how do you use salt, or sodium chloride?*

melted chloride salts for coolant ...have fuel for control jets ...fill tanks hydrogen from this water

Connie sometimes forgot to whom she was speaking. Comments like this would bring back the reality that this was a traveler for whom most planetary systems were fuel stops.

She said aloud, unnecessarily, "Litan, I have to go talk with Brad. We will figure out how to bring you salts."

B-rad good at problem solve ... make good ka-unit

"Ka-unit?"

yes ... ka same as pilot commander ... Litan is Ka-Litan

She said, "Oh, yes. Soon. Brad and Connie will come to talk. To talk about salts. We cannot come too soon, or we will put Ka-Litan in danger."

Without a summary good-bye, the presence near the back of her skull was gone. She knew she was alone with her thoughts. A log truck blew by a little too close, buffeting her car and bringing her back to the present. The Tallahassee FM station she'd been listening to broke for a weather update. After the annoying mantra, "In this, the capital city, a new hour begins," three klaxon bursts sounded, indicating a weather emergency broadcast. "We have a weather update on what is now Hurricane Kate. Hurricane hunter planes based in Miami reported at the one o'clock update that the storm's position was approximately 185 miles east-northeast of Camagüey, Cuba, and 420 miles southeast of Miami. The storm has continued to intensify since the last observation and now has sustained winds of one hundred miles per hour and is moving westerly at eighteen miles per hour. It is expected to graze the northern coast of Cuba Tuesday morning. With the mountains of central Cuba coming into play, the National Hurricane Center is unsure of the course of the storm after Thursday." The broadcast then reverted to news in progress. "In other news, President Reagan's visit to the Geneva Summit leads world news as his conversations with Soviet President Mikhail Gorbachev seem to point—" She punched another station up and found some music.

November 20, 1985
Wakulla Beach

The Hitchens household once again was filled with laughter bubbling from trivial kitchen conversations. With Lucy still out west, Susan and Bradley spent mother-and-son bonding time in the yard, trying to get control of the overgrowth of azaleas and weeds that lined the foundation and driveway. Nearly a decade of neglect had allowed the showy shrubs to obscure windows, block paths, and cover planting beds. Looking up from his work, Brad noticed a familiar silver sedan near the end of the driveway. Peering closer, he saw that he was looking into the large black iris of a telephoto lens. He turned and, willing himself not to give the man the single-digit salute, found Susan in the backyard.

"Mom, he's back again. The guy from National Enquirer is at the end of the drive."

"I just don't understand, Brad. What in the world would make anyone buy a paper with a picture of me in cutoffs and an old T-shirt?"

"It's not that, Sue. You know that. They're waiting for me to look for something, go somewhere, or do something interesting. Who knows? Maybe the sucker is writing a book on the side, and something about us is just so interesting that thousands of people will keep turning the pages to find how Southern folk burn azalea trimmings."

She gave him a playful punch on the shoulder. "I don't think that's what he's writing about."

He responded, "Knowin' the Enquirer, he doesn't need any actual facts to write a story. All they need is the whisper of an idea to weave a whole story out of speculation, guesswork, and outright lies." He kicked at an oyster shell near the back steps, wondered idly if it was one from the last bag of oysters he and his dad had shucked, and said, "I think I have a plan for getting away from him. Simple, really. I'll tell you about it after it's done," he grinned, "or you can just watch from the porch. He may be lip reading or have a parabolic mike in there or something. Just know that when he would really want to follow us, he won't be able to."

"Have you got your equipment ready, hon?"

"Yes, ma'am. Chase is putting the gear together for us; we're being watched too closely." He picked up the oyster shell out of idle curiosity. "Mom?" He handed the shell over to her. "The night before Dad was killed, he and I sat here on the back porch and shucked a few dozen oysters for dinner." She took it from him as if the common coastal Florida paving unit had suddenly gained a gold lining. "I hope I can dig into a bushel of oysters someday without thinking about Dad and what happened."

Susan dropped the shell and hugged him close. He was almost a full head taller, but the embrace still comforted him as much as Lucy's motherly hugs always had. He found himself fortunate, after all. He'd lost a father but had ended up with two loving mothers.

She pulled back and asked, "When do you think you're going to get back out to the pool?"

"Prob'ly soon as I can get the stuff over here from Apalachicola. Connie said Chase was going to try to bring the stuff over in a few hours. Most of it looks like regular boat stuff anyway."

"Just be careful, sweetie. I don't think you are in physical danger anymore, but these reporters are dangerously aggressive, and I still don't think the military is totally out of the picture."

Brad shrugged. "I don't know. The last I heard from Jenks was that he was going to quit the Air Force. He'll be out at the end of his current contract. Not so much because he didn't do what he was told; more like he no longer wanted to do that kind of work."

"Really?"

"Yeah, he called, I don't know, three or four weeks ago and tried to apologize for everything that happened."

"You don't say? You didn't yell at him, did you?"

"No, he actually sounded contrite. Like he had been conflicted for a while and was almost glad that the whole cover-up stage was over. Now that the 'cat was skinned,' as he put it."

Susan, visibly surprised, straightened a crick in her back and said, "Well, waddayaknow?"

"We talked for a while. I think he was legit." Brad scanned the windows on the house. "I think we need to get some plywood on hand, just in case Kate comes this way."

"Where is it? I thought it was heading for New Orleans."

"It was at the last advisory. Only thing I know for sure right now is that it's in the middle of the Gulf and it has to hit something. Last report I heard said it was going to be affected by a front, and it would start to curve to the northeast. The target area right now is anywhere from Mobile to Panama City."

"Should we be worried?" Susan, the parent, had begun to look to her son as the new man of the house.

"Well, not worried, but at least prepared. It's at cat three and pretty dangerous, and we're on the east side of it. If you can get me a check, I'll get some plywood for the windows. I have a list working in my head."

"A list? Already?"

"Simple stuff: gas for the chainsaw, fill up the car and truck and generator gas, at least two full propane bottles for the cooker, rice and dried beans, a week's worth of bottled water ..." He dusted his hands on the back pockets of his jeans. "Usual hurricane stuff."

Susan looked at her son with pride and admiration. "I'll go for the groceries; you get the plywood. How much time do we have?"

"Couple of days, but if the storm turns this way, there won't be anything left on the shelves." Brad peered around the side of the house, saw that the reporter's sedan was still near the end of the drive, and walked over to the workbench in the pole barn. "I'll be inside in a minute, Mom. I've got a little project to finish." Looking around, he found a scrap of one-by-four pine and a box of two-inch nails.

~ ~ ~

Tim Murray had been staking out the Hitchens homestead for over two weeks and was beginning to think that his effort to scoop the networks was going to be fruitless. The only thing good, he thought, was that the weather was considerably better than in Chicago. *Middle of November,* he thought, *and the temperature has been running from the fifties to the eighties.* He had asked just about anybody he had come in contact with for a personal angle on the big "alien artifact" story and come up dry. His attempts to get a relationship angle between the Hitchens boy and his girlfriend had seemed a little too close to voyeurism, but, hell, she was cute and you never knew. He might get some front page pics to build a story on.

Murray was going over his notes and the telephoto shots at the hardware store. Big deal, half the county had been to the hardware store getting chainsaws sharpened, hurricane clips for window inserts, sixty-gallon trash barrels for water storage, and other inexpensive feel-good investments in case the hurricane came that way. The thought occurred to him that he should call to see if he could sell exclusive shots of Kate's landfall. Of course, that depended on where landfall was going to be. He turned on the radio to get a weather update.

He looked up from the dial and was surprised to see the Chappell chick walking toward him. "Crap!" He realized there was no way to disguise the fact that his passenger seat and backseat were covered with takeout pizza and doughnut boxes, crumpled burger bags, and yesterday's laundry.

Connie was wearing short shorts and a man's shirt with the tails tied up to reveal a firm, supple belly. He was transfixed, and she was smiling!

Connie walked up to his rental Chevy and leaned over, hands on the door frame. She made a point of allowing the shirt to fall open to reveal just enough cleavage to ensure that his eyes would be trapped between her eyes and her chest. "Hi," she said and extended her hand. "I guess you know I'm Connie Chappell. We've seen you around a lot." She tried to sound homey.

The reporter fidgeted to get his right hand out the driver's side window to take her offered hand. "Yes, I've been here for about a month now. Wasn't trying to be too intrusive, but my editors want me to stay on the story." His eyes fought to retain hers in spite of the almost open shirt. Finally he said. "Hi, I'm Tim, Tim Murray."

She took the hand and flashed a captivating smile. "So, do you plan to follow us everywhere? We would like a little privacy from time to time." *My smile is immaculate, perfect.* She thought he looks foolish, embarrassed.

Trapped in the car, he had to look up at her. She knew she found it hard to keep his gaze focused on her face and not let it drop to her shirt. It did, and she knew that although his attention was divided, it was totally on her. He mumbled something about the damned editorial staff; he really wanted to get his resume beefed up and work for some real press like Time magazine. He stopped rambling; trailing off.

"Well, Tim, it'd be good for you to find some high ground up in Tallahassee, 'cause this area floods if we get a hurricane anywhere near here. Lots of trees come down, and this county's pretty slow at getting the roads cleared again. You could get stuck in this car for a lot longer than you'd like."

Murray noticed a movement in his rearview mirror. Hitchens was almost at the car. Wow! he thought. Maybe I can get an interview with both of them.

Hitchens simply said, "Con, are you ready?"

Murray asked, "Hey, you guys? Do you think I could get a shot of you? Promise I'll go away for a coupla days and not be a bother at all. Guys?"

Murray craned his head back to try to make eye contact with Hitchens, but Connie was no longer leaning against his door, and before he knew it, they were both walking back up the driveway. Cussing at himself for not being more assertive, he watched as they walked back into the house. He did snap a few shots of them walking back toward the house.

A few minutes later, they emerged and both were in blue jeans and T-shirts. He heard the pickup start up in the backyard. He turned on his own ignition and waited. He knew he'd have to turn around to follow them out to the highway, but he wanted to make sure they weren't headed down to the local beach.

As the brown-and-tan F-150 pulled out, both Brad and Connie waved at Murray. He managed an embarrassed wave back and put the little Chevy rental in gear. As soon as the car moved forward, he heard a low pop, some hissing, and a clunk. He stopped, puzzled, and then felt the back of the car settling to the ground. His heart sank, too, as he realized he wasn't going anywhere. He got out of the car and saw the small board full of nails attached to his now flattened tire and jammed up in the wheel well. He'd been had. Cussing aloud now, it wasn't until he went to pull out the tiny spare that he realized that both rear tires were flat.

~ ~ ~

They left the F-150 in a small trailhead parking area just down the road but well out of sight of traffic on the coastal highway. Connie sounded just a little worried. "Brad? How far away is the hurricane?"

Brad made a show of looking up at the clear blue sky and said, "I'd say at least two or maybe three days."

For this, she punched him hard in the biceps. "Thanks, buddy. Seriously, how far out is it?"

"I heard a report on the way over; it's still about two days, maybe a day and a half out, and the strike zone is anywhere from Panama City to Cedar Key. They still don't know how much the steering currents are going to affect her course overnight." He wasn't trying to sound overly confident. Although he had spent most of his high school and college years in the Southwest, he had watched the track of every hurricane that ever entered the Gulf. As a lifelong addict of the weeklong news events that were potential hurricane strikes, experience told him that the Big Bend of Florida, the region between Cape San Blas and Steinhatchee, was rarely hit. They almost always seemed to hit from Panama City to points west, with New Orleans and Galveston or, especially, Corpus Christi having hurricane bull's-eyes painted on them. A direct hit in the Big Bend was a rarity. He asked, "Chase didn't mention it. Is your mom worried? How are people getting ready over there?"

"Most of the fleet is going go up the river and ride it out. A lot of the houses on Bay Avenue are already boarded up. There's no bottled water left in the stores, and all the tourists have been ordered to get out of town and off the island by tomorrow morning."

"Fat chance that'll happen." He snorted. "A lot of 'em would stay over just to experience it. Even though it's supposed to go down to a cat two tonight, ya just never know."

Several hundred yards from Litan's pool, they began to feel the familiar presence.

B-rad and Ka-nee ... hello, friends

They both responded at about the same time. *"Hello."*

friends close ... no visit ... hard to talk in distance

Brad, leaning back against his usual cypress trunk, replied, "There are others who might do you extreme harm if they found out about you. We want to help you get out of the ground so you can be free, but we do not want our military to dig you up. They will not treat you well." He looked up from the pool. "Connie, can he understand all that?"

She was nodding with a little uncertainty on her face, but Litan answered, *Litan understand words, but not military not treat Litan well*

"Litan," Connie asked, "does your kind have enemies?"

yes Coalition forces fight Errans ... Errans fight all Dzuran Coalition force ... Errans fight Dzura long

She felt stupid, remembering the stories that Brad had told her she continued the conversation. "Earth military has never seen other intelligent species before. If you are captured, you would be studied, possibly killed. You would not be allowed to leave Earth when you wanted."

if free Litan look for Dzuran Navy ... Litan look for other Dzuran Coalition planets ... Litan not know if Erran fighters win this sector

Connie asked, "Litan, you have been missing a long time. Do you think you will find any of your kind?"

not know ... my ship much old now ... new weapons much danger

Brad and Connie looked at each other, and Brad asked, "So you think new technology would be very dangerous for your ship?"

yes ... maybe Erran ship sensors better

After a short pause, they both felt something that felt like humor.

maybe Erran pilots still stupid

The two humans laughed. Brad asked, "Litan, we have come to talk about your crash. We know that a piece of your ship was broken when you crashed. I found a piece a long time ago; it is now proof to my people that other species exist."

Litan exist

The thought expressed to both of them was a statement, but it had a hint of question embedded in it.

"Humans, our species, have never had physical proof that your species or any other species from another planet exists."

easy prove ... Litan show humans ... Litan exist

Brad smiled. There was almost an innocence here, or was it hubris? Did Litan think he was above human weapons systems? "Litan, if scared, humans could use very powerful energy weapons to hurt or kill Litan."

Litan use shield ... Litan need get chlorides from earth ocean called gulf ... chlorides help restore shield

"We have been thinking about that," Brad replied. "We may be able to bring chlorides to you. Are you exposed to water under this pool? *Are you completely covered in dirt, soil ... hmm, non-liquid?"*

Litan not know about liquid ... humans not go into water ... water bad for humans?

Suppressing a laugh, Connie replied, "Yes, Litan. We can go into the water."

Brad looked at her. "You know, we're planning to do this in the middle of a hurricane? Right? You still in? I can do this—"

She said, "Will you stop?" She shook her head at him in disgust. "You think I'd stop now? When did I become a girly-girl?"

He backed away, as far as sitting three inches away from her would allow. "OK, OK. Got it, we'll just need to get a little bit of primitive human technology to bear here."

Litan like human technology ... Litan want free from rock ... shield will break rock ... like tell you before ... need sodium chloride coolant for shield power reactor

Connie looked at Brad, they had the plan and it was about to hatch and her father was busy gathering the materials as they spoke.

Brad looked into the unknowable something in the depths of the pool, "Litan, the piece of your ship that broke off, is it necessary to your ship for flight? Is there more damage that we do not know about?"

Feeling like they were playing twenty questions, the two humans were able to provide a description of the found piece to Litan who was not quite able to tell the humans what its purpose was. They finally realized that it was a sensor for deep-space communications and that another of the appendages was available on the ship in its retractor slot. Having only one would just decrease his range and limit direction-finding abilities.

In more question-and-answer, Litan told Brad and Connie of another piece that he felt was missing. It might be in the rock with him and damaged or, more likely, had been snapped off the same way the antenna mast had been broken.

Brad stood and looked beyond the thicket at the general layout of the forest around him. He moved to the shallow end of the pool and faced away from the deep end. This would be the direction of the crashing ship's approach. He saw that in line with this direction was the upended cypress tree's base. The antenna mast had been found there. If anything else was on or near the surface, it would most likely be on that alignment in the direction of the coast or coastal flats to the south.

Although it wasn't necessary—it just felt right—Brad knelt and faced the deep end of the pool. *"Litan, I will search for the missing piece soon, and we will also bring some of our simple machines to help get you free."* He thought that maybe this was a good time for a hurricane after all.

Chapter 23

Then was heard the low rumbling of distant thunder, then the
lightning quivered, and then the darkness of an hour seemed to have
gathered in an instant.
Charles Dickens

November 21, 1985
Hurricane Kate, 1:30 a.m.

Tim Murray had used his press card to avoid mandatory evacuation and checked into a small bed-and-breakfast in Port St. Joe, about an hour west of the Hitchenses' home. Port St. Joe was predicted to be on the high-wind side of the expected landfall forty or fifty miles west along the coast. He was excited. He stayed up for the 1:00 a.m. National Hurricane Center's forecast based on the late-evening flights through the storm's eye. Central pressures had increased slightly, indicating that the predicted weakening was happening as the storm center moved into cooler waters in the northern gulf.

He felt good about a weakening storm. He had become a little apprehensive and was glad that he could have the experience of a hurricane without worrying about dying. His inn was not on the beach but across the highway from a large bay, which was why he picked the location, especially with storm surge predicted at over six feet. It was on an intersection on the coastal highway, allowing him to track east or west if predictions changed at the next update. Or he could escape at all haste due north toward lower wind speeds and no chance of surge.

Satisfied that he was going to get some great coverage of the effects of Hurricane Kate's landfall, he tried to tell himself to get some sleep. Heck, even the locals were still open for limited business. The bar downstairs was doing a great business in, what else? Tequila Hurricanes! Kate's center was still 180 miles away and moving at 10 miles per hour; he had plenty of time. It would be a long night after the storm came ashore; he lay back, closed his eyes, and tried to imagine one-hundred-mile-per-hour winds. He could not imagine that the story of a lifetime was unfolding just down the road from the stakeout he had abandoned two days ago when the wrecker showed up and hauled him and his rental car off Wakulla Beach Road. He allowed his memories to drift toward the image of Connie leaning on his window and fell asleep.

~ ~ ~

At dawn, about a mile down the coastal highway from Wakulla Beach Road, Brad pulled off to find Chase waiting for him. The off-road package was complete: a well-muffled modified golf cart with a small utility trailer attached. The low-rise utility trailer had been cut down to a thirty-inch bed from the standard forty-eight to fit on forest trails. It was loaded with a small pile of lumber, a two-and-a-half-horse Johnson Sea Horse outboard motor, a new metal detector, a shovel, his wet suit and goggles, a gas-powered mud pump, two cases of five-pound bags of salt, a wooden truss assembly, and a few spare items.

Brad helped back the golf cart off the truck bed and hooked up the trailer. Connie drove Brad's Ford behind some trees where it couldn't be seen and met him at the trail head. She looked to the southwest, as if the violence centered 140 miles offshore could be conjured to mind.

Leaning out of his truck window, Chase called, "Connie, Brad? I want you two to be careful, ya hear? There's a big storm out there, and I've got to go back to protect the boat and keep Lou Anne calmed down." He paused to ensure he had Brad's attention.

"Brad?" Chase leveled a serious man-to-man look at him. "I know you will look out for Connie. She is my one and only daughter, and if anything should happen, you know I'll come looking."

"Yes, sir, mom's house is battened down safe, and it's just down the road. If it gets rough, we can go hang out there. The house may be old, but it's been through some pretty rough storms before."

Chase climbed into the cab of his truck and looked at them both. "Just be smart and be careful!"

He drove off to a chorus of, "We'll be careful."

They headed into the woods onto a fairly wide path staked and maintained as part of the Florida Trail. A half-mile further they pulled off the Florida Trail and onto a thinner trail he had prepared to get golf cart access to the pool. Connie asked, "Tell me again why we're doing this with a hurricane coming?"

"It's still twelve hours or more out, and that's if it's coming our way. Lucy and Sue are spending the night up in Tallahassee. They're not likely to get anything from this storm; chances are it's going to dive inland at Destin and all we'll get here is rain and a few downed power lines." He pulled to a stop and turned off the golf cart. "And, besides," he added, "the storm has all the reporters looking out to sea instead of at us, and the sheriff is more than busy chasing tourists out of the county." He waved both hands skyward. And the Refuge? Shoot, the Refuge Rangers are all hunkered down at their houses like any other sensible person would be."

He hoped that sounded sufficiently nonchalant; the last news reports were a little more ominous than he'd hoped. But then, so often when he'd perversely wanted to thrill to the experience of a hurricane, they usually turned away to the west.

He reached into the trailer and pulled out the metal detector. Overhead, low gray clouds scudding across the treetops and a persistent rise in humidity were the only indications of any oncoming inclement weather. Lining up on Litan's pool and the base of the cypress tree, he sighted along the line and aimed at a distant tree. He pointed south and said, "Connie, imagine that his ship bounced a hundred yards south, one last time before plowing in. That depression might have been where the rod was broken off, it filled with sediment, and at least one cypress tree—that one—took root." He didn't know if he was right, but the elegance of the explanation was satisfying. He adjusted the shoulder straps to Connie's back and pointed out the line. Armed with a small garden spade, she started to walk in an undulating S-pattern, swinging the broad base of the detector back and forth. Soon, she was walking off into the woods, concentrating on the neutral hum in her earphones.

Brad began to unload the equipment and set up for the rescue. He had been blocking Litan's attempts at conversation because he had a plan in motion and didn't want the distraction. He set the mud pump on the bank near the deep end and attached a suction hose that he hoped would be long enough. Donning his wet suit and goggles, he slid into the water for an exploratory dive. Without sunlight, the pool was dimly lit, but, as yet, he had not stirred the mud. His flashlight soon revealed that there was a mud layer over everything. What should he have expected after a few centuries of silting, the activity of boring and burrowing creatures, and falling and decaying leaves from above?

Surfacing for air, he again felt the presence. Litan was in his head, but this time, it was different. He lowered his goggles back under the waterline and was shocked to see—no, sense, was the better word— the location of the ship. His first reaction was an involuntary gasp, which left him choking and gagging and hanging on to a protruding root. He coughed up the accidental bit of water, took a breath, and submerged to look again. He knew X-ray vision was impossible, but there, within the mud, soil, and displaced chunks of lime rock, was a large, almost triangular oval. Its long axis was a little off horizontal, and there appeared to be random lumps in its surface. The more he stared, the more it seemed to take on depth. "Thanks, Litan, I don't know how you did that … but that helps me see where you are."

B-rad try help Litan … Litan try help B-rad … B-rad linked with hull status sensor

"Well, it worked. I have to get some breathing aids for underwater, and I will be back."

~ ~ ~

Martin Jenks pulled up beside the tan-and-brown F-150 and smiled at how easy this was going to be. Acting now as the military advisor of a reorganized, off-budget special investigation unit of AFOSI, Jenks now enjoyed more field autonomy and better logistical support. He had all the support he could put on a virtually unlimited charge card. He also enjoyed the salary level that civilian contractors could charge the military. He had no idea what civilian pay grade he was listed as, but he netted something close to midrange for a full-colonel making combat hazard pay.

His assistant, Frank Fischetti, was also a former field agent from the disbanded B-Team at Edwards AFB's Groom Lake facility. Fischetti, "Fish" to his friends, looked at the aging truck with a wrinkled brow. "Is that the same truck from your surveillance reports?"

"Sure is," Jenks responded, suppressing a grin. "Nothing like telling the world that your unit has been disbanded to drop the levels of paranoia." He reached into the backseat and pulled a small zippered bag to the front. He handed Fischetti a thick, dark wax crayon. "You wanna start with brown or olive?" Fish took the olive crayon, smudged a thick layer onto his thumb, and began to smear streaks onto his forehead and cheeks.

"Hey, Marty, anything not in the file that I should know about?" He took another look in the rearview mirror and smeared a band of green into a broader area to provide color base. "Seems to me we're going to a lot of trouble to find some more of that sample."

"Judging from the stuff Miss Chappell's father put together, they are doing some serious searching for something out there in the woods, and I don't want it to disappear only to show up again on national television."

Jenks was smearing a broad band of lighter green and making leaf dapples across his cheeks and chin. "That object, the now-famous artifact, had always been sampled from the broken end. From what we've seen, most of the samples were identical, like neighbors on a continuously consistent bar, however exotic." He looked across at the transforming face of his partner. "The piece left in the electron scope at FSU was the original broken end, and it's now stressed beyond analysis of how it originally was attached. Now, the other end, that's what's interesting. It looks like something was attached to it. It reminds me of the cubed end of a ratchet driver, only it had a triangular head. It even had a dimple on two sides where some piece of equipment was attached."

"So we're hoping that they find whatever was attached to the undamaged end?"

"We're hoping to acquire whatever they find." Jenks shook his head in recollection of hundreds of hours of surveillance. "Those little snots have been eluding me, lying to me, and generally, pissin' me off for the better part of nine years now, and I finally want to win a round." He checked the rearview mirror for his dehumanized face and looked over at Fischetti. "Come on, Fish, you're as fussy with that stuff as a teenager on prom night."

They left the car keys under a rock beside a significantly large pine and headed down the trail. Overhead, pine tops swayed in a brief harbinger gust.

~ ~ ~

Connie was puzzled. Her earphone was responding with a whine that blended with a screech when she pointed the coil end of the metal detector toward a clump of palmetto, but she had expected to find a depression—maybe not one as deep as Litan's pool but something that looked like something heavy had bounced off it.

There was no doubt about it, though. A definite screech and wow alternated as she waved the wand back and forth. She looked back to make sure the palmetto clump was in line with the base of the cypress and the pool. She realized they would need a backhoe to excavate those palmettos later. At the moment, she just had to find out if whatever was causing the sound was something interesting or merely a beer can. She tied a piece of pink flagging tape to a branch and moved on in her line of survey.

~ ~ ~

Brad was back in the water with the business end of the mud pump. The three-inch-wide suction hose was stiff and hard to maneuver, and it took some time to position. When he finally got it near the mud wall that separated open water from his "vision" of Litan's ship, the pump suddenly stopped. He surfaced to see what had gone wrong.

Connie was standing at the rim of the pool setting up an impromptu picnic for two. Brad looked up at her, surprised. "That time already? Guess I've been busy."

They sat on the bank, eating and wondering at the still air overhead. Connie said, "I think you were right, Brad. Looks like Kate went somewhere else."

"Let's hope. Did you have any luck with the detector? Find anything?"

She winced slightly, skewed her mouth to one side, and answered, "I got two hits, one is deep in a clump of palmettos; take a bulldozer to get it out. The other one was an old Pepsi can so far from any trail that there's no telling how long it's been there." She reached into her belly pack and pulled out the flattened remains of a can so old that it predated the molded one-piece aluminum cans. She tossed the can into the back of the trailer. "How 'bout you? Any luck down in the pool?"

Brad looked down at the dark water and said in a tone that understated his wonder, "Strangest doggone thing happened. As soon as Litan figured out that I was in the water and looking for him, it's … it's …" He faltered and looked back at Connie. "It's like he knew I was looking for him, and he wired me into one of his sensor circuits. I could just about see where the ship was. At first, maybe it was like I could sense the mass, then, the profile. As I looked, it was as if he was imprinting some sort of sensory system so I could, I don't know, visualize the ship in 3-D. And, Connie, the thing is pretty big!" He spread his arms. "Like bigger than a school bus big!"

Her eyes widened. "Any clues as to how to get him out?"

"Well, I'm not sure if I'm reading or understanding what I'm seeing— or sensing," he corrected himself, "but there appears to be a port of some kind, and I'm going back down to get at it with the suction hose. It's like he's giving me instructions, a map, and feedback."

They set to work after lunch with renewed enthusiasm. Overhead, an occasional gust shook the canopy as low clouds continued to slide by, perhaps a little more rapidly than earlier. They hadn't noticed that most of the wildlife had sensed steadily decreasing barometric pressures and grown quiet. Most creatures with burrows or nests were securing them and shutting down.

~ ~ ~

A hundred and fifty yards away, two crouching figures lay in a bed of ferns and creeper vines watching the activity. Frank Fischetti maintained vigil with a pair of hooded binoculars. Despite his concentration on Hitchens and Chappell, he had the particular sensation that he and Jenks were being watched. He could not shake an uncomfortable feeling that something behind him had watched them approach, sent out some passive-aggressive sense of hostility, and then settled to watch them. He didn't relish feeling like prey; he had spent his entire career being the hunter.

Martin Jenks knew that if approached, Brad would just shut down. They would not find out what they were about until he had actually accomplished his goal. Jenks planned to wait it out. They could certainly outrun a golf cart. He pulled a small two-way transceiver from his camo breast pocket, pulled a thin wire from its receptacle, and inserted a tiny earphone. Quietly, he called in to get a weather update. Per the one o'clock NOAA hurricane center update, Hurricane Kate was now only about 120 miles southwest of their location, moving north-northeasterly and curving to a more easterly track. He subtracted about a seventy-five mile radius for significant winds from the hundred and twenty miles and realized that the effects were not far away and would soon be overhead.

~ ~ ~

In the next few hours, Hurricane Kate would give Tim Murray the scare of his life as she came ashore a few miles west of him and the eastern eye wall passed just up the road. He would submit the best story he'd done in years. He was so preoccupied with post disaster cleanup photo opportunities and stories of property loss and human anguish, that he would miss the biggest story on the planet. A few hours later, Kate would pass close to Tallahassee, the supposedly safe haven Brad's aunt and mother had gone to only thirty miles to the north. Tallahasseeans would remember this storm as "the big one" or simply "Kate" and it would serve as a benchmark reference for disaster planning for decades.

~ ~ ~

In the murky haze of silt and debris, there was very little that Brad could see. His sense of sound was obliterated by the alternating hiss and burble of his breathing equipment and the thumping rhythms of the mud pump. The pump's vibration on the adjacent embankment made it into the

404

water around him. Silt disturbed by the pump's vibrations had turned the little pool into a thin brown gravy. He could feel the pump more than hear it as the jerking cycles of its piston-induced vacuum passed down the suction hose. His plan was working, and he was making headway as the working end of the suction hose made steady left and right passes around the area of what Litan was telling him was an important intake scoop. Something flashed bright in the brown water, startling him. A rumbling boom passed through air, earth, and water, and he realized that it had only been lightning and thunder. His excitement was all-encompassing now. Even though actual visibility in the pool was worse now than it had been in the *Lou Anne*, the 3-D spatial link to the ship from Litan made the work possible, and Litan's silent encouragement and the steady progress he was making in removing centuries of silt totally occupied his thoughts.

Above, by the side of the pool, Connie alternately watched Brad's bubble stream and the steady stream of brown water emerging from the pump. She had gone to the golf cart to retrieve his second tank and a bright-yellow waterproof rain suit just before the first shower passed over the area. It was brief and chilling. The pock, pock of the gas motor seemed loud enough to call in the wildlife rangers from all over. She did not know for sure whether the St. Marks National Wildlife Refuge permitted gas-operated equipment, but she was pretty sure they would *not* permit any of what was happening in the refuge today.

The pump beside her seemed to hiccup. The intake hose jumped on its mounting ring. Underwater, Brad found something solid and the suction end of the hose grabbed the hull. He pulled against the suction and managed to free it. By holding it at an angle to the solid surface, he found he was able to clear more of the caked mud off the side of the buried ship. With Litan's guidance, he moved the hose to clear a pair of small openings of encrusted mud. He heard a minor mechanical whine, and a small scoop appeared out of the formerly smooth surface of the hull. In flight, the ship could extend the scoops wide for atmospheric intake or keep them close to the hull for liquids. In combat, they would be retracted entirely flush with the smooth-sided hull.

Brad had no idea of this but accepted the running array of images Litan supplied as he worked. Moving the suction hose up the surface of the hull, he uncovered a small hole, which when cleared, surprised him with a small amber light that glowed dimly and then startled him as it flashed bright before fading back to a dim glow again.

He felt something that reminded him of humor in his consciousness. Was Litan trying to be funny?

Yes ... trying funny ... almost ready

As this thought was completed, a water jet blew from one of the openings in the scoop, which Brad could now sense was partially extended.

"Well, that's good, my friend, because I am almost out of air," Brad responded in thought.

He could not see his dive watch in the murk, but he could feel the back pressure on his regulator. He was running out of air, or soon would be. He tasted the bitter metallic taste of tank as it released its last few quarts of over-pressured gasses. He popped to the surface and gasped for clean, fresh air. He was surprised at how dark it seemed.

Connie said from behind him, "About dang time! I was about to go down and grab a leg to pull you out. You gonna need this tank?"

"I don't think so." Brad pulled himself up onto the bank, shed his tank, and sat facing her across the pool. "Anybody around here going to do any leg-pulling, it's gonna be me." He raced around to the other side. Connie shrieked and made a show of running away, but not fast enough to evade him, and was soon tackled. They collapsed laughing in the rain-dampened tall ferns. What might have developed from the moment of release and accomplishment was interrupted by a rolling grumble that could be felt passing from south to north overhead. A pair of mockingbirds left their nest in a tall cabbage palm and dove for the better protection of a palmetto thicket. The thunder was a wake-up call to the fact that it was now mid-afternoon and a hurricane was due to make landfall soon less than a hundred miles west. With the leading edge of the storm extended north and east, this would give them a maximum of three or four hours before they should be indoors. They incorrectly thought they had about three hours to get out of the woods in, four max.

"Come on, hon. Let's get phase two going." They got back to the trailer and pulled ready-made pieces of a truss from the bed. They struggled to get the pieces through the well-traveled path through the titi trunks and attached them to form a thirty-foot truss that spanned the narrow pool. The truss, when assembled, had a two-by-twelve plate mounted at the midpoint that doubled as a splice for the two sections and a motor mount for the outboard motor. Brad pulled the small two-stroke Johnson from the trailer and placed its clamps over the extension of the two-by-twelve. The little motor provided an industrial-strength mixer for the small pool of water.

Connie arrived with the first two of the bags of salt. A sustained flash of lightning strobed overhead and was followed immediately by another long stanza of rolling thunder.

Brad looked at the heavens and noted the movement of treetops overhead. Sustained winds at the canopy were beginning to pull the remaining end-of-season leaves from their branches, and waves of amber blew through the air, falling more horizontally than vertically. "We haven't got much time, Con. We need to get this done or get out. What do you want to do?"

"Do? I've wanted to leave since before we got here." She looked up at the swirling leaves, felt rather than heard the thrashing of the cabbage palm leaves nearby, and tried to gauge her response. "Brad, we are so freaking close. We are rigged and ready. If we had to, we could add the salt and get out of here. If it works, Ka-Litan will get what he needs and get out of his hole in the ground."

"Don't you want to see him?" He clasped her by the shoulders. "Connie, I want to see him. I have worked for this moment for a long time. And you and your family have all been a part of this. This thing, his release, his reality! If he can get out of the ground and prove his existence and recharge all of his systems? Man! That will be the biggest thing to have hit the world since, since, umm, your press conference with Tom Brokaw!" He shook his head for emphasis. "Don't you want to be a part of this, to witness it?"

Connie looked at him in earnest. "I, uh, Brad, I want to go. I really want to get the hell out of here." Another long deep-throated rumble of thunder rolled overhead, emphasizing her thoughts. "But you're right." She glanced at the pond and projected: *I want to see you, friend* Her face broke into a beaming smile. She almost cried at the wordless emotional response that reflected back from the pool. She looked up into Brad's eyes. "Yes, I'm staying with you. If we have to, we can shelter in the pool. It's chilly, but there's no wind!"

"I don't think so, Con. We'd need to shelter for a few hours, into the night, and we'd get hypothermia by then."

"Well?"

"Well, we will deal with it when we have to. Kate may be passing by as we speak. He pointed up at the swaying treetops. "This might be it, plus some rain." To himself, he thought, *or it might be heading right for us.*

Connie set her mouth in the firm, thin-lipped line that meant she had made her decision and turned back to the golf cart. "Come on," she said over her shoulder. "Grab some salt, will you?"

~ ~ ~

From their vantage in low cover, Jenks and Fischetti were uncomfortable and becoming more so by the minute. Fischetti's headache was distractingly prominent. It had started in the back of his neck, risen to the nodes behind his ears, and made concentration difficult. For the past hour or so, he'd had the ridiculous feeling that they were being watched by a predator. As he slowly moved a camouflaged hand up to the top of his neck and rubbed at the base of his skull, he noticed Fish take a quick glance behind him. "What? What are you looking at? Our objective is in front of us."

"It's the creepiest thing, boss." Fischetti looked worried. "I've felt like we're being watched ever since we got into position." He nodded at the two subjects who were hauling something that looked like sugar or flour bags to the pond. "Those two definitely aren't looking at us."

"No, indeed." Jenks was almost relieved, but he could not admit to the same haunted feeling. Haunted? He thought that sure as heck felt like what was happening. He had been suppressing the thought of leaving on grounds of weather for an hour or so, but it wasn't fear of weather that bothered him. Hell, unless a tornado came through, the average forest was safer than the average house in a hurricane. But this feeling of being watched was damn creepy, just like Fish said. He thought all of this in seconds but said only, "Eyes forward, Airman."

Both agents turned to look at the two kids who seemed to be oblivious to the gathering storm, lost in their own moment. "You know, Marty, they don't know the hurricane turned east."

"Yeah, I know. Ignorance is bliss."

"So how long do we have?"

Jenks looked at his watch. "Two hours, three on the outside, probably less."

~ ~ ~

In just a few trips, Brad and Connie had assembled a small pile of salt bags at the edge of the pool. The small motor was mounted and ready. Brad yanked on the pull rope, and the motor coughed quietly. On the second pull, it started. It would be an overstatement to say the tiny outboard engine roared into life, but Brad soon had it in gear and set it just above an idle; it was much quieter than the mud pump had been. As he looked to Connie, she handed him the first bag. He cracked its back on the truss and poured the contents into the swirling eddy just behind the motor's prop. A hundred yards west, the two watchers looked incredulously at each other.

"Here you go, Litan, sodium chloride solution. The concentration will be coming up soon." Brad expressed the thought as he cracked open another bag and slowly poured its contents into the eddy. They continued to empty their supply of salt into the pool and sat huddled at the edge of the pool out of the gusts whipping by overhead. As the moments stretched toward an hour, straining patience and resolve, the weather above worsened.

Below, at the other end of the pool, a panel of instruments lit up. Three columns of lights illuminated from top to bottom. Beside each indicator, icons and text were backlit in turn. No human eye would be able to decipher the symbolic labels. The central holo screen, dark for centuries, began to glow red around the edges, as nav systems activated. Sensors for liquid salts extended into the slow current passing through the liquid intake ducts. The ship waited. Hydrogen and oxygen had long ago been pulled from fresh water leached out of groundwater and separated out. The ship's chem tanks were restored. Only their periodic use had allowed the ship to maintain power for so long without firing up the fusion units. Using the main reactor at anything below minimal power would require superheated liquid heavy salt as a coolant. Filter banks now continually cleansed and backwashed a constantly richer stream of saline solution, separating out the much needed sodium chloride heated to liquid state for coolant. The third indicator from the bottom left column blinked slowly at first, and then as the concentration of halides was improved, its color changed from amber to blue, and the blink rate increased.

On the surface, weather was beginning to deteriorate rapidly. Two rain bands had swept through, soaking all four humans. The watcher below, oblivious to weather for centuries, was preoccupied with system status reports as ramped-up power allowed long-lapsed processes to be rebooted. The little outboard had long since pockety-pocked to a stop. The silence revealed a continuous surrounding whistle through the higher branches of the canopy. Occasionally, wands of palmetto, untested by the breezes of summer, broke loose and sailed to the forest floor. Cracks and crashes, heard over the general sound of wind and rain, indicated a few trees had lost the battle and come down.

Brad and Connie moved out of the water and found some small comfort huddled behind the flimsy shelter of the golf cart, conflicted with indecision. The brave face of two hours ago had diminished as the long wait set in. They had no idea how long it might take Litan to replenish the required minerals he needed. Maybe it would take days. The forest around them creaked and moaned while above, the wind and nearly continuous thunder preceded squalls of unbelievable intensity. Brad had determined that it would be safer to overturn the golf cart and create a shelter in its lee rather than continue to sit in it and wait for a gust to blow it over. They were now within its frame, wrapped in ponchos and facing hypothermia in spite of the warm rain soaking the Florida flatwoods.

Their calm refuge, long known to the two of them as Dreamland, was taking on the characteristics of a nightmare. Brad remembered a thoughtful moment several years back when Lucy had wondered why hurricanes always seemed to do their worst in the dark. They weren't kind enough to show their bad side to the light of day. They only revealed the results of their raucous terrors in the calm of dawn. A staccato blast of lightning and the following thunder announced the approach of another rain band. The pressure wave of thunder so close, they could all feel it in their bones. A crash in the treetops a few hundred yards away signaled a lost branch and a thud, its landing. A shout rang out. Brad looked up into the swirling darkness. Another human? Here?

Frank Fischetti had taken a three-inch branch square in his left thigh. He had become terrified by the strengthening storm, more afraid than he had ever been while on assignment. In third-world hot spots, he had experienced high mission anxiety or extremes of apprehension before going out on missions, but this steadily increasing violence superimposed on a terrific medullar headache was becoming too much. In this dark, wet, and windy maelstrom, the chunk of pine tree bouncing off the flesh of his thigh might as well have been the sudden first violent bite of a Florida gator. He jumped up and yelped, hurling into the maelstrom a string of cuss words that would have made any Bronx father proud. In another accent entirely, one familiar to both Brad and Connie, a violent reprimand was shouted back into the wind.

Jenks wondered if it was possible over the noise and rain that the loss of cover by Fischetti could have been missed by Hitchens and Chappell. Fish had recovered from the shock and jumped back down into position. Jenks counted to ten quietly and then slowly so that the motion would not stand

410

out in the sea of motion around him, he raised his head above the low brush that had been their cover. He saw Brad's head peering over the side of the cart looking off in another direction. "Okay, so they know someone's out here, but they don't know where."

Fischetti hissed a whisper, "Sorry, man, I thought something just took a bite out of my ass. Tell me again why we're staking out these woods with a hurricane just around the corner."

"Fish, that was the stupidest thing I've seen you do since you got married. What the hell were you thinking?"

"I got spooked. Hell, it's spooky out here. Next thing you know, whole trees gonna start comin' down like that big sucker over there." He nodded toward the fallen cypress.

"Just be cool, Fish. Calm down." He could tell Fischetti was spooked because his New York accent was coming back strong.

Jenks looked again and saw that Hitchens was standing now and looking in the opposite direction. He was looking toward the little pond. Hitchens reached down and tapped at something. Soon Chappell stood, bracing herself against the roof of the cart. They both were staring at something out of his sight. He reached for the back of his head. "Christ! What a headache!" He lowered his head and heard a low moan coming from Fischetti. Frank had his hands over his ears as if he were blocking out noise. Crap, he thought. He's scared. Jenks took stock of his situation. Hell, I should be scared. He looked back up again. The girl was holding onto Hitchens in the wind, and they were moving away from the cart. "What the heck are they looking at?" In response to his thought, he heard, *Ka-Litan*

"What?" Fischetti hissed.

"I didn't say anything."

Fischetti said, "What's caylitan?"

"Caylitan?" Jenks realized that Fischetti had heard what he had heard. Where it had come from, he couldn't guess.

I am Ka-Litan ... friend B-rad ... you not friend B-rad

"Da hell wid this!" Fischetti started to break cover again.

Jenks put his hand on Fischetti's back and pressed him back down into the grass. When he looked up again, he couldn't see the kids anymore. He thought, *this is quickly getting out of control.*

~ ~ ~

Down in the pool, there had been changes taking place while the humans above tried to take shelter from the growing storm. Invisible in the blowing rain, steam had been boiling off the top of the pool and blowing away. When Brad first noticed, the water level had dropped below the level of the outboard motor's prop. Standing to see what was going on with the pond, he saw a swirling rainbow of light at the deep end in pulsing color bands through the brown soup of the pool. Leaning down to shout above the wind, he tapped Connie on the shoulder and helped her stand.

In the low light of near dusk, the pulsing colors flashing through the muddy water were muted, but beautiful. "What's he doing?" Connie asked.

Brad gave a little snort, unnoticed by anybody, and shouted over the wind, "Only guess I've got is that he's boiling off water!"

"Boiling off water?" she shouted back into his ear.

"If he fires up engines underwater, the steam could cause an explosion." Connie nodded, absorbing the power that was developing just below the rapidly dropping water level of the former pool.

Brad looked at the wooden truss and the motor still in position, but totally out of the water. "Here, help me pull this out of the way."

With the truss gone and the water level receding, the pool bottom was now looking more like a trench with a steep side at the deep end. Steam roiled off the surface and disappeared in the mist of blown rain. A wall of boiling water rose from the exposed edge of the hull, backlit by swirling color. The two stood transfixed by the signs of unknowable power coming to life in the bottom of their pool. Buffeted by howling wind, they sat on the edge, staring into the pool, awestruck by the glowing, shifting colors visible beneath the boiling surface. The indentation, growing deeper as the water level receded, sheltered a thin layer of steam that further obscured the source of the light show.

Chapter 24

Any sufficiently advanced technology is indistinguishable from Magic.
Arthur C. Clarke's Third Law

November 21, 1985
Jai, 7:00 p.m.

The National Hurricane Center's advisory from Miami had reported that Kate officially made landfall at Panama City, and that winds in the leading quadrant were reduced to a sustained speed of only ninety miles per hour. According to the news feeds, one of them originating from field reporter Tim Murray, this "reduced" wind speed was still ripping off rooftops; downing trees, power lines, and gas station canopies; overturning mobile homes; driving boats from their moorings; and generally creating havoc on the thin margin of coastline inhabited by humans.

Most real estate inland from the coast was owned by paper companies or were national and state forests. No news reporters contemplated the terrors experienced by the deer, hogs, owls, bears, gulls, and hundreds of other species that occupied the spaces shown on the maps of Florida as "empty."

By 8:00 p.m., any moonlight that might have shone through forty thousand feet of cloud deck was gone. Darkness anywhere beyond the pool of light created by Hitchens's lanterns was absolute. Martin Jenks had the flat of his palm firmly on his partner's back. The tough, streetwise New Yorker was obviously just hanging on to his wits in the roaring reality of the subtropical hurricane. Between the nearly crippling headaches that both were experiencing and the sixty- to seventy-mile-per-hour winds ripping through the trees above, both felt like they had drawn a cosmic short straw for getting this duty.

"For Christ's sake, Frank, get a grip." Frank had again announced his intention of getting the hell out of there. Jenks reassured him, "It's just a windstorm; we're barely getting any rain here now. Some of these storms are nonstarters. All hat and no cattle." The peculiarity of the westernism got

Fischetti's attention. He looked over in the direction of his partner in the darkness and smiled. It often surprised him that this black man who had such an easy time adopting Southern personae or using the streetwise lingo of the urban north was actually a former MP from Montana.

It had grown dark even before sundown, but now, these woods were blackout dark. This was not the dark of a suburban forest with moonlight through clouds or backscatter from a nearby city. This was an absolute moonless darkness with heavy clouds and without human habitation for miles. The absolute darkness bred fears the were only mitigated by the overhead flashes of lighting that illuminated the overhead flailing of branch and frond. Thunder crashed nearly continually and so close Jenks thought the ground was trembling. Something preternatural was throbbing beneath the soil. The small light that had apparently been coming from a camper's lantern brought by Hitchens had faded and gone out. The winds, if they had varied at all over the last half hour since darkness fell, seemed to be increasing. Jenks made a mental note that they had gone from scream to howl to screeching howl. What description was left for the winds sawing through the palmettos? How would his report read?

The raucous flailing of palmetto fronds would have been bad enough, but when added to the rippling thunder rolling nearly constantly, it was almost too noisy to think. The two watchers could keep track of the activities around the pool only by the lightning above and around them which punctuated the darkness.

Fischetti crept closer to Jenks's side to make conversation a little easier. They were not sure if Fish's earlier indiscretion had been recognized as a human cry or if Brad and Connie had assumed it to be the frightened cry of some wild animal. For their part, the kids had not come looking. They actually seemed to be huddled out of sight for the time being. Peering into darkness, Martin Jenks thought he could make out the profile of shapes in the approximate area of the small pool that had been the object of their attentions all day.

Earlier, they had observed Connie Chappell taking an apparent sight line and then heading off to the south with a metal detector while Hitchens set up equipment at the pool. Jenks had concluded that they had previously discovered some other part of the alien artifact, maybe the missing end, in the little pond. This conclusion was born out by the use of the pump. Perhaps they were trying to lower the water table to get at the artifact. And, of course, they had waited for today to mask the sounds of a gas engine when the entire coastline would be under evacuation orders.

When the truss and outboard were rigged, Jenks's grudging admiration for Hitchens's natural creativity heightened. He reasoned that they were blowing away mud and sediment trying to uncover a piece of unknown size in the bank of the pond. Way to go, kid. Came prepared for two avenues of attack, he thought. He was about to share these conclusions with Fischetti, in an effort to calm him down and engage his rational processes, when the dim outlines that he thought were caused by a campers lantern seemed to brighten.

The glow initially looked like the flickering light of a campfire. This was clearly not a possibility in a gale-force wind accentuated by bands of heavy, driven rain. He almost forgot the background level of pain at the base of his skull. *What is with this freakin' headache?* He looked over at Frank Fischetti, who was leaning on his elbows, skull clasped in his hands. He realized he could actually see Frank without the flickering aid of lightning. There was more light out than there should be.

He looked back toward the pool; there now seemed to be a steady glow coming from the little encampment in the titi thicket. But it flickered now and then and seemed to be changing between colors in the red-orange-yellow range. He considered that cover for their current positions had been chosen in the full light of day. There was plenty of wind to cover the sound of their movement, and he was pretty sure that with the glow of their lantern or their fire, or whatever, illuminating the slender titi branches, that the kids wouldn't be able to see into the darkness beyond.

He tapped Fish's shoulder, got up into a low crouch, and began to close the hundred and fifty yards to the edge of the thicket. He moved to a place beside what looked like a well-worn path through the tangle of branches and crouched down. Fischetti moved up beside him. The golf cart was beside them, and they could take partial shade from the wind gusts in its overturned chassis. From the new vantage, they could clearly see Hitchens and Chappell crouching just inside the edge of the pool where water had been. But the light seemed to be coming from down in the water. As if coming to the same conclusion at the same time, Fish asked in a whisper, "Where's the water? Isn't this a sinkhole?"

"Well, they did pump a lot of water out of it," Jenks said.

"Aren't these things connected to groundwater?"

"Usually, I guess. I don't know, my specialties are criminology and psychology, not geology; maybe it takes a while to seep back in." They settled in to maintain the surveillance. Both of them found that their headaches had increased to something just this side of tolerable.

~ ~ ~

Brad heard-felt Litan clearly: *your not friends come closer ... hiding in dark ... not friends Mar-Tee ... Fish ... watch in dark* He found it hard to not look out into the darkness for the humans called Mar-Tee and Fish. Mar-Tee must be Martin Jenks, as he and Connie had figured earlier; Fish must be a second. It would have been harder not to look, but the irresistible beauty of the emerging energy field around the ship was incredible. The glowing, iridescent bubble seemed to throb or pulsate. Its surface modulated and swirled, reminding him of a huge, electrified soap bubble or the surface reflections of gasoline floating on water. Impacting raindrops immediately hissed into nothing, and the remaining water in the pool formed a line of vapor that bubbled out from under the ship and blew rapidly away on the wind.

Connie, staring into the pool, cried, "This is just awesome!" She pointed into the pool. "What color do you think it is behind the shield bubble?"

"Hard to say—almost like a dolphin gray."

"That is exactly right!" She nudged him. "Behind all the aura light, the colors, that's just about the color I'd say. Bottlenose-dolphin gray."

They felt the warning from Litan at the same time. It was wordless, but both of them felt the instruction to move away from the pond. Connie started for the path through the thicket they had always used and felt Brad's grip on her forearm. "No, we need to go this way." He looked down into her eyes to make sure she understood and mouthed, "Jenks is out there; he's close by." Her eyes widened with understanding. They moved away from the edge of the pond, making their way through tangled branches. They got clear of the trees and were able to back away. The light show at the bottom of the former pool ramped up suddenly in intensity. The pulsing red, orange, and yellow flashed to blue-white and then an intense pure white.

The noise rose now, above the maelstrom in the trees. The pulses of driven rain flashed into steam on contact with a growing bubble of light. The light coming out of the pool-turned-ditch gained an intensity that felt more like the intense glare of stage lights or the invisible heat from a jet exhaust. On both sides of the pool, the two groups of humans backed away in awe.

416

One pair knew what they were watching; the other, awestruck, was beginning to understand. Beneath them, a low rumble in the soil amplified to heavy, long-period throbbing vibration. The saturated soil easily transmitted the long thrum, thrum, thrum pulsing up from below. Trees immediately around the pond began to fall outward or downwind in a tangle. The glowing ball of the ship's energy shield began to emerge from the mess of roots and liquefied soil.

The noise from the rising ball of energy overcame the howl of wind through palmetto branches. The Skeeter, about fifty-five feet long by twenty feet wide and maybe twelve feet high, hovered just above level ground. Its shields formed a layer about three feet off the smooth edge of the hull. Sliding off the energy shield, clumps of soil and root fell into the hole remaining at the end of the pool. Brad and Connie could see large rectangular openings that they figured must be thrusters, but they were not like the cones they might have been used to seeing at the business end of aircraft or rockets of human design. All that was visible through the glowing shield was a gridded array of interlocking triangles. Brad's first description of the ship's shape would have been an elongated jellybean cut off nearly vertically at the back. The ship began a slow rotation on its vertical axis, and slowly, its front came into view. A view screen, nearly black but slightly backlit by cockpit instrumentation, became visible and then rotated out of view again.

Small ports began to open at the base of the hull, and blue-white spurts of flame erupted, rocking the ship left and right. Similar jets appeared in holes in the side that had previously seemed like solid hull metal. The ship responded by sliding back and forth. Brad leaned into Connie and shouted into her ear to be heard over the din of the ship and storm. "It looks like he's taking the ship through test procedures." When he backed away to look at her, he saw a look of entranced rapture.

She shouted back without turning her head, "It's absolutely beautiful! I am so glad we stayed." She was bouncing on her toes in excitement, grinning like a village idiot.

A jet near the nose blasted a small charred hole before its reaction slowly tipped the ship back on its rear thrusters. Then the array of triangular thrusters began to glow: deep red at first and then quickly running through the yellow to white and blue hot. The ship began to move slowly at first but then, roaring with sudden acceleration, rose rapidly to several hundred feet and remained motionless, unaffected by the seventy-mile-per-hour winds still blasting above the tree line.

With no video camera, Martin Jenks lay on his back looking up at the ship, unable to record an event he would never forget. It was stupendous, and he found himself laughing. He had the same sense of awe and wonder he'd had when watching a shuttle launch at the cape. Looking around, he saw that Fischetti was gone. He didn't know when Fish had left and didn't care. He had no idea what the kids had done to facilitate the emergence of what must have been a long-buried alien craft, but there it was. He was joyous!

During its centuries of imprisonment in solid rock, the ship had been without the ability to use its field effect generator to break open the confining limestone. Now above ground, Jai, the ship's computer, ran through a series of diagnostic tests on support systems, weapons systems, chem directional and attitude thrusters, and finally, gravity-effect drivers. The roaring of the thrusters abruptly stopped.

On the other side of the ship, Connie was crying from awe and bliss. Beside her Brad was laughing. Nine years! He corrected, almost nine and a half years of unimagined and undeserved hardship to achieve this. He and Connie had done it! There was the ship.

Then, suddenly, it was gone. They had felt the sensation of motion and assumed that it had gone up into the cloud deck—gone! Looking up, they saw a diminishing glow that thinned to black in the overhead cloud layer like the vanishing dot on a sixties television set.

The darkness was sudden and immediate. They had felt safe and secure in Litan's growing, glowing presence. They had somehow felt that despite the oncoming wrath of the hurricane, there was some moral stance that would protect them from the elements. Both Connie and Brad had been given the same calming, soothing mental images or sensations. That was gone.

Litan was gone? The dark, the rain, the wind, and the noise persisted.

In the psychic vacuum remaining, the three humans found their legs, and began to move toward a common center. Aided by nearly constant flashes of lightning, they approached cautiously at first. An unspoken need to share what had just happened drew them all toward edge the fallen mass of titi branches covering the golf cart. Through instants of flashing white

418

from overhead lightning to the dimmer, suffused glow of more distant flashes, they appraised each other. All wore unquenchable smiles.

Jenks spoke first. "Well done, Hitchens, very well done!" He extended a hand and moved toward Brad. Uncertainty, with a flash of suspicion, passed across Brad's forehead. Slowly, he reached out and took Jenks's hand. Jenks then extended his hand to Connie, who was hanging on to Brad's left shoulder. Surprised at herself, she allowed Jenks to take her hand, and in a momentary darkness, she felt her hand being shaken by a man she had just minutes ago loathed. "Chappell?" Jenks was saying—shouting through the din. "That was absolutely, freaking amazing!"

Had he been talking? A man, obviously Jenks's partner, approached in the darkness and stood a little farther back from the group. Fischetti, as shaken as the rest of them, began to feel that he was becoming a center of attention when a light above them illuminated the scene. They all looked up as a stationary light shone above backlit clouds rushing overhead. It brightened as the ship lost altitude, dropped below the cloud deck, and dimmed. A row of white lights, pulsing inline from front to back, was the only indication of its location. The ship descended slowly into the clearing beside them. At treetop level, three intensely blue landing lights illuminated the area in thin cones of white. Landing pads appeared from sockets in the hull, and it settled to the ground.

Brad estimated that at rest, it nearly hugged the ground but was at least fifteen feet tall at the cockpit. Brad reaffirmed that the craft he had come to know as a skeeter had the overall shape of a slender, jelly-bean-shaped oval, flattened on the bottom and cut out at the rear for main drive thrusters. But, as they had just seen, its aerodynamic shape concealed functional moving parts. They all heard or felt the internal communication. Jenks's mouth dropped. Fischetti stepped back a pace or two.

systems check complete … B-rad come close … please Ka-nee wait

Brad kissed Connie on the forehead and approached the ship. Handholds appeared in the side of the ship as sections of the hull surface retracted inward about three inches. He received messages of reassurance as he took one handhold and then another. As he touched the hull, the energy field reactivated and increased in depth to include him and about eight or ten feet immediately adjacent to the ship in all directions. Immediately, the rain and wind stopped buffeting him. He climbed. As his hand hit the top handhold, a line appeared just below a blacked-out canopy, and it clam-shelled open from the opposite side.

B-rad ... Jai must explain about Ka-Litan ... please not be afraid

Brad looked into a dimly lit cockpit. A suited figure was strapped into a forward seat; a rear seat was empty. The helmet on the strapped in figure lay at an odd angle on the chest of the pilot.

B-rad ... ka unit damaged on impact with earth ... Litan survive long time in stasis ... no help ... no water ... Litan now with Maker of Lights

Brad was stunned. Speechless, he hung onto the edge of the canopy. The uniform below him was motionless. He was about to ask *"Who?"* when he received the answer.

Jai unit ... name Jai ... your books say ship computer

Brad looked back across the thirty yards to Connie. She looked hopeful. She hadn't been getting the communications from Jai. He looked back into the ship's fore and aft cockpits. The rear seat was empty.

"Why did you tell us you were Ka-Litan? Was he alive when we first met you?"

no ... Litan go to Maker of Lights long time

"Why? Why did you say you were Litan?"

There was a pause. *"You say 'embarrassed' ... maybe humans afraid ... not talk with machine*

Brad thought about it. He had never imagined he could communicate with, empathize with, and care for a machine.

that my fear ... Jai talk for Ka-Litan

"Okay, okay, I forgot you can read my thoughts. Is that how you and your pilot communicate?"

yes ... and instruments and weapons controller ... and tactical controls A pause and then, atmospheric water not good for control systems ... must use energy for field effect ... B-rad come in

It was not a question. Brad realized he had been standing over the open cockpit for a few minutes, and Jai was keeping the energy field deployed to keep the interior dry.

He looked up at rain splashing and hissing on an invisible bubble that seemed to swirl around the perimeter of the ship. He thought that if he had to describe the shield, he would say that it looked like a cross between a soap bubble and the aurora borealis. He looked into the rear cockpit at the array of lights, toggles, pressure pads, and what looked like a control stick. He said. "Can Jai teach Brad to fly ship?"

yes ... B-rad friend ... soon teach Ka-brad

This is unreal, Brad thought. "Jai, does the ship have a name?"

yes ... Jai

Brad's thoughts were in a jumble; "You are the ship?"

Jai ship computer ... ship brain

He looked out through the rainbow swirls of the shield. Connie, Jenks, and another camo-clothed man were standing in buffeting gusts of wind-driven rain. He was soaking wet, but protected now by the shield. Litan, the real pilot of the ship, was still suited up and strapped into the forward seat. The friend connection he had was with a machine, not a biological survivor. What were his allegiances now? If he were to get into the ship, where would it go? He would not want to leave Connie alone in the wind-blown forest. Should he remove Litan's ancient corpse for Jenks's people to examine?

He was used to tackling one or two major issues at a time. Now, with multiple issues cascading through his brain, he was approaching decision point overload. He couldn't settle in on one problem. Connie, leaning into a forty-mile-per-hour gust, began to walk closer to the edge of the shield. Okay, first things first. "Jai, can you let Connie into the shield?"

Momentarily, the colors faded; rain began to splatter through, and the shield disappeared entirely. He pointed to Connie and waved for her to come to him. She ran to him, and Brad thought, *Jai, shields up* Immediately, the colored force field popped back up, and the rain overhead stopped, for them only. He was impressed.

~ ~ ~

Anyone else out of doors in the eastern Florida Panhandle and a majority of Georgia's southern-tier counties was getting a good soaking. Hurricane Kate was out of fuel and spending her stored-up water in torrents of rain. Of course, anyone outdoors was either looking at damage that had already happened—lost homes or roofs— or was just nuts, out trying to extract the most memorable experience out of these rare tropical events. Semi-rare in this location, at least. It was a rare year that a hurricane or tropical storm did not enter or get spawned in the Gulf of Mexico. It was unusual, though, for a specific location to get hit more than once every ten or so years—sometimes more often, sometimes less, but a decennial near miss and a close hit every twenty years was a good average. And, it was rare for a hurricane to form and make a Gulf coast landfall after November 5th.

By 9:00 p.m., Tallahassee was nearly dark. The eighty-mile-per-hour winds of the degrading eye wall's feeder bands had passed over the northwestern half of the city, downing ancient water oaks, pines, magnolias, and virtually every other kind of tall growing thing, either in specimen or in ranks. Often, the only evidence that there had been power and telephone service in any given neighborhood was the line of parallel poles lying across road or yard. Tornadoes embedded in a feeder band had wreaked havoc in some neighborhoods. Lucy Hitchens and Susan Delaney were hunkered down in Susan's darkened neighborhood. Power had flickered in warning at about 7:30 and was gone for the week five minutes later.

~ ~ ~

Thirty miles south of Tallahassee at 9:00, winds were dropping to less than thirty-five miles per hour, rain was intermittent, and Jenks and Fischetti were standing ankle-deep in water that had flooded in with the storm's surge. After carefully and respectfully laying Litan's corpse on the ground, Brad and Connie had simply climbed into the ship inside the colored bubble of the energy shield and left. The ship had gone straight up. It had hovered long enough to retract its landing pads and gone, risen into the clouds. Jenks pulled out his military-issue flashlight, removed the red lens cover, and went over to investigate the area where the alien ship had been. They found stretched out on the ground a space suit, or rather, the desiccated remains of an alien in a pressure suit. Litan's arms were folded across his chest in a familiar position of repose.

The only things that might have been different about this suit from one containing a human were the shortness of his legs relative to his torso, that his helmet was too long, and that his gloves had only three digits across from an opposable thumb. Looking more closely at the gold-tinted faceplate, which showed no details within, he saw only his reflection looking back.

Joining Jenks with his own flashlight, Frank began to look for a release on the helmet. "No, Frank, wait! Let's keep this thing contained until we find out what condition it's in. It may have millions of toxic organisms that are fatal to humans, or for that matter, anything that shares our double-helix DNA. We'd be reamed for sure if we opened this suit to the atmosphere without precautions."

"Right," Fischetti responded. "As much as I'd like to look, I'm not sure I want to see whatever's in there." He looked down at his feet again. "Where the heck's all this water coming from?" Water was now a little higher than their ankles and seemed to be flowing across the ground.

Jenks looked up at the sky. "Well, either there's a storm surge coming in or a hurricane's been raining for six hours and it's flat as a plank out here. Come on, let's see if we can't figure out how to get this guy out of here."

Chapter 25

What's past is prologue.
William Shakespeare (The Tempest)

November 21, 1985
McDill AFB, Tampa, 2112 Hours

"Sergeant Banks, look at this. We've got a bogey smack in the tail of that hurricane." Airman Schiff was staring intently at his multiple display screens. "It just showed up."

Banks, the NCO in charge of monitoring Gulf traffic for unidentified aircraft, had had his team on alert because the Yucatan-to-US drug routes often went active in the wake of a storm. Assuming that all eyes would be on weather and that some stations might even be down, the little planes came in following the tail of big storms. Hugging the water to avoid long-scan radar out at sea, their daredevil pilots had to rise above treetops as they approached land but were usually spotted over a hundred miles out. This particular bogey with no transponder signal had just appeared over the Florida swamps and didn't appear to be going anywhere. Banks was skeptical. "What are you saying, Airman? This bogey just showed up? Or do you mean you just noticed it?" As he stared at the zoomed-in view of their radar sweep he wondered at the chopper pilot who could maintain position so well in thirty-five- to fifty-mile-per-hour gusts.

There were unusually few aircraft over the eastern panhandle of Florida. The hurricane had cleared out all scheduled flights in the region and grounded all private aircraft. The Tallahassee commercial air traffic tower was down and, unsurprisingly, not reporting. It could have gone down because of loss of power or lightning or a dead emergency generator. Or, it could literally be down on the ground. They had not made ground line contact with TLH yet. Moody AFB also was blacked out. Also not surprising, since the center of the storm had passed just to the northwest of Valdosta minutes ago.

So what was the bogey doing on the radar screen? The bright yellow triangle was absent all number ID, meaning there was no transponder, just a radar signature for something made out of metal. Banks slapped the side of the blank screen, which should have had the Moody tower displayed as if the signal was stuck and would somehow show up if you tapped it like when his dad would hit their old Zenith console TV. It didn't work.

"Schiff, see if you can pull up the Rucker feed. One of their ATCs should be able to see it too. Use a landline, if you have to, to get their attention." The airman tapped his keyboard but received no response from Fort Rucker. More taps and he got a "no-radar signal available" message from Tyndall.

"Sarge, it's gone."

"Rucker's gone too?" Banks was getting frustrated.

"No, Sarge, the bogey." Airman Schiff sounded frustrated as well.

"Whadaya sayin'?"

"It's gone!"

"You didn't see it all day. It shows up out of nowhere in the backwash of a hurricane, and now it's gone?"

"Sarge, you saw the signature, right?" He was exasperated. He knew what he'd seen; it was legit. "You want me to pull the backup tape?"

For the next twenty minutes, he tried to reestablish contact with some of the military bases that went off-line as Kate passed by. Tyndall came back first. They had been down and were just getting the machinery back online. The Air Force radar at Cape San Blas called back, too. There had been an unusual blip south of Tallahassee on their screens. No, they didn't know what it was, maybe a civilian search-and-rescue or medevac helo with a dead transponder unit. Definitely not military. Definitely not the 1st Air Cavalry out of Ft. Rucker..

Schiff was working up his report on the sighting, when he looked up at what should have been a blank screen. "Sarge! The bogey's back!"

Staff Sergeant Banks sprinted across the com room. "Put a lock on that bogey." He picked up a phone and tapped in an access code. "This is Narc two-three-two, requesting visual and track on a bogey located one niner dot six miles from TLH radar tower at bearing one-six-one. Bogey is stationary at approximate altitude one-five-oh." Banks repeated the location and request into his hand mike.

The panel speaker responded in a combination of static and fuzz common to aging military sound systems, with the addition of electrostatic interference from the numerous lightning strikes in the trailing feeder bands of the dying storm. "Narc two-three-two, this is Tyndall ATC. Is this an absolute necessity? All units are on-call status in coordinated emergency response at this time. We've got civilians on rooftops going crazy."

"Tyndall, that is affirmative." Banks affected his best command tone. "Have reason to believe a narco helo is shadowing the storm in from an offshore base. Request visual approach and interdiction. We are clearing all civilian emergency response units in that area at this time to ensure that sighting is not EMS." Banks's adrenaline was up now; he'd have some sheriff's ass if an emergency responder was up in this weather with damaged electronics. He finished his transmission with, "Bogey displays no readable transponder and should be considered an incoming narco until cleared."

There was a moment of silence before Tyndall ATC came back with, "Narc two-three-two, take a look at your screens. Please verify readings."

Banks leaned over the monitor and scanned the info box that popped up as Schiff scrolled over the yellow blip. As he looked at the display, lat longs wavered slightly in the second decimals, but altitude was scrolling. Banks whispered an oath not allowed on military airwaves. The bogey was traveling straight up. It had just passed forty-five thousand feet and was still climbing.

Schiff muttered, "Sure as heck ain't no helo."

Banks swore again, softly to himself, in disbelief. "Altitude's scrolling past fifty-K and climbing."

There was an uncomfortable silence in the McDill control room as Banks, Schiff, and a now-curious small gathering looked incredulously at altimeter and rate of climb numbers usually associated with a cape launch. As they watched in near-breathless silence, the altimeter readings stopped at just over one hundred thousand feet. Only rare spy planes had ever flown that high, and the instrumentation wasn't calibrated to go any higher. The McDill control room, known as narc two-three-two, remained silent; a pop sounded on their speakers as one of the other air traffic towers keyed its mike as if to make a comment, and then the room was silent again.

Sometime later, the speakers sounded again: "Narc two-three-two, this is Tyndall Air Traffic Control. We're scrubbing recording traffic tapes per Dreamland protocols. Suggest you do likewise."

Airman Schiff cleared his throat with an uncomfortable choke and said, "Sarge, should we hand this off to Cheyenne Mountain, see if they can fix it with a satellite array?"

Sergeant Banks, clearly out of his depth and belief systems, hesitated. "No, uh, I don't think that's necessary. Don't scrub that tape just yet. If anyone asks, we'll show them, umm, we'll show them whatever that was."

~ ~ ~

Martin Jenks and Frank Fischetti carried the remains of former Coalition squadron command pilot Litan on a makeshift stretcher fashioned from some of Hitchens's left-over lumber. They had slogged through a shallow storm surge that had risen to their knees and finally made it to dry land and the Coastal Highway by 2:30 in the morning. By 10:00 a.m., they had made the hundred miles to Tyndall, stopping often to assist locals in clearing trees from roads. By noon, Litan's suited corpse was on a transport to Nevada.

~ ~ ~

Jai had taken his two humans high enough for them to see the planet as a circle. Cities were bright spots that winked and twinkled. There was no bright spot immediately below them where the region around Tallahassee was blacked out by cloud and massive electrical distribution failures. In fact, the entire region from Apalachicola to south-central Georgia was dark. Kate had taken a toll on civilization, and thick cloud banks obscured anything still shining in the darkness.

As the ship continued to gain elevation, scaled now in tens of miles, the portion of the planet to their relative east reflected moonlight from the crescent moon that had just "risen" in the east over the Atlantic. In a few more minutes, a bright band of atmospheric blue lit the western horizon, and the sun rose brightly in a reversed sunset behind the western side of what was now a spherical view of the earth. The two humans, sensing that motion was slowing, made sense of the holographic array in front of them as it displayed the shrinking ball of their home planet with images of the neighboring moon, surrounding planets, and the sun displayed on an outer shell of the display.

Jai asked them both to place a right thumb and three of their fingers in a palm rest to the right of each seat *"for better communication."* Doing so wordlessly, Brad and Connie felt their minds sharing thoughts, felt Jai cautiously probing, consensus building.

Jai asked in a voice free of implication, but full of possibilities, *where Ka-Brad and Jen-Ka-nee want to go?*

THE END

If you've enjoyed *Dreamland Diaries*,
look for the exciting sequel, *Orion's Light*
at Amazon Books, and other ebook outlets.

And be patient reader, the final chapter in the Dreamland Diaries series,
Part 4 entitled, *PASS-FAIL* will be worth the wait
as Brad Hitchens' saga is not over yet.

And as always, if you've enjoyed the journey,
Please provide a review on Amazon books and/or on Goodreads.com

Author's Note

There really was (is) an Area 51. Officially a US Air Force secret testing facility utilizing several airfields in the badlands of Nevada, Area 51 is simply its cartographic designation on old maps of the desert wasteland. Its front door was Edwards AFB in the southern desert of California. It had more removed access at Creech AFB in Indian Springs, Nevada, about forty-five miles south of the Groom Lake secure area. The complex was developed and used as a testing area for new airframes and power systems that brought us the most advanced aircraft our planet has ever produced. It was dubbed "Dreamland" by its test pilots because they got to fly planes most pilots could only dream about flying. It is believed that, because of the publicity and scrutiny of these facilities, these testing activities have been moved to the Dakotas and Creech AFB and Groom Lake are now involved in "normal" desert training exercises.

A pile of wreckage, assumed by UFOlogists to be a crashed alien ship found near Roswell, New Mexico, *may* be a wrecked high-altitude balloon designed to drift silently above Soviet airspace out of reach of tactical surface-to-air defenses; at least that's the official story. An internet search for Dreamland, Area 51, and UFOs will unearth myriad sites that repeatedly cross reference and internally reference themselves so that real research on the web is virtually impossible to verify initial sources for any information presented.

There really was a project Blue Book. Operating out of right-Patterson AFB in Ohio, the project ran from 1947 to 1969 with the official function of tracking down claims of UFO sightings. After twenty-two years of inquiry in a sighting-rich environment, it concluded, "There was no evidence indicating that sightings categorized as 'unidentified' were extraterrestrial vehicles." Persons wishing to report UFOs are requested by the Air Force at www.af.mil to contact their local law enforcement authority. Sure, go ahead.

There really is an AFOSI. The Air Force Office of Special Investigations maintains Detachment 206 at Nellis Air Force Base in Nevada. A critical part of the facilities that were known collectively as Area 51, Nellis AFB's facilities in the northeastern suburbs of Las Vegas and the publicly accessible Creech AFB in Indian Springs provide no indication of the operations or facilities located at the Groom Dry Lake installation where this story locates the detachment's "B-Team" interrogation and detention unit.

There really is a DISCO, or Defense Industrial Security Clearance Office. Its stated public mission is to provide clearance eligibility evaluations of potential employees, contractors, etc., involved in military-associated activities requiring clearances. Like many civilian contractors in the employ of the United States, it is not a long stretch to consider that mission creep might take their operations into activities that we might find questionable.

As a fiction author and cynic, I would not and could not advise any reader on the reliability of any sources reporting to be authorities on alien contacts with this planet. I agree with Carl Sagan's assumptions that the numerical odds favor intelligent life in other planetary systems. Whether they are accessible in our time and physical space is another question. If evidence were ever discovered by our government, I do firmly believe that any and all information supporting such a discovery would be suppressed with prejudice. Like the X-Files' Fox Mulder, I do believe.

There really is a beautiful natural beach in Wakulla County, Florida, where the intertidal zone is a grassy shallow nearly devoid of wave activity on normal weather days. It and the nearby miles of diurnally submerged grassy flats are spawning grounds for literally hundreds of varieties of marine life from shrimp to sea bass to shellfish. It might be hard to imagine a child of this environment acclimating to the arid regions surrounding Phoenix, Arizona, if it were not for the special beauty and complexity of that entirely different ecosystem.

The universities listed in the effort to confirm or refute a terrestrial origin of the artifact are some of the best institutions in the world for advanced metallurgical study. Any reader interested in this field would do well to consider their curricula.

Specific locales created in this work of fiction resemble or are based on real places located throughout the coastal region of Florida's Big Bend region. For instance, although there is a home located a few hundred feet down Wakulla Beach Road from the Coastal Highway, it bears no resemblance to the Hitchenses' residence, which is very similar to hundreds of such structures expanded over succeeding generations across the rural southland. Any resemblance to real persons other than the nationally known news personality named is entirely coincidental.

Sanitized Copy

Made in the USA
Middletown, DE
28 January 2022

59888397R00245